DARK
RESOLUTION

Tyner Gillies

Also by Tyner Gillies

The Watch

DARK
RESOLUTION

Tyner Gillies

Dark Dragon Pub-   lishing
Toronto, Ontario, Canada

Dark Resolution

Dark Dragon Publishing
313 Mutual Street
Toronto, Ontario
M4Y 1X6
CANADA
www.darkdragonpublishing.com

Printed in the United States of America.

For more information on Tyner Gillies

www.tynergillies.com

For my Dad
Gone but never forgotten.
Thanks for all the books.

ACKNOWLEDGEMENTS

To Jay Clarke and my Uncle Jack, for having the words I needed.

To Jason, Christine, Rose, kc, Kathy, Laura and Mummy Pam.
My friends. My people. My tribe. For endlessly being in my corner.
I love you guys.

CHAPTER 1

The dog, a deep chested Rottweiler, picked her head up off her paws and looked at the front door of the cabin, a growl rumbling in her throat.

Dean Springer turned from his small writing desk and the antique typewriter he had been clacking away at. "What is it, Betty?" he asked, looking down at the dog beside his chair.

She came to her feet, legs spread wide, eyes locked on the rough panels of the door as her hackles lifted and her lips peeled away from white teeth. She lowered her head, and still staring at the door, the growl in her throat rose in both pitch and volume.

Dean stood and picked up the Remington shotgun that leaned against the rough, log wall beside his desk. He stepped next to the dog, his wiry hands gripping the stock of the shotgun as he pumped a round into the chamber.

"They've finally come for us, have they?" He stepped forward and put his hand on the latch of the cabin door and looked down, addressing the dog. "You write enough letters to the mayor, get enough attention, annoy enough people and they always come for you. But they came for the wrong people this time, didn't they girl?"

The dog turned her big head and snapped at the air, slobber flying from her jowls. Every muscle in her body vibrated, her claws digging gouges in the wooden planking of the floor as she kept her eyes locked on the door.

"That's right. Fuckers are messing with the wrong people." Dean threw open the door and stepped aside. "Get 'em, girl!"

The dog did not move, but her growl pitched up even further until it sounded like an undulating whine.

"What are you waiting for?" he asked, surprise causing his voice to take on a mewling note he did not care for. He gestured towards the open door with the black barrel of the shotgun. "Get out there and teach those assholes a lesson."

The dog took a shuddering step backwards, her haunches shaking so badly it made her claws clatter on the wooden floor. Dean realized she was not shaking with righteous fury—the kind he was constantly filled with—she quaked in fear.

He snorted. "Never mind. I'll do it myself." He snatched a heavy, square flashlight off a narrow shelf besides the door and stepped into the dark summer night.

It was not him who should be scared, it was the interfering fuckers outside, trespassing on his land. He always knew that if he wrote enough letters to the paper—whether they printed them or not—and pissed off the Mayor enough, the government would come for him. They might even send the aliens he knew they were consorting with. Let them come, he thought. They were in for a surprise.

"Who the fuck goes there?" he shouted as he stepped onto the porch and swept the darkness with his flashlight.

He was isolated, high up on a mountainside where government interference was minimal, and he liked it that way. The downside of his isolation was he had no neighbours, no phone and no one to help him if he got into trouble. This was foremost in his mind as his dog whined behind him and his flashlight cast a feeble light that did little to cut through the darkness.

"Come out where I can see you," Dean said to the dark air, far less strength in his voice than he would have hoped. The dog's panic got to him, made him nervous. He'd never seen her like this, never seen her scared.

He swallowed, his throat feeling tight and pinched. The beam of the flashlight shook slightly. "I'm warning you, I'm armed."

The beam of the light swept back and forth, hitting the trees, Dean's old pickup, the dirt and grass of his driveway, then more trees. There was nothing unusual to be seen, nothing that would cause his dog's panic. He glanced behind him. The dog had inched further away from the doorway, her growl turned fully into a whine.

Dean wet his lips and tried to speak, to tell the dog she was being silly, but his mouth felt dry and chalky. He cleared his throat, the sound loud in his own ears. "There's nothing there, you dumb dog," he said, unsure whether he believed his own words or not.

He swept the light across the space in front of the cabin once more, then flicked it off and turned back towards the interior of the cabin. As he turned, he paused. Something, a small movement, caught the corner of his eye. He turned back to the yard and switched the flashlight on, sweeping the beam across his field of vision. There, off the rear end of his truck, he saw a shape.

He lifted his shotgun and settled it across his forearm so he could keep one hand on the light. "I see you, asshole!" he yelled. The shape, what looked like a big man wearing a long, hooded coat, did not move. "You step forward where I can get a look at you. You're on private property." The shape stepped forward.

The moment the shape moved, Betty let out a frantic yelp and fled towards the back of the house, her claws scrabbling for purchase on the floor. Dean glanced behind him at her disappearing form, and then looked back at the shape that stepped slowly towards him. With each pace the large man took, Dean was more certain he had made a terrible mistake.

"That's far enough," he shouted, his voice cracking. The shape kept approaching slowly, and Dean dropped the light so he could grip his shotgun in both hands. The flashlight bounced off the edge of the porch and tumbled into the grass in front of the cabin. The beam of light, obscured partially by the grass, shone uselessly into the trees, but the shape was close enough now that Dean could see it.

"I told you to stop."

The big man in the hood gave no indication he had heard Dean and kept taking slow, deliberate steps towards him.

"One more fucking step and I shoot." Dean depressed the safety on the shotgun with his index finger and tucked the stock into his shoulder, sighting along the barrel at the centre of the intruder.

The man stopped. The hood tilted up and down, as though he were taking Dean's measure, before he took another step forward.

Dean pulled the trigger on the shotgun. The roar of the gun hammered into his ears and the muzzle flash left a white streak in his vision. He blinked several times, trying to clear his sight, and looked at the space on the ground where he expected the big man to lie.

Nothing.

He stepped off the porch and picked up the flashlight with a shaking hand, his heart beating against his rib cage. He swept the light across his property, tendrils of gun-smoke still floating in the air.

"Where'd you go?" he tried to yell, but it came out as a child's nervous whisper. There was no answer, no movement, anywhere he could see. He turned the flashlight on his old pickup, and thought about the keys hanging on the hook beside his writing desk. He licked his lips and swept the light across the yard again. "I gotta get the fuck out of here," he said to the darkness.

Dean turned towards the porch, planning on grabbing his cowardly dog and getting the fuck off the mountain. The police would have to listen to him now, those silly bastards. If a man who didn't die when you shot him wasn't proof of alien life, or at the very least a good government conspiracy, then nothing was.

There was a crackling in the trees to his right and Dean

turned just in time to see the shape rush out of the shadows and slam into him. Both the light and the shotgun flew from his hands as Dean pin-wheeled across the lawn, coming to rest against the front tire of his truck.

A distant corner of Dean's mind, the one that tells you when it's time to shit your pants and run like hell, pummeled him. *Get up!* it screamed. *Run!* it yelled. Dean tried to obey, but he could not seem to get a breath. The right side of his body burned with a heavy, throbbing pain, and his mouth felt as though it had been filled with pancake syrup.

He turned his head and saw the big man in the hood coming towards him with slow, deliberate steps, and halting before him. Through the white flashes in his vision Dean could make out the outline of a face in the hood. The big man shook his head.

"Is this the best this place can do?" he asked.

He had a deep, pleasant voice, Dean thought, but there was something wrong with it. There was something beneath the dulcet tones, something almost hidden that grated his eardrums and made him want to gag. Dean raised his hands in front of his face, as though he might be able to fend off the sound of his voice.

"If this is your best defense," the big man said, "then you've no defense at all." He looked side to side. "This place will be easy to take, and they won't be able to hide."

The big man looked down, shaking his head, and casually raised his foot high in the air; a man making ready to crush an ant.

Summoning the last of his breath, Dean screamed.

On the other side of the Rivers Inlet, high above the lights of Resolution Cove, a small blonde head snapped up, blue eyes wide beneath long, silky hair. The wind carried a horrible sound: a long, undulating scream that sounded as though it had been ripped from the throat that produced it.

The slender girl, just shy of her teens, stood up from the

seat of the picnic table she had been sitting on. "Daddy?"

A lean man, all hard angles and sinewy bulges, turned from the camp stove he had been working over and brushed long, shaggy black hair out of his eyes as he looked out over the inlet. "I know, sweetheart," he said. He turned back to the chicken strips in the frying pan on the camp stove. "I heard it, too."

The child moved several steps closer to her father, her hands clasping a round medallion that hung from a leather cord around her neck. "I thought you said it would be safe here." She looked up, tendrils of hair drifting across her face in a breeze that cut across the narrow campsite. "I thought you said we wouldn't have to run anymore."

"I said this town had a Guardian, my love. I hope we'll be safe here, but you know we never have guarantees. We might have to keep moving."

"Will the Guardian help us?"

"We talked about this already. When we find him, we'll ask him. That's the best we can do."

She sighed, and twisted her small mouth as she stared out over the water of the inlet. As she stared, her small hands worked continuously around the dull, copper-coloured metal of the medallion. "I hope he helps us," she said.

Her father kept his eyes on the chicken in the frying pan, his shoulders sagging with unseen weight. "I hope so, too."

CHAPTER 2

Constable Quinn Sullivan ducked as a frying pan flew over his head and crashed into the wall of the small, filthy kitchen behind him.

"Jesus Christ!" he yelled. "Would you stop that?"

"I'll stop it once I hit that son of a bitch." The small, wiry woman opposite Quinn snatched another, larger skillet off the cluttered countertop and cocked it up above her shoulder. "I'm out working all day and he's in bed, drunk off his ass, with that whore from next door. I'm gonna cut his nuts off and shove 'em in my purse, is what I'm gonna do."

A rotund man, his gut bulging out from under his John Deere t-shirt, hair unkempt, nose red from liquor, bobbed and weaved on the other side of Quinn. "You heard her, officer. She threatened me."

Quinn had to suppress a strong urge to hit the man himself. "Shut up, Frank," he said. "You've done more than enough talking for one day."

"Yeah," the wiry woman said, shuffling her feet, trying to get a clear shot with the skillet. "You talked that bitch right into my bed and let her smear her fat ass all over my clean sheets."

Quinn doubted very much the sheets were clean, but kept his thoughts to himself.

When he had pulled up to the small, ramshackle house in Resolution's south end, a relatively obese woman had been fleeing from it, her clothing in hand and her bulk flapping in the wind. The idea of her and Frank in bed together was not a pleasant thought, and he had to sympathize with the small woman who was busily trying to brain her husband.

"Irene, you need to calm down," Quinn said, holding up his hands in a gesture of placation. "If you do manage to hit him, I'm going to have to arrest you for assault with a weapon. And if you hit me, I'm going to get really mad."

"You should arrest him," Irene yelled, gesturing at Frank with the skillet, causing the fat man to duck again. "You should arrest him for bad taste. Running around with that fat cow and giving up this." She cocked out one bony hip and gave her narrow ass a slap.

"Go ahead and arrest me," Frank said. "Get me away from her God-damned nagging."

Irene sucked in an indignant breath through thin, pinched lips and closed one eye to improve her aim.

Quinn grabbed the radio microphone hanging from the d-ring on his ballistic vest and pressed the transmit button. "Charlie Three from Charlie One, you mind stepping it up? I could use a little help here."

As Quinn released the radio mic, Dave McLeod, the intended recipient of his call, stepped in through the front door. "Frank," he called amiably. "Who'd you fuck this time?"

"This time?" Irene asked, her face growing redder by the minute. "What do you mean 'this time'?"

Quinn dropped his hands and glared at Dave. "Really?"

Dave shrugged and lunged at Irene as she let out a screech and charged towards Frank, skillet flailing above her head. Quinn intercepted her, ducked under the skillet and caught her around the waist. As he hoisted her from the ground, her legs kicking in all directions, Dave snatched the skillet from her hand.

"You see that, officers?" Frank asked. "She's crazy. She tried to kill me."

"Shut up, Frank," Quinn and Dave said in unison as they pinned Irene face down on the floor and clicked handcuffs onto her narrow wrists. The skinny woman kicked and spat and gnashed her teeth as she struggled with the Mounties, straining towards her husband. Despite the fact there were two large policemen holding his wife down, Frank cowered in the corner of the kitchen, his hands still up in front of his face.

"What do we do with her?" Dave asked, as he wiped sweat off his forehead with one hand and held onto Irene with the other.

"We gotta take her in, man," Quinn said. "She tried to brain her husband and threatened to kill him half a dozen times. We don't take her, Raife will have our asses."

Nodding, Dave helped Quinn haul the spitting woman to her feet. "Okay, you're right. You transport her and I'll see if good ol' Frank here wants to give me a statement."

Careful not to get kicked in the shins, Quinn pulled Irene from the front door of the small house and guided her down the rickety wooden steps to the overgrown front lawn. All the while she yelled abuse at both her husband and her rotund neighbour, who peeked nervously—and, thankfully, fully dressed—out through her living room window. Quinn managed to get Irene into the back of his marked patrol car, a task similar in scope to stuffing a bobcat in a pillow case. Despite the fact Quinn was a big man by most standards, more than twice the size of the angry little woman in his grip, he was sweating freely and cursing profusely by the time he finally got the car door closed on her writhing form.

"Sweet Jesus," he muttered, as he wiped several rolling beads of sweat off his forehead with a meaty forearm. Once he had caught his breath he opened the driver's door of his car and leaned across the driver's seat to turn the ignition key. With the engine running, he stood up straight and depressed the switch to roll down the back window, which emitted a fresh string of Irene's cursing. Wincing against the barrage of noise, he took his notebook from his vest pocket, flipped it open to the first blank page and leaned on the car to speak into the open window.

"Okay, Irene," Quinn said, reaching into a pocket on the inside of the notebook to pull out the laminated card that held the Charter Rights and Police Caution. "I'm gonna read you something and I need you to pay attention. Okay?"

Irene had her face pressed against the bars across the window of the backseat, her mouth sticking between them. "You need to read that fat fuck his obituary 'cause I'm gonna kill him once I get out of this car."

Quinn sighed. "Right. Okay, you are currently under arrest for assault with a weapon and uttering threats. Do you understand?"

"Fuck you!" Irene yelled.

"Right," Quinn said, marking down the response in his note book. "'Fuck you'. You have the right to retain and instruct counsel, in private, without delay. Do you understand?"

"I'm gonna kill you, Frank!" Irene shouted, spit flying from her thin lips.

"'I'm gonna kill you, Frank,'" Quinn repeated as he wrote down the response. "Irene, do you want to talk to a lawyer?"

"Save your lawyers for after I chop his nuts off!"

"Right," Quinn said, and sighed again. "You are not obliged to say anything to me, but anything you do say will be given in evidence. Do you understand?"

Seemingly out of steam, Irene sagged back against the seat of the car, still casting glares out the window at both her own house and the neighbour's. "Yeah, fuck, whatever. Just take me to jail. It's no good being here anyway."

Quinn made another notation is his notebook. "Okay. Try to take it easy and we'll get you a lawyer when we get back to the office." Irene made a harrumphing noise and sagged further down in the seat so only the top of her head was visible through the bars of the window.

As Quinn used the toggle on the driver's door to roll up the back window, Dave came out of the house, scribbling in his own leather-bound notebook.

"How'd it go?" Quinn asked, slamming the driver's door

before leaning back on it with folded arms.

"Frank was all gung-ho to give a statement until I told him he'd have to show up in court and miss a day of drinking. Then he caught a sudden case of amnesia and said he couldn't remember what happened."

"Perfect," Quinn said, rolling his eyes.

"What you wanna do with her now?" asked Dave, tilting his lean chin towards Irene while he scratched at the black stubble on his scalp.

Sighing, Quinn looked into the car. "We'll still take her back to the office and put a charge through. Crown will likely bounce it without a victim statement, but we still have enough to go with the charge from what we saw."

Dave opened his mouth to reply and then paused, his head cocking to the side and his eyes going up to the mountains south of Resolution. "Did you hear that?"

Quinn nodded. "I did." A gunshot, low and echoing, bloomed across the valley and echoed among the mountains. "Where do you think it came from?"

Dave shrugged. "Somewhere up on the hillside. There's lots of homesteaders up there that might want to shoot at something." He frowned down at his watch. "It's a little early for hunting, though. We're not halfway through June, and the season doesn't start until September."

The two men stood side by side, their eyes sweeping across the mountains and their dense covering of trees. As they stood, Quinn heard another sound: a faint, high-pitched scream.

"Uh, that's not good," Dave said as the two Mounties looked at one another.

Frowning, Quinn scanned the hillside. There were numerous camps, cabins and tent cities among the trees. Unless they heard the scream again it would be impossible to pinpoint where the sound came from. He folded his arms across his chest, still scanning the hillside, when he felt a sudden flare of heat coming from the small of his back.

He groaned, thinking he had pulled a muscle in the struggle with the snaky little woman in the back of his car, and then remembered the object he had secreted under his uniform shirt. Donell's dagger, the artifact given to him by Autumn Donnelly, was getting hot, the pulsing heat growing with his every heartbeat.

More than two years had passed since Quinn had discovered, with Autumn's help, the existence of a demon in Resolution Cove. With Dave at his back, Quinn had gone to find the creature and destroy it. He had only been able to do so because Autumn had given Quinn the dagger, carried by her ancestor, Donell of Inverness. The dagger, Autumn told him, had been used by Donell, a wandering knight, in service of the Light. The weapon, now imbued with Donell's power, had been guarded by her family for dozens of generations.

When Quinn had fought the demon the blade had burned with a white fire; a fire that consumed the creature when Quinn stabbed it. After the battle, and a warning from Autumn that this might not be the last time they would encounter something black in the shadows of Resolution, Quinn had a sheath made for the dagger and carried it with him everywhere he went.

For two years he had kept it with him constantly and the dagger had been dormant, nothing more than a sharp blade. Today was the first time it had grown hot to the touch since he had killed the demon.

"Dude, you okay?" Dave asked, as he studied Quinn's face.

"You remember the knife Autumn gave me?"

Dave jerked his chin back, apparently surprised. "You mean the one you used to kill the...you know, the thing?"

They had seldom spoken of their experience facing the demon, in the basement of a drug dealer's house, only a few blocks from where they stood. When they did speak of it—among themselves or with the other members of their watch, Charles Raife and Sandy Harding, who had also seen the thing—it was in hushed tones and with hurried words while they cast glances over their shoulders to be sure no one listened. The thing had caused Sandy to attempt suicide, and had nearly killed Quinn, Dave and Raife in the dirt floored basement of Joe Robowski's house. They had worked hard at forgetting. Only Autumn's warning, and the belief that he would rather be prepared if it ever happened again, had caused Quinn to carry the dagger at all times.

"Yeah," Quinn said, in response to Dave's question. "Well, it's hot."

Dave spun, his hand dropping to the pistol at his hip, his eyes scanning the houses around them and the trees behind. "Do you think there's, you know, another one of the things?"

Quinn shook his head, his eyes also searching the shadows among the drooping, dingy houses. "I don't know, man. It hasn't done this, or anything, since that night. I don't know what it means."

As the two men stood there in the dark, the heat faded from the dagger, leaving it cool to the touch again. He dropped his hand from the small of his back and rested it on his pistol, shrugging his shoulders to ease the building tension.

"It stopped," he told Dave. "Whatever made it hot is gone."

"I don't like that, dude," Dave said, still looking around. "That shit freaks me out. I don't ever again want to fight something that doesn't die when you shoot it."

"Me neither."

Dave looked at Irene, who must have sensed the tension in the Mounties and stared at them through the window.

"You two okay?" she asked, her voice muffled by the glass. "It looks like you saw a ghost."

"Fuck me," Dave said, turning and walking towards his car. "Let's get out of here. I'm getting the willies."

Climbing into the driver's seat of his car, Quinn dropped it into gear and pulled away from Frank and Irene's house. He glanced into the rear-view mirror and saw Irene leaning forward in her seat, not saying anything, a puzzled expression on her face as she studied Quinn's face in the mirror.

"You sure you're okay?" she asked, all the previous venom gone from her voice.

"I'm fine."

She shrugged. "If you say so." She turned her head and looked out the window.

Quinn took several turns, careful not to meet Irene's eyes in the rear view mirror, and drove down the street where the charred husk of Joe Robowski's house still sat. Only the foundation and a few random sticks of lumber – nothing more than a few blackened fingers reaching towards the dark sky - had survived the inferno that had burst from the demon when it died. The City had erected a portable fence around the site, but had not paid to have the place demolished, and no one had purchased the lot. It was as though the old memories of the place kept potential buyers away, as if they could feel the evil that had burned there two years previous. The place still haunted Quinn—brought back vivid memories of the night he and his friends had almost died—and he avoided the house whenever he could.

He slowed as he drove by, examining the remains of the house. The fence stood intact and the piles of charred lumber appeared undisturbed. The dagger remained dormant, with no heat emanating from it at all as he passed the site. It did not appear the demon he had fought was making a reappearance.

So, if it wasn't that, what was it?

Questions in his mind, he sped up and turned north to head to Resolution detachment.

Once Quinn had gotten Irene into the cell-block, took pictures and fingerprints, and lodged the now sullen woman into a cell, he walked through the hallways of Resolution detachment and into the general duty pit.

Sandy stood behind her recruit; a skinny, pimply faced youth named Gerritt Hauk, while he sat, hunch shouldered, at one of the office computers. He had come out of Depot only a few weeks before and stared at everything in utter bewilderment.

"No, Gerritt," said Sandy, her ample patience apparently

wearing thin and lending an edge to her voice. "For the thirteenth freaking time you have to write the report in chronological order, and no one cares if you were hungry when you were doing the traffic stop."

The youth nodded, but did not appear convinced of Sandy's instruction. He hit the backspace key on the computer's keyboard several times.

"How's it going?" Quinn asked as he dropped his prisoner report and Dave's handcuffs on his own desk.

Sandy rolled her eyes and gave Quinn a large, false smile. "Just fantastic, Quinn. How are you? I heard you and Dave had to arrest Irene so she didn't beat Frank to death with a frying pan."

Quinn snorted. "I'd almost say he'd have it coming if she did, but yeah, she's in lockup now." He looked down at Gerritt, who stared at his computer screen with an expression of profound dismay on his face. "How you doing, newbie?"

Looking up and scratching at a newly brewing pimple on his face, Gerritt gave a weak smile. "Good, Constable Sullivan. How are you?"

"Jesus, kid. I keep telling you, you can call me Quinn. We're all the same rank here."

"Oh, right," Gerritt said, not sounding particularly convinced. "I'll remember, Const—I mean, I'll remember, Quinn."

Quinn suppressed an urge to shake his head and turned towards his own computer. He tried to remember that everyone started out clueless, but the kid was just this side of hopeless.

As Quinn typed out the opening passages to the report to Crown Counsel for the charge against Irene, Dave hurried into the pit.

"Dude," he said. "Did you see that black SUV out in the parking lot?

"SUV?" Quinn asked. "No, I didn't. Why?"

"I think it's the District Officer's truck," said Dave, worry making his words short and clipped. "Did we fuck something up?"

Dave's disquiet was infectious and Quinn felt himself growing nervous as well. "Jesus, I hope not."

Since Resolution detachment was big enough to have a commissioned officer—Inspector Green—in charge of it, there was seldom any need for the District Officer, Chief Superintendent Cameron Crowley, to show up. When he did, it usually meant that someone had made a mistake of monumental proportions and Crowley was there to hand out an ass kicking. Quinn looked at his watch and saw it was after ten o'clock at night. If Crowley was out here now, making the drive of several hours from Prince George, the ass kicking was going to be vigorous indeed.

Footsteps sounded in the hallway leading from the back door, and all the members in the pit did their best to look busy. Crowley appeared at the opening to the corridor. A lean man of average height, with a smoothly shaved face and his grey hair shaped in an immaculate, military-style haircut, he wore his dress blues, with his officer's forage cap under his left arm.

Sneaking a look, Quinn frowned. Every other time he had seen Crowley, he had been dressed for duty, with his working uniform, body armour and gun-belt on. His appearance in regimental dress, at this time of night, was deeply concerning.

Another man stepped up behind Crowley; a short, portly man with thinning hair, dressed in a navy suit with the RCMP emblem on the left breast. Crowley spoke a few quiet words to the man behind him and then walked into the pit and directly up to where Quinn sat. He stood, but resisted coming to attention, as the superintendent stopped in front of him.

"Constable Sullivan, isn't it?" Crowley's manner was rigid and formal. "I believe we met when you and Constable McLeod received your commendations for bravery two years ago."

"Uh, yes, sir?" Quinn's heart-rate increased at being addressed directly.

"Is Inspector Green here? His wife said he was working

late."

Swallowing thickly, Quinn looked over the cubicles to the door of Green's office. A faint light shined beneath the closed door, a sign that the inspector worked with his desk lamp on.

"I haven't spoken to him, sir," Quinn said. "But it looks like he is in his office."

Crowley nodded and turned for the closed door, the portly man behind him.

When they were out of ear shot, Dave peeked around the wall of his cubicle. "What do you think that's about?" He asked from the side of his mouth.

"I have no idea," Quinn said. "But I hope it doesn't involve me."

Crowley knocked softly on Green's door, and then stepped through, the portly man following. The door closed behind them.

For several minutes Quinn's eyes darted from his computer screen to the closed door, fearful of what fuckery was being discussed inside. If Crowley was here, dressed as he was, with the strange hanger-on following him, there must be a severe shit storm brewing on the horizon. Quinn wiped damp hands on the legs of his uniform pants and tried to focus on the computer screen in front of him.

A handful of minutes later, the door to Green's office opened and Crowley walked out, his mouth and eyes turned downwards. Through the open door, Quinn could see the man in the navy suit patting Green on the shoulder. Green sat, his chair pushed away from his wide oak desk, looking at his hands lying limp in his lap.

Sandy, walking behind Quinn's chair on a trip to the photo-copier, stopped. "Isn't that the force chaplain?"

Quinn turned and looked at her. "Who?"

"The guy in the inspector's office."

"I don't know. Is it?"

Dave peeked around the wall of his cubicle and took another look. "You know, Sandy, you might be right."

As the constables watched, the man spoke a few more

words to Green, too softly for them to hear. Green nodded, still staring at his hands. With another pat, the chaplain straightened up and walked out of the office and towards the back door.

Quinn shared a look with his two partners, and then stood up and walked towards the inspector's office. As Quinn reached the office door, he rapped his knuckles against the jamb. Green looked up slowly, his eyes red and bloodshot.

"Sir," Quinn said. "Are you all right?"

Green shook his head, and lowered his gaze back down at his limp hands. His shoulders shook slightly, as though he were crying.

"Sir?"

"It's my son, Quinn," Green said and looked up, his eyes red and puffy, his cheeks shining. "He's dead."

CHAPTER 3

The nickel-plated spurs on their boots clicked in unison as the six men in red serge walked slowly, in step, down the centre aisle of the church. Quinn kept his eyes on the broad back and bald head of Charles Raife, and concentrated on the weight they carried together. The casket on Quinn's shoulder, bearing the body of Constable Patrick Green, was a heavy burden.

Only months previous, Inspector Donald Green had proudly announced his son's graduation from Depot, the RCMP training academy, whose gates had borne witness to the making of tens of thousands of new Mounties. Patrick's first posting had been the small town of Cranbrook – an isolated town in the British Columbia interior – and Inspector Green had kept his members updated, nearly daily, with his son's exploits and blunders as the newest member of the Cranbrook detachment. Patrick's death, by his own hand, had been a shock to them all.

The conversation in Inspector Green's office, a week prior to the funeral, burned in Quinn's mind as he bore Patrick's body toward the front of the church.

"It's my son, Quinn," Green said, raising his head. "He's dead."

Quinn felt the strength fade from his legs, and his face felt sud-

denly too heavy. *"Dead? How? Was it on duty?"*

Now Dave stood at Quinn's shoulder. Green glanced from one man to the other, then back at his lap to shake his head. "No. Crowley said they found him in the little apartment he'd rented. He'd hung himself."

Of course, the moment there was the vaguest whisper of a member of the RCMP committing suicide, the media descended on it like a pack of starving dogs. Pictures of Patrick's apartment had been leaked, apparently by the coroner's office, and had promptly been plastered all over every newspaper that was classless enough to publish them.

The apartment had been covered in strange symbols and odd articles. Black candles, pentagrams, posters and paintings of dark scenes, were everywhere in the small dwelling. Patrick himself was painted with odd symbols, things Quinn did not recognize when he saw the pictures, though he did not look at them long enough to get any clear sense of what they were. Once he had realised that Patrick was not, in fact, painted with symbols, but carved with them, he felt as though he might vomit. The thing that affected him most was that Patrick still held the scalpel he had used to rend his own flesh, and how it glinted sharply in the flash of the crime scene photos.

As the honour guard carrying Patrick's casket drew nearer to the altar, and the priest waiting there, Quinn allowed his eyes to leave Raife's back, and instantly wished he had not. They drifted to Donald Green's face. The pain in the twisted features and the red, puffy eyes, stabbed at Quinn so hard it made his breath catch in his throat. His eyes met the inspector's for the briefest of moments and in that moment Quinn learned everything he would ever need to know about sorrow.

In front of the altar sat the stand for the casket, and the honour guard walked to either side of it, so it sat directly below the long burden they carried. At a whispered command from Raife, they turned inward, as one, and lowered the casket to the stand.

Over the top of the casket, directly opposite him, Quinn

saw Dave McLeod. His eyes reflected the misery Quinn felt building behind his own. They broke eye contact quickly. Quinn feared that if he looked at his friend for too long he would break down—crumble under the weight of the sadness that lay across him—and he would not have that.

Quinn, and the entire Resolution detachment, had grown close to Patrick over the last two years. After the confrontation with the demon two years previously, Inspector Green had changed dramatically. Gone was the political schemer and absentee commander, to be replaced by a conscientious leader who possessed a renewed enthusiasm for his job and who genuinely cared for his members. That renewed enthusiasm generated a strong interest in police work for the inspector's son, and the boy, not long out of high school, began spending the majority of his free time in the detachment office. He put in volunteer hours, participated in the auxiliary constable program, and did everything he could to set himself up to walk in his father's footsteps. Not only Inspector Green, but the whole detachment was proud to see him onto a plane to Depot to begin his journey into the ranks of the Mounties.

Now that pride had come to an awful end and lay in a wooden box in the small church.

The honour guard stepped back from the casket, turned, and marched away from the altar, the plates on the bottoms of their boots clicking sharply on the stone floor. They paced quickly, their arms swinging in unison, and headed for the seats that had been reserved for them at the back of the church.

Carrie Dawson, dressed in traditional black with her long dark hair loose about her shoulders, was already seated and waiting for them. Quinn took her hand as he sat between her and Raife. As he gripped her firm hand in his own, he turned his attention to the robed priest who stepped up to the pulpit and began addressing the crowded little church.

Trying to focus, Quinn attended to the voice of the priest, hoping he could reach some kind of closure, come to some sort of understanding through the clergyman's words, but the blood pounding in his ears, a reflection of the tightness in his face, drowned out every other sound.

The service might have lasted ten minutes or an hour; time was meaningless to Quinn, as his eyes endlessly bounced between Patrick's casket and the face of a grieving father. He found himself staring at the long box when Raife grabbed his elbow and pulled him gently to his feet to follow the parents of the dead boy out of the church.

As he walked down the centre aisle, Quinn looked over his shoulder to see two ushers push Patrick's casket through a door behind the altar; a final farewell that brought him no comfort.

At the entrance to the church, Inspector Green stopped and stood at the head of the stairs, his weeping wife at his shoulder. He spoke to everyone who passed him, shaking hands and sharing an occasional hug, thanking people for coming. Quinn hung back, Raife and Dave near him, unwilling to step forward, as though this final act would be admittance that Patrick was gone. Gradually, the crowd thinned and Quinn found there was no one standing between him and the inspector. Quinn stepped forward, his hands at his side, and forced himself to look Donald Green in the eye.

Two years previous, when Quinn had faced the demon and Inspector Green had undergone his change, something had passed between the two men. Green had worked hard to keep a lid on the fact that his members had fought a supernatural being, something he never questioned Quinn about, and thereby preserved their careers and kept the detachment running. Quinn was acutely aware that without the Inspector's intervention they would have all—Raife, Dave and himself—been fired and soundly prosecuted for the things they did while combating the dark force that had tried to destroy their town. That shared experience, the violence and struggle, had brought them all very close together.

As Quinn stood on the stone steps of the church, looking into Green's face, he felt that binding like a great weight in his chest.

Donald Green gave Quinn a single shake of his head, and then extended his right hand. "Not now, Quinn," he said, his voice a gravelly whisper. "We won't talk now. We'll do it later."

Quinn was not entirely sure what the inspector meant by that comment, but nodded and clasped his hand. The inspector's wife, Geraldine—a short, round woman with a puff of thin, curly blonde hair—stepped past her husband, softly kissed Quinn's cheek and hugged him briefly, her arms around his waist. Carrie embraced both the inspector and his wife, and then squeezed Quinn's hand. Raife and Dave stepped forward to give their whispered condolences, and then followed Quinn and Carrie down the stairs.

"I've seen a lot of bad days in my time," Raife said, and ran his thumb and forefinger over his bushy, handlebar mustache. "But ain't nothing ever compared to this."

Quinn gripped Carrie's hand as they walked towards Raife's truck, and could not help but agree.

Across the street from Raife's black truck, in the parking lot of a small grocery store, a young girl and a lean man watched the three men walk out of the church and towards the vehicle.

"Is that him, Daddy?" asked the girl. She wiped a small hand across her face, pushing her silky blonde hair over her ear. "Is one of those men the Guardian?"

The angular man holding her other hand, her father, rubbed his free hand against several days of black beard grown on his face and worked his jaw, chewing at the inside of his cheek. "I think so, Abby, one of them anyway."

"Should we go and ask them?"

He watched the three men, dressed in scarlet, climb into a black pickup. "I don't think so. Today is not the day to be asking favours. Their day has been heavy enough as it is, and I don't think they have anything left to give."

Abby nodded in apparent understanding. "Do we still have time, Daddy?"

He looked around, taking in the trees and mountains that were visible from every inch of this town. There were a lot of places to hide in those mountains; both for them and the one who hunted them. "I think so, sweetheart. I hope so, anyway."

CHAPTER 4

A week after his son's funeral, Donald Green returned to Resolution detachment. Quinn was on duty, sitting at his desk, when the inspector came in and slouched his way between the back door and his office.

The inspector looked terrible. His face was drawn, as though he had lost weight, and his already thin hair seemed significantly thinner. He had always had bad posture from years of sitting behind a desk, but his shoulders were caved forward so far he almost seemed to be folding in on himself. If Quinn had to describe exactly how the inspector looked, he would have said he appeared to be diminished.

The pit was empty except for Quinn, the other members of 'C' watch out on the road dealing with one thing or another. Quinn stood from his desk and walked towards the inspector's office. Green was signing on to his computer and looked up, black circles under his eyes, when Quinn stepped into the doorway—much as he had two weeks prior when Green had been informed of his son's death.

"Quinn," the inspector said, a small smile turning the corners of his mouth. "Come in, we need to talk about something."

Thinking the inspector would want to unburden himself concerning his son's death, Quinn took in a deep breath, closed the office door behind him and sat down in one of the visitor's chairs in front of the inspector's wide oak desk. This was going to take a while, and it was probably going to hurt, but he was ready.

He was completely surprised when the inspector slid a legal sized piece of paper across his desk, and followed it with a pen. "I need you to sign your transfer papers."

"My *what?*"

"Your transfer papers. I need you to sign them."

"I'm getting transferred?" Quinn asked. He could feel his own eyes going so wide they hurt, while his eyebrows felt as though they were trying to climb off his forehead.

"In a manner of speaking, yes."

All thoughts of a difficult conversation with the inspector were forgotten. "What do you mean, 'in a manner of speaking'? Am I getting transferred or not?"

"You're getting transferred from the senior constable position on 'C' watch, to the corporal position. You're getting promoted." The inspector reached into his desk drawer and pulled out several sets of blue corporal's epaulettes, the double chevrons indicating the corporal's rank stitched on them in gold thread.

With no small amount of effort, Quinn closed his mouth.

Inspector Green said nothing for several heartbeats, only studying Quinn across the desktop.

Pulling in a large breath through his nose, Quinn looked at both the transfer form and the epaulettes. His tongue felt sandpapery in his mouth and his face felt too tight. Finally, he worked his jaw loose and looked up at the inspector. "So, you're fucking with me, right?"

That drew a small, stingy grin from the inspector and he shook his head. "No, Quinn, I'm not fucking with you. As of now you are a corporal."

"But..." he said and looked around the room. He felt like he was waiting for someone to jump out and tell him he was the butt of an extremely large joke. "But, I didn't apply for it. I didn't even know there was a corporal's vacancy that needed to be filled."

Green nodded. "Raife has been promoted to sergeant to fill the operations NCO position, so Steve Faulk can stop doing it and take care of the job he's supposed to take care of. I've arranged for you to receive a promotion by exemption and you're going to fill Raife's spot."

"Sir," Quinn said, nervousness strolling in to fill the seat recently vacated by incredulity. "I'm not qualified for the position. I don't have a fucking clue how to be a corporal."

Green leaned forward and rested his elbows on his desk while he tilted his chin down and looked at Quinn. "Now you're the one full of shit, Sullivan. What does Raife do that you don't know how to do?"

Quinn opened his mouth to respond, and then closed it with a click of his teeth. Come to think of it, there wasn't any specific duty that Raife performed that Quinn was completely uninformed about. In fact, he had filled in for Raife, on a temporary, 'acting corporal' basis, several times.

His mind started reaching. "Well, then, it's...uh...a matter of experience." He thought for a moment that his argument almost sounded reasonable, but the inspector continued to regard him as though he were looking at the village idiot trying to figure out how to put a space shuttle together.

"Quinn, you have nearly eight years service. You've passed the corporal's exam and you've proven that you can be a leader. You're a far better cop than I was at your service and the guys all look up to you. If this job had been advertised and open to applications, I was going to tell you to put your name in and you'd have gotten it anyway."

A niggling realization began chewing at the leg of nervousness, and Quinn felt his eyes narrow. "Wait a minute," he said. "Why wasn't this job advertised? You'd probably have a hundred applications."

Green shrugged. "I called in a few favours to see that it didn't go to the promotions board, and ensure you got it."

"Uh-huh. And why did you do that?"

"I need you to do something."

There it was, Quinn thought; The Catch. He felt like jumping out of his chair, pointing at the inspector and yelling 'Ah-ha!' But there was no jest on the older man's ashen face, and Quinn grew fearful of the 'something' the inspector wanted from him.

"Okay," Quinn said, slowly, speaking in a voice he would use when talking to an especially angry dog. "What do you need me to do?"

"I need you to go and investigate my son's death."

Shock, almost as great as when the inspector told him he was being promoted, slapped Quinn in the face. "Sir, I'm afraid I don't understand."

The inspector leaned back and folded his hands over his protruding gut while he looked at the top of his desk. After a few moments he looked up at Quinn. "Do you remember two years ago when Sandy tried to kill herself and you couldn't accept it? And you went and found...whatever it is you found in that basement?"

Did Quinn remember? How could he forget? After coming into contact with the demon in Resolution, Sandy was so tormented by what she had seen that she put her own gun to her head and pulled the trigger. She had jerked away at the last second, shooting herself in the neck instead of the temple, but she had fallen into an unnatural coma that she could not be pulled out of. It was not until the demon had been killed that she had awakened.

"Yes, sir," Quinn said. "I remember it very well."

"Yeah, well, just like you couldn't accept that, I can't accept this." Green leaned forward, the lines of his face hard. "You knew Patrick, Quinn. Did he go in for all this mystical, angstful, devil worship kind of shit? Did he walk around with his fingernails painted black and wearing eye liner? No, he didn't. His favourite band was Bon Jovi for Christ's sakes." The inspector rubbed a shaking hand over his tired face, and smoothed back his thinning hair. "You saw the pictures as well as I did. That wasn't the Patrick we knew. Something is wrong about this whole thing and no one who investigated it seems to give a fuck."

Quinn hated to admit it, but the inspector was right. "Okay, so what can I do about it?"

"You know about this stuff, Quinn. You've seen it before. You're the closest thing we have to an 'expert'. I need you to go and dig through what happened and get to the truth of it."

"Sir, I am far from an expert. I did that one...thing." Even two years later Quinn had difficulty describing exactly what had happened in the basement of Joe Robowski's house.

"Yeah, maybe so," the inspector admitted. "But out of anyone I know you're the only one with any kind of experience at all. And you've got that lady from the book store to help you out."

Autumn Donnelly, who had pointed him in the right direction and made him see what was actually happening in Resolution two years previous, was a resource that could not be overlooked. The inspector's decision began to make sense, and Quinn did not care for it.

"Okay, so why the promotion?" he asked. "You know if you'd asked me to do this I would have just gone. You didn't have to give me hooks." He gestured to the epaulettes bearing the two chevrons that gave rise to the term 'hooks'.

"I wanted you to apply for the position anyway, Quinn. But then this..." The inspector paused, took in a great, shuddering breath, and blew it out through puffed cheeks. "Then this happened. I pulled a few strings and called in a few favours and made it happen right away.

"As you've experienced before, people don't like to see closed investigations opened again. It makes them look bad. I figured you'd have an easier time of it as a corporal than as a constable."

"So, you anticipate some difficulty?" Quinn didn't really know why he was asking. He already knew the answer.

"This is gonna look like a wounded father looking for answers," Green said. "Which is exactly what it is. Only, I believe the answers are actually there and it's not just the grief talking. I've talked to a few people with more authority than me, and I've gotten you a point of contact in the Cranbrook detachment so you'll have access to the file." He paused again. "Although I don't know how happy anyone is going to be to see you."

"Right," Quinn said. The inspector was asking a lot, and was likely throwing him into a viper's nest of political bullshit and assholes with wounded pride. Yet, the man had saved his career two years ago and had since become a valuable friend. Quinn owed him this.

"Okay," Quinn said after several moments. "When do I leave?"

"How soon can you pack a bag?"

Quinn stepped out of Inspector Green's office several minutes later, after discussing travel plans and his point of contact in Cranbrook. The Force plane, apparently, was scheduled to be in Prince George the following day. Quinn was to drive there as soon as possible and catch a ride to the Kootenays.

As he stepped out of the office, he closed the door behind him and looked down at the objects gripped in his hand: the epaulettes the inspector had given him. He had signed the transfer form and was now officially a corporal. In most cases, this should be cause for celebration, but right now all he felt was dumbfounded shock.

He glanced up as Dave walked into the pit and towards his desk. The lean man stopped and looked at Quinn.

"Dude? Are you all right? You look...well you look ridiculous."

"I just got promoted." Quinn said, holding out the epaulettes tentatively, like a child who had found an especially strange caterpillar in his back yard.

Dave jerked his chin back, like he was avoiding a punch, and shook his head. "You got what?"

"I got promoted. The inspector just told me now."

"You didn't even tell me you applied." Dave looked offended.

"I didn't. I mean, I didn't apply. It's a promotion by exemption."

"Really?" Dave scratched his head. "What the fuck?"

Quinn shrugged and looked down at the epaulettes again.

Sandy entered the pit, her recruit slouching along in her wake, and stopped when she saw Quinn and Dave both looking down at Quinn's hand.

"Are you okay?" she asked.

"Quinn just got promoted," Dave said.

"You're fucking kidding me," Sandy said, and walked towards them.

"Congratulations!" Gerritt said, clapping his hands together once and pumping a fist in the air. He stopped celebrating when the other Mounties glared at him. "What?" he asked.

"Go check the tire pressure on the car, Gerritt," Sandy said.

"Again?" The recruit slumped his shoulders even further and turned to shuffle out of the office.

When Gerritt had turned the corner and was out of ear shot Sandy turned back to Quinn and took her turn to look offended. "You didn't even tell me you'd applied."

"Fuck," Quinn said. "I didn't apply. The inspector just handed it to me."

Sandy's eyebrows drew together. "I'm guessing there is a catch."

"Yeah," Dave said. "A hook that's got you right here." He bowed his legs and pointed at the area behind his scrotum.

"Pretty much," Quinn said, nodding. He looked over his shoulder at the inspector's closed door, and then jerked his head towards the other side of the pit. Both Sandy and Dave nodded and followed him to stand behind a bank of filing cabinets. Quinn looked around to make sure no one was near, before he told his two partners the details of his conversation with the inspector.

"So, he thinks what happened to me also happened to his son," Sandy said, summarizing when Quinn finished.

He swallowed and paused a moment, the memory of

31

Sandy lying on the floor of her house, a gunshot wound in her neck, swam across his vision. "I don't know," he said. "But he certainly doesn't believe Patrick killed himself."

"I don't blame him," Dave said. "Patrick didn't really look to me to be the kind of kid who would carve a fucking mural into his chest and then drop off a chair with a cord around his neck."

"No," Quinn said. "I didn't think he was either."

"So what are you going to do?" Sandy asked.

"What can I do, but go? If the situation were reversed, you know that Green would do it for one of us. I think I owe it to him."

Dave and Sandy both nodded in agreement.

Dave asked, "Do you know where you're going to start when you get there?"

"I haven't a clue," Quinn admitted. "I owe it to the inspector to go, but I don't know what I'm going to be able to accomplish. I don't know the town, I don't know the people and I don't know where to start."

Dave shrugged. "Start at the beginning."

Easier said than done, Quinn thought, but nodded anyway.

They stood silently for a moment, each thinking their separate thoughts. After several heartbeats, Sandy reached down and took two blue epaulettes from Quinn's hand.

"Well," she said, as she reached up to unbutton the bare epaulette on his uniform shirt and slip the corporal's hooks on it. "You might as well be happy about getting promoted."

Dave took the other epaulette and put it on Quinn's other shoulder. "Yeah, even if you have to eat a shit sandwich to do it."

CHAPTER 5

You're going where?" Carrie asked Quinn as she crossed her muscular, tattooed arms and glared at him from the foot of the bed they shared. The weight of her stare made him deeply uncomfortable.

"Cranbrook." Quinn tried to step around her to get to the dresser, but the bedroom in Carrie's little house, the house they now shared, was tiny and didn't leave much room to maneuver. He was forced to stand and bear the weight of her eyes.

"And why do you have to go?"

"To look into Patrick's death."

"Yes, I understand that Quinn," she said, the edge of her voice getting a little sharper. "But why does it have to be *you?*"

Quinn shrugged and stuffed his hands into the pockets of his jeans. "The inspector asked me to do it."

She made an exasperated sound, looked up at the ceiling and ran her hands through her long hair. "You know what I mean, Quinn. Why is he asking *you?* Why does it always have to be you?"

"The inspector thinks I'll be able to handle it, I guess. Because of what happened...you know...before."

Carrie was well aware that Quinn had faced something

unnatural, on the night he, Dave and Raife had killed the demon in Resolution, but they had never discussed it openly. Carrie had seen the claw marks on Quinn's neck, noticed the wounds the other men carried, and had walked in on the hushed tones they used on the rare occasions the incident was ever discussed. Despite the fact it went unspoken, it was clear Carrie did not want to know too much, and it was enough that Quinn had dealt with whatever it was needed dealing with. She never asked any questions and he never volunteered any information.

"So, what?" she asked. "You figure out one weird thing, you can figure them all? No, Quinn, you're not going."

"Carrie, I have to. I owe him—"

"I don't!" she yelled, leaning toward him and clenching her fists. "I don't owe him, Quinn. I don't owe him you. I almost lost you before, *twice*, and I'm not going to risk losing you again." She turned away, putting one hand on her slender hip and the other across her eyes.

"Carrie," Quinn said and stepped close to her to wrap his arms around her waist. "Carrie, you're not going to lose me. This isn't a big deal. I'm just going to go and look into Patrick's suicide. I'll ask a few questions, piss in some cornflakes, make a few people angry and help the inspector feel better."

As Quinn said the words, he did not know if they were necessarily true. The truth was he did not really know what he was going to do. He was a street cop, the Queen's goon, and had always thought of himself that way. What Green had asked him to do, to find the holes in the investigation concerning the death of a commissioned officer's son, was outside his realm of experience. He was going because he felt compelled to do so, but he really did not know what he was going to do when he arrived, or even where he was going to start.

Carrie looked up at him, strands of her black hair falling across her suspicious face. "Are you sure that's all?"

"I'm sure."

"It's not going to be like last time?"

"Not like last time."

She studied his face, as though she were looking to see if there was a lie somewhere on it. After several moments of narrow eyed scrutiny, she nodded. "Okay. Just make sure you come back in one piece, okay?"

"I will."

She stood on her tip toes and put her arms around his neck, pressing her face below his jaw. "I love you, Quinn," she said, her lips pressed close to his skin. "I can't be without you. I need you here with me."

Slowly, her whispered words turned into teasing kisses on the tender skin below his ear. A shiver ran up his spine and a steady heat bloomed in him.

"Mmmm," he said as her kisses traced the line of his jaw towards his chin.

Her hands slipped from around his neck, reached below the hem of the grey t-shirt he wore and ran across his hard stomach to his lower back. Her lips moved up from his chin and found his mouth.

He turned his head to the side as her lips traced the other side of his jaw. "Carrie," he said, his voice thick, his blood pounding in his ears and elsewhere. "I don't know if I have time for this."

Her right hand slipped from his back, deftly undid his belt, and flicked open the button of his jeans. She flashed him her even, white smile. "Shawn is still at school, and I'm not going to see you for a few days. You can make a few minutes for me." She hooked her thumb in the waist of his jeans and shoved them down to his upper thighs, then gripped what she revealed. A low moan rumbled out of his throat.

"Maybe just a few minutes," he said between heavy breaths.

Her smile got wider. "I'll be done with you in no time."

Quinn backed his Chevy Tahoe out of the gravel driveway of the house they shared. He'd had to give up his single man's sports car as he and Carrie grew more committed, and her son,

Shawn, had grown. A hockey bag did not fit well in the trunk of a two door Mitsubishi.

Quinn wished he'd had more time and could say goodbye to Shawn—the boy he was coming to think of as his son—but he was in school for two more hours and Quinn needed to get some miles under his wheels so he could make his flight. He was running short on time and still had another stop to make.

A few minutes later he pulled into a slanting parking spot in Resolution's down town business area and put his truck into park. He looked up at the store in front of his bumper: Nature's Song, Books and Gifts.

As he got out of the truck and approached the entrance, a familiar poof of curly blonde hair appeared behind the partially frosted glass of the door. Autumn Donnelly pulled the door open and stepped back, allowing Quinn entry.

"How do you always do that?" Quinn asked.

"Do what?" Autumn let go of the door and folded her hands in front of her.

"Meet me at the door every time I show up here."

She shrugged as the door closed and gave Quinn a smile. "I just get a feeling when you're coming around."

He shook his head, and smiled in return. "How did I know you were going to say that?"

"You do the same dance enough times, you memorize the steps." She turned and walked towards the back of her shop, past the pale wooden shelves that lined the walls and were filled with a myriad books, crystals and baubles. "What brings you by, Quinn? I haven't seen you in a while."

He followed her through the store, his eyes roaming about the shelves of odd objects. "I've got a job to do for the next few days and I wanted to see how you were doing before I got to it."

She reached the counter at the back of the store, with its ancient cash register, and turned back towards him. She leaned the small of her back against the thick, lacquered wooden surface of the counter, and folded her arms, tucking her hands into the sleeves of her voluminous scarlet blouse.

She regarded him, as she often did, with a small smile as though she was waiting for him to ask a question. He studied her face in the light of the old, green-shaded lamp beside the cash register. He did not like what he saw. There were always fine lines around the corners of her pale blue eyes from constant smiling, but today they appeared cavernous in the light of the lamp. There was a weariness etched on her face that he had never seen.

"Autumn, are you all right?" He reached forward to touch her elbow, then drew his hand back and stuffed it in his pocket.

"I haven't been sleeping well," she said, glancing at his withdrawn hand.

He studied her, waiting for her to add to her explanation.

She squirmed slightly under his gaze. "I've been having bad dreams." She turned and walked behind the polished surface of the cash counter. The wall behind the counter was covered in framed pictures, all of them hand-painted and with small price tags in the corners. She fussed with several of them, straightening the frames by minute degrees.

Each of her small, fidgety, nervous movements deepened Quinn's concern.

"Autumn?"

She turned from the wall, her hand shaking slightly as it paused in the act of straightening a small, water colour picture of a fairy creature.

"What kind of bad dreams?"

She took shook out her hands and ran one palm over the curls of her hair as she looked past him, through the bright front window. She leaned her elbows on the polished surface of the counter, clasped her hands in front of her and blew out a big breath through pursed lips.

"Dark ones," she said. "I keep dreaming of a shadow that settles over me, and it is cold inside the edges." Her eyes narrowed as she studied the street, like she was waiting for someone to walk up to the door. She looked at Quinn and shook herself, her eyes widening slightly and the smile returning to

37

her face.

She reached out to touch one more frame then walked back around the counter to stand in front of him, arms crossed and one curved hip propped against the counter. "What about you, Quinn? How are you doing?"

"That is a little complicated," he said, rubbing the short hair on the back of his head.

"Complicated?"

"Well, I got promoted."

Autumn studied him a moment, her eyes moving around his face. As always, he felt vaguely uncomfortable under her scrutiny, as though her gaze were moving like feathers over his skin. They had developed a certain camaraderie, begun when Autumn convinced him there was an evil force in Resolution Cove that was causing the surge in violence the town had experienced. After she proved to be right about the demon, he had learned to trust her instincts and had come to her for advice on a couple of files. Despite the odd bond they had, Quinn was always reluctant to think of Autumn as his friend, but regarded her more like a bead wearing, incense burning consultant.

The fact that she had kissed him once, and he sometimes wondered what it would be like if she did it again, did just this side of nothing to settle his nerves.

Her examination apparently concluded, Autumn ran her tongue over her teeth. "Should I be happy for you? I'm guessing there is a catch somewhere in that promotion."

Quinn crossed his arms and blew out his own heavy breath. "Your guess would be correct. Did you hear about our Patrick Green's death?"

Autumn nodded. "Yes, I'm afraid I did. There was a haze of pain that looked like a cold mist hanging over your office. It still hovers there. Even if I hadn't read about that poor boy in the paper it was easy to see that you and yours had suffered a loss." She paused and looked at the floor. "I wanted to come to the funeral, to be there for you when you carried your friend, but I didn't think it would be appropriate since the only person I'd really know there would be you." Her gaze landed on his face again and he unconsciously reached up and brushed at his own cheek.

"Well," he said, trying to work past his discomfort. "Inspector Green gave me my hooks so I'd have a little more authority when he sent me to investigate his son's death."

Autumn's eyes widened slightly. "You're leaving?"

"Yeah, I'm on my way right now. I wanted to stop and talk to you a minute before I left."

She uncross her arms and laid one hand flat on the polished surface of the counter, leaning towards him slightly, her eyes fixed on his face. "I don't think you should leave Resolution, Quinn. I have a bad feeling."

Conversations with Autumn always involved auras, portents, strange feelings and a list of other things that Quinn still didn't particularly understand and wasn't too interested in learning. With a great effort he kept himself from rolling his eyes, but he could not quite keep the annoyance out of his voice.

He leaned both palms against the counter and made a show of studying the pictures on the back wall. He was avoiding her gaze, but could still feel it on the side of his face. "I'm only going to be gone for a couple of days, Autumn. It really isn't a big deal."

"No, you're wrong, Quinn." She still regarded him intently. "I think it is a big deal. I think something is happening. Something black. And you, as the Guardian of this place, need to be here to face it."

"Autumn, you say that every few months and nothing has ever happened." On a regular basis, several times over the last two years, Autumn had sought Quinn out at his home—much to Carrie's annoyance—or at his office, always convinced there was some kind of threat in Resolution. Immediately after the confrontation with the demon, Quinn had jumped when Autumn showed up, alerting Dave and Raife that they might have another fight on their hands. Each of Autumn's suspicions had proved baseless and nothing had ever come of them.

It was as though she was getting more paranoid the less she had to worry about.

"Just because nothing else has happened, Quinn, doesn't mean it won't." She looked out the front window, both hands lifting to push her hair back from her face. "I know I've over-reacted before, but this time is different. My dreams, the weather, even your visit here, it all fits."

He took his hands off the counter and raised them, palms upward. "What about the weather?"

"It's June, Quinn, and you're still wearing your coat. Remember how cold it was while the demon was growing beneath the floors of that house in the south end?"

"We live on the coast, Autumn. We have ten months of shitty weather and two months where it gets vaguely less shitty. This isn't unusual."

She shook her head and clasped her hands in front of her. "I thought we'd be past this."

"Past what?"

"Past your miserable disbelief," she said, and reached out and tapped the middle of his forehead. "Past your thick skulled grumpiness. Did everything you saw two years ago teach you nothing? Why are you making this so difficult?"

He squirmed again and crossed his arms, because, truthfully, he did not know. He knew what he had seen in that basement, and still bore the scars of it. The memories, like the scars, were fading and he was ready for those memories to disappear. To Autumn, he thought, the battle with the demon was a justification of her belief; proof that the things she told him about, and was still telling him about, were real. To him, the event was a nightmare, where he had killed three people and nearly died himself. He wanted to move on, away from any thoughts of demons or boogeymen, while Autumn seemed to be gripping tight to a buoy in a sea of other people's disbelief.

"It's over, Autumn," he said, finally. "We killed that thing and burned the house it was hiding in to the fucking ground. It's done. You need to let it go."

"Yes, Quinn, that demon is gone, but there is nothing to prevent another's coming, and I fear that coming is upon us. You really should not go."

"I have to, Autumn. The inspector asked me to do this for him. I can't say no. I owe him."

"And you're not one to leave a debt unpaid, are you Quinn?"

He wasn't sure if there was an alternate meaning to her question, but he shook his head. "No, I am not."

She sighed and rubbed a hand over her face, and it made her look all the more weary. "All right, Quinn. Do what you have to and come back quickly. I think you will be needed here." She regarded his face for a moment, and quirked one eyebrow. "Is there anything else you wanted to talk about while you were here?"

He thought, very briefly, of telling her about the heat in Donnell's dagger and decided almost immediately against it. It would only add to her paranoia and insistence he not leave the town. She was crazy enough all on her own. She did not need him to throw fuel on her nut-log fire.

"No, Autumn," he said, forcing a smile and tucking this thumbs into the pockets of his jeans. "I'm all good, I just wanted to stop and see you, since it'd been a while."

She nodded and stepped past him, close enough that her skirt brushed the back of his hand, towards the door. He followed, the scent of her wake—of flowery soap, the stronger smell of some kind of spice—wafted across his face, and he clenched his teeth and felt his brows scrunch together. He did not like that he enjoyed it so much.

She pulled the door open and stood aside so he could pass, but as he did she put her hand on his arm and stood on her toes to kiss his face. Her lips landed on the line of his jaw, and he drew in a sharp breath as he felt the heat of her so close to him.

"Luck to you, Quinn," she said, just as she had said when he went to fight the demon two years ago. "I hope you won't need it."

"Thanks, Autumn," he said as he stepped through the door. "I'll come see you when I get back."

He got into his truck and backed up from the curb. He slapped a hand on the gearshift to put the vehicle in drive and pulled away, raising a hand to the blonde haired figure in the window of the little store. As he finished his wave, he brought his hand to his face and rubbed at his jaw, where the outline of Autumn's kiss still burned.

From the wide, open lawn on the mountainside south of Resolution, the town was nothing more than a vague outline; squat buildings and the grey scars of roadways carved into the surrounding trees.

A pair of narrow eyes studied the shape of the town, as the owner held a thick bone to his lips and sucked at the remaining bits of putrid meat clinging to the pale surface. He pulled the bone from his mouth and turned his eyes down to study it. Finding nothing worth pursuing, he tossed it to the bristling dog that lay at his feet.

His eyes had seen hundreds of towns in his long life and wide travels, perhaps thousands. He had visited many countries of this world, always moving, always seeking. Of all the places he had seen, he had never encountered a place so *ripe*.

This place, this dwelling of men, was small, but it had a depth of feeling, a raw energy that he had never found before. This town was a confluence, a meridian point, a meeting of streaks of power running through the earth that he could feel thrum beneath his feet. For a settlement so young, the history of this place ran deep, and that depth brought a power that was unimaginable.

For many of a man's lifetimes he had walked, seeking a key, delving for it in the cities and the lives of men. Now, as he sat studying the town, he felt as close as he had ever been. That key was almost in his grasp. It would not be kept from him much longer. They could not run forever.

His long travels had left him weak, but he had fed well in

the past days and was ready for the final leg of his journey. He would go into this town and walk among its people, hidden in their plain sight, and find the one he sought.

He pulled the ragged, stained cloak—nothing more than an old blanket—from his shoulders, tossed it onto the ground and reveled in the feel of the wind on his bare skin. He stretched his arms above his head, thick muscle and tight sinew creaking as he rolled his shoulders in their sockets. He could not go like this, he realised as he finished his stretch and looked down at his naked body. He would have to disguise himself, similar to his prey, if he was to be successful.

He bent and picked up the garments previously worn by the thing he had been eating. There was a weight wrapped up in the fabric of the stained material, and he reached in to find a hand. He examined the hand for a moment, wondering how he could have possibly overlooked it, and set it aside for later. He examined the blue work-shirt he held and decided it would not do. The red stains of the previous owner's blood would draw far too much attention he did not want. He tossed the shirt aside and walked into the cabin.

A few minutes later he re-emerged, dressed in a pair of worn blue jeans and a thick, red-checked flannel shirt. He stooped down and pulled on the boots he had left outside the door, shaking them out first to ensure there were no lingering scraps of the one who had worn them before. He stood and stretched again, with less enthusiasm this time, now that he was constrained by clothing.

He trotted down the wooden steps and onto the matted grass, stopping to pet the massive, growling dog that lay beside the piled bones of its former owner. The dog had been a shaking, miserable thing when he found it, but he had made several improvements and she was something to behold now. He regretted not being able to take her with him into the town, but that, once again, would draw entirely too much attention.

With a final, fond glance around the place he had spent the last several days, he slipped into the trees and towards Resolution Cove.

CHAPTER 6

"Excuse me, Sergeant?"

Raife turned away from his computer screen, about to correct the elderly volunteer that stood in the doorway to his small, grey-walled office, when he remembered that he now wore sergeant's epaulettes. He was still surprised when he looked down to see the extra chevron with the crown above it. Green had told him yesterday—only a few minutes after he had sent Quinn on a wild fucking goose chase to Cranbrook, of all God-forsaken places—and he was still getting used to the idea that he was no longer a corporal.

"Hi," he said, as he glanced down at his epaulettes again, just to make sure they were still there. "What can I do for you?"

"There is a man here to see the inspector," the woman said, her blue-veined, liver spotted hands dry-washing each other nervously.

Raife waited. "Yes?"

"Well, the inspector isn't here, but I'm afraid to turn this gentleman away."

"Okay," Raife said. "Who is he?"

The old woman looked over her shoulder, and then stooped a little further into Raife's office, her voice dropping with her posture. "He says he's the Mayor."

Raife frowned, the corners of his mustache dropping to tickle his chin. "Did he say what he wanted?"

The volunteer shook her head and reached up unconsciously to pat her tight perm. "He just asked to see the Inspector."

"Okay," Raife said, as he stood to shuffle around his faux-wood desk towards the door. "I'll go talk to him."

As he walked to the front counter of the detachment, past the clusters of cheap cubicles and rows of filing cabinets, Raife saw the Mayor; a slim, straight-backed man in his mid-thirties, dressed in a dark suit, his short hair carefully styled. The young man—young to be a mayor anyway—was leaning easily on the counter, his elbows on the glass surface, as he reached down and tapped his finger on a newspaper in front of another, elderly, be-spectacled volunteer who was undoubtedly someone's grandmother.

"I think twelve down is 'Napoleon'," he said, then rubbed his clean-shaven jaw, apparently in thought.

"Oh!" the volunteer said in a reedy voice. "You're right."

The mayor looked up at Raife and straightened as the volunteer jotted down the answer on the newsprint. The mayor stuck his hand out as his eyes flickered briefly to Raife's shoulder. "Good morning, Sergeant," he said. "I don't think we've met. I'm Jay Drummond."

"Charles Raife," Raife said as he clasped the mayor's hand, enclosing it in his hairy-knuckled mitt. The smaller man had soft hands, but his grip was solid, without trying too hard.

Unlike the previous mayor, Raife actually did not mind this one. He had only been in office for eight months, winning by a landslide over his predecessor—who had experienced a fairly severe falling out with Donald Green when he had attempted to rid the city of the RCMP and bring in a municipal police force. Drummond had been supportive of the detachment, agreeing to an overdue budget increase in trade for the inspector agreeing to try out some crime prevention initiatives Drummond had come up with. The man was young and energetic, almost to a fault, and had not, yet, turned out to be an asshole.

"What can I do for you, Mr. Mayor?" Raife asked when he released the smaller man's hand.

"Please, call me Jay. I was hoping to see the Inspector. Is he in?"

Raife shook his head. "Sorry, no. He's not here today."

Drummond nodded. "Still dealing with the loss of his boy?"

Raife believed, very firmly, that a man's grief was his alone, and was not to be discussed unless that man wanted to talk about it. "He's not in," he said.

The mayor nodded, smart enough to take the hint and let the subject drop. "Perhaps I could speak with you about something, then, if you have time."

Running his fingers over his mustache, Raife tried to think of an excuse not to talk to the man. He was all for crime reduction, but that was not his kind of police work. He was hoping to finish the administrative tasks expected of his new position and then get out on the road with his team and do something useful.

"Sir, if you need to discuss one of your initiatives, perhaps you'd be better off speaking to the Inspector when he returns to work or Staff Sergeant Faulk sometime next—"

"No, no," the mayor waved a hand, interrupting Raife. "I'm not here for any of that. I actually have a request. An odd one."

Raife examined the mayor's face. Despite himself, he was curious. "Please," he said, swinging open the waist high door that gave access to the lobby. "Let's sit in my office."

They walked quickly across the open area of the pit, towards Raife's office. Halfway there Raife saw Dave McLeod enter the pit from the hallway leading to the cell block. Dave looked from Raife to the mayor and back again, and raised one hand slightly, palm up. Raife cocked one eyebrow in reply, indicating he did not know why Drummond was there, either.

Once they had entered Raife's office and he'd closed the door behind them, the big sergeant squeezed himself in behind his desk—he still didn't know why they insisted on designing these spaces for midgets—and folded his hands on his desk top, waiting for the mayor to speak.

Drummond fidgeted and shifted in his seat, looking at the floor, at the pictures—Arnold Friberg prints and a picture of the Queen—arranged on the grey walls, at Raife's big hands, everywhere but at the face of the man across from him.

Growing impatient, Raife blew out a breath through his nose. "So, sir, what is it I can do for you?"

"Well, Sergeant," Drummond said as he shifted in his seat again. "I feel somewhat silly coming to you with this." His eyes flickered to Raife's face once, and then skittered away again, the confidence and ease he had displayed in the detachment lobby completely gone.

Raife leaned back in his chair, heard it creak with his weight – another piece of office furniture made for midgets – and pinched the bridge of his nose between thumb and forefinger. Thoughts, awful ones, raced through his head, imagining all the possible scenarios the mayor was about to lay in his lap. Raife had an inclination a dead hooker might be involved and Drummond was looking to get his ass saved.

"Mr. Mayor—" Raife began.

Drummond cut him off. "Please, Sergeant, call me Jay."

"Okay, Jay. You need to tell me why you're here before we can decide if the reason is silly or not."

The mayor nodded. "Right. Well, do you know Dean Springer?"

This question, Raife did not expect. He leaned forward in his chair and rested his elbows on his desk. "Dean Springer? The crazy bastard that lives up the forest service road south of town? Yeah, I've dealt with him before, usually when he's convinced himself there is a sasquatch in his crawl space and wants us to arrest it for trespassing."

The mayor looked sheepish and rubbed one index finger beneath his nose like he had an itch. "Well, Mr. Springer has been sending me two or three letters a week for the last eight months, ever since I was elected."

Drummond paused. Raife waited for the space of a couple breaths then said, "Yes. And?"

"Well, two weeks ago," the mayor continued, "the letters stopped."

"Okay?"

"And I'm a little concerned."

Raife sat up a little straighter and ran his hand over his bald head. "Just so we're clear, Jay, you're in here to complain that a man who has been sending you, what I can only assume are, rude and ridiculous letters for the last eight months has stopped?"

"See? I told you it was silly."

"Okay," Raife said. He had several sarcastic and caustic remarks on the tip of his tongue, struggling to wriggle past his mustache, but he bit them back and cleared his throat. "I'm confused, sir, as to what the problem is."

Drummond shrugged. "Well, I guess I'm worried something has happened to him." Raife started to speak but the mayor held up a hand, halting him. "I know it sounds stupid, Sergeant, but I don't have anything against Mr. Springer. His letters are ridiculous, of course, but I've come to look forward to them. In fact, I read them out loud to the staff and council at the town hall every time they come in. We all get a laugh out of them. When the letters stopped coming everyone noticed, and I started to wonder if maybe something had happened to him. He lives way out there," the mayor waved his hand in the air beside his head, "all alone, and he doesn't have a phone – I know because I tried to call him – and he can't call for help if he needs it."

The mayor paused and ran a hand across his smooth face. "I guess I'd feel bad if something had happened to him and I didn't speak up."

Raife watched the mayor for several moments, letting the younger man's words roll around in his mind. He was impressed he had to admit, to himself if no one else, that the mayor would give a shit about a man who made a hobby out of harassing him. Maybe the kid wasn't as big an asshole as most elected officials were inclined to be.

"You have a point, sir," Raife said. "I know where Dean lives. I'll go and check on him, make sure he's all right."

Drummond's easy smile returned and he let out a breath he had been holding as he stood up. "That would be fantastic, Sergeant Raife."

"Just Raife, please, Jay," Raife said as he stood. "That's what everyone calls me."

"Raife, then," Drummond said as he stuck out his hand and gripped with the big sergeant. "No need to see me out, I know the way." He opened the door and took two steps out of the office, then turned back. "You'll call me and let me know how it turns out?"

Raife nodded and hitched his gun-belt up. "I will."

Drummond smiled again, then turned and walked briskly towards the front door.

When he was gone, Dave stood up from his cubicle and approached Raife. "What was that about, boss?"

"The mayor was worried about something."

"Worried, huh?" Dave asked. "What'd he do? Kill a hook-er?"

Raife chuckled and shook his head, then related the complaint Drummond had made.

"Spinger? Really?" Dave asked. "I don't know who's crazi-er; Dean for his letters, or the mayor for being worried he isn't getting them anymore."

"That's an even race, and I don't know which horse to bet on."

Dave grunted. "You want me to go up and check on him?"

Shaking his head, Raife grabbed his hat off the rack beside his office door. "Nah, I've known Dean for years. I'll go have a talk with him. See if he's got any new photographs of blurry shadows that he swears are a sasquatch."

"Make sure you don't tell him the mayor was worried about him," Dave said, with his even grin. "He'll think it's some kind of conspiracy and start shooting at you."

Two hours of windy, switch-back mountain roads later, Raife pulled his white Chevy Suburban, the RCMP crest emblazoned on the doors, into Dean Springer's driveway. It took him only moments to realise there was something wrong.

As Raife got out of the truck, he unsnapped the retention straps on his holster and rested his big hand on the butt of his pistol. He stood behind the open door of the truck and studied the front of Dean's cabin. The door was open, there was a pile of trash beside the stairs up to the front porch, and all the windows facing the yard were dusty and dark. In the times Raife had been up to the property to speak to Dean, he had been nutty as a shit-house rat, but he was a neat rat. The trash strewn about worried Raife more than anything else.

He suddenly wished, very much, that he had asked Dave to come along, to keep him company on the ride. Keeping his eyes on the house, he leaned across the driver's seat of the truck, picked up the radio mic from its cradle beside the steering wheel and pressed the transmit button.

"Resolution, this is Charlie-Five-One," he said and released the button.

A few seconds later a blast of static sounded through the radio's speakers, a voice hidden somewhere in the noise.

"Resolution, this is Charlie-Five-One, can you copy me?"

More static, the voice made an unintelligible reply.

"Resolution, if you can hear me, I need cover up here."

Raife felt stupid almost as soon as he said it. It took him two hours to drive up a road he was well familiar with, in a truck designed to handle it. It would take Dave, or anyone else working, as long or longer to get up to him if he needed help. For now, and the foreseeable future, he was on his own.

He reracked the radio mic, pulled his pistol out of the holster and gripped it in both hands as he stepped around the open door of the truck. He did not slam the door closed. If there was someone in the cabin—someone who had done something to Dean—he did not want to give them any more warning he was coming.

His gaze flickered over the windows in the front of the house, the open door, the space under the porch, watching carefully for any kind of movement. He shook his head in irritation as a drop of sweat, despite the cool weather, rolled down his bald head and past the corner of his right eye.

He reached the bottom of the stairs and held his pistol at eye level as he pointed it at the dark gape of the front door. Something in the pile of trash beside the stairs caught his attention. He did not want to lose sight of the door, but risked a glance down at the trash to see a clump of bloody clothing, entangled in a pile of bones - big bones, with small bits of red flesh still attached. He looked up at the door again, worked his mouth, and sucked at another drop of sweat tickling his mustache.

The stairs creaked under his bulk as he stepped onto them, the sound sending a hot spike into his chest. He gritted his teeth as his heart beat crashed in his ears, and decided that any attempt at stealth was useless. In two big steps he launched himself up the stairs, onto the porch, and pressed himself up against the wall beside the open door. He sucked in a deep breath, steadied himself and then wheeled into the doorway and to the side of it, so he wasn't silhouetted in light of the entrance.

He had his pistol up, even with his gaze, and swept it across the room. The space was dark after the brightness outside, and it took several seconds for his eyes to adjust to the shadows in the small cabin. The place did not look like it had been lived in for weeks. There were leaves and debris on the floor, the old couch in front of the rock fireplace looked like there was an animal living in it, and the typewriter on the desk contained a piece of paper that was wrinkled and fluttering.

There was no movement, though—except for the slightly fluttering paper—and Raife held still for several seconds, holding his breath and straining to hear anything else in the dwelling. When he heard nothing, and the silence stretched on, making him increasingly jittery, he moved forward towards the small kitchen. He had just glanced behind the worn, arborite counter, when a noise from the small bedroom at the back of the cabin made him turn.

The click of claws on the wooden floor.

Dean had kept a dog, Raife remembered. There was no sign of its master, and the poor thing must be half starved and terrified. The presence of another creature settled Raife and he let out a whooshing breath as he stepped around the kitchen counter to halt beside the table.

"Where you at, dog?" Raife asked the shadows at the back of the house. "It's all right. You can come out. Maybe tell me where Dean's gone." He began to crouch, to make himself look less threatening, but stopped halfway down.

In the doorway to the small bedroom, was a darker shadow. The curtains in the room were closed, but a crack between them allowed enough light to outline a large, hulking shape filling the bottom half of the doorway. Dean's dog had been a Rottweiler, Raife remembered, a heavy, gentle dog that Dean had insisted was trained to attack, but had been about as vicious as a rose petal. The thing in the doorway was half again as big as the dog had been, with heavily muscled shoulders that gave it an almost comic appearance. This was not Dean's dog. This was something else.

Raife stood from his half crouch and brought his pistol back up to eye level again, aiming at the dark shape. It was time, he decided, to get some help and start a search for Dean. He and his dog were certainly not here, and whatever was staring Raife down now had settled in and taken up residence. He thought, looking at the outline of the heavy shape in the bedroom door, of the pile of bones by the front steps and swallowed heavily.

He took one, slow step backwards and, as his size fifteen boot scraped the floor, the massive head of the thing in the doorway lifted and the body shifted forward, the big muscles in the chest and shoulders vibrating. The thing snapped at the air in front of it and Raife heard the splatter of its slobber hitting the floor.

"Ah, fuck," Raife said to himself, as he moved his finger from the frame of his pistol and onto the trigger.

He took another step backwards and the thing lunged, the huge body hurtling across the distance between them. Raife let out a snarl, almost as deep as the creature attacking him, and pulled the trigger of his pistol rapidly while he backpedaled. He got off four shots, too close to miss, but the momentum of the thing carried it to slam into him. He stumbled out the door and fell heavily on his back, the smooth planks of the floor beneath him.

The thing on top of Raife was a blur of dark hair and scrabbling claws, and he felt a crushing pain as the thing clamped its heavy jaw down on his left arm. He still had his pistol in his right hand, and fired up into the dark shape. The body jerked and the grip on his arm slackened. He thrust his hips upwards and heaved with his bitten arm, tossing the thing over his head and down the stairs. He rolled onto his knees and saw the thing that had attacked him, and had likely eaten Dean, clearly for the first time.

Struggling to his feet, he rubbed a bloody hand across his eyes. On the ground, at the bottom of the stairs, was Dean's dog, only it was not the same dog anymore. The animal was much bigger, the muscles in the jaw and shoulders far more pronounced, but the basic shape was the same and the colouring was identical. There was a pink collar around the thing's neck, stretched tight with its bulk. Raife was willing to bet there would be a little brass tag on the collar with the name 'Betty.'

Despite all the bullets Raife had put into the animal, it was still alive. It rolled and thrashed on its side, its wide, black eyes fixed on his face as it snapped and snarled. Blood and saliva flew from its jaws. Its scrabbling feet churned the darkening ground beneath it to mud.

It tried to stand, to crawl towards Raife, mindless, animal fury plain in all its painful movements. Before its frantic efforts were successful, Raife scrambled down the stairs, slammed his heavy boot down on the thing's head and shot it once more, through one of its furious black eyes. The dog spasmed once, its body curling and rigid, before becoming still.

Raife staggered backwards and sat heavily on the stairs. He looked down at the dog, then at the ragged tear in his flesh of his arm and the blood running freely down his left hand. "Mother fucker," he said as he wiggled his fingers, making sure his hand still worked.

Once he had a handle on the pain, Raife stood up walked towards his truck. He realized he still gripped his pistol in his right hand, the dull grey metal smeared in dark blood. He looked over at the dog, which had not moved, but shot it one more time, just in case it got any ideas. He dropped the nearly empty magazine onto the ground, pulled a new one from his belt with his bloody hand, and jammed into in the grip of the pistol.

He holstered the pistol and walked to the rear of his truck, where he opened the rear hatch and pulled out a large, yellow tool-box that said 'First Aid' on it. After wrapping several lengths of gauze around the jagged punctures in his arm, he opened another bag: the emergency survival kit the inspector had bought for all the detachment vehicles the previous year. He opened it and quickly found what he was looking for: a small black box with a dial on it that said 'On'. He turned the knob, and a small red light beside the dial began pulsing steadily.

He walked back towards the front of the truck and slid the emergency beacon onto the dash, then settled in to wait. The search and rescue teams that operated in Resolution, both in the port and in the area around the town, would pick up the beacon in short order and come to see who had set it off, with their chopper, if he was lucky. Those boys would have satellite phones, and he would be able to the call the detachment and get a hold of everyone who needed to know where he was and what he had seen.

His arm was not that bad and he could have driven down the mountain to fetch help, but that would have left a crime scene unguarded. He did not feel right driving out of there while Dean was unaccounted for. Although, as he eyed the pile of bones beside the stairs, he figured that accounting would come quickly enough.

He leaned against the hood of the truck, stretching his bandaged arm out and letting it throb as he examined the huge dog he had killed. The sight of it brought back memories that he had hoped were done and gone; of people who were not as they were supposed to be, of strange things living beneath the floors of rundown houses, and of red eyes in the dark.

He wiped at a crust of blood in his mustache, and thought this was a very bad time for Quinn to have left Resolution.

CHAPTER 7

uinn clenched his teeth and gripped the headrest of the seat in front of him. "Fucking planes," he muttered.

He hated to admit it to anyone, least of all himself, but he hated flying. Being several thousand feet in the air with nothing beneath you but a few layers of flimsy metal was not a natural state for a man to be in. He especially hated little planes with engines roughly the same size as his lawnmower.

He gripped the headrest in front of him a little harder and bit back several curses as the plane hit another pocket of turbulence, threating to knock them out of the sky, or so Quinn assumed. Once he had swallowed back the contents of his stomach, he cleared his throat.

"How much longer, do you figure?" Quinn shouted forward to the pilot, trying to keep the high pitch of panic out of his voice.

"Another twenty minutes." The pilot, a heavyset man named Melvin, turned in his seat and looked through the open cockpit door to where Quinn sat in the second row of passenger seats. "You all right there, Corporal? You look a little green."

"I'm fine," Quinn said, resisting the urge to throw something at the pilot. "I'll be better when I'm off this fucking thing," he said in a tone that would not be heard over the noise of the single engine at the front of the aircraft.

Quinn's drive from Resolution Cove to Prince George had been uneventful, if a bit long, and he had located the hotel the detachment office manager had arranged for him. He had arrived at the Prince George airport at shortly after six a.m. and the pilot had been eager to leave.

"What did you say you were doing in Cranbrook?" Melvin asked. "Sounds like a lot of strings were pulled to get you there."

"You have no idea," Quinn said, thinking of his recent, unexpected promotion.

"What's that?" Melvin asked, shouting over his shoulder.

"Oh, nothing."

"Right. So what is it you're doing?"

Quinn ran his tongue across his teeth and looked out the small window beside his seat. He studied the green carpet of trees, with the bright splotches that would be lakes or ponds, and wondered silently just what it was he was supposed to be doing.

Undertaking a special investigation? Well, if you stretched it a lot, maybe. Catering to the wishes of a grieving father? Certainly. Quinn really did not believe that he was going to do any good with this trip to Cranbrook, not in the sense of investigating Patrick's death or the circumstances surrounding it, anyway. He trusted the investigation would have been done properly the first time and there would not be much for him to do, except bring some peace of mind to Inspector Green.

What was the Inspector hoping to achieve by this, anyway? Did he hope to prove that Patrick had not actually committed suicide? Did he think that Quinn would uncover some conspiracy and discover that his son was actually alive? The Inspector was looking for a miracle. Unfortunately, Quinn did not have one to show him.

Turning away from the window, Quinn looked back at Melvin, who stared at him, peering over the top of his aviator sunglasses.

"I'm going to look into something," Quinn said.

Melvin shrugged. "We're gonna land soon."

Both grateful that the trip would cease, but terrified that the plane would invariably crash upon landing, Quinn leaned back in his seat, wiped his sweaty palms on the legs of his jeans and grabbed the arm rests. Melvin lowered the landing gear, banked sharply, and then landed smoothly on the black air strip.

The plane taxied across towards a squat, single storey building that Quinn could only assume was the airport. Once the plane had stopped, he stood up and grabbed his duffle bag from the overhead bin. Melvin got out of the pilot's seat and opened the door so Quinn could get out. The door doubled as the stairs, and gave a faint hiss as they lowered towards the ground.

"I'm only getting fuel and then taking off again," Melvin said as Quinn shuffled past him. "I'm heading to Vancouver, but I'll be back to get you in three days."

"Okay. Thanks for the lift."

Melvin nodded. "Good luck with...whatever it is you're looking into."

Quinn gave a tight grin as he ducked out the door. Luck was something he figured he was going to need.

The heat outside the plane, radiating off the blacktop in shimmering waves, surged up off the ground and slapped Quinn in the face the moment he stepped through the plane's narrow door. The contrast in temperature from Resolution to Cranbrook startled Quinn. Sweat popped out on his forehead.

He wiped a hand across his face and checked to make sure his badge was attached to his belt, just in front of the pistol on his hip so that no one at the airport made any panicky 9-1-1 calls about a man in a grey t-shirt walking around with a gun. He stepped down the portable stairs onto the blistering tarmac.

Wondering where he was supposed to go, he moved away from the plane and started walking towards the building. He did not have to wonder long. He saw a slender woman with straw coloured hair, dressed in dark slacks and a wine coloured blouse, standing with crossed arms beside a black Nissan Altima. A badge hung around her neck and a gun on her hip that matched the one Quinn wore on his own.

"Corporal Sullivan?" she asked when Quinn got close. It still confused him to be addressed by his new rank, but he nodded and stuck out his hand.

"Yeah. Hi."

The woman shook hands with him. "I'm Clara Morgan," she said, and released his hand. Her grip was firm, her palm slightly calloused. Quinn had a lingering sensation of pressure in his hand. "Inspector Ferguson asked me to come down here to meet you and bring you to the detachment."

"This our ride?" Quinn tilted his chin towards the Nissan.

Clara nodded and opened the driver's door. Quinn walked to the passenger side, threw his bag on the back seat and climbed in the passenger side. Clara drove away from the airport building, across a few hundred meters of tarmac and onto a service road that led to a two lane highway.

"It's about twenty minutes to get to the office," Clara said, as she drove, one hand gripping the steering wheel easily, while the other arm leaned on the centre console. Her eyes flickered from the road, to her rear view mirror, to Quinn, and back again. He caught her looks out of the corner of his eye, but did not say anything. He waited.

"So, why are you here?" she asked after a few minutes of silence.

There it is, he thought. "I'm here to look into Patrick Green's death." He had anticipated the question and decided a simple answer would be best. He did not know what kind of environment he would be walking into at Cranbrook detachment, but he knew how he would feel if some asshole came into his house to crawl all over one of his files. He would want to push the prick down the nearest set of stairs.

"Look into what?" Clara asked, turning her head and focusing her pale blue eyes on his face. "The file was investigated already. What are you supposed to be looking for?"

Judging by her plain-clothes attire, Quinn guessed that Clara was one of the Major Crime investigators for the detachment and would likely have been part of the investigation. He did not begrudge her the questions. They were the same things he would be asking if he sat where she was.

He shrugged. "I'm not sure, to tell you true. I was asked to review the file and have a look for myself, and that's what I'm going to do."

"His dad asked you, didn't he?"

Something in the way she made the comment made him pause before answering. She had said 'dad', not 'father'.

"He got you promoted, just so you could come and do this, didn't he?" she asked, her eyes still on the road.

Quinn watched the road as well, one elbow on the door rest, his hand rubbing the space beneath his bottom lip. "Did you know Patrick?"

"You didn't answer my question."

He turned from the mountainous view in front of him and looked at Clara, while she stared, conspicuously, at the road. "Yeah. Patrick's dad sent me. The promotion, so I was told, was coming anyway."

She snorted and looked out the window on her left, hunching her shoulders a little.

"So, did you know Patrick?" Quinn asked when she did not look back at him.

She turned her eyes back on the road. "It's a small office. Everyone knows everyone."

"You know what I mean," he said, still studying her face. As he watched, it reddened significantly.

"Yeah, I knew him," she said, and wiped beneath her eye with one finger.

"Were you..." Quinn suddenly felt very uncomfortable with the question he had been about to ask. If this girl had been romantically involved with Patrick, his death would be like a fresh wound, and Quinn did not want to be the asshole pissing in it.

He did not have to finish the question. "No, we weren't

dating," she said. "We were friends. A lot of the members in the detachment are older, with kids and families, and it's hard being a cop in a small town 'cause everyone knows who you are. Patrick and I were the same age, and when he got posted out here I was so relieved to finally have someone who..." She paused and wiped under her eye again. "He was my friend."

"I knew Patrick, too," Quinn said. "He spent some time in the office, volunteering and what not. We all knew him. We were all close." As he said it, he was thinking of how close he had been to Patrick when he carried the boy's casket down the red carpet of the church.

"So, what do you think you're going to find?"

Originally, Quinn had planned to stay somewhat aloof, conduct the review the inspector looked for and then get the hell out of there, but Clara knew Patrick and called him friend. That friendship, Quinn thought, would come before her ire at having her team's investigation scrutinized.

"Really," Quinn said, "the only thing I'm expecting to find is closure for Patrick's family. His dad asked me to do this, and the man has been good to me, so I didn't feel I could refuse."

"Okay, so why you?" she asked. "Why would he promote you so you could do the review? Do you have some kind of special skills? Something to do with all the stuff that was found in Patrick's apartment, and the symbols that were—" She stopped talking, swallowed thickly. "With the symbols that were...there?"

Telling her his main qualification for this job was that he had once killed a demon in the basement of a drug dealer's house probably was not his best course of action. "I guess Patrick's dad wanted someone he knew, that answered to him, to do it."

She nodded and seemed to accept Quinn's explanation.

They passed the rest of the drive in silence. The thunderhead on Clara's face gave Quinn the inclination that more questions would not be wise, and he decided to look out the window instead of push her.

The view was not hard to look at. If he had not been visiting the town for such a miserable purpose he might have actually enjoyed the drive. Where Resolution Cove was surrounded on all sides by thick, dark rainforest, the countryside of Cranbrook was composed of tall pine trees, rolling, scrub-covered foothills and the cold sentinels of the Rocky Mountains in the distance.

The town itself, as they entered it, was dominated by red-brick buildings—hardly any of them over three stories tall—and small "mom and pop" style business storefronts; much like Resolution Cove.

Clara drove the Nissan past the front of the RCMP detachment – a squat, single story building – and around to the back. "The inspector will be expecting us," Clara said as she pulled into a parking stall and put the car into 'park'. "You can leave your bag in the car. I'll be dropping you off at your hotel later."

Quinn climbed out of the car and followed Clara through the back door to the detachment, which led into a narrow hallway. The layout was similar to Resolution's detachment. The long hallway branched into several other corridors, including the cell block, locker rooms and what appeared to be a small gym.

Clara led Quinn briskly down the hallway, past a large space with several cubicles—what Quinn assumed was the general duty pit—and finally to an office in the front corner of the building. There was a plaque on the tall window beside the open door that said 'Commanding Officer'.

Clara knocked on the door-jamb and a deep voice said, "Come in."

Leading the way into the office, Clara entered and stepped aside. Quinn followed. She held a hand out towards the L-shaped wooden desk in the corner. Facing them, across the longer branch of the desk, was a fit, clean-shaven man with his dark hair carefully slicked back over his skull. The man wore the white shirt of a commissioned officer, and watched Quinn with a less-than-impressed expression.

"Inspector Ferguson," Clara said, "this is Corporal Quinn

Sullivan."

"Good morning...*Corporal*," Ferguson said. He did not stand up, extend a hand in greeting, or invite Quinn to sit in one of the chairs in front of his desk. Quinn kept his face smooth and clasped his hands in front of him.

"Good morning, sir."

Ferguson leaned forward on his elbows, dark eyes under heavy, tanned brows studying him openly. "I'm going to be plain, here. I do not know why you are here, nor understand the necessity for your *investigation*, but I have been instructed, by people several pay grades above me, to make this fracas happen. I don't know what strings he pulled, or favours Donald Green called in to get you a promotion I doubt you deserve, but here you stand before me despite any protests I might make.

"The investigation into Patrick Green's death was done promptly and properly. I oversaw it myself. Patrick was a strange kid, but he was one of mine, and the very slightest implication that I would have allowed something to be overlooked in the inquiry into his death is horribly insulting."

Ferguson gestured to Clara with the expensive-looking pen in his tanned hand. "Constable Morgan will get whatever it is you think you'll require and give you access to our files. See that you make use of them quickly, and then go away." Ferguson looked at Quinn for several moments. A vein in his left temple pulsed slightly, before he turned to the computer on his desk and studied the screen intently.

Quinn had expected a certain amount of push-back to his visit, but he had not anticipated open hostility. Once he had recovered from the verbal ass kicking he had just received, Quinn remembered that he could be an obstinate prick as well. "Thanks much, sir. I'll be sure to include your helpful commentary in my report. I'll be in touch if there is anything else I need you to provide. I'll keep you apprised of what your involvement in this process will be, and I'll let you know when you need to know something."

Quinn waited, just for a moment, to see the blood climbing up into Ferguson's face, adding a tinge of crimson to the inspector's tan, then turned on his heel and walked out the way he had come in. He knew he was currently poking at an already angry bear and he did not know where the authority for this review had actually come from, but Ferguson had not come out of his office and shot him in the back. Quinn could only assume that whoever the orders had come from sat very high on the food chain indeed.

"You're a bit of a shit disturber, aren't you?" Clara asked from over his left shoulder as she struggled to keep up to his brisk pace.

"I've been known to make friends with my abundance of charm."

He could not see it, but he thought he heard a grin in her voice. "Okay there, charmer. Where do you want to start?"

Quinn looked over his shoulder at her. "At the beginning."

CHAPTER 8

"Good God, you look like you've been stuffed in a bag of wild cats," Dave said as he regarded Raife, who was stitting on the rear bumper of an ambulance.

"And your arm looks like you fed it into a meat grinder," Al Blaker, a chubby paramedic—a dead ringer for Elmer Fudd —said as he finished wrapping a clean bandage around Raife's left forearm. "Doesn't look like there will be any disability in the limb, Raife, but you need to get to a doctor and get stitched up. You're probably gonna take twenty sutures."

"Okay, Al," Raife said, getting up from bumper of the ambulance, causing the springs to squeak violently. "I'll head down there once everything here is wrapped up."

Half an hour after Raife had turned on the emergency beacon, a search and rescue helicopter had landed in an open meadow fifty yards from Dean Springer's cabin. Ninety minutes after that Dave McLeod and Steve Faulk, the second in command of the detachment, had pulled up in Dave's patrol car. Two more hours had seen the coroner, an ambulance and the detachment's lone forensic identification member at the cabin, as well.

"How you doing, Raife?" Steve Faulk asked, as he walked up to the ambulance. Steve was nearly as tall as Raife, but half as wide, and had a square jaw and neatly trimmed mustache that would be well at home on a souvenir post card.

"I'll live," Raife said, as he touched his arm gingerly. "Bloody thing throbs like hell."

"I'm surprised you have an arm at all," Dave said. "Did you get a good look at that fucking dog? It probably could have bitten through a telephone pole."

"What did Springer do to that poor thing?" Steve asked as he looked over his shoulder to where the ident girl was setting out markers and taking pictures of the dead dog and Raife's shell casings. "What was he giving it that would make it that big, and then drive it into killing and eating him?"

Raife shrugged, an odd prickle running down his spine as he looked at the dead animal. He had a dark memory of a young man named Brandon Williams, who had tried to murder Quinn and had died in the process. Brandon had gone from a scrawny junkie to a hulking, enraged behemoth in a matter of weeks, and it was not caused by anything in his food. Brandon had been changed, horribly, by something that Raife, Quinn and Dave had met, and fought, beneath the floor boards of a shit hole house.

"Maybe it wasn't Dean who changed it," Raife said, and glanced surreptitiously at Dave.

The younger man caught the glance and gave a barely perceptible nod, apparently laying hold of Raife's drift. Steve had not been part of the battle with the demon in Joe Robowski's house and knew nothing about it.

Steve snorted. "If not Dean, then who?" He shook his head. "No, Dean, with all his conspiracy theories and hunting for bigfoot, finally lost it enough that he fed that dog something he shouldn't have and it turned on him. It's just lucky the mayor reported Springer missing so Raife came up here to deal with the dog before it got hungry and ate someone else."

"Uh, Staff Sergeant Faulk?" the coroner, a dark haired, olive-skinned woman named Raj Perhar, called from across the yard where she knelt beside the pile of bones.

"Yes?" Steve answered and walked towards her. Raife and Dave followed in his lean wake.

"We've got a problem," the coroner said.

"What's that?" Steve Faulk asked.

"These bones are human."

Steve stopped beside her, thumbs tucked behind his gun belt, and looked down at the long bone in her hands. "Yeah, we figured that. The remains of the occupant, Dean Springer."

Raj looked up at Steve. "There are teeth marks in them."

"Yeah," Steve tilted his chin towards the dead Rottweiler. "From the dog."

The coroner shook her head. "No, Staff Sergeant. The teeth marks in these bones are human."

Steve curled one lip and whistled through his teeth.

Dave gave a wide, even grin and clapped him on the back. "Looks like this just turned into a murder."

No matter what she did, Autumn Donnelly could not get settled, could not rest. She leaned against the counter of her shop, crossed her arms, signed, and moved around among the shelves. She turned a crystal, turned it back to its original position, then moved it to a new shelf altogether. She ran her fingers through her thick hair, shook out her hands and stretched her neck from side to side. She needed to do something, but she didn't know what. Since Quinn had left her shop the day before she had not been able to concentrate on anything other than the huge mistake he had made in leaving.

She knew that she jumped at too many shadows, saw the presence of evil in inane events, but this time she was certain she was not overreacting. This time there really was a shadow creeping into Resolution Cove. Now was the time Quinn was needed most.

She stood in front of a wide book shelf, rearranging titles that didn't need to be rearranged, when the bell above her shop door jingled. She sighed, wishing she had locked the door and put up the 'closed' sign.

She turned away from the books and faced the door. "I'm sorry. I'm not open right now. I apologize, but I forgot to the lock the door."

Inside the entrance way stood a lean man dressed in worn jeans and an old work shirt with patches at the elbows, longish dark hair pushed back over his ears. A girl, about ten years old, blonde hair in a long braid down her back, stood at his right hip holding his hand. Autumn felt a hot tingle below her breast bone.

"Can I help you?" she asked. She studied the pair and tried to figure out what it was about them that had her hair shivering on her scalp.

"Hi," said the man, his voice deep and smooth. "I'm Kord McRae and this is my daughter, Abby." The girl waved a small hand and gave a shy smile. "We've been in town for a few days and we're wondering if you could point us towards someone."

The tingle grew more intense and her heart punched at the inside of her chest as Autumn looked at Kord McRae's lined, weather-beaten face. It was like the feeling she had the first time she met Quinn. "Who are you looking for, Mr. McRae?"

Kord brushed at his shaggy hair and glanced around the small shop, taking in the shelves of books, crystals and other uncommon apparatus. He blew his breath out through puffed, stubbled cheeks. "I hope you don't think I'm crazy here, but you"—he gestured to the shelves with his free hand—"seem like the most likely person to be able to help us."

Autumn nodded and crossed her arms, sliding her hands into the wide sleeves of her crimson blouse. "I will help you if I can, but you need to tell me who you're looking for."

"I don't know his name." Kord looked down at Abby and then back at Autumn. "But, I'm looking for the Guardian. Do you know who that is?"

Drawing in a great, shuddering breath, Autumn felt the tingling from her scalp crawl down her neck and clasp her spine. "I know very well who you mean, Kord. Why do you need him?"

The lean man looked down at the girl again. "My daughter and I...well... let us say we're on the move."

"You mean you're being hunted." Autumn did not mean it as a question. There was a tired, haggard look about the pair that gave the impression they had had little rest.

"I guess you could say that," Kord said. "I just don't want people to think we're running from the law."

"I understand," said Autumn.

Kord nodded and slipped his free hand in the pocket of his tattered jeans. "So, do you know where the Guardian is?"

Autumn frowned, her trepidation at Quinn's departure from Resolution grew into a near fit. Here, standing in her shop, was proof that he never should have gone. Here, finally, was the need she knew had been coming for the last two years. "He's not here, right now," she said, her voice sullen in her own ears. "He is out of town, investigating something for his...commander. He's a policeman."

"Yes," Kord said. "We knew that."

"We saw his scarlet coat," Abby said, in a surprisingly strong voice for such a small child.

Autumn turned her gaze from Kord, to Abby and back again. "I have to ask, Kord, how did you know to come here—to Resolution Cove—I mean. How did you hear about the Guardian?"

The thin man shrugged. "I'm like you, I think, a little anyway. I know where to listen and what to look for. I can't quite explain it, but there were signs and they all pointed here. You can still smell the stink of the thing the Guardian killed when you drive into this valley and get close to the inlet. We've been looking for a safe place for a long time. First my wife and me, and now me and Abby, were hoping we could find it here."

He pulled his hand from the grip of the child and put his arm around her thin shoulders. "Do you know when the Guardian will return?"

Autumn wanted, terribly, to ask about Kord's wife because she saw no band on his finger, but the look on his face as he studied his daughter told her that would be unwise. "A few days, he said when I last talked to him. He didn't think that his business would take him very long."

"All right," Kord said. "We'll be okay until then. I think." He smiled and turned towards the door. "I thank you for your time."

"Wait," said Autumn, stepping towards him. "I can help you. I know the Guardian. Quinn is his name. I've helped him before, and I want to try and help you."

"I appreciate your offer, uh..."

"Autumn," she prompted.

"Autumn," he confirmed. "But you don't want to get in the way of what's coming for us. I've tried to face it down before, when I was a younger man, and failed horribly. The only thing left for us now is to find the Guardian and see if he can help."

"What is coming for you, Kord?"

He glanced down at the child, a mere flicker of his eye, but enough that Autumn caught it. "It's a thing, a black thing that would have you believe it is a man. It wants something that I am intent it shall not have, but it is persistent. It keeps getting harder to keep ahead of it." He turned away again and put his hand on the door, pulling it open so the child could step through onto the sidewalk.

"Kord, who is this thing?"

The angular man stopped. "You will know it when it comes, and when you have that knowledge it will already be the time of your death. Stay clear of this, Autumn. Tell the Guardian I need to speak with him when he returns, and I'll look for him soon." He stepped into the gray afternoon, released the door with a tinkle of the brass bell, and was gone.

Standing in the in the centre of her shop, Autumn watched his shape flicker behind the frosted glass of her front window as her heart hammered. She felt she was going to be ill. The shadow over Resolution had become deeper, but Quinn was not there to cast a light.

Clara Morgan took Quinn to the hotel that had been arranged for him, where he dropped off his bag and slapped some water on his face.

The girl at the front desk had taken in the gun on his hip with a concerned look, but said nothing when he checked in. She said more nothing as he left his room and walked briskly down the hall and through the lobby, towards the parking lot where Clara waited for him.

Never having worked a Major Crime section, or ever having any kind of desire to wear a suit and tie to work, Quinn did not have a long investigative resume. He had not ever been the lead investigator on a murder, cracked an international drug ring or infiltrated a human trafficking group, but he was not an idiot. Having had the benefit of a field trainer, an Amazonian woman named Mikayla Taylor who had worked in Major Crime, she had beaten certain concepts into his thick skull.

One thing she had always told him: start at the beginning. Whenever you look at an investigation, start at the first point you can possibly think of. Once you have your starting point, get the concrete beneath your boots, talk to some people, and do some God-damned police work.

In this case, Quinn was not investigating a break and enter or an assault, or even a murder. He was here to figure out why a cop, who was barely more than a kid, had carved himself up with a scalpel and then hung himself from a ceiling fixture. Despite the circumstances of the investigation, the steps would be the same and Quinn must start at the beginning. Everything else would stack up from there.

He walked out to Clara's black Nissan, opened the passenger door and got in.

"So, now that you've impressed the hell out of the inspector, what do you want to do?" Clara sat easily, leaning towards the driver's door, her arm draped over the sill of the open window.

Her ease made Quinn slightly uncomfortable, as it contrasted so sharply with the tension that seized the muscles of his back. Despite the fact he did not feel particularly qualified for this job, he wanted, very badly, to do it well. He owed it both to Inspector Green and to Patrick's memory. There was no room for mistakes or half measures.

He settled himself in the seat beside Clara and tried to match her casual posture, letting some of her calm wear off on him.

"Did Patrick finish his recruit field training? Did he get signed off after his first six months?"

Clara shrugged. "Yeah. So?"

"Okay," Quinn said, nodding. "I want to talk to his field trainer."

"His field trainer?" Clara turned the corners of her mouth down. "What would you want to talk to his field trainer for?"

"Patrick's trainer would have spent twelve hours a day trapped in a car with him for the first three months. Even after he was out on his own, the trainer would still see him every day. If Patrick was acting odd, then the trainer would have seen it."

Clara appeared doubtful.

"Who was his trainer?" Quinn asked.

"A guy named Gerry Barnes."

"Is Barnes working today?"

Clara pursed her lips, lifted one eyebrow and looked up at the roof of the Nissan. "Uh, yeah, I think he is, actually."

"Good. Find out where he is and take me to him."

"Do we really need to do that?" Clara lifted her hand off the window sill and snorted a little. "I mean, what is that going to prove? Patrick hung himself. Of course he was acting weird. Can't we just leave him in peace? What are you going to accomplish by digging up all this shit?"

"Shit?" Quinn felt his face flush, Clara's nonchalance striking heavily on his last frayed nerve. "What do you mean, 'shit'? Patrick's father is a man in a world of hurt and he asked me to come and look into the death of his only child. Whether I find anything or not—even if I don't think there is anything for me to find—I plan on covering off everything I can and doing this job right. You say you were Patrick's friend and, of all fucking people, you should be behind this." Quinn paused to catch his breath, the heat of his anger making his heart thump. "Now, you find out where Patrick's trainer is and drive me there. That is a fucking order, Constable."

Clara had looked out the window during Quinn's rant, the index finger of her left hand pressed under her nose. Quinn said nothing else, but stared at the side of her head while he let his heart slow and tamped down the bile that had risen in his throat. For some reason, talking about Patrick in the past tense made him feel ill.

"Okay," said Clara. She took a *Blackberry* out of a holder on her belt. "Whatever you say, *Corporal.*"

Quinn waited while she dialed a number and began asking someone on the other end of the line the location of Gerry Barnes. She used short, clipped sentences and did not glance at him. He could feel the anger flowing off her, but did not care. If he had to get angry and yell to pay Patrick his due, then he could make that happen.

Ten minutes, and a silent, awkward drive later, Clara pulled the black Nissan behind a marked police vehicle in a residential area of Cranbrook, and put the car in park.

"There he is." Clara took up her same position of ease and gestured to the police car in front of her. She said nothing else and made no move to get out of the car.

Her inactivity troubled Quinn, not because he expected anyone to help him in this particular enterprise, but because as Patrick's friend she should be taking more interest in the investigation. It occurred to Quinn that, perhaps, she was affected by Patrick's death more deeply than she had let on, and was not doing well as she would have people assume. Perhaps her exaggerated show of nonchalance was a way to distance herself from the investigation and the memories it would undoubtedly bring up. Quinn made a mental note to call a division representative and put Clara in touch with a counselor, since it was obvious that Inspector Ferguson was not going to do it.

There was a stigma around the suicide of police officers, Quinn had found in his eight years on the job. In the beginning, immediately after the event, there was a great deal of caterwauling about the mental health of the members. Often psychologists were called, counseling was offered to the people left behind, and there was a great show of support from the greater policing community. Then, about ten minutes after that, it was all very quickly forgotten. *The guy was mental*, people would say. *Selfish prick for leaving his wife and kids to deal with this*, others would grumble. After the initial urgency of the response to the suicide, everyone who was even loosely associated with it put as much distance between themselves and the recently deceased as they could.

Quinn could not say he was any different, but now the loss was personal. Patrick had been a friend, someone he had known, someone who had talked to him across the dinner table. Patrick might not have died in a gun fight, but he was one of the fallen nonetheless, and his memory deserved more than a dismissive grunt and a half assed inquiry. He deserved to be remembered.

Opening the passenger door to the Nissan, Quinn swung his feet out and set them on the ground and then looked back at Clara. She did not move for the space of two breaths, then rolled her eyes and opened her door as well. Quinn got out and closed the door with a click. He approached the marked police car, which appeared to be occupied, and walked towards the centre of the back bumper where he was sure he would be seen in the rear view mirror. A forehead was visible to Quinn in the mirror. As he approached the car, a set of eyes looked up before the door opened and a uniformed Mountie got out.

The man, who Quinn assumed was Gerry Barnes, was about Quinn's height, but had at least a hundred pounds on him. Barnes had thick arms and shoulders, with a protruding gut that jutted out past his gun belt and made the blue shell of his body armour look like a sports bra. As he got out of the car, he had to stop half way, appearing to get stuck between the seat and the steering wheel.

Clara followed in Quinn's wake and stopped beside him. "Gerry," she said as the heavyset cop wrenched himself out of the car. "This is Corporal Quinn Sullivan."

Gerry stuck out a meaty hand and Quinn gripped it. Gerry's shake was firm and he looked Quinn in the eye. "You're the guy Patrick's dad promoted to come out here and look into Patrick's suicide."

Gerry Barnes, obviously, was not a man who let himself be limited by the constraints of tact. "Yeah," Quinn confirmed. "That's what I hear."

"What are you thinking you're gonna find?" Gerry asked. There was no challenge in the comment, no sarcastic ire or cutting angst. He actually wanted to know and was not trying to be a disingenuous prick about it.

"I'm not sure, to tell you the truth," Quinn said with equal candor. "I'm just trying to cover off everything I can."

Gerry nodded and seemed to accept this, then rubbed his double chin. "What can I do for you, then?"

His tone of voice, the set of his eyes, even his posture—besides being rotund—made Quinn think of shrewd competence. Gerry might not have been in peak physical condition, but it was evident to Quinn that there was nothing wrong with his thought process.

"Can you tell me about Patrick?" Quinn asked. "Was there anything that set you off about him? Did he do anything recently that seemed out of character?"

Looking at the gravel off the toe of his boots, Gerry leaned his wide body back against the trunk of his car and rubbed at his chin some more, the stubble made a rasping sound against his fingers. "Well, I don't know, really. I'm not sure that I can say I knew Patrick really well."

The comment struck Quinn as odd. "You were his trainer, weren't you? You spent a lot of time with him. I figured you'd know a few things about the kid that rode around with you every day."

"Well," Gerry said, considering the comment. "I can tell you that Patrick was smart, no doubt about that. He picked up everything I told him the first time and didn't have to ask many questions, but, he didn't really ask many questions in the first place, and didn't talk much at all."

That did not sound at all like the Patrick Green that Quinn had known in Resolution. From Quinn's experience, Patrick was a fount of never ending questions, constantly looking over someone's shoulder and asking what they were doing. More than once Raife had threatened to gag Patrick if he couldn't find a way to shut up for two minutes.

"Did he not do well here?" Quinn asked, seeking a reason for the change in his behaviour.

Gerry shrugged. "He seemed to do all right when he first got here, to be honest, but he wasn't here long before he kind of started shutting down."

"What do you mean, 'shutting down'?" Quinn crossed his arms and leaned forward slightly.

"Well, when he first got here he was sociable enough and would come out to the watch functions and so on, but after about a month he stopped."

"Do you know why?"

Gerry shrugged. "I don't know for certain. I think it had something to do with him being an inspector's kid. I think he might have thought he had something to prove to everyone, you know, to show us that he got here on his own merits and not 'cause of his dad. He got razzed a couple of times, all just harmless comments, about following in his old man's footsteps and getting his white shirt. He didn't really take that well. Afterwards, he kind of closed up, put some distance between himself and everyone else."

Quinn rubbed his chin, thinking. "Was there ever a problem with his performance?"

"Never," Gerry said, shaking his head, making the flesh beneath his first chin jiggle. "He was fine on the road, had no problem dealing with people, knew how to do his paper. He didn't call in sick, and was never late..." Gerry paused. He looked uncomfortable for the first time, shifting his weight and pulling up his gun belt in an exaggerated manner. "Well, except for the day he didn't show up at all." He sniffed and rubbed one sausage-like finger beneath his lower lip. "No, his work was good. He was just more and more impersonal as the weeks went on. When he got out on his own and wasn't riding with me anymore I wouldn't see him for the entire shift. I'd hear him taking calls on the radio, and he'd submit all his field training stuff to me to review, but he never talked to me, never came out for coffee, nothing."

Quinn could feel his eyes narrow and his face burn. "And you didn't think there was anything wrong with that?"

"How the fuck would I know?" Gerry asked, meeting Quinn's eyes, heat in his voice. "His work was good so I didn't worry about it. If he wanted to be left alone, I figured I'd leave him alone. I didn't really know there was a problem until the day he didn't show up for work and I went to his apartment to check on him."

Another angry question died on Quinn's lips as he looked at Gerry's face. The heavy man was looking at his boots again, both thumbs tucked between his gut and his belt. Understanding flooding Quinn; it was Gerry who had found Patrick after he had hanged himself. Quinn looked over at Clara, who had her arms folded and glared at him accusatorily.

Embarrassed, Quinn tried to stammer out an apology, but was interrupted when Gerry looked up, his eyes damp.

"Do you really think that if I'd thought there was something wrong with Patrick that I'd have just let it go?" Gerry's voice was on the verge of cracking and he pulled in a deep breath. "If I thought for a minute that kid was gonna do that to himself, with all those fucking symbols and weird shit, I'd have kicked down his door and dragged him to the hospital. It's easy for you to come out here and do your little inquiry and stand there with your fucking promotion, but where were you? I heard you knew Patrick. So where were you when he was sick in his head and thinking this shit? Nowhere, asshole.

That's where. How many times did you phone him? How many times did you go to his house and see how he was doing with his move?

"You didn't do fuck all, either, so don't stand there with your outraged expression and your fucking questions and think that you're doing something for Patrick. You should have done something for him when he was alive, just like I should have."

The force of the man's anger made Quinn step backwards. The sorrow, the guilt written on Gerry's round face was a hot glow and it made Quinn's eyes sting, threatening to send him into tears to match the heavy man.

Quinn shook his head, the questions he had been about to ask dying in the back of throat. "I don't know what to say, Gerry. I'm sorry."

"Fucking rights you are," Gerry said, and turned away from him. "We all are."

Standing mute, Quinn watched Gerry walk back to the driver's door of his car, get in, and drive away.

Hands hanging at his sides, Quinn watched the dust from Gerry's departing wheels settle on the legs of his jeans. The anger that had been heaped on him made Inspector Ferguson's outburst pale in comparison. Quinn's face burned with shame and guilt, all the righteous anger he had felt drained away to lay with the dust around his feet. He did not know what he had expected, but it certainly had not been this.

Beside him, Clara cleared her throat, a heavy, exaggerated sound. "So, Corporal, how's your little inquiry going so far? You get what you were looking for?"

Quinn clenched his teeth, unsure who he was angrier at; her or himself. Before he could decide and say anything stupid, he turned and walked back towards the Nissan, the remembered weight of Patrick's casket heavy on his shoulder.

CHAPTER 9

Raife's arm throbbed in time to his footsteps as he walked down a bright, central hallway of Resolution Cove's hospital. He was the proud owner of almost twenty stitches in his arm and now that he was bandaged up and sent on his way, the freezing was starting to wear off. With every step he took he wished he'd shot that dog a few more times.

He arrived at the end of the hallway, occupied by a single, wide elevator door, and hit the down button. He was at the back of the hospital now, in a corridor that was seldom traveled by patients. The elevator in front of him had only one destination. As the doors opened and he stepped inside, he hit the lone button marked with a single word: Morgue.

The elevator made a slow, brief, trip downwards. When the doors opened, Raife was greeted by a familiar, unwelcome smell. The morgue, whether it had a good stinker in it or not, always smelled like a combination of disinfectant, rotten hamburger and dog farts. Raife took in a breath through his mouth and stepped out of the elevator.

A short, wide hallway led to a set of double doors—the kind that swung in both directions so you could push a cart through without worrying about pulling a door open—and then into a broad room, about ten big steps across. Tall steel doors, leading into coolers, sat in each wall.

Usually, the morgue was silent, occupied only by the off-tune humming of the strange, thin, sharp-nosed doctor who did the autopsies and medical examinations. Today, however, it was filled with the hum of a dozen voices, all talking at once. The buzzing seemed all the louder as it bounced off the shining doors of the cadaver coolers.

The room was close-packed with people, most of them wearing suits. On Raife's right, he saw Sandy and her recruit standing beside a shining, steel table bolted to the wall. On the table, in a rough approximation of a human skeleton, were the bones located outside of Dean Springer's cabin.

On his left, a group of plain clothes Mounties, their badges hanging from chains around their necks, stood talking to each other or into their phones, scribbling into their black, ledger sized note-books. Between them was an assortment of random people, who Raife could only assume were either hospital staff or police personnel he did not know. All told the place was a yapping mass of humanity that seemed about as organized as a flea market. Raife's head began to throb in time to his arm. He began silently counting the years until he could retire.

Dave McLeod peeled away from the wall and came to stand beside him. "How you feeling, boss?"

"Like an enormous dog tried to rip my arm off." Raife looked at his blood splattered watch. "It's almost eight o'clock. What are you still doing here?"

Dave looked up from his pocket-sized notebook that all general duty police officers carried. "Staff Sergeant Faulk asked Sandy and me to come down here and help the Major Crime team." He indicated the trio of suits with a tilt of his chin. "They've got their hands full until the Provincial guys get here."

"Uh-huh. And what have we got, so far?"

Dave turned and pointed towards Sandy and the steel table with his pen. "Oddly enough, the northern branch of the University of British Columbia has a graduate class in town doing a dig in an ancient Coast Salish village. The anthropology professor in charge has some experience in forensics and the Coroner knows him and called him in as a personal favor. He seems to know what he's talking about and confirmed that both the bones and the teeth marks in them are human."

Raife hitched up his belt and began shuffling across the room, squeezing through the knots of people who were all talking at once and getting in each other's way. He managed to make it across without squashing, or punching, anyone and folded his heavy arms as he stood at Sandy's shoulder.

Sandy held her notebook in her hand and listened with profound concentration to a slender, slightly balding man in a white dress-shirt with the sleeves rolled up. The man wore medical gloves and examined each of the bones, one by one, laying them out to re-shape the skeleton. Gerritt stood behind Sandy, his face extremely pale as he held his own notebook with nothing written on the page, and tried very hard not to look at the articles on the table. Dave sidled up to the recruit, slapped him on the back and gave him a hearty grin.

The boy grew paler, with a touch of green creeping into his bloodless cheeks, and swallowed hard.

"How's it going, Sandy?" Raife asked when there was a break in the explanation by the balding man.

"I'd say it was good, but that doesn't seem appropriate considering the condition of our recently eaten friend, here." She finished scribbling a note down in her book and gestured to the slender man who was hunched over examining one of the bones. "Boss, this is Doctor Jordan Kane from the university. Doctor, this is Corporal...I mean Sergeant Raife."

"Hi, Doc," Raife said.

The doctor grinned and wiped a wrist across his forehead. "I'd shake your hand, Sergeant, but, you know." He held up one gloved hand that had small bits of gore on it and wiggled his fingers.

"Understood, Doc. Can you tell us anything?"

Doctor Kane set down the bone he held, almost reverently, on the table in front of him. "Well, they're obviously human." He gestured to the mostly formed body. "And I'd say, from the size and structure of the pelvic bone, most likely a forty or fifty year old male. They are not old, meaning they have not been sitting out long, and the flesh seems to have been stripped, mostly, from the bones."

Raife nodded. "I understand you confirmed the teeth marks on there as human."

"Well, yes and no, Sergeant. That is a bit of a complicated answer."

Complications were not good. Raife did not like them. "Uh, would you mind explaining how it's 'complicated'."

"Well," the doctor said and picked up the thickest bone on the table. "This is a femur, about the strongest bone in the human body."

Dave pointed over Gerritt's shoulder. "Look, you can see a big piece of meat on there." Gerritt turned and ran down the hallway, his hand clapped over his mouth. Sandy turned and swatted at Dave who laughed so hard he looked like he might fall over.

The doctor glanced from the laughing constable to Raife, who shrugged. "What can I say," Raife said. "It's like having a bunch of children...with guns."

"Indeed," the doctor said. He did not look impressed. "As I was saying, this is a femur." He held it up and tilted it slightly to catch the light differently. "And these"—he ran his little finger along the surface of the bone— "are teeth marks, which appear to be human." He looked up at Raife.

"Okay," the big sergeant said. The surface of his thin patience began to crack. "Where does this get complicated, Doc?"

The doctor slid his finger a little higher, to the centre of the bone. "This is a large crack." He tapped the crack with his finger, which was now obvious to Raife. "It looks like the crack was made posthumously, and is not an old injury."

The three Mounties stood looking at the doctor, his belief that he had made a great conclusion apparent on his narrow features.

"Okay, Doc," Dave said, scratching at his stubbled head. "You lost me here. What does that mean?"

The doctor rolled his eyes a little, as though he were explaining the concept of the wheel to the village idiot. "It appears to me, from my examination, that whatever stripped the meat off these bones also bit this femur hard enough to crack it. These teeth marks might look human, but no human jaw could do that."

The confusion that had whispered across Raife's brain fell away as the doctor's words sunk in to his weary head. "So, what do you think it was that did this, Doc?"

"I don't know," Doctor Kane said. He set the femur down on the table. "I'd like to give you an explanation, but I don't have one. I'd like to say that another animal came along after this person was dead and had its way with the corpse, but there are no other marks on here that would indicate the bones were chewed by an animal. I don't know what it was, but I know it's giving me the creeps."

"That goes double for me, Doc," Dave said from behind Sandy, who looked almost as pale as her recruit had.

Raife saw the shade of her face and could only imagine it matched his own. She knew what had lived beneath the floor of Joe Robowski's house. She knew what it was like to look into the face of something evil. Raife, Dave and Quinn had faced that evil too, had sent it back to wherever it came from. They all carried the scars, both mental and physical, of those confrontations.

Looking down at the bones on the table, Raife had a prickly sensation at the base of his neck that told him another fight was coming.

Raife drove away from the hospital under a sky that was as black as his mood. It was just shy of nine o'clock at night. It should still be light enough for the local kids to be playing softball in the park beside Resolution Detachment's office, but the fields were deserted and Raife had to turn the headlights of the big police truck on to navigate his way into the parking lot.

This town grew dark, and it was not just the weather. The pile of bones in the morgue gave testament to exactly how black it could get. Raife predicted a very bleak shade indeed. He thought, for the tenth time that day, Quinn should be here. That young man, despite his reluctance and insistence otherwise, had a way about him. He was a level head in a churning room and he would know what to do about this. Though he viewed the boy as one of his own children, Raife was reassured when Quinn was around, especially when something fucking weird, like a man being eaten, was on the agenda.

As he pulled into a parking spot at the rear of the detachment and turned the truck off, Raife thought of what he would say to Green to make him bring Quinn home. Raife knew Patrick's death still ate at the inspector. Raife did not begrudge the man's search for some piece of mind, but they could not spare Quinn on that job any longer. They needed him back.

He climbed out of the truck and walked through the back door of the office. The building was nearly deserted. The watch on duty must have been all out on the road and every other member of the detachment at the morgue, craning their necks to get a look at the recently discovered skeleton. The silence bothered Raife. It made him uneasy. It felt like the calm before a storm of complete of fuckery that lurked on the horizon.

Raife reached the main area of the General Duty pit and wondered how big the shit storm might be. Inspector Green came down the hallway from the back door and into the pit, Bill Davis and a team of plain-clothes investigators on his heels.

"Raife," Bill said and stuck out his hand.

Raife gripped it and nodded. He had not thought much of Davis when he had first met him. The Major Crime sergeant had been interrogating Quinn over a justified shooting. Although he had proved to be a solid investigator, he had treated Quinn fairly. Eventually, Raife decided, Davis wasn't as big an asshole as initially suspected. "Hi, Bill."

"You got promoted," Bill said, looking at the sergeant's epaulettes on Raife's shoulders. "No surprise there. I heard your man, Sullivan, got his hooks to fill your spot."

"That's right," Raife said. "No surprise there, either."

"No, there was not," Bill agreed. He looked down at his smart-phone, which showed pictures of the partially formed skeleton on the steel table at the morgue. "What can you tell me about this?"

The idea came to Raife, but only for a brief and foolish moment, of telling Davis that there was some kind of boogey-man roaming the hills of Resolution and eating people. While Raife tried to think of a suitable explanation that would not sound too crazy, a stoop-shouldered, elderly man—one of the detachment volunteers—gripped Raife's elbow in a gnarled hand.

"Sergeant Raife?" The man's voice sounded like two pounds of gravel being scraped with barbed wire.

"Yes?"

"There's a hippie girl at the front counter, wants to talk to you."

"A hippie?" Raife asked in obvious confusion.

"She's wearing bloody tie dye and beads. Looks like she wants to set up a tent and occupy something while cursing England and damning the Queen."

Raife did not know the name of this particular volunteer, but instantly liked him. "She say what she wanted?"

The old man shrugged. "Said she needed to talk to you about something urgent. In my day I'd have tossed her on her dope-smoking ear, but apparently I'm not allowed to do that."

Raife could feel his mustache quivering as he stifled a laugh. "Okay. I'll talk to her."

"If she gives you any lip, let me know and I'll give her a stern piece of my mind. I'll bet if she went to get a job she wouldn't be down here harassing you." The old man turned and walked back towards the front desk, mumbling something in his rough tone about liberals and how they were bringing the country to ruin.

Raife turned back to Bill Davis and his team, to see faces showing a range of emotions from bald shock to uproarious humour.

"If I ever get back to uniform," Bill Davis said, between fits of burbling laughter, "I wanna come here."

Turning away from Davis and his giggling team, Raife trudged towards the front counter. The woman he saw there, with her heavy mop of blonde hair and deep lines around her eyes, could only be considered a girl by someone as old as the gravelly volunteer. She had her hair tied back with a bright scarf and her wrists were covered with softly clinking bangles.

Raife put his meaty hands on the counter and tried not to slouch as his arm throbbed, exhaustion weighting him down. "Hi," he said. "I'm Sergeant Raife. You wanted to see me?"

The woman extended a slender hand. "Sergeant, I'm Autumn Donnelly. I'm a friend of Quinn Sullivan."

As Raife gripped her soft hand in his own, recognition tapped at the back of his brain like an unexpected visitor. This was the woman who had told Quinn about the demon in Resolution and had given him the knife he had used to kill it. Quinn had spoken of her more than once, but to call her his friend, Raife thought, was a bit of a stretch.

"What can I do for you, Autum?" he asked as he released her hand.

She took her right hand back and gripped it with her left, wringing it like a dish rag. "Do you know when Quinn is coming back?"

That tingle at the base of his neck started up again. "I think he's scheduled to be gone a couple more days. Why?"

She pressed her mouth into a thin line, her disappointment obvious. She shook her hands out for a moment, and then continued to wring them together. "It is very important that I speak to him. Something has happened that he needs to hear about."

"You don't know how right you are," Raife said, before he could stop himself. He saw Autumn's eyes widen, and shook his head. "If you tell me what you need to talk to him about I'll pass it on to him and get him to call you."

She shook her blonde head. "I don't have a phone for him to call, although I'm strongly rethinking that decision. No, this is something that I would prefer to talk to him about directly."

Raife had heard himself described as a grumpy bastard, on more than one occasion, and while he denied the 'bastard' portion of that description he was well aware that he trusted almost no one, besides other cops, and liked people even less. His desire to be standing there and talking to this woman, who Quinn had described as crazy on more than one occasion, bordered on just this side of fuck all. Quinn had also said that she had helped him more than once and had not steered him wrong when it came to the thing they had fought in the basement. Against his better judgment, he decided to take a chance on her.

He glanced over his shoulder to ensure the volunteers were out of easy hearing distance and dropped his voice to a whisper. "You remember two years ago, when you gave Quinn the knife he carries? And what he fought with it?"

She nodded, her hands still wringing.

"Don't forget that I was there. I was with Quinn when he killed that thing, and after the weird shit I've seen today, I've been putting a lot of thought into giving Quinn a call."

"Does that weird shit have to do with what happened to your arm?" Autumn asked and pointed at the white bandage.

"You could say that," Raife said. He flexed his fingers, sending jolts of pain through the shredded flesh beneath the dressing. "What do you need to talk to Quinn about?"

"Do you understand what Quinn's role is, here in Resolution?"

He had a feeling she was not talking about his new rank as a corporal. He leaned closer and lowered his voice. "Quinn told me that you think he is some kind of protector for this town. Something about destiny."

"A Guardian," she said. "I believe that Quinn is here for a reason. Like I've told him before, Sergeant Raife—"

"Just Raife," he said.

"Okay, Raife. Like I've told Quinn before, this town, this valley and inlet, has as a strong energy, as powerful a will, as I've ever felt, and I've moved around a lot in the last twenty years. That energy is in the very ground and has drawn people to this place. Their lives, their struggles, have added to the energy of this town until it has built up layers of power. Just like the people who are drawn here, other things are drawn here, too, which is how you came to meet a demon in the basement of an old house."

At the word 'demon' Raife turned quickly and looked over each of his shoulders, again. The only person near the front counter was the gravelly volunteer. The old man did not seem to be paying any attention to their conversation, although he still mumbled to himself and cast the occasional stink eye at Autumn.

The blonde woman, apparently, understood Raife's trepidation and lowered her voice. "I believe that fate drew Quinn here, to this place, to be its Guardian and face the things that are drawn here, like what you met in that basement."

"Okay," Raife said. "Quinn told me a bunch of this stuff already." He had wanted to say 'shit' instead of 'stuff', but his wife always criticized him for his lack of tact and he was trying to do better. "What has any of it got to do with why you need to talk to Quinn?"

"Today, two people came into my shop: a man and his daughter. They said they'd heard there was a Guardian here and they needed to talk to him."

"What?" Raife asked. The tingling in his neck turned into a full-on itch. "How the fuck did they hear about Quinn?"

"I don't know," Autumn said. She shook her head, her blonde hair swaying. "They didn't know who Quinn was, or even his name. They only knew there was a Guardian in this town and they needed him."

"What do they need him for?" Raife asked, thinking of the pile of bones that used to be Dean Springer.

"They said they'd been running, that something was chasing, *hunting*, them and, whatever it is, they told me that I want no part of it."

He drummed his fingers on the counter, the thick digits making a dull, hollow noise. "You think they're nuts, or is there something to this?"

"I don't think they're nuts," Autumn said. She glanced down at Raife's drumming fingers. "I've met a lot of odd people, Raife, probably almost as many as you have in this job, but this man wasn't odd. He was lucid and clear, and wasn't in a hurry to convince me of anything. He just saw my store and figured I might be a little more aware of what he was looking for."

"This thing that's hunting them, he say what it was? Or what it wanted?"

"No." Autumn shook her head again. "He didn't say what it was, but he said he'd faced it before and gave me the impression that he was scared. What it wanted, he didn't get into. He had his daughter with him and I had an idea it might have something to do with her, but that is only a guess."

"Right," Raife said, chewing over the information in his mind. "Did he say what his name was?"

"Kord," he said. "Kord McRae."

"Okay. I'll call Quinn as soon as I get clear of this place and let him know. Anything else you want me to tell him?"

She chewed her lip a moment and looked down at Raife's bandaged arm. "Tell him to be careful, and tell him to hurry."

Turning to leave, she paused and reached out to touch Raife's bandaged arm. The tingle that had been buzzing in his neck leapt to the skin beneath the bandage. He shivered beneath her touch.

"Heal quickly, Raife," she said before she turned for the door and was gone.

Raife stood for several moments, his fingers continuing to drum on the countertop, as he looked out the window at the dark grey sky.

He heard the squeak of a boot behind him and turned to see Dave McLeod, his lean face concerned. "You all right, Boss? You're even paler than Gerritt, and he's been puking in the parking lot for the last twenty minutes."

"I'm a long way from all right," Raife said, and turned for his office. "Get Sandy. We need to talk. Then we need to call Quinn."

The conversation with Gerry Barnes left Quinn disheveled and raw, like a cat who had had its fur rubbed backwards by an over-zealous three year old. He needed to rest, he needed to regroup, and most importantly he needed to think about what Gerry had told him - or accused him of.

When the conversation had started, Quinn had his accusatory pointing finger all ready to jab at the first person he could lay some blame on. He looked forward, even though he hadn't previously admitted it to himself, to finding some detail he could take back to the inspector that would give the man some closure and heap fault on an individual, or group of individuals, who was not Patrick. When Gerry had said that Patrick had been strange and distant, but no one had said anything or gotten the kid some help, Quinn thought the "X" on his treasure map of fault had been reached. Then Gerry balled up the map, wiped his ass with it and threw it in Quinn's face.

The problem, as Quinn saw it, was Gerry was right. Quinn, and all the other people who knew Patrick from Resolution Cove, had largely ignored the kid after he had been posted to Cranbrook. It was not anything intentional, Quinn thought, but it was certainly neglectful. When Patrick had volunteered at the office, riding with the members as an Auxillary Constable, he had been present and real. When Patrick had gone to Depot, in Regina, he had sent them all weekly updates of his progress and the comic ridiculousness his instructors put him through. When the emails popped up on your screen it was easy to take a moment and write a few lines to wish the kid well. When Patrick had graduated, the inspector invited Quinn's Watch to come to the ceremony. They had flown to Regina as though they were going to a big party and toasted Patrick's success, welcoming him to their scarlet ranks.

When Patrick had moved to Cranbrook and got busy with his own life, the emails had stopped. Neither Quinn, nor any other members of the watch, had made sufficient effort to keep in touch with a kid who they had regarded as the office mascot. It was lazy. It was unforgivable. It might have led to Patrick's death.

Quinn went back to the Nissan, opened the door and sat heavily in the passenger seat. He slammed the door and said nothing for several minutes while he stared out the front window. Clara sat in the driver's seat, making an obvious show of not looking at him.

Her face was as blank as any professional poker player. When she had picked him up and they had talked briefly of Patrick, she had spoken of the friendship she shared with the boy and had leaked out some carefully bottled emotion. In her, Quinn thought, he had found a bit of an ally; a resource to use as he looked into Patrick's death. Now, as she sat beside him in the confined space of the car, he could almost smell the smugness rolling off her as his inquiry led to nowhere but self-doubt.

Clara let out a pronounced sigh. When Quinn turned to look at her, she ran a hand over her loose blonde hair. "So, what do you want to do now?"

What he really wanted to do was find a hole to hide in for the next three days, with his self-pity and bloated guilt for company, but he was not built that way and he had a job that needed doing. He had let Patrick down in life. He would not fail Patrick's father in the boy's death.

"The other guys who are working now," Quinn said. "Did they work with Patrick as well?"

Clara nodded. "Yeah, this was his team. The inspector considered splitting them up, giving them a change, or even a transfer, but they all said they were okay to keep working."

"Let's see where they are," Quinn said. "I'll talk to them, too."

"After that conversation with Gerry, are you sure you wanna do that? I think you've had enough for one day. Maybe you should try it again in the morning. You know...quit while you're ahead."

"I'm not ahead," Quinn said. "So there's no point in quitting."

Clara pulled the *Blackberry* off her belt and made a phone call to the dispatcher. She pulled a ledger sized notebook out of the interior pocket on the driver's door and scribbled a few lines. Once she had finished the conversation she put her notebook away, started the Nissan, dropped it into gear and pulled onto the quiet street.

She said nothing as they drove, and Quinn was happy to sit in silence and look out the window. They rode down a wide highway—the same one they had taken when they came into town from the airport—and past Quinn's hotel. Then, Clara made a right turn and drove through a residential area and across a set of wide rail tracks. Quinn, with his gaze still cast out window, whistled softly through his teeth.

The change the town undertook as they crossed the tracks was as dramatic and clichéd as any old Hollywood movie. The other side of those steel rails saw the socioeconomic scale drop significantly. The houses turned from neat homes with well-kept lawns, into run down shacks with tiny, unkempt yards - several with three or four dysfunctional cars in the driveway. The ugly little residential area further transformed into an industrial district with small factories, mills, truckyards and warehouses.

"Where are we now?" Quinn asked as he took in the grubby sights.

"Slaterville," Clara said. "Our equivalent of skid row."

They passed a group of buildings, most of them charred and burned nearly to the ground. In fact, only one structure in the skeletal cluster stood and appeared whole, although all the windows and doors were boarded up with plywood, most of it stained with graffiti.

The lone building was squat and ugly and had a decidedly menacing appearance. The sight of the place brought back flashes of memory and the rundown house occupied by Joe Robowski.

Clara looked at Quinn before following his gaze to the buildings. "That's the old hospital," she said. "It's been unused for years, but some squatters burned it merrily to the fucking ground about a year ago."

"And what building is that?" Quinn pointed through the windshield to the remaining building.

"That," Clara said, "is the old psych unit, where they locked up the freak shows. It was shut down years before the hospital closed. Someone decided that segregating the mentally ill in an old, ugly building was cruel, so they added a new wing to the hospital and stopped using that place in the seventies. The only thing there now is gatherings of those fucking Goth kids who do weird shit in the cemetery." She pointed to the small cemetery beside the abandoned hospital. "They go to 'commune with the spirits' in the old loony bin."

She put her face closer to the driver's window and examined the building, her lips peeling back from her teeth in an expression of distaste. "They're supposed to bulldoze that shithole soon, but not soon enough."

Quinn studied the old building. After his experience in Resolution, he wondered what lurked in the subterranean floors of a building like that.

After a few more minutes of driving they reached an abandoned house with two marked police vehicles out front: a Chevrolet Pickup and the ubiquitous Ford Crown Victoria. The two members there were shuffling along a group of, what Quinn assumed were, squatters who had set up housekeeping in the tiny, dilapidated building.

The conversation with the two constables was brief and unremarkable. They had both known Patrick, had not talked to him much, but thought he was a good worker. When he was done, Quinn felt no closer to any kind of solution and even more worn out.

"So, now what?" Clara asked when they were back in the car.

He looked down at his watch. It was well after seven p.m. He had travelled a long way and felt all kinds of shitty. "I think I'm done for today," he said, rubbing a hand over his face. "We can pick it up in the morning and go from there."

She did not say anything, but Clara looked relieved as she started the car and drove through the pot-hole ridden streets towards Quinn's hotel. She did not offer any words of encouragement or ask him if he wanted any company for dinner. As they arrived at the hotel and she brought the car to a stop, he reached for the door handle without any parting words.

She reached out with her right hand and touched his elbow, making him look back at her. "Look," she said. Her eyes moving down towards the gear shift of the car. "Look, I know I've been kind of a bitch today and haven't been helping you at all, but I don't want you to think I don't care." She paused again, removing her hand from his arm and gazing out the windshield at the other cars in the parking lot. "I think like Inspector Ferguson. Patrick was one of ours. He was my friend. The thought, the *accusation*, that we didn't do a proper job looking into his death is a slap in the face. For all of us." She turned her head and looked into his eyes for the first time since they had stopped. "Have you ever lost anyone you worked with?"

His jaw clenched involuntarily as he thought about the day Sandy had tried to kill herself after her confrontation with the demon. She had nearly died, and would have if he had not kicked down her door and clapped his hand over the bleeding wound in her neck. He remembered, very well, the feeling of awful, hopeless frustration as he sat beside her hospital bed, hoping she would wake up.

He realised he was grinding his teeth, as Clara stared at him, her head cocked to one side. He shook his head, as much a gesture to loosen himself up as to indicate the negative. "I've come close, once, but no one I've ever worked with has died."

"Then you don't know what it's like," she said, tilting her head the other way. "You knew Patrick, but you never rolled this city with him. You never bled with him at a file. We did. He was here with us, not you. It's not personal, but we all want you to get this over with and go the fuck away so Patrick can rest without you digging him up."

She turned from him and looked out the driver's window, seeming to pretend he was not there. Having no idea what he should say, Quinn opened the door to the Nissan and got out. He had not quite managed to close the door before Clara pulled away.

He walked into the hotel, across the black tile of the lobby and towards the restaurant. The girl at the reception desk, who had not made mention of his gun and badge, looked up at him with a smile when he walked in. She put down the magazine she had been reading and leaned against the front counter expecting him to stop. Quinn slowed his steps and veered towards the desk.

"Hi," she said when he was in front of her.

"Uh, hi," he said in return.

"So, you're a cop, right?" Her eyes flicked down to the gun on Quinn's hip and the badge attached to his belt. She wore a great deal of black eye-liner and it made her eyes appear wider than they really were, giving her a bit of a doe-ish look.

"Uh, yeah," he said. "Is there something you need to tell me?"

She pushed her loose hair back over her ears with fingers bearing black nail polish. Upon closer inspection, her hair showed light roots where the black dye was growing out.

"Well, I kinda wanted to tell you I get off at ten."

Quinn rubbed a hand across his forehead and let out a heavy breath. "I'm sorry, uh..."

"Mandy," she said, and put her hands on the desk in front of her hips. She straightened her arms so her elbows pressed into her breasts and made the smooth tops want to pop out of the low-cut black shirt she wore.

Resist as he might, Quinn felt his eyes drift towards the

sight, which was not at all unpleasant. "Right, Mandy," he said and shook his head. "I'm sorry, I'm practically married."

She quirked her mouth and gave him a half smile while she looked him up and down in an obvious, exaggerated fashion. "That's too bad," her eyes flickered to the screen on her desk, "Mr. Sullivan. You're kind of cute." She picked up the magazine she had been reading and fanned herself, making her dyed-black hair flutter away from her chest, once again exposing her cleavage.

Quinn was about to turn away again when he saw the cover of the magazine. "What are you reading?" he asked.

She stopped fanning and looked down at the cover. It depicted several young men and women, all with black hair, pale skin, eye liner and long, dark coats. The title said 'Bleak Hope.'

"This?" Mandy asked, and opened the magazine to a page near the middle. "It's a local thing, done by a guy in town. To let people know about alternate culture in this cramped place."

"Alternate culture?" Quinn asked.

"You know, the kinds of things outside the box. The stuff the Corporate Overlords don't want out in public where people can see it."

"Corporate Overlords? You know you work for a massive hotel chain, right?"

She snorted. "I just work here. I don't subscribe to their doctrine of suppressed sexuality and boring corporate shackles." She toyed at the corner of her mouth with one black fingernail. "People like me, and like the editor of this," she waved the magazine, "we're free spirits. I let my sexuality run where it wants." She looked him up and down again. "Which is why I wanted you to know I'm off at ten."

"Okay," Quinn said, drawing the word out as though it had a lead weight attached to it. He rubbed at his face again while he turned towards the restaurant, deciding it was best to leave before she had a chance to say anything else that was ridiculous. "Thanks. I'll see you tomorrow."

"Only if you're very lucky, Mr. Sullivan," she said to his back.

Quinn had not eaten since the hasty McDonald's breakfast he had picked up on the way to the airport in Prince George, but the sick feeling he had had all day while looking into Patrick's death had kept hunger at bay. Now, when he walked through the doorway of the restaurant, identified as Mickey's by the sign above the door, the smell of cooking food hit him. His stomach rumbled so loudly that an elderly couple sitting by the door looked up at him, disapproval on their wrinkled faces.

There was a bar with high stools across from the entrance and Quinn sat at one, studying the menu-board high on the wall.

"What can I get you," a middle aged woman in a black collared t-shirt asked him.

"Uh, the burger platter, please, and a pint of whatever you've got on tap."

The beer arrived in short order and the food not long after. There was a television on above the bar, but Quinn paid no attention to it. He was far too busy shoving fries and cheeseburger into his mouth.

"That's disgusting," the waitress said, one fist on her round hip.

It took a few seconds for Quinn to realise she was talking to him and another moment to notice she watched the television mounted on the wall above the bar, not referring to his eating habits. He swallowed hastily and wiped his mouth with a paper napkin. "What is?"

"The news," the waitress grabbed a remote control from under the counter and turned up the volume on the television. "They found human remains in a little town out on the coast." She pointed at the television with the remote. "The news girl said it looks like there were human teeth marks in the bones."

Quinn turned his attention to the television and his hand stopped, a French fry half way to his mouth, as he saw what was on the screen. Inspector Donald Green, dressed in uniform with his name on the screen beneath his face, spoke to the camera.

"I can confirm," said the inspector, "that we have located human remains at a remote residence in the mountains south of Resolution Cove. I don't have any other details to share, other than that we are in the early stages of what is likely to be a complex investigation."

A disembodied voice came from the television as well. "Inspector, what about the rumor the remains have marks on them made by human teeth."

The inspector shook his head. "You said it yourself. It's nothing but a rumor and I have no idea how it started."

"What about reports that one of the officers in your detachment was injured while recovering the remains?" the voice asked.

"One of my members suffered cuts to his arm during the course of the investigation," the inspector said. "But will suffer no lasting or permanent injury."

The inspector disappeared from the screen and the disembodied voice started prattling about the police investigation. A wooden porch with crime scene tape on it flashed onto the screen. They did not show enough of the house for Quinn to be able to recognize it, but a distinct feeling of dread crawled into his belly to join the cheeseburger.

He stared at his mostly empty plate, his interest in the meal severely diminished, when his phone rang. He pulled it out of the pocket of his jeans, looked at the screen and saw a picture of Carrie. He slid his finger across the screen and held the phone to his ear.

"Hi," he said, a grin creeping across his face.

"Hey, baby," Carrie said. He could hear the smile in her voice. "How did it go today? How was your trip?"

"The trip was fine. The day sucked ass. Do you have the TV on?"

"Yeah," she said. "Why?"

"Change it to a channel that has some news on it." He

looked up at the television which still played clips of crime scene and showed pieces of interviews with locals.

"Okay," she said. He heard Shawn's squawk of protest as the background noise of the television changed.

"Did you find anything yet?"

There was several heartbeats worth of silence on the other end of the line, and then Quinn heard a sharp intake of breath. "Oh my God," Carrie said. "That's disgusting."

"Yeah," Quinn said, still looking at the television and wondering if they were watching the same broadcast. "It's bad enough that it's not just on the local news, but out here as well. Did you hear anything from the guys? My team is still working today."

"No, none of them have said anything to me."

"So, I guess you don't know who got hurt, then?"

"Someone got hurt?" Carried sounded slightly alarmed.

"Yeah, Inspector Green said so in an interview clip."

"I'm sorry, I didn't hear anything. If I do, I'll let you know."

"Okay. How's the boy?"

Quinn heard Shawn's voice in the background asking if he could change the channel back. "He's fine," she said. "He misses you already. We both miss you. Are you going to have to stay out there long?"

"No longer than I expected. I feel kind of dumb to tell you the truth. It's obvious that the members in the detachment don't want me here. They think I'm tarnishing Patrick's name with this inquiry, and it doesn't look like there is anything to find anyway. If it weren't so important to the inspector, I'd probably come back now."

Her sigh whispered through the phone. "I'm sorry it's not going well. Do what you think is right, then come back to us."

"Okay, I'll talk to you tomorrow. I love you."

"I love you, too."

Putting his phone back into his pocket, Quinn drank down his last few gulps of beer, dropped a twenty dollar bill on the counter and walked down the hallway towards the elevators. The hotel only had four floors, so the ride to the top was short. As he stepped out into his hallway, his phone buzzed in his pocket again.

The number showed as blocked, but he answered it on the third buzz. "Hello, Quinn speaking."

"Quinn, it's Raife."

"Hey boss, I was just going to call you."

"You're on speaker phone and Dave and Sandy are in my office. Are you somewhere private?"

The tone of Raife's voice made the cheeseburger take on a hateful personality, clawing at the walls of his gut. He reached the door to his room and fit the key card into the slot above the handle.

"I will be in a second. What's up?"

"We got troubles, son. All kinds of 'em."

"Okay," Quinn said, as he opened the door, stepped through, and shut it behind him. He sat down on the edge of the hotel room bed, his anxiety rising with every moment that Raife was silent on the other end of the phone. "Right," he said, when he was settled. "Lay it on me."

"Whatever weird shit was happening in this town before..." Raife said, letting out a heavy breath.

Quinn heard Dave clear his throat. "Well," he said. "It looks like it's come back."

CHAPTER 10

Autumn Donnelly walked, her steps brisk, from the Resolution Cove RCMP detachment, through the quiet, darkening streets and back to her shop. She knew when she walked to the detachment that Quinn would not be back to his office, yet, but that did not stop her hope that she would find him there. The conversation she had had with Kord McRae earlier replayed over and over in her head. Each repeat showing in the theatre of her mind made her all the more uneasy.

Seeing that there was some kind of police incident, and that the big man, Sergeant Raife, had been injured, almost set her teeth chattering.

An inky stain spread across this town, like it had two years ago. She was horribly fearful that without Quinn here to stem the flow the whole town would soon be covered.

She saw very few people on her brief walk from the police station to the downtown business district, but she shied away from everyone she met and kept jumping at shadows. She experienced a huge surge of relief, the heat of it warming her chest, when she finally returned to her shop and slid the key into the lock.

She opened the door and stepped inside, and knew instantly something was wrong.

The air in the shop did not taste quite right. She would never have been able to explain it if someone had asked her, but there was a taint to it, a spice that was not like any of the familiar smells. It was like walking into a strange house for the first time and smelling the life of another person. It set her scalp tingling.

She let the door close, the bell above it ringing as it had when she had opened it. If there was someone in her place, they already knew she was here and there was no way to hide her coming now. She looked about the shadowed bookshelves, barely illuminated by the sparse light outside. There was nothing that she could see to be used as a weapon against any intruder, if there was one. She hoped, as she walked further into the store, that she was only being paranoid, that her imagination was running away with her.

The further she got into the store, the stronger the strange smell became. It was not a dirty, unpleasant smell. It was clean and wild, like the loam in a pine forest. It set her at ease, somewhat, but she still walked cautiously.

She reached her small cash counter and stopped. There was a quartz crystal sphere, about the size of a grapefruit, on a little brass stand. She picked it up and weighed it in her palm for a moment. If worst came to worst she could try and brain the intruder. With the sphere held at her side, beside her right breast, she walked through the door behind the cash counter and started up the stairs to her loft apartment.

She put her foot on the first stair and looked up. She screamed in shock, the sphere flying from her hand to shatter on the cement floor below the stairs. Sitting in the centre of the stairs, his feet two steps below him, was a dark haired, broad-shouldered man.

The man had been reading a book, his elbows on his knees and the book sitting on his open hands. "I'm sorry I startled you, witch." He closed the book and stood up, towering above her on the stairs. "But I did not want to wait in your shop where I might be seen, and I did not feel it right to sit in your home," he gestured up the stairs with the book, "without being invited. This was the only other place."

She put a hand on her chest, her heart hammering against her palm, while she gripped the stair railing with the other. "What did you call me?" The title he had used, without the normal accusatory tone that usually came with it, was even more startling than his appearance in her shop.

"I called you 'witch'. That is what you are, is it not? Though your kind is not what it once was, you still carry the trappings." He lifted the book slightly. "And you have the..." he took in a great breath through his nose. "You have the smell of the old magic about you."

The way he sniffed, closing his eyes as though savouring the smell, set her scalp back to tingling.

"Who are you?" she asked. She took her one foot off the stair and backed away the few steps the small space would allow.

The dark haired man gave her a horribly handsome, awful smile and started down the stairs. His muscular arms swung beneath his heavy shoulders. He moved with a vital, animal grace. He reminded her of Quinn, except the shadows pooled around him so heavily it made her vision dim.

"Who I am is not really important. What I am concerns you a great deal."

Autumn retreated another step until her back was against the wall. The inside of her mouth felt chalky and dry. She worked her tongue over her lips several times before she could speak. "What are you?"

The man lunged forward, a streaking motion so fast she could scarcely follow it with her eye. He stopped short, his body pressed against hers, his nose touching her cheek. "What I am," he said, and then breathed in the scent of her hair, closing his eyes as he did it. "Is something that can hurt you very badly."

The pleasant scent Autumn had detected when she first walked into her shop lay about this man like a blanket, pouring off him in waves. Now that she was close, it was no longer pleasant. It smelled of rot and decay. Of violence. Of death.

He spun away, as fast as he lunged at her, and took in another deep breath. "You've had a visitor here, Autumn. Two of them, in fact. A man and a girl child. Where are they?"

"I don't know what you're..." the lie came to her lips easily, but died quickly as he turned and looked at her over his shoulder, his brown eyes narrow. Lying, she decided, would be a bad idea. She worked her tongue over her lips again and pressed her palms against the wall behind her to try and stop her body from shaking. "What...what do you want with them?"

He turned, then, his eyes flashing red beneath the dark brown. "YOU DO NOT ASK ME QUESTIONS!" he roared. The sound was powerful enough to make the bells on her cash register hum and her ears ring. "You answer me when I give you opportunity. Now, I asked you, where are they?"

"I don't know," she said, her voice cracking behind a sob. "They only came in here for a moment. I don't know where they've gone."

He stepped close to her again, slowly this time, his body pressing close to her. "You know, I'll be able to smell your lies."

She closed her eyes tight and turned her head away, the smell of him making her want to gag, the hard tension of his body making her want to squirm.

He laughed in her face, his spittle hitting her cheek. "You tell Kord McRae, when next he comes crawling in your shop, that he cannot hide from me. I will find him soon enough." The man turned and strode lazily through her shop. He stopped at the front door and turned back, in the same spot that Kord McRae had stood to give her his warning. "And you tell that sorry fool you call a Guardian, if he ever returns, that the first time we meet will be our last. Tell him what a bloody meeting it will be." The man pulled open the door and walked out into the street.

Autumn stood shaking for several moments, staring at the place he had been, remembering the red flash of his eyes at the peak of his fury. Slowly, she lowered herself to the floor, letting her back slide along the wall. She crouched there a long time, her arms wrapped around her legs, tears rolling down her face. She wished, for the first time in her long, happy, solitary existence, that she did not have to spend the night alone.

Turning off his phone, Quinn gritted his teeth and tossed the device on the bed-spread beside him. He had spent the last hour talking with Raife, Dave and Sandy, about both the remains of Dean Springer, and the conversation Raife had participated in with the terrified Autumn Donnelly.

The conversation, instead of bringing about any kind of conclusion, had only served to make Quinn more frustrated. The three people on the other end of the phone were looking to him for answers. He could hear their anticipation through his phone as they perched around Raife's desk like solution vultures waiting for him to produce something tasty.

You need to come back, they had all said. We need you here, they told him.

I can't, he'd replied. I'm not done yet.

He understood where they were coming from. There was something strange happening in Resolution, just as it had happened two years ago, and they did not know how to handle it. The problem was he did not know how to handle it either.

He had pulled the knife—that once belonged to Donnell of Inverness—from the small of his back and looked at it during his conversation. Sure, he could fight a demon if another one showed up. He could stab it with this knife and consume it with fire, but they did not even know if there was actually anything to fight. If there was an enemy, no one knew who it was.

In the end, he had convinced them he needed to stay. There was something about Patrick's death that did not sit right. There was something about his behaviour that set off that cop instinct that always lurked in the back of Quinn's, and every other cops', head. He needed to look a little more, to dig a little deeper. That and the inspector had asked him to do it.

After he had resolved to stay, to the reluctant agreement of his team back in Resolution, he hung up the phone. He stripped off his gun, spare magazine, handcuffs and sheath for the knife, and dropped the items in the drawer of his bedside table. Then he peeled off his clothes and climbed into the shower.

He stood, letting the hot water beat away at his concern, his confusion and his anxiety for more time than his exhausted brain could calculate. Eventually, once his fingertips had grown wrinkly and the skin on his shoulders were near to scalded, he climbed out of the shower, wrapped a towel around his waist and stepped into the larger space of the hotel room.

The window in the room did not show much: the parking lot of the hotel, the highway, the residential area and Slaterville, with its rundown shacks and abandoned loony bins. Quinn wondered, as he leaned against the window frame, if the answer to Patrick's death lay somewhere out there. He wondered if there was some kind of closure, something that could be made to answer for the ruin of such a young life. No matter how long he stood there, or how hard he stared into the night, no answer would come.

Throwing the towel over the back of the faux-leather office chair, he crawled between the crisp sheets of the bed and turned on the television. He flicked aimlessly between the channels of putrid reality TV and turbid, complicated dramas that he did not understand and did not care about. He hoped the flickering, mindless lights would lull his frantically moving brain into some kind of relaxing trance, but after another thirty minutes of the incessant channel surfing he gave it up and turned off the lights.

He did not know how long it took, but, eventually, he fell asleep. Dreams came to him, indistinct as shadows, the concepts as elusive as fish beneath dark water. The only thing he clearly remembered later was confusion, violence, and loss.

They were dreams he quickly tried to forget upon waking.

He swung his legs from the bed and walked slowly, exhaustion settling bars of lead in his thighs, to the balcony window and saw a streak of pink light on the eastern horizon. He stood there for a while, studying the same view he had the night before, and concluded that nothing looked any clearer in the fingers of daylight creeping across the town.

He washed his face and dressed in the previous day's jeans and a clean t-shirt, strapped on his gun, Donnell's dagger and other gear, and then went down into the lobby of the hotel. It was full daylight now, not quite six a.m. The lobby was deserted except for a skinny youth with carefully styled hair and a crisp white shirt, seated behind the reception desk. He looked up when Quinn stepped out of the elevator and gave him a polite grin.

"Good morning, sir. Sleep well?" the youth asked.

"Fine," Quinn lied. "Can you call me a cab?"

The youth, who had a tag on his shirt with the name 'Will', leaned back a little and looked up. "There appear to be two cabs already outside, sir." He looked back at Quinn. "There is always at least one waiting for any early morning travelers."

Quinn nodded, assuming there was some kind of monitor for a security camera on the wall above the desk. He turned and headed for the doors and had gone three steps when clerk cleared his throat. Quinn turned back and looked at him.

He pointed a slim finger towards a table at the back of the room, laid out with fruit, pastries and bottled beverages. "Continental breakfast," Will said. "I can see you're in a hurry, so feel free to take some to go." He reached below the counter and produced a foam take-out container.

"Uh, thanks," he said. He accepted the container while he made a mental note to tell the manager to give the kid a raise.

He filled the container from the table, taking two muffins, a banana and some yogurt, and a bottle of orange juice. He turned for the doors again, waving to the clerk and went outside to find a ride.

There were two cabs parked near the front doors; one yellow and one white. When the double sliding doors opened and Quinn stepped onto the sidewalk, both drivers looked up from what they were reading, reached for their gear shifters and lunged towards him. The yellow cab was a fraction faster and lurched to a stop in front of Quinn, cutting off his opponent and nearly causing a collision. The driver of the white cab honked his horn, yelled and made several rude gestures.

Quinn stared at the spectacle and had to suppress a chuckle. He made eye contact with the driver of the white cab, who still yelled and swore, gave him an apologetic shrug, and climbed into the back seat of the yellow cab.

The driver, a huge fat man, wearing a fisherman's vest and appearing to have only one leg, looked in the rear-view mirror at him. "Where can I take ya?"

"The RCMP detachment, please," Quinn said and looked through the back window at the still-yelling driver of the white cab. "You guys get competitive here in Cranbrook."

The driver pulled away from the curb and shrugged. "Early bird doesn't look like an asshole, or so they say."

"So they say," Quinn agreed. He bit into a muffin. Who 'they' were was as unclear to him as why they might have such a saying, but he thought it best not to argue with a one legged cab driver in a fisherman's vest.

The drive to the detachment did not take long. Quinn paid the driver, telling him to keep the change, and walked to the front door of the detachment. There was a small button beside the door. Quinn pushed it and heard a chime inside the building. It took several minutes, but eventually he saw a wary face peer around a cubicle wall and squint at the door.

There were few things a cop hated more than a walk-up complaint to the front counter. Generally, it meant one of two things: the person were either crazy and wanted to rant at a police officer in person, not content to do it over the phone, or it meant something horrific had just happened and someone would be bleeding on the front door, causing grotesque amounts of paperwork.

Once the member in the office saw that Quinn was neither bleeding nor ranting, he cautiously came and unlocked the front door.

"Can I help you?" asked the member, a short, athletic-looking man in his twenties.

Quinn turned his right hip forward so the member could see the badge and gun on his belt. "I'm Constable...I mean, Corporal Sullivan. I'm here for—"

"I know why you're here," the member said as he stepped back from the entrance and held the door open. The tone of his voice led Quinn to believe that the member's knowledge of Quinn's purpose did not bring agreement along for the ride.

He stepped through the door, waited for the member to close and lock it, and then followed him through the office lobby and into the interior.

"Do you need anything?" asked the member, his voice just a shade below civil. Quinn was happy to know he was making so many friends during this little venture.

"Yeah," he said. He dropped his now empty breakfast container into a garbage can. "I need a computer terminal and access to your file room."

The member pointed to a vacant cubicle. "You can use that computer. The file room is over there." He pointed behind him to an open door beside a row of offices. "It's not locked."

Quinn was saved the trouble of saying 'thank you' when the member turned and walked away without another word.

The only other people in the office were the on-duty members hiding in the back of the general duty pit. Those members, Quinn figured, would be conspicuously ignoring him, so he would have some privacy and space to think for a couple of hours. He sat down at the computer and went through the logging-in process, and then logged onto the PRIME file system. When the system was up and open, he punched in Patrick's name and date of birth. There was only one file that came up, and it was labeled as a 'Coroner's Act', which was the classification for every suicide.

Normally, a file involving an RCMP member, beyond something simple – when they were victims of a minor crime like vandalism, or were driving a police vehicle and got into a collision – would be privatized so no one, except for the primary investigators could see the details of it. In this case, the strings Inspector Green had pulled had afforded him access to the electronic file, as well as the hard copy.

There were dozens of reports on the file from all the various members who had some hand in the investigation. Quinn started at the beginning, reading the synopsis of the event, and then the entire individual occurrence reports from the members and the coroner's report that had been scanned into the file. There was nothing here that he had not expected to find. It was all reflective only of the scene and Patrick's condition when they attended. There was not a single word about his behaviour beforehand. The file was sterile and clinical. Quinn needed something more that he would not find there.

Once he had read the file through again, to be sure he had not missed anything, he memorized the file number, and then walked into the file room. The Cranbrook detachment file room was much like the one in Resolution cove. Most of the files never saw paper. The ones that did were a few sheets at most. It took Quinn approximately six seconds to locate Patrick's file, which filled a brown banker's box, and pull it off the shelf.

He carried the box back to the desk he had occupied and set it on the surface. He put his hands on the lid and stared at it for a moment. Reading about the file on a computer screen gave some distance from the event. It was not near as real when looking at it through an impersonal electronic eye, but when you had paper in your hand that someone else had touched and produced, it provided a human connection. That connection brought several emotions surrounding Patrick's death, the ones that had surfaced the day before during the conversation with Gerry Barnes, crashing into the walls of Quinn's calm.

He curled his fingers around the edges of the lid, took a

deep breath and lifted it. The weight felt immense as the square of folded cardboard came free, as though it were the lid to Patrick's casket and he was digging him up to poke at his mangled body. Quinn took another breath that caught and shuddered as he looked down into the bundles of paper bound together with clips. He felt as though Patrick's memory stared back at him. It had nothing nice to say.

The first bundle he pulled out was a collection of photocpied notebook pages from the various investigators that had been there. He sat down at the desk and began flipping through them, but did not have the patience to sit and try to decipher the hieroglyphic handwriting of most of the members. He put them aside to look at later.

The next bundle was the coroner's report and autopsy. This, he opened and read carefully, his eyes touching every word. It was clinical and detached, as such reports always were. As he scanned the pages he felt for a moment like he could pretend it was someone else, besides a boy he had known. After several pages he got to the part of the report he was interested in: the toxicology screening. The report advised there were no foreign substances in Patrick's body. No drugs—prescription or otherwise—and no liquor. He had been sober and straight when he had hung himself from the ceiling fan. Quinn could not point to any chemical interference to account for the event. He read on, gleaning what details he could, making notes in his own leather notebook as he went.

His detachment held until he reached the pictures.

After the coroner's report was a bundle marked 'images'. He had been flowing through the task of reading the file and had not hesitated to pick up the folder and open it. When he did, he could not help the tears that sprang to his eyes, making the pictures in front of him blissfully blurry.

The first shots were of Patrick and the inside of his apartment. Quinn had seen the images before, briefly, but had not taken much of a look. He had only seen enough to know that it was Patrick and he had disfigured himself before taking his own life. The scalpel Patrick had used still rested in his half-open hand as he hanged, his toes only an inch from the ground. Now, Quinn thought of the job he had to do, swallowed hard and did his best to shove his emotions aside and lock them away behind the iron of his will.

There was a close up picture of Patrick. Quinn studied it closely, doing his best to avoid looking at the odd angle of the boy's neck and the bloated tongue sticking out from between his purple lips. He focused, instead, on the symbols that were carved in Patrick's torso, the tops of his thighs, even his arms.

The landscape of gaping, jagged images was dominated by an inverted pentagram in his chest. It was so stereotypical and clichéd that if Quinn was not looking at it himself, below the distended, mottled face of a boy he once knew, he would have thought the pictures were from a movie poster. There seemed to be no semblance of order to the other symbols. They were uneven and oddly spaced, as though they were made in frantic haste, and they did not appear to be similar or related to one another. He did not recognize any of the symbols, beyond the pentagram, and decided he would have to consult with someone to find out what the symbols meant.

He looked down at his watch and saw it was now after seven a.m. He pulled his phone from his pocket and hit the speed dial for Raife's number.

The big man picked up on the second ring. "Sergeant Raife here," the baritone came through to Quinn's ear.

"Raife, it's me."

"Good morning, Me. How you feeling today?"

"Uh, like I've been stuffed in an outhouse and shoved down a set of stairs?"

"Are you asking me, or telling me?"

"A little of both."

"Very colourful." Raife snorted into the phone. "What's up, son?"

"I'm gonna fax you a couple pictures." Quinn flipped through the stack of pictures until he found some that depicted the symbols up close without showing Patrick's face. "I need you to take them and show them to someone."

"You know I love you, boy, but if you send me naked pictures of yourself to show Carrie, I'm gonna drive out there and kick your ass 'til it's humped up around your ears."

Quinn laughed. It was a good, honest laugh, and it helped to cut through the misery he had been feeling since he got off the plane and started walking around this town. When he had controlled himself enough to speak again he said, "No, it's for the investigation."

"I'm willing to bet it's still something I don't want to see."

Quinn sighed. "That's a bet you'd win, Boss. They're pictures of Patrick and..." he paused, running his tongue back and forth across his bottom lip as he looked at the pictures again. "They're pictures of Patrick and what he did to himself. I need you to take them and show them to Autumn."

"Autumn?" Raife's voice dropped another octave. Quinn heard a huffed breath in the phone. "Why?"

"I don't understand any of the symbols, Raife, and she might know them. I'm hoping if we can figure out what they mean, we can get a bead on what was going on in his head at the time."

There was silence on the line, save for the heavy breath of the big man. "Okay, son," Raife said finally. "I'll take them to your crazy lady. You need anything else?"

Quinn thought for a moment about saying goodbye and hanging up the phone, but the sound of Raife's voice, the steady depth of it, brought him a large measure of comfort. He didn't know if he was ready to end the conversation yet.

"I..." he hesitated, worried he would sound stupid. After a moment he decided that once a group of people, Dave and Sandy included, had seen and shared as much as they all had, there was not any room or need to hold much back. "I wish you were here, Raife, to tell you true. This job sucks as bad as anything I've done in eight years on the force. I could use a friend to watch my back and shore me up."

There was a slight growl on the other end of the line. "I wish I could be there, too, Quinn. Or that Green had sent me instead of you. It's an awful burden to carry, something like this. I don't think it was reasonable for the inspector to lay it on you, but he believes you can do it and so do I. Probably none better. It's a shitty job, without doubt, but I know you can manage it."

Like all of Raife's pep talks, it was short and plain, but it got the message across – although with fewer threats of violence than was customary – and, for a moment, it made Quinn feel like he were in a familiar place. Like he was home.

"Thanks, Raife."

"No thanks needed. I'll get these pictures to the hippy chick and I'll let you know when she tells me something. You call me if you need anything."

"I will," Quinn affirmed. He hung up the phone.

"What the fuck are you doing here?"

Quinn turned in his chair to face the voice behind him. Clara Morgan stood dressed in dark maroon slacks and a black blouse, her short blonde hair held back with clips. There was a tall Starbucks cup in her hand and she had a decidedly displeased look on her face.

"Uh, what?"

"I went to your hotel to pick you up and the skinny kid at the front counter said you'd already left." She set her cup on the desk beside her and crossed her arms. The glare she cast at him was hard enough to scratch glass.

"I couldn't sleep so I came in early to get a start on the day," Quinn said, a little surprised by the force of her anger.

"What the fuck are you doing in here by yourself? Looking through our files?"

Annoyance flashed across Quinn's mind and he felt his jaw clench as he stood, thrusting himself up from the chair. "You're forgetting something here, Clara; I'm a cop, too. I also have top secret security clearance, and, whether you like it or not," he reached out to put a hand on the rim of the file box, "this is now my file, not yours. So, if I want to read it naked, in a tree, while eating powdered donuts, I'll go right ahead and do that."

With every word he spoke, her face got flatter and flatter, until the utter lack of emotion was so startling it spoke of the fury beneath her countenance. Quinn ran a hand over his face, frustrated, knowing that getting into a verbal pissing contest with Clara was certainly not going to aid him in his investigation. He sucked in a breath through his nose and calmed himself.

"I need to make something clear," he said. He held up his hands in a gesture of placation. "I am not here to hurt anyone. I'm not here to piss in your ear or made you look bad. I'm just looking into this investigation so I can bring some peace to Patrick's family, and because he meant something to me, too. I don't really want to be here anymore than you want me here, which is quite obviously not at all. So, if you can help me out and see this done, I'll be on my way and be nothing but a vaguely disinteresting memory."

Her expression did not change as her eyes made subtle movements, apparently scanning his face.

"Does that sound reasonable?" he asked. "Can we make that happen?"

She uncrossed her arms, slowly, her eyes narrowing minutely. Then she picked up her coffee, took a sip, smacked her lips and looked at him some more. She must be a reasonably good interviewer, Quinn thought as he felt a little like squirming under her gaze, but his horribly stubborn streak, a gift from his father's side of the family, steadied him.

"Yeah," she said, after another sip. "We can do that."

He would never allow it to show on his face, but Quinn felt a substantial amount of relief. Doing this investigation at all was hard enough without having to fight every single person he came in contact with.

"Thanks," he said.

"Yeah." She leaned back against the desk, resting her butt on the edge, and took another sip from her cup. "So, what do you want to do now?"

Quinn had been considering that very thing as he read through the file. He was having the symbols carved into Pat-

rick's body looked at, but he could not sit around waiting for
Raife to get back to him with the results of his conversation
with Autumn. He needed to do something in the meantime,
but what?

His eyes flickered to one of the pictures of the scene and a
thought formed in his head. "Has anything been done with
Patrick's apartment?"

Clara shook her head. "We're not still guarding it as a scene, if that's what you mean."

"I wouldn't expect so, but has it been cleaned?"

"I'm not sure," she said. She pursed her lips as she looked
up, apparently thinking. "I'm reasonably certain that we didn't
clean the place out. I think we were waiting for Patrick's family to come and take care of his effects." She looked down at
him. "But they sent you instead."

The dig was obvious, but Quinn ignored it. "So it might
still be as it was when you guys released the scene."

Clara shrugged. "Yeah, maybe."

Quinn bent over the desk and began replacing the bundled paper in the banker's box. "Let's head over there. I'd like
to have a look for myself."

Raife pulled his Chevy Suburban into one of the slanted parking spots in front of Autumn Donnelly's shop and shoved the
gear shift into park. He leaned forward and looked up at the
front window of the store: 'Nature's Song'. What a stupid
name for a store, he thought as he rubbed his mustache and
stared. But, that was the kind of name you came up with when
you sold hippie bullshit, he supposed.

He was cranky this morning, even more than usual, because he was feeling better, and he did not like it. He looked
down at his bandaged arm and flexed his fingers. He had
peeled the bandage off his arm this morning to wash the
wound and change the dressing. He had found it much im-
proved; much more than it should have been. It was still a
long way from back to normal, but the burning ache of it was

now down to a dull throb and the wounds looked like they had been healing for several days, instead of just overnight. He was not a religious man and did not believe in miracles, so there was only one thing he could reasonably attribute his healing to: Autumn Donnelly's touch.

He felt a distinct dose of ire because he did not want to attribute anything, let alone his abnormal healing, to the tie-dyed hippie woman. He had tried to deny it when he examined the wound, but once he had run through the other options, his mind forced him to accept the final deduction – logical or not.

Raife considered himself very much self-aware. Knowing he was set in his ways, anything new upset him, and when he got upset it translated very quickly into anger.

He had seen a great deal of new things, most of which he wanted very much to forget, since Quinn Sullivan came to Resolution Cove— a demon that had appeared in the basement of a shit hole house in the south end. He did not want to believe in the things that went bump in the night, even though he had seen them with his own eyes. He fervently wished he could go back to the days when his life was simple; see the bad guy, thump the bad guy, arrest the bad guy. He did not want the bad guys to make people crazy, have red eyes and burst into flame when you stabbed them with glowing knives.

The worst thing, in the last couple days of renewed strangeness, was that he felt like he owed this Autumn woman, and he hated owing people, especially of the hippie, tie-dyed variety.

He flexed his arm again, sighed and opened the door to the truck. As he slid out of the driver's seat, he grabbed the manila folder he had left on the dash. He was very careful not to open it and look at the contents.

He glanced down at his watch as he walked up to the front door. It was after nine in the morning, but the interior of the store was still dark. The closed sign on the door still faced the street and there was no movement inside. The crazy broad did not have a phone, so he could not even call her to see if she would come let him in. He was about to turn back for the truck when he got a closer look at the door and realized it was open several inches.

He transferred the folder to his left hand, so his gun hand was free, and pushed the door open.

The bell above the door rang and Raife started, shoulders climbing up towards his ears. He let the door go and immediately stepped to the left of it, close to the shelves, so he would not be silhouetted by the glare from the grey light outside. His hand on the butt of his pistol, Raife slowly walked towards the back of the store.

There was no movement and no sound. The tingle that had invaded the back of his neck the previous night started up again. As he reached the narrow cash counter at the back of the store, its ancient cash register perched on it, he slid the folder onto the surface so he would have both hands free.

There was an open doorway, in the wall behind the cash register, and he stepped to one side of it. Pieces of broken glass, or perhaps shards of rock, littered the floor. From where he stood he could see a bolted door to the alley behind the building, and a blank wall on the right. To the left he saw the bottom of a wooden staircase that lead upwards. He pivoted around the door frame and started up the stairs. He felt a bead of sweat pop out on his bare scalp and start running down to mingle with the tingling on the back of his neck. He tightened his grip on his pistol and undid the snaps on the holster.

When he was halfway up the stairs, a shape, a darker mass against the shadows, appeared on the narrow landing at the top. There was a slender, pointed shape in its hand that glinted dully in the filtered light from the doorway below. Raife took a step backwards, nearly missing the stair, but regained his balance and yanked his pistol from the holster.

"Show me your fucking hands," he roared. The sound boomed in the small space. He pointed his pistol at the dark shape. "And drop the knife."

"Sergeant Raife?" the shape asked in a decidedly shaky, feminine voice.

Raife lowering his pistol slightly, but did not re-holster it. "Miss Donnelly? Are you all right?"

He saw the shape move back towards the doorway it had appeared out of and then a light above the stairs flicked on. The shape was, indeed, Autumn Donnelly, and she looked terrible.

Raife holstered his pistol and walked up the rest of the stairs to be greeted by puffy eyes and a drawn, pale face. The woman looked like she had aged ten years since he saw her last night, and he thought she might be in imminent danger of collapse.

"What happened to you?" he asked as he put out a hand to steady her. "You look like shit."

"Such a charmer," she said, and gave a thin, haggard smile. "You must be an absolute hit with the ladies."

She turned from him and walked into the doorway she had come out of. Raife followed cautiously, completely unsure what an insane hippie woman might keep in a room above her magic shop. He was pleasantly surprised to see a small, neat apartment, as he followed her past a sitting area and into a tiled kitchen. Although he was a little worried that Autumn still gripped a long knife.

He pointed to the blade. "You can probably put that away and tell me what happened. You're safe now."

She looked down at the knife as though she had forgotten it was there, nodded, and set it on the counter beside a small sink. "I'm sorry," she said. She ran her pale hands through hair that was even frizzier than Raife had seen it previously. "It was a bit of a rough night."

He tried to summon the nurturing part of his brain, the one that could see she was suffering. "I'm not gonna lie, but you look like you've been stuffed in a shit box and shoved down the stairs." His mother had always told him he did not have much in the way of couth, so he did not expect much of himself.

"Like I said, you're a charmer."

"Did you sleep at all last night?"

She shook her head.

"Tell me what happened."

She stepped away from the door and to a set of wide leather chairs surrounding a low table, just inside the entrance to the small apartment. She sat down, set her elbows on her knees and put her head in her hands. After a few moments, she rubbed the heels of her hands against her eyes and looked up at Raife.

"Remember when I told you about my conversation with that man yesterday? Kord McRae?"

Folding his arms, Raife moved to stand on the other side of the low table and nodded.

"Well, the thing he said was looking for him and his daughter, that I didn't want any part of? I got some of it last night. It came here looking for McRae."

"Looking for him?" Raife uncrossed his arms and ran a hand over his bald head, while surprise made his voice climb in both pitch and volume. "How the fuck did it know to come here?"

Autumn pushed one handful of hair back behind an ear. "It said it could smell him. It also said it could smell my fear."

The tingle that had been on Raife's neck since he came into the store now felt like a gripping hand and it made his head ache. "Why are you saying 'it'? Was it like that...uh...that thing from before?"

"The creature you faced with Quinn? No, it wasn't like that. It looked like a man, a handsome one, but it was certainly not human."

More questions popped into Raife's head, but if anyone could identify a boogeyman, he figured it would be the woman sitting in front of him. "What did he, or, I guess 'it', say?"

Autumn took in a large breath and held it for a moment. "It said to tell Kord McRae that he could not hide. And it said to tell the Guardian, Quinn, that their first meeting would be their last."

"So this thing, whatever it is, knows this McRae guy was here, and it knows about Quinn?"

"I don't know if it knows Quinn's face, but it certainly knew Resolution has a Guardian, and it did not sound worried."

Raife turned away for a moment, rubbing his mustache to consider his options. The stakes in this little game just got a little steeper. It certainly appeared there was another boogeyman in Resolution. If the thing knew who Autumn was, enough that it would come to her shop and terrorize the fuck out of her, then it was obviously under the impression that she was important. If that was the case, she would not be safe here on her own. She was likely the only one who had any idea what the fuck was going on.

"Okay," he said, turning back to her. "You need to pack enough stuff for a couple of days. You can't stay here. I'm gonna find somewhere else for you to go."

"What?" she asked, looking up at him. "Go? Go where? This is my home. Who's going to look after my shop?"

"The shop will be fine for a couple of days until we get this sorted out. For now, you can't be here by yourself. Not if that thing comes back."

The mention of the thing, whatever it was, seemed to reach through Autumn's resistance. "Okay," she said. She got up and walked to a closet at the back of the room, set in the wall that would be above the front door. She pulled out a small over-night bag, and set it on the narrow bed beside the closet. Quickly, she gathered a few items of clothing and things from the small bathroom set between the bed and the sitting area. While she packed, Raife paced back and forth in front of the entrance, tugging on his mustache, thinking furiously.

Where was he going to take this woman? He certainly could not bring her back to the office and tell people she had been threatened by a fairytale creature with red eyes. They would both be locked up and certified as insane. Inspector Green could certainly help them, but it would be best to keep him somewhat distanced so he could deny any knowledge later if he had to pull their asses out of any fire. He was still thinking when she came and stood in front of him.

"I'm ready to go," she said. The activity and preparation had leeched some of the panic out of her face and she looked far more composed. Although she had the appearance of a hippie version of Mary Poppins with her hair tied back and the old fashioned travel bag in her hand.

"Right." Turning, Raife led the way down the stairs and towards the front of the store.

"Sergeant," Autumn said behind him. "Is this yours?"

He stopped and turned back. He saw that Autumn held the manila folder he had left on the cash counter. He had been so engaged in trying to decide what to do with her, and the baggage under her eyes, that he had completely forgotten why he came here to begin with.

"Those are pictures," he said, walking back to stand beside her. "Quinn faxed them to me this morning and asked me to show them to you."

She started to open the folder but he reached out with a wide hand and pinched the open side closed with his thumb and forefinger.

"I need to give you a warning before you open it." He paused, rubbing the forefinger of his free hand under his nose. "The stuff in there is hard to look at. I've been on the job more than twenty years and those pictures make my gut turn."

"Is it to do with your inspector's son?"

He nodded. "When the boy was found, he'd carved himself up in all kinds of weird symbols. Quinn asked me to get you to look at them and tell us if you know what they mean."

"I'll make it through," Autumn said. She tugged the folder gently from Raife's grip and opened the cover.

The only indication he got that she was troubled was the clenching of her jaw, the muscles on the side of her face standing out slightly. She reached over to the lamp beside the cash register and flicked it on, then held the pictures under the light as she looked at each one in turn.

"This is...odd," she said after examining the pictures for several minutes, holding each one close to her face as she studied it.

"You're telling me."

She looked up at him and shook her head. "No, I mean this is odd beyond the fact that a boy marked his body like this. As far as I can tell, these symbols don't really mean anything."

Raife frowned deep enough that his mustached tickled his chin. "What? What do you mean?"

She spun one of the pictures, one that thankfully did not show Patrick's face, and pointed to it with a slender finger. "This is a pentagram, about the most obvious and misunderstood symbol on the face of the planet." She moved her finger. "These are old Celtic Ogham. These here are Norse runes. This line looks like it's written in Japanese, but the characters are badly muddled, so I can't be sure."

"Okay," Raife said. "What does it mean?"

"It doesn't mean anything," she said. "It's the symbolic equivalent of gibberish. As part of a greater mass of symbols they might mean something, but here, like this, it's like looking at alphabet soup and trying to find the meaning of life."

"Great," Raife said as he gathered the pictures and slid them back into the folder. "This whole thing just gets weirder by the minute." He grabbed her bag off the floor by the cash desk and turned for the door again.

"Wait," Autumn said, following him. "What about Kord McRae. If he comes back and I'm not here, we won't be able to warn him."

"Don't worry about that," Raife said. "I'm already working on finding him. It's you we need to worry about right now."

He pulled his cell phone from the holder on his belt and flipped through the contacts until he found the number he was looking for. He dialed it, waited, and was shortly answered.

"Hi, Carrie? It's Raife."

Autumn Donnelly looked up at him, concern creasing her brow and making the lines around her eyes even deeper.

"Are you busy?" Raife said into the phone as he opened

the door to the back seat and tossed Autumn's bag in, along with the folder, and then opened the passenger side door for her. Autumn looked distinctly uncomfortable as she climbed into the seat.

"Well," Raife said, casting a glance at Autumn. "I hate to impose on you, but I need a favour."

The condo building Patrick Green had lived in was in a relatively nice part of town, on the right side of the tracks, and was completely innocuous. The building was square with the ubiquitous beige siding used on many modern condominiums. The units appeared small, closely packed, with narrow, black-railed balconies jutting off the front like a series of small sores. Quinn got out of the passenger side of the same Nissan Altima Clara had been driving the day before and looked at the building over top of the door.

Clara got out of the driver's side and stared over the roof of the car at Quinn. "Something wrong?" she asked.

"I guess I'd expected something different," Quinn said, studying the building.

"Different how?"

He shook his head. "I don't know. Maybe I'm being stupid, but when you think of a place that means nothing to you but bad, I guess you picture it different. This building is a lot more...normal than I expected it to be. Not the kind of place I imagined a kid would hang himself."

He glanced across at Clara, her face blank. He closed the door without another word and walked towards the front door of the building.

"Do you have a contact to get in?" Quinn asked as he eyed the call panel beside the front door.

"Don't need it," Clara said. She pulled a folded brown envelope from the pocket of her short coat. "We've got keys." She dumped the contents into her palm; one small brass key and a wider silver key. The silver key she stuck in the lock on the front door, turned it and pulled the door open.

Quinn followed Clara through the small lobby - complete with old newspapers and a couple of ugly chairs - to the twin elevators on the other side. He pressed the silver call button set in the wall between the two doors and the one on the left opened immediately. They entered the elevator and Quinn saw buttons for four floors. Clara pushed the button for the third.

"You ever been in here before?" Quinn asked.

"Nope."

He looked over at her. "I thought you and Patrick were friends. You've never been to his home?"

She shrugged. "He was a solitary person. He didn't invite people to his house often, or ever, that I heard of. I didn't even know where he lived until this file came in. I've only ever seen pictures of it."

"You know anything about the building? Many calls here?"

"Not really," Clara said. "In fact, I don't think I've ever been here before."

The elevator slowed, came to a smooth stop and the doors opened. Clara stepped out, Quinn on her heels, and pulled the brown envelope that had contained the keys from her coat pocket. She looked down at it. "Three-twenty-one," she said out loud. She glanced up and down the hallway, before turning to the right.

A dozen steps from the elevator they came to a clean white door. There was no police tape or any other sign to indicate that a boy had died inside. As he looked at the door, Quinn pulled in a heavy breath and rubbed a hand across his stubbly chin. How could something that affected him, and many other people so deeply be forgotten so quickly?

Clara put the key in the lock and paused to glance at Quinn. "You all right?" she asked.

"I'm fine." He tilted his chin towards the door. "Let's have a look."

The lock opened smoothly as Clara turned the key, opening the door to step inside. Quinn's heart spiked a little, a warm bloom moving out from the centre of his chest, when he stepped over the threshold. He was not sure why he was so affected by this part of his inquiry. He had been in houses were people had died before, dozens of times, perhaps hundreds, and once more should not bother him. Yet, for some reason, he felt hesitant, almost frightened.

The front door opened into a small entry-way, with a closet on the left side and a galley style kitchen on the right. Straight ahead of Quinn was a bedroom with an unmade bed and a few articles of clothing scattered around the floor. It looked as though the occupant had gotten up that morning, gone to work and would be back at the end of the day.

Quinn stepped into the narrow entry of the unit, while Clara closed the door.

There was an odd smell in the small space, though, like ripe garbage, with enough rotten stuff in it to be stinky.

"Here we are," she said, putting the keys back in her pocket. She folded her arms and looked at him. When he did not move, she shrugged. "Where do you want to start?"

He felt vaguely silly, waiting for her to do something when it had been his idea to come to this place. He brushed across his upper lip with the side of his finger, took the three steps down the hallway to get a look at the rest of the place Patrick had lived, and died.

On the left, just beyond the closet was a small, mostly clean bathroom. The clutter was minimal, but the smell present in the front hallway became stronger. Quinn turned right and walked into the kitchen and was greeted with a small armada of fruit flies, jittering through the air above the sink. He opened the cupboard door below the sink and saw a half-full garbage can. The smell that had been in the entry way must have been sourced from the reeking pail in front of him. A full -on army of flies swarmed out from under the sink and into the air around Quinn's head. He stepped back and waved them away.

"No one thought to take out the garbage?"

"Do you take out the garbage at every suicide you go to?" Clara asked, her manner derisive.

Grudgingly, Quinn had to admit she had a point. The fact that the garbage had not been removed pissed him off because he imagined Inspector Green and his wife coming here to collect Patrick's effects and having to smell the trash and fight off the horde of fruit flies. He was angry, but knew that picking a fight with Clara over the issue would be stupid, so he let it drop.

He closed the cupboard door and walked out the other end of the kitchen, which opened into a small, carpeted dining area. There was a small, round wooden table, holding two place mats and several pieces of unopened mail. Looking up from the table, Quinn turned to his left and into the living room. There, he stopped and the hot bloom in his chest returned.

In the middle of the living room ceiling was a fan, half ripped away from its moorings. Below the fan, broad dark spots stained the pale carpet.

"This is the place, is it?" Quinn asked, mostly himself, but he saw Clara nod out of the corner of his eye.

"Yeah, this is it."

He stepped away from her, trying hard to keep her behind him and out of his vision. The spot where Patrick had ended his life, where he had made his last movements, experienced his final, frantic, terrified thoughts, horrified Quinn. It made him want to run from the suite, but he needed to feel the place, to try and get a sliver of what Patrick went through in those last moments. Quinn needed to understand what drove Patrick to mutilate his own body before hanging himself.

He circled the spot in the centre of the small living room, staring down at the floor, careful not to disturb anything. The initial investigation and processing of the scene had already been concluded, all the evidence collected, but the place felt like a humid tomb and Quinn was reluctant to jostle the dead.

He looked up at the wall furthest from the front door and saw a bookcase, the same one that was behind Patrick in the pictures. He turned his back to it and faced the way Patrick had faced when he died. He closed his eyes and raised his arms slightly, reaching out into the room to try and collect what presence of Patrick was still there. He tried to imagine what Patrick had thought, what he had gone through, what the boy's misery had felt like during his final, awful moments. He opened his eyes, to try and see the last thing that Patrick had seen. The feeling was shattered, irretrievable when Quinn looked up and saw Clara standing there arms crossed and one hip cocked out. She had one sculpted eyebrow raise and looked at him as though he was off his gourd.

Quinn quickly turned away and examined the rest of the room; a new television, a single, black leather couch, a scattering of black and red candles, and finally the bookcase. Not much there to see.

He stopped as he passed the book case and reached out for one book he saw there, plucking it from the centre of the shelf. He laid the small volume in the palm of his hand and looked down at it.

"Did you find something?" Clara asked. Her look of caustic judgment was replaced by intense interest.

"What?" He looked up. "No, not really. Just a book I gave Patrick when he left for Depot. A book I read while I was there myself."

"What is it?" she asked, stepping closer.

"*The Hagakure*," he said and held up the small black book, red writing on the cover. "It's more or less a rule book for samurai, for warriors. Patrick was learning to become a warrior and I thought he could use it."

"A warrior, huh?" Clara asked and lost interest. "Is that what we are? Last time I checked I was a cop."

Quinn shrugged and slid the book back into its space on the shelf. "Same thing."

He moved from the living room, through the kitchen, and followed the short hallway into the small bedroom. He looked through the dresser drawers, under the bed and in the closet, but did not find anything but rumpled sheets and dirty laundry.

"Are you about done?" Clara asked, standing by the doorway, arms crossed while she leaned against the wall. "The guys who attended here initially went through all this stuff already."

"Yeah," Quinn said. "I'm done."

Uncrossing her arms, she pulled the front door open and stepped out into the hallway.

He turned to follow her, when a piece of paper sticking out from beneath a dirty, white undershirt on the dresser, caught his attention. A small section of the page was visible and showed part of a logo, and the word 'gathering'. He picked up the piece of paper and unfolded it. The top of the sheet said: *Gathering of the Enlightened. Throwing off the shackles of the corporate overlords in the company of the like-minded.* There was a picture of several youths, dressed in the dark colours and the dreary expressions of the goth culture. Below the picture was a small logo and the words: Presented by 'Bleak Hope' magazine.

The magazine the hotel girl was reading? Quinn thought. What the fuck would an advertisement for some goth party be doing in Patrick's bedroom. He looked over the flyer again and in the bottom left hand corner, in very small writing that Quinn thought was Patrick's, was "Old Hospital, 2100hrs." There was no date.

"What now?" Clara asked, leaning back into the condo from the outer hallway, exasperation thick in her voice.

"Huh?" Quinn asked. He dropped the paper onto the dresser. "Nothing. I'm coming."

She rolled her eyes and disappeared back into the hallway.

Quinn hastily picked up the flyer, folded it in four and stuffed it into the front pocket of his blue jeans.

CHAPTER 11

R aife pulled the big supervisor's Suburban away from the curb in front of Autumn's shop and turned in the direction of the mid-level residential area where Carrie lived.

"I'm just going to take you to stay with a friend for a couple of days," Raife told Autumn, keeping his eyes on the road.

"A friend?" Autumn asked.

He could feel her eyes on the side of his face. "Yeah. A friend. Carrie."

"Is this Quinn's Carrie?"

He looked over at her. "Is that a problem?"

She turned to stare out the windshield, folding her arms. It was likely his imagination, but Raife swore he saw the digital temperature reading on the inside of the truck drop a couple of degrees. He could feel the chill radiating off her like mist out of an open refrigerator. He turned his head towards her, wondering where all the unseen ice chips were coming from.

"No," she said, this time not looking at him. "Not a problem at all."

Rubbing at his mustache, Raife turned his gaze back to the road and thought that Quinn's life was about to get significantly more interesting. It would be high comedy if it was not so tragic.

They drove in silence for several blocks, each in their separate head spaces, when their respective trains of thought were interrupted by the crackle of the car's police radio. "Charlie Five-One, from Charlie Two."

Raife reached down for the radio mic. "That's Dave calling me," he said, glancing over at Autumn who nodded. He keyed the mic. "Go ahead for Five-One."

"Raife," Dave's voice said through the radio speaker between the seats of the truck. "We got something you need to come and see."

"Copy. What is it?"

"We got a call of a suspicious pile of bones behind the Welcome Beaver hotel." There was a pause. "And we just found a skull." Another pause. "A human one."

"Fuck me," Raife muttered, glancing over at Autumn, whose pale face had turned a previously unknown shade of white. "Okay, I'll be right there."

The Welcome Beaver was a few blocks away in the shadier district of town. Raife was reluctant to drive out to Carrie's and then turn around to come back.

"Will you be all right if I go and have a look at this?" he asked. Autumn was already haggard and strained. He feared she would break if he looked at her too hard.

She surprised him, apparently reading his thoughts, when she gave him an even-toothed smile. "I'll be fine, Sergeant. I'm not made of glass."

He nodded, hit his right turn signal, and headed further away from the water and towards the Welcome Beaver.

When he pulled up to the mouth of the alley that led behind the hotel, he saw Dave yelling at a skinny, pot-bellied man, while Sandy cordoned off the area with police tape. Gerritt stood behind Dave, his thumbs behind his belt, looking extremely uncomfortable.

"Wait here," Raife told Autumn as he put the truck in park. "I'll hopefully just need a few minutes to lock this down and then I can get you where you need to be."

"I'm fine, Sergeant. Really." She gave him a spare smile. It seemed to add some colour to her pale face.

Nodding, he blew out a big breath through his nose, opened the door and climbed out of the truck.

As he walked the fifty feet down the alley towards Dave, he could see the argument was escalating rapidly.

"I don't need a fucking warrant, Cecil," Dave shouted at the skinny man, who stood with his thin, bony arms folded above the odd looking protrusion of his stomach. "I'll search this alley if I want."

"The alley gives access to my building, McLeod," Cecil, who had a ridiculous looking tattoo of a spider on his forehead, shouted back. "And for the last fucking time, my name is 'Spider.'"

"That's ridiculous," Gerritt said from behind Dave, a look of annoyance on his pimply face.

"See?" Dave asked. "Even the new guy knows. You can't stop us from locking down this alley, Cecil. And if you don't get out of my fucking face, I'm going to arrest you for obstructing a peace officer."

"You lay one finger on me, McLeod, and I'll sue."

Raife stopped beside the squawking little man, who had not looked in his direction yet, and then looked at Dave, who shrugged. Blowing out another big breath through his nose, Raife jabbed Cecil in side of his bald head, extremely hard, with one meaty finger. Cecil gave a shrill little yelp, slapped a bony hand over the spot where Raife had poked and spun towards him.

"What the fuck?" Cecil cried, his voice climbing to a new octave on every word. "That's assault you gigantic asshole. I want your name and your badge number."

Raife had been told, several times, that he was quick for a man so big, and he used that speed when he reached out one broad hand and latched onto the top of Cecil's head. Raife dragged Cecil up to his own chest, so Cecil's face was pressed against the embroidered name tag on his vest.

"I am Sergeant Charles Raife, you horrid little man," he said, still pressing Cecil's face against the name tag. Cecil squealed and flailed and tried his best to get away, but he looked like a snake that had a truck parked on its head. "You can get the spelling of my name from your face later." He let Cecil go. There was a definite imprint of the name tag in Cecil's cheek.

The little man fingered the indents in his cheek while he stared at Raife with open-mouthed shock.

"Now," Raife said, hitching up his gun belt. "Are you the proprietor of this..." he looked up at the building, "...establishment."

"You're fucking right I am," Cecil shouted, his fists clenched and his pale arms rigid and shaking. He glared at Dave, extending one finger from his quaking fist and pointing it at him. "And you're fucking trespassing."

"And, are you the one who reported the human remains in your alley, Cecil?"

"No," Cecil said. He folded his arms in a petulant manner. "Some guy who lives in one of the rooms upstairs called you assholes." He glared at Dave again. "And my name is Spider!"

"It really is not," Raife said to Cecil, and then turned to Dave. "So, we've established that there are human remains outside this...establishment?"

"Looks human to me, Boss," Dave answered. Gerritt nodded from beside him, his eyes wide.

Raife turned back to Cecil. "And you've disclosed that one of your...guests reported the discovery to police."

"Yeah," Cecil said, drawing out the word as his eyes narrowed.

"Then there is one clear course of action for us," Raife said, allowing a big, toothy smile to lift his mustache.

"Yeah," Cecil whined. "You assholes get off my property."

"No, Cecil," Raife said. He stepped close to the little man, who backed away, his eyes growing wide and his jaw working. "What we do is arrest you for obstruction, first of all. Then we get a warrant to search this miserable shithole, in case there is evidence of a murder inside." He looked up at the red brick walls above him. "It's a big place, but I'm willing to call in a

Major Crime team to help us. We'll clear out every one of your rooms, shut you down for a week, and tear this place apart, brick by brick." He looked down into Cecil's eyes, which grew wider. "So, you wanna keep yapping about warrants and getting in my way? I'll get a warrant, and then search this alley without it anyway. Or, you can go get the guy who found these bones, get out of my face and we'll sort this out as quick as we can." He lowered his voice a little more. "So tell me, Cecil, what you wanna do?"

"The guy lives in suite 202," Cecil said in a voice barely above a mumble. "I'll go get him for you."

"That's what I thought you were gonna say."

Raife turned back to Dave, Sandy and Gerritt as Cecil turned and scuttled through an open door to the building.

"That was awesome," Gerritt said in a breathy voice.

"Isn't that the little bastard you and Quinn had a run in when..." Raife tailed off and glanced over at Gerritt, who had not been pulled into their circle of confidence, and whose mind likely could not handle the notion that the people he worked with had killed a demon.

"Two years ago?" Dave finished for Raife. "Yeah. Same guy. He wanted to complain, but the inspector told him to go away. He's had a hard-on for me and Quinn ever since. Gets in our way any chance he gets."

"Well," Raife said, rubbing his mustache and thinking angry thoughts. "Fuck him if he can't take a joke." He looked behind Sandy to the end of the alley protected by the crime scene tape. "What have you guys got?"

"Same as up at Dean Springer's place," Sandy said, slipping under the tape and holding it for Raife and Dave, who ducked under as well.

"Gerritt," she said to the youth as he moved to follow. "You're guarding the scene. No one comes down this alley without Sergeant Raife's say so. Got it?"

"But I wanna be here when Sarge goes over the scene," complained Gerritt.

Sandy pointed towards the mouth of the alley. "Junior

134

man, prove," she said. "Go."

He let out a heavy breath and plodded towards the intersection of the alley and the street with his gaze on his boots.

The three other Mounties watched him go and when he was out of ear shot Sandy let out a weary sigh. "He's a good kid," she said, "but he's slower than molasses on a cold morning, and he couldn't remember his own name if I wrote it backwards on his forehead and issued him a mirror. I have no idea how he get through Depot on the first place."

"Dave got through, so we know the system is flawed," Raife said.

"Ouch," Dave said. He slapped a hand over his heart and put on a pained expression.

Raife looked from Dave to Sandy. "The kid'll be fine once he has some more service. Or when he gets his ass kicked by some scrout-bag because he's not paying attention. Don't worry about it. Now, once again, what have we got?"

"Like Sandy said," Dave said as he moved to point at a heap of bones behind a reeking green dumpster. "It looks just like Dean Springer's place. We got a 9-1-1 call from the payphone in the hotel lobby." He jerked his chin towards the Welcome Beaver. "The caller said he'd found a heap of bones in the alley."

"We thought it might be someone jumping to conclusions," Sandy said. "But the details about the stripped human bones didn't make it to the news last night, so we figured it wouldn't just be someone over reacting. Then we drove down here and saw this."

She pointed to the pile, sitting between the wall and a rusted, green dumpster and Raife moved forward for a closer look. It was certainly a pile of bones, stripped in the same manner as Dean Springer's remains had been. The top portion of a human skull sat beside the pile, giving the Mounties a mocking half-grin. Raife did not get close enough to be absolutely sure, but it looked like there were teeth marks on the bones. He was willing to bet his mustache the marks on these bones would match those found on Dean Springer's.

"Son of a bitch," Raife said. "How the fuck are we ever going to ID this guy?"

"Boss," Dave said. "There's a set of human bones, with a set of human teeth marks in them, behind a hotel called The Welcome Beaver, and you're worried about how to ID the victim? Are you drunk?"

Raife shook his head, and ran a hand over his bald pate. "We need to ID him so we can figure out where he came from, Dave. We have some nut running around our town, eating our residents. We need to know where he is and what he's doing before we can even think to lay a hold of him."

"Or 'it'," Dave said.

"Precisely," Raife agreed.

"What about this Autumn woman," Sandy asked. "Was she any help with those freaky symbols Quinn sent you?"

"Well, yes and no," Raife said.

"I fucking hate that expression," Dave said, tilting his head back. "Which is it? Yes, or no?"

As he often did, Raife thought Dave McLeod could use a good beating, just to get his attention.

"She looked the pictures over," Raife said, working desperately to keep his hand by his side, instead of laying it across Dave's face. "Said they didn't mean anything. The symbols are a mish-mash of shit from different places. Norse, Celtic, Japanese, fucking everything. She said that put together the way they were they're just gibberish."

"So where does that leave Quinn?" Sandy asked.

"I haven't the foggiest fucking notion," Raife said. "I know it still leaves us without the guy who is supposed to be able to kill the fucking things that do shit like this." He pointed to the pile of bones. "I have to talk to him and tell him what's going on, after I get Autumn to Carrie's place."

"You're taking her to Carrie's place?" Dave asked. "What for?"

Caught up in the activity of sorting out that little shit, Cecil, and having a look at the gnawed bones, Raife realised he had forgotten to apprise his two constables of what had happened to Autumn Donnelly the night before.

"So, the thing that was looking for that Kord guy came to her place?" Sandy asked, once Raife had relayed the story of the attack on Autumn.

"And we think it's the same thing that did this?" Dave asked, tilting his head towards the pile of remains.

"I'm willing to make that leap," Raife said.

"He was here, Sergeant. I can smell him."

Raife turned on his heel to see Autumn Donnelly standing at the edge of the crime scene tape, her arms wrapped around herself as though she was cold.

Sandy looked past both Raife and Autumn to where Gerritt stared at the sky. "Gerritt!" she yelled. The youth turned and looked at her. "I thought I told you to keep everyone out of this alley."

Gerritt gave an exaggerated shrug, indicating, in a normal person, that he did not particularly give a fuck, but with Gerritt it was unclear what the gesture meant. He turned and continued looking at the sky.

"Is he...you know...slow?" Autumn asked.

"He's something," Raife said, walking to where Autumn stood. "What did you say about smelling?"

She turned back to him, her arms still wrapped tightly around herself, gooseflesh standing out on the pale skin of her neck and arms. "The thing that was in my shop last night had a very unique smell. I smell it now. It was here."

Dave and Sandy had walked up behind them and heard the brief conversation. Dave turned and faced back down the alley, giving a loud sniff. Raife did the same and was about to wave Autumn off, smelling nothing other than the garbage in the dumpsters, when he caught something. Just at the edge of his senses, where he would not even know it if he was not looking for it, he caught something beneath the reek of the alley. It smelled like horses, or sweaty animals, a faint scent, just a spectre of recognition playing at his mind, but it was there.

"Yeah," Dave said. "There is something. It smells

like...animal."

"I've got it too," Sandy said. "Just underneath the garbage smell."

Raife turned back to Autumn and lifted the crime scene tape so she could duck underneath to join the Mounties in a huddle.

"Okay," the big man said. "So, we've got a guy and his kid come into Resolution looking for Quinn 'cause they think he can protect them from something. That something, a smelly bastard by all accounts, comes to Autumn's place looking for these refugees. That same thing then eats someone and leaves their bones in an alley."

"Don't forget Dean Springer," Sandy said.

"Right," Raife said. "This thing eats both Dean and another unfortunate individual, while he's looking for this Kord McRae guy. So, now what?"

"What's with the eating people," Dave asked. "If he's that hungry, I'll buy him a cheeseburger."

"It's not just eating," Autumn said. "It's *feeding*. Just like that thing you faced two years ago. Only instead of eating what's inside you, this one eats everything else."

"So, it's getting bigger," Sandy said. She crossed her arms as she shivered. She knew what a demon's feeding was like first hand.

Autumn shook her head. "Not necessarily bigger, but certainly stronger. The last demon you faced, I believe, was trying to gain enough strength to get out of that basement. This one is already well past that point where it can move around and appear human. Any feeding it does is only going to add to its power."

"Great," Dave said. He rubbed a hand over his stubbled hair. "This fucking thing is stronger than the last one and getting badder by the minute."

"What do we do?" Sandy asked, casting her worried eyes to each of the faces around her.

They all stood in silence for a moment, Autumn staring at the bones - a haunted, haggard look on her face – while the

Mounties all looked at their bootlaces and rubbed at various parts of their faces.

"Here's what we do," Raife said after he'd had his moment. "We cannot tell anyone about what is really doing this. They'll think we're nuts and discount us; maybe even take us all off the road. We have to stay in the game where we can do some good. Right now, our working theory is a serial killer. We put that out where the media can get a sniff of it and they'll jump on the idea like a pack of dogs on a gut wagon."

Dave nodded. "Once they see another set of bones they'll get there by themselves, anyway."

Raife pointed a thick finger at him. "Good point." He looked around to ensure no one else was within ear shot. "Our next job is to let Quinn know what's going on and get him back here. If he's this Guardian—"

"He is," Autumn interrupted.

Glancing at her, Raife smoothed his mustache. "Right. He's the one these people are looking for, so he needs to be back here to do the job. Next, we need to find these people the thing is looking for, Kord McRae and his kid, and get them where we can keep an eye on them." He looked over at the piles of bones. "If anything that does this kind of shit wants something, I'm disinclined to let him have it."

"Okay, so who does what?" Dave asked.

"You two carry on as normal," Raife said, pointing at Dave and Sandy. "You do whatever it is Major Crime wants you to do and we'll connect again later. I'll look after informing Quinn and finding these two people. I'm not even supposed to be your boss anymore, Quinn is, and I can go do as I please easier than you can."

"What about the inspector?" Sandy asked. "Do we let him know what's going on? Or do we leave him out of it."

That was something that Raife had not considered during the rapid planning in his head. He thought for a minute, chewing on the inside of his cheek. "No, we leave him be. He's got enough on his plate and I'm sure he'll pick up on it sooner or later, anyway. We only bring him in if we get something we can't handle ourselves, or it gets so fucked there are going to be uncomfortable questions coming his way."

Dave looked worried. "We're going to have to tell him when we ask Quinn to come back early."

Raife shrugged. "We're going to have to hope that Quinn can sort out what he needs to and find a flight back."

"What do you want me to do?" Autumn asked. "I want to help."

"No, I need you to hide," Raife said. "None of us can have you with us all the time, it would raise too many questions, and it is far too dangerous for you to be left alone. I need to get you to Carrie's place, where, hopefully, this thing won't come looking for you. If there is something you can do, I'll know where to find you."

Reluctance was obvious on her pale face, but she nodded.

"Is everyone clear?" Raife asked, and all assembled nodded. "Good, now get busy and stay alive."

"What do you mean the symbols don't mean anything?" Quinn asked Raife through his cell phone as Clara drove the Nissan towards the centre of town. Raife had called shortly after Quinn had left Patrick's apartment, the odd flyer he had found crinkling in his pocket. Raife had said he was on speaker, with Autumn, in his truck, and Quinn could hear traffic noises and the growl of the police truck's engine through his phone.

"Just like I said, boy," Raife's voice rumbled through Quinn's earpiece.

"Quinn, it's Autumn," came her voice from the phone. She sounded tinny and far away. "I didn't research the symbols enough to know what the individual meaning of each one is, but I'm relatively sure they don't make up any words. It looks like Patrick just picked a bunch of symbols at random and carved them into his body."

"Are you alone, Quinn?" Raife asked.

"I just left Patrick's apartment with the member they've

assigned to help me out."

"Hmmm..." Raife said. Quinn could hear the bristly sound of Raife rubbing his mustache - which is what he always did when he needed a moment to think about something. Quinn had an idea where his thought pattern was going; the big man wanted to talk about things that were better left between only them.

"Okay," Raife said. "You need to come back here. We're running short on the team, and you need to come fill your spot. The one only you can fill."

Running short? Quinn thought to himself, puzzled. They had as much manpower as they always did. There was no shortage. Then he caught on to Raife's drift and realised he was not talking about manpower issues.

"I'm working as quick as I can here, Boss."

"You need to work faster," Raife said. "That thing you saw on the news last night? It happened again."

"You mean you found more bones?" He glanced over at Clara, who glanced between him and the road. The news that a set of human bones with teeth marks in them had been found in Resolution was now common knowledge to most people with a television or internet access. The discussion of it would not set off any alarm bells for Clara, or so Quinn hoped. She already thought he was an asshole. He did not need her to think him crazy as well.

"Yeah," Raife confirmed. "Another set out behind the Welcome Beaver."

Quinn almost laughed at the mention of that particular hotel and the memory of his previous confrontation with Cecil.

"We figure that whatever did it is going to do it again," Raife said.

"And get better at it," Autumn chimed in.

"You need to come back here, son," Raife said. "You need to be here so we can deal with this."

Quinn rubbed a hand across his forehead and listened to the silence on the other end of the line while he drew several conclusions. They thought whatever was eating people was going to get better at it, meaning it was going to get stronger the more people it consumed. They also believed that he was the only person who could face down whatever had come to their town.

Just as Autumn had done two years ago when she was trying to convince him that a demon was lurking somewhere in Resolution, they were heaping an authority and a responsibility onto him that he did not want. He did not want to be this Guardian that Autumn kept talking about. He did not want the pressure of having to look out for Resolution, all the time, against something that he scarcely understood.

Beyond his reluctance to accept the apparent responsibilities of being this so called 'Guardian', he did not want to leave the review into Patrick's death incomplete. Now that he had the pamphlet to some kind of weird gathering that the kid had apparently been interested in, he felt as though he had something to look in to, something that might be important.

"I'm not finished here, yet," he said into the phone. "There are still a couple of little things I need to do before I can say the job's done."

A sigh so heavy it felt like a shove came through the ear piece on his phone. "Can you finish it today and then catch a flight out tomorrow?"

"The Force plane isn't due to pick me up for another forty-eight hours," Quinn said, trying to remember the flight schedule the pilot had given him.

"That's too long, Quinn," Autumn said. "There is something awful on the verge of happening in this town. I don't know exactly what it is, but it is going to be bad."

Quinn let out a sigh of his own. Autumn had been constantly convinced that something was about to happen in Resolution for the last two years. The only difference he ever saw in her behaviour was the level of catastrophe she expected.

"I can try to get a commercial flight out to Prince George tomorrow, "Quinn said. "I think I'll be able to finish what I need to get done tonight."

In the driver's seat, Clara let out an audible sigh of relief. Quinn did his best not to glare at her.

"Okay, son," Raife said. "That'll have to do."

"Be safe, Quinn," Autumn said.

"Yeah, thanks," Quinn said. "I'll talk to you guys later on tonight."

He hit the 'end call' button on the screen of his phone and settled in his seat.

"Your boss screaming at you to get back?" Clara asked.

"Yeah," Quinn said. "They found another set of bones with the meat stripped off them. They've already classified it as a serial killer and they need everyone back so we can deal with it."

"Okay, so where does that leave this thing you're doing?"

He noted, very conspicuously, that she did not refer to his review as an 'investigation', just a 'thing'. He shrugged and did his best to keep his ire down below his breast bone so it could not burble up his throat and come out his mouth as something rude. "I've gotta figure out what bases I still need to cover, and then get them all done tonight. They want me to fly back tomorrow."

"So, do you have a game plan, or are you still just winging it?"

Another dig, he thought, considering the word 'still', as though she were implying he was making everything up as he went along.

"Do you think it would be possible for you guys to loan me a detachment car?" he asked. "Then I could make my stops without tying you down anymore. I could drop it off in the morning and hitch a ride to the airport."

Clara stuck her tongue in her cheek for a moment, apparently thinking. "Let's head back to the office. You can see about booking your flight and I'll talk to the inspector about a car."

Quinn nodded as he touched the scrap of paper in his pocket and thought about what to do next. It was barely noon and he had nine hours to kill before he could go to the old hospital to see if there was anything to this poster, or if he would just be standing there in the dust by himself. He had a funny feeling it would be the latter.

When he had agreed to do what Inspector Green had asked of him and come out to this little town to conduct a file review he was not remotely qualified for, he had felt like he would be doing something good. He would be giving closure to Donald Green and his wife by making sure their boy was seen to properly.

But that was not what Quinn had experienced.

What he had found in Cranbrook was contempt, apathy and disregard. No one seemed to have meant Patrick any harm, but no one wanted his memory to linger around them any longer than it already had. Patrick was an old ghost that they had exorcised and Quinn was the nuisance who had shown up to invite the spectre back in.

Quinn had been looking for Patrick's ghost so hard he had found it. Now it rode on his shoulder, its shadow as heavy as Patrick's casket had been. For the life of him, Quinn could not seem to shake it off.

"So, tell me again why this is a good idea," Carrie said. She stood in the front door of her house and glared up at Raife. The upward angle did nothing to take any of the edge off the black haired woman's look. Raife, standing on the front step, felt like a small child who had wandered to the wrong house while trick-or-treating, wanted to twitch a little under her stare.

"It's just for a little while, Carrie," Raife said. "She was at-tacked at her shop, and we need some place safe for her to stay."

"I get that, Raife," Carrie said, looking over her shoulder to the kitchen where Autumn sat at the kitchen table and chatted with Shawn. "But don't you guys have somewhere to take her that isn't my house?"

"I'm sorry, but we don't." It was unclear to Raife how

much Quinn had revealed to Carrie about the incident in Joe Robowski's house two years ago. Raife had told his wife almost nothing about what had happened. "This is kind of a unique circumstance. We're not sure how to proceed and it is more than a little complicated."

Carrie crossed her muscular arms, the tattoos standing out on her taut skin. "Unique circumstance, huh? How unique?"

Raife smoothed his mustache, his mind working feverishly to try and find a plausible explanation. "Well," he said, still searching. "You see..."

"Does it have something to do with what happened two years ago?" She cut off his train of thought.

His already faltering process derailed completely. "Er..."

"Look, Raife," she said. "I know something fucked up happened back then. I know the inspector told everyone that you, Quinn and Dave all got hurt trying to pull some asshole out of a house fire at three in the morning, but I believe that almost as much as I believe that you're Santa Clause and Donald Green is the Tooth Fairy."

Raife patted his stomach. "That idea is not too far outside the realm of possibility." He was hoping for a laugh, but didn't even get a smile.

"I know the bullshit the inspector came up with was to protect you guys from whatever it was you did. I also know that Quinn called me, just before the three of you miraculously stumbled upon a raging house fire in the south end of town, where you had no reason to be.

I know what Quinn was doing that night had to do with whatever had attacked Sandy and put her in a coma. I know he went to that house for something, and he came back with burns and stitches and fucked up memories that still make him wake up in the middle of the night. I also know whatever was in that house nearly killed him, and probably sent Brandon Williams into my house to kill us all."

He thought about arguing with her, but he knew it would be more or less useless. Carrie had grown up around cops, lived with one and could pick out a lie and a half truth as easily as he could.

"All I need to know right now, Raife, is do I need to be worried? Do I need to be worried about Quinn, about Shawn and me, with this woman in my house?"

"Carrie," he said, "I'm not going to bullshit you. We ain't got no time for it. Quinn and Dave, and me, too, went down into the basement of that house two years ago and we found something black. Black as I've ever seen. And be damned if we didn't kill it and leave it in that house to burn. Now, something else has come to this town, and it brought a whole bunch more black with it."

"Is it as bad as it was before?" Carrie asked.

Raife shook his head. "No. It is not. It is far, far worse."

"So why is this woman in danger? I know she helped Quinn before—he's spoken of her, but not much—but why does she have to be kept safe?"

Raife shrugged. "This thing that's come, it thinks she knows things, and until we get this sorted out she needs to stay out of its way."

"And what are you going to be doing?"

"Trying to sort this out."

That, finally, brought a hint of a smile to her mouth. "Should I be on the lookout for anyone?" She paused. "Or anything?"

"I haven't told anyone but Dave and Sandy that I was bringing her here. So if anyone but us comes looking for her, you got problems."

"What do I do?" she asked. She was not scared, only cautious. Raife could not help but think she would make a good cop if she ever decided to take up the profession.

"Does Quinn keep guns in the house?"

She nodded slowly, running her tongue across her teeth. "Yeah, after he was nearly stabbed to death, he went and bought a shotgun, and got me a pistol that takes really big bullets." She tilted her head towards the hallway behind her. "They're in a safe in the closet."

"You know how to use them?"

She nodded again. "Quinn taught me how to shoot when he bought them, just in case there was a 'next time'."

"Okay, then. Anyone else comes here looking for Autumn, you take one of those guns and put as much lead into it as you can."

She started nodding, then paused. "You said, 'it'. Not him or her."

Raife nodded, up and down, once.

"Great," Carrie said. She turned to look back at the kitchen table, where Autumn sat beside Shawn, going over his homework with him. "Does Quinn know about all this? I haven't talked to him yet today."

"I talked to him before I came here. He's going to wrap up what he's got going on in Cranbrook and fly back tomorrow." He turned and walked down the concrete steps to the sidewalk. "If anything happens, I'll let you know."

"Am I going to regret this?" he heard her say from behind him.

"I think that is a definite possibility, kiddo."

"I had a feeling you'd say that," she said and closed the door.

Autumn watched Carrie's conversation with Raife with some trepidation and the distinct feeling she was not welcome. When Carrie closed the door and turned back into the small house, Autumn braced herself for a verbal assault and made ready to flee. It had been a mistake, she was sure, for Raife to bring her here.

Carrie walked to the edge of the kitchen, put one hand on her hip, and combed the fingers of her other hand through her long, black hair. She blew out a breath through puffed cheeks and made eye contact with Autumn.

"How you doing?" asked Carrie. She sat down across from Autumn and put her elbows on the table.

"I've been better," admitted Autumn. "I'm not excited about having to leave my home. I'm not a big fan of running."

A smile tugged at the corner of Carrie's mouth. "I hear that, but sometimes it's the best option you have."

"I'm sorry I'm here, Carrie," said Autumn, aware that Shawn looked back and forth between the two women. "This was not my idea. I don't want to be an imposition in your home."

"No, it's fine," Carrie said and turned to at Shawn. "I think you've worked hard enough on your homework for now, shorty. Why don't you go see if there's anything good on TV?"

The boy stood up slowly, his gaze moving between Autumn and his mother, then shrugged and gathered his books to walk the short distance into the living room.

Once he was out of ear-shot, Carrie turned back to Autum. "Raife said it was important for you to be somewhere besides your shop, and you're welcome here." She clasped her hands on the table in front of her and leaned forward. "I have to ask, though, what are you to Quinn?"

If it had not been for the idea that Carrie might use her muscular arms to break her into little pieces, Autumn might have smiled. She knew the question was coming. It was a matter of when.

"I'm not trying to be a bitch," Carrie said. "Quinn might not be my husband, yet, but he is mine, and he's talked about you before. I always let it go because it was somehow related to work. That and whatever happened to him and his team two years ago. But now you're in my home and it's not limited to work anymore, so I want to know what your relationship is with him."

Autumn breathed deep, choosing her words carefully. "I sometimes see things that other people don't."

"Like a psychic?" Carrie asked. There was no challenge, as though she did not believe what Autumn said, but only a simple question.

"Not exactly," Autumn answered. "I get feelings sometimes, like I can read other people's emotions. I can see their energies if I look at them right. When I met Quinn, something awful was happening in this town and I believed he might be

148

the only one who could stop it. So, I helped him as best I could and tried to point him in the direction I thought he needed to take."

"And what direction was that?" The tone of Carrie's voice dropped and she lowered her chin.

Autumn's mouth dried up and she had a strong urge to look away from Carrie's face. "I thought he needed to look at the problem from a different angle; to see it as he didn't see it before." She paused, thinking. "He is hard headed, your man, and he needed to open his mind. I tried to help him do that."

Carrie leaned back in her chair and folded her arms. "Is that all?"

Autumn nodded. "Yes, Carrie, that is all. Trust me when I say to you that I am a friend to Quinn and nothing more." She thought it would be a bad idea to mention that she'd kissed Quinn once and thought about doing it again every time she saw him. She did not think that would make Carrie, or her, any more comfortable.

Carrie nodded, apparently accepting Autumn's answer. "What you said before about him being the only one who could stop what was happening two years ago; why did you think that?"

"It's hard to explain, but when I first met Quinn, saw him for the first time, I knew he was not like other men. He is special in a way he himself does not understand."

"That is certainly true," Carrie agreed. "I don't understand it either, but I know it's true. Did he tell you he was so drunk the first time he asked me out that he puked in my pub?"

Autumn shook her head and stifled a laugh. "No, I didn't know that."

"Yeah, he barfed up about fifty dollars' worth of beer behind the pinball machine and then asked me if I'd have dinner with him the next night. Any other guy I'd have told to pound sand, but Quinn...I just couldn't resist him. I still can't."

Autumn nodded and remained silent.

"Anyway," Carrie said and stood up. "I just wanted to talk to you a little, and make sure you know you're welcome here.

If Quinn calls you a friend, then so will I.

"You want some tea?"

"Love some," Autumn said. She breathed a small sigh of relief as Carrie got up and walked towards the sink. It appeared the confrontation she had feared had been avoided and that some of the ice in the look Carrie had given her when she appeared on the doorstep with Raife had melted. She looked down when Shawn returned from the living and touched the back of her hand. He pointed to the open page of the book he was reading.

"What does this word mean?"

She looked down. "'Maleficent'?" she read from the page. "It means evil."

CHAPTER 12

After working in Resolution Cove for almost eight years, Raife knew every camp site, rest area and wide spot on every back country road for fifty kilometers in every direction. After driving those bumpy roads in a fruitless search for the entirety of a cloudy afternoon, he and his sore ass were ready to give up.

He had set Dave and Sandy the task of taking care of the new crime scene and keeping Major Crime busy, while he went to look for this Kord McRae guy and his kid. So far he had checked almost every place he could think of, but did not find anyone matching the description Autumn had given him. He had started with the hotels, then the motels and the hostels, then the campsites in town and eventually the Forestry camp sites surrounding the inlet. It grew late, his empty stomach grumbled, and he became more and more pissed off with every pot-hole and empty camp site he drove into.

He was ready to pack it in as he drove into a clearing beside a small lake. It was not a Forestry camp site, so it was not maintained and there would be no outhouses, but the local kids were fond of coming up here and getting drunk, so there were a bunch of fire pits and a make-shift boat launch.

As Raife guided the Suburban down the narrow road and into the clearing beside the lake, he saw a beat-up old Ford camper-van, with a folding table set up beside it. In front of the van, close to the water, stood a slim man in worn blue jeans and a dark green work shirt. Beside him was a skinny blonde girl with her long hair in a single braid down her back. The girl held a drawn sling shot, aiming at some tin cans set up on a stump about ten feet away. The man turned to face the truck as it pulled into the clearing.

As Raife stopped the truck, the girl let her stone fly. One of the tin cans pin-wheeled into the air and she thrust one small, triumphant fist above her head.

"That was a fine shot," Raife said as he climbed out of his truck and slammed the door. The man gave him an easy grin, but watched every movement he made. The girl lowered her fist and stared at Raife with wide eyed intensity.

"Good evening, Sergeant," said the man after a glance at Raife's epaulettes. "Is this campground off limits? We didn't see any signs."

Raife stopped a few paces away from the pair and crossed his big arms. The man still wore a grin, but it was pasted on and it did not touch his eyes. His right hand rested on his hip, just a little too far back. Raife wondered what kind of a weapon the man had concealed in his waist band. The man likely knew, as well as Raife did, that there was no problem with him and the girl camping beside the lake, but he was making small talk, filling the uncomfortable silence that stretched out as the two men measured each other. He waited to see what Raife wanted before he volunteered anything.

"Your camp is fine," said Raife. "But I'm looking for a couple of people."

The man's hand shifted back a little further. Raife dropped his own hands to his belt, the heel of his right hand only a few inches from the butt of his gun.

"I'll help you if I can," the man said. "What do you want with them? If you don't mind me asking."

"They came to a friend of mine, looking for help. She wasn't able to point them in the right direction, but I might be able to."

"Is he the Guardian, Daddy?" the little girl asked.

The man whipped his head to look at her and gave a small shake of his left hand, indicating he did not want her to say anything else.

"I am not," Raife said. "But I know the man who is. He's a friend of mine as well. His name is Quinn."

The man's eyes narrowed. He appeared to be examining Raife again. "Were you one of the men who carried the casket of that poor boy a couple weeks ago?"

Raife nodded. "I am. The boy was a friend of mine. Why?"

The man dropped his hand from his hip and let it dangle against the front of his thigh as he let his weight rest on his right leg. He nodded. "I thought one of you was going to be the man we were looking for, but I wasn't sure." He stepped forward and extended his hand. "I'm sorry to be rude, but I have to be careful. My name is Kord McRae. This is my daughter, Abigail."

Raife gripped the man's hand. It was calloused and warm. "Charles Raife."

"How did you find us, Sergeant Raife?"

"Just Raife. Autumn Donnelly, the woman whose shop you went into yesterday, came to talk to me. She knows Quinn, too, and said you were looking for him. I've been checking hotels and camp sites all day hoping I'd find you."

"Here we are," Kord said. "What can I do for you?"

Raife wondered, for a moment, how much he should reveal to this man. He had an innate mistrust of everyone, developed after twenty years of police work. He certainly did not know, from a thirty second conversation, if he could trust Kord McRae as far as he could throw him. Despite his nature, his logical mind told him the man had meant no harm to Autumn and had only come looking for help. He sensed only caution, not aggression, as he spoke to Kord, and did not believe him to be a threat. Although he had been wrong before, which led to his inherent mistrust of everyone.

He made a hasty decision and smoothed his mustache. "Last night, after Autumn came and talked to me, something came and talked to her. It was looking for you. I've had to hide Autumn because she thinks this thing will come back. It knew to look for you in her shop. Said it could smell you there. Now I'm worried that it'll be coming for you."

"You are right to worry," Kord said. "We've been running from that thing for over a year, just one small step ahead. It's found us everywhere we go." He looked down at the child. "If you're not the Guardian, then you can't help us. You'd be better off getting away from us, right now, and staying away. If it comes, no one can help us."

Raife had a thing, a horrid thing, for people telling him he could not do something, especially when it involved kicking someone's ass. "I've seen this kind of thing before, Kord," he said. He hitched up his gun belt. "We found it, we killed it and we'll kill this thing, too."

"No," Kord said, shaking his head. "The Guardian killed it. You might have been there, but the Guardian, the man named Quinn, he was the one who killed it."

"I was there," Raife growled. "I know what happened. Quinn was the one who stabbed it, but we all fought it, so I know what we're up against."

Kord nodded. "So do I. I've fought this particular thing, and lost. So, believe you me when I say, you cannot stop it. Only the Guardian can do that and only if he's lucky."

Raife believed wholly in being practical, but this guy was starting to get depressing. "Whatever it takes to put this thing down, we will, but we need to get you somewhere safe until Quinn gets back here and we can sort this all out."

"You cannot protect us, Raife. We are safest where we cannot be found. Once you leave here, so will we. We'll find a new hiding place."

The set of Kord's stance, the way his body read, told Raife he would not be an easy man to move, either physically or mentally, and it would not be done with direct force. He needed to think of something to lead the man to his way of thinking.

"Daddy?" The little girl, Abigail, reached up and tugged at

her father's hand.

"Abby?"

"Couldn't we stop running for a while?"

The lean man shook his head. "No, Abby. It's better when we move. We can't put any one else in danger just to serve ourselves."

It struck Raife that the child looked tired. Horribly, bone weary exhausted. She appeared as though she had been carrying around far more weight than anyone so young had a right to.

"Why is it you're running, Kord?" Raife asked. "Why does this thing want you so bad?"

The man looked at Raife, then down at the little girl. "It's not me it's after," he said. "It's my daughter."

"Abby?" Raife asked, pulling his chin back in surprise, to avoid the punch of Kord's words. "Why?"

"That is a long, complicated story. Not one I'm sure I'm up to telling."

Abby shifted forward slightly, just out of reach of her father. "I can do things," she said.

"Abigail," Kord said, a warning note in his voice.

"The thing wants me because I can do things. It wants me to do things for it," the girl said.

"What kinds of things?" Raife asked, wondering what could be so special about a skinny little twig of a kid.

Abby looked back at her father, who gave a heavy sigh, his shoulders rolling forward. The man appeared to be nothing, if not defeated. "All right," he said. "Show him if you must."

"Are you going to hurt us, Mr. Raife?" Abby asked, her pale blue eyes locking on Raife's. There was a depth in that stare, the experience of years that he had not seen in people twice his own age. It sent a chill spider crawling up his spine.

"No, Abigail," Raife said, once the spider had passed. "I'm not going to hurt you. I'm going to help you if I can."

She looked down and nodded, as much a confirmation to herself as a communication with him. She crouched and picked up a small stone off the ground. "Okay, then," she said.

"Hold out your hand."

She was still five big steps away. Raife stood and waited for the child to get close to him.

"Go on, hold it out," she said.

Raife looked to Kord, who nodded once, and rubbed his hand over a face that was slack and exhausted. Shrugging, Raife did as he was told and held out his right hand, palm up.

Abby reached beneath the threadbare t-shirt she wore and pulled out a bronze medallion, about the size of miniature donut. The medallion was rough, its edges not completely uniform, and there was a primitive impression of a feather in the middle of it. Abby gripped the medallion in one hand, held the small stone in the other, and stared at Raife's open palm.

For several seconds nothing happened. Abby just stood there, a little ahead of her father, her face an ivory mask of vibrating concentration. Raife felt a sigh gurgling up from his guts and was ready to tell Kord to be serious, when the sigh was stopped as suddenly as a train rolling off its tracks.

From inside Abby's hand, the medallion began to glow.

It was faint, at first, but grew until bright streamers of light lanced from between her fingers. The light forced back the rapidly falling shadows of dusk. Raife had to squint against its glare.

As the light stopped growing and burned steady, Abby extended the hand with the stone, the small object held between her thumb and forefinger, her face still a mask of concentration. She let the stone drop and as the stone passed through the light, it disappeared.

A moment later it plopped gently into Raife's open hand.

He snapped his hand closed in surprise and felt the shape of the stone there. It was freezing cold, so cold it hurt him to hang on to. He kept his hand shut tight, afraid to open it and see what was there, because what he thought he had witnessed was not possible.

Once she had dropped the stone, Abby let her other hand relax and the light from the bronze medallion died. He had seen that light before, Raife thought. Two years ago he had seen it, in the basement of Joe Robowski's house, when Quinn pulled out the dagger that Autumn had given him and rammed it into the neck of the demon that had nearly killed them all.

Raife opened his hand and stared at the stone for several moments, working his mouth as he tried to think of what to say. He reached up a hand to smooth his mustache. He pulled his gaze from the stone to glance over to Abby McRae, and then shifted it to her father. "What the hell did I just see?"

"I told you," Abby said. "I can do things."

"Now do you understand why this thing wants my daughter?" asked Kord.

"If I said I understood what was happening, I'd be telling a filthy lie," Raife said. "But I think I'm starting to get a bit of the picture."

That drew a smile from the slender man, but it looked like he was pulling it from some place that was hard to reach. "I must admit I don't quite understand it myself, but I know this thing wants Abby bad enough to kill anyone that gets in its way. I also know that it must not have her."

"No," Raife agreed. "I would have to say that it should not."

Raife was about to start another round of debate to try to convince Kord that he and his daughter should come with him, when the slender man's eyes widened. He scrambled for his back pocket. Raife snatched his pistol from his holster and pointed it at Kord, thinking he was going for a gun, but all the man pulled out was what looked like a set of brass knuckles.

Raife would not have been concerned in the least if they had not been glowing bright white.

"What the fuck?" Raife asked out loud. The glow was the same as Quinn's knife and that produced by Abby, although a little less bright.

"It's close," Kord said, as he slipped the brass knuckles over the fingers of his right hand. "Get behind me, Abby."

Raife spun and looked into the dense trees that surrounded the campsite. His pistol felt about as useful as a squirt gun and he put it back in the holster. With three big strides he was at the door to his truck. He pulled the door open, grabbed the key from behind his gun belt and leaned across the driver's seat to stick it into the ignition. Once the truck was started and running, he hit the release for the shotgun rack and pulled the big gun from its mount. Straightening up and stepping away from the truck, he pumped a round into the chamber.

"Your gun can't kill it, Sergeant," Kord said, as he scanned the trees.

"No," Raife agreed, as he tucked the stock of the shotgun into his shoulder and clicked off the safety. "But it'll sure as fuck slow it down."

As they stood debating, the sun had dipped closer to the horizon, until only a faint inclination of light remained to the west. The shadows beneath the trees had become almost as deep as nightfall. Raife could not see more than a few feet outside the clearing.

"We need to get out of here," he said. "Get in my truck. I can get us out of here faster than that jalopy of yours will go."

Kord swiveled on his left foot, hands up before him like a boxer, his right hand tucked beneath his chin. He looked back and forth between Raife's new Suburban and his battered van. "It's our home," he said, his jaw stiff.

"If we're still alive tomorrow we'll come back for it," Raife said. "Now, for fuck's sakes, get in the truck."

Growling once, Kord grabbed Abby's hand and ran for the suburban.

As he moved, something burst from the trees. Raife pivoted towards it and pulled the trigger on the shotgun. The big gun roared and blinding fire leaped from the muzzle. The thing that had charged at him veered away and back into the trees. He pumped another round into the shotgun and fired again at the thing's fleeing back.

It was the size and shape of a man, but it moved faster than anything Raife had ever seen. He barely had time to register the movement when it charged at him from behind

Kord's van. He brought the gun to bear and fired, hitting it almost point blank in the chest. The thing faltered, but only slightly. Its momentum carried it into Raife.

The shape was far smaller than Raife, but he felt as though he had been hit by a bus and was thrown backwards, colliding with the side of the Suburban. White spots burst in his vision as the shotgun flew from his hands and he tumbled to the ground.

Through the starbursts before his eyes, Raife saw the thing that had hit him stop in front of him. He looked up from a pair of worn boots, to a dusty pair of blue jeans, to a red plaid shirt that was stained with dark splotches and looked too tight. The thing appeared as a dark-haired man with broad, handsome features, but Raife could tell immediately it was not human. It had a thick animal smell about it and its eyes burned like two coals in its face. Sick waves of memory washed over him as he struggled to stand.

"You are not the Guardian," the thing said in a deep, pleasant voice, then tilted its head to one side. "You've met my kind before, though. I can smell it on you. So, if you're not ignorant, why would you bother to fight me?" The thing shrugged. "No matter."

The demon lifted one of its feet high in the air. Raife scrabbled for his pistol with numb fingers.

A bright light streaked through Raife's vision. Kord McRae rushed around the back of the truck, his right hand blazing in the dark. The thing turned, but with its foot high in the air, its balance off, Kord struck it with a vicious punch. His fist, clad in the glowing brass knuckles, crashed into the thing's face. Fire, like a rag soaked in gasoline, burst from where the blow landed and the thing staggered backwards. Kord pursued it, his fist lashing out with practiced efficiency, landing several more blows and bringing more gouts of flame.

The creature regained its balance and lashed out with one muscular arm. The wild blow caught Kord in the shoulder with enough force to send him spinning through the air. The thing lunged towards the fallen man, but Raife found his feet and pulled his gun from his hip and started firing. The hollow point rounds punched into the demon's body. The thing screamed in frustration, an awful, screeching, feline sound and charged at Raife again.

The thing did not go down, but the damage done to it, by both Raife and Kord, seemed to have slowed it down a little. When it hit Raife this time, he had his feet spread and was ready for it. He dropped his empty pistol and grappled with the creature, using his empty right fist to hammer into the thing's head.

Although weakened, the demon was still strong , pushing Raife back until he was pinned up against the side of the truck. The thing's hands, the hair singed off the skin by the fire from Kord's brass knuckles, flailed at Raife's face and then latched onto his throat.

Raife dropped his chin and heaved against the smaller body. He may as well have been heaving against a Buick for all the good it did. The thing continued to squeeze.

A flash of light appeared in Raife's vision and he feared he was about to pass out. He glanced away from the thing's blistered, ruined face and looked over its shoulder. He saw Abby, crouching beside a very large rock, that incredible glow spearing from between her fingers. She saw him looking and gave him a slight nod, then laid her hand on the rock. With desperate effort, Raife twisted and lunged sideways just as the rock, which must have weighed close to four or five hundred pounds, appeared in the air above the creature's head and landed on it.

The demon lay on the ground, the right side of its body pinned beneath the massive weight of the rock. It howled and clawed at the stone with its left hand, its nails leaving white scratches in the dull surface. Raife sucked in ragged breaths through his battered throat and looked around for something to finish the demon off, but could see with every wild convulsion it worked itself closer to freedom.

"Abby," he croaked, his throat still tight. "Get in the truck!"

160

The girl leapt to obey and sprinted for the Suburban, her braid a pale streak in the dark behind her. Raife, battered but mobile, shuffled past the flailing thing and to where Kord lay in the dirt. The slender man was groggy, trying to roll to his knees. Raife reached down with one broad hand, grabbed the smaller man's belt and hauled him to his feet. Once up, Kord was able to stagger forward on his own and climbed into the passenger seat of the truck.

Raife stooped to pick up his pistol off the ground and made his best attempt at a run. He threw himself behind the steering wheel, yanked the truck's gear shift into drive and hit the gas, letting the momentum of the vehicle close his door. He drove forward as far as he could, cranking the wheel, then stopped to back up. As he moved backwards, heedless of where he was going, Kord sat up in the passenger seat and looked over Abby's head in the back seat, out the back window.

"Raife," he yelled. "It's up."

Raife looked in his side mirror and saw a mangled, blistered face glowing red in the truck's tail lights. He hit the gas a little harder and felt the impact as the truck struck the creature and it tumbled from sight. He slapped his big hand down on the gear shift, putting the truck into drive and peeled out of the small campsite.

Raife drove as fast as he dared down the narrow bush roads, pushing the truck, and himself, to the limit. He checked his mirror every few seconds to see if they were being pursued.

"Is that thing going to stay down?" Raife asked. Fear made his voice louder than he had planned.

Kord shook his head. "Not likely. I've done worse to it before, and it's still here."

"You fought that thing before?" Raife asked, risking a glance over at his passenger.

"Once, a year ago," Kord said, rubbing his left arm where the thing had hit him. "That's when we lost Abby's mother." He glanced over at Raife, who looked in the rearview mirror.

The girl gazed out the back window and gave no indication that she had heard.

"I'm sorry, Kord. I didn't know."

"No, you didn't. How could you?" He turned in his seat and looked back at Abby. "Sweetheart, are you hurt?"

"No, Daddy," the girl said without turning around.

Kord nodded and turned forward, his face a tight with pain. He shook the brass knuckles, which were now dull, no longer glowing, into the cup holder of the centre console. Then he continued to rub his arm and sucked in a hissing breath.

"Raife, I think my arm is broken."

Gripping the wheel in hands slick with sweat, Raife pushed the accelerator a little harder, the Suburban down the road, between the dark shapes of the trees. "We gotta get back into town and get some support. Then we'll get you to a hospital."

"Can you trust the hospitals here?" Kord asked. "Won't they have to report this to your bosses?"

"We have a special relationship with one of the doctors in town," Raife said. "And I'm sure she'll be delighted to see us."

Quinn spent a long and wasteful day waiting for the sun to go down. Clara had returned him to the Cranbrook detachment and had gone to speak to Inspector Ferguson about lending him a car.

"He said if it makes you go away any faster, you can have anything you want," she told him when she dropped the keys to a car on the desk he occupied.

The car they had given him was an old Pontiac Grand Prix that had roughly ten million kilometers on it. Quinn had only driven it a few blocks before he was convinced they had given him the car in hopes he would kill himself and cease to be a nuisance.

He filled his time by doing a canvass in Patrick's building, talking to the neighbours and asking if they knew the new

Mountie from down the hall. They all said much the same thing; they had seen him in the building, but had not really talked to him and could not say they knew him. They had not heard any disturbances coming from his suite and he did not cause problems for anyone.

Quinn checked with some of the nearby businesses to see if they had ever seen Patrick. Once again he got nowhere. No one remembered Patrick, or anyone matching his description coming from the building.

No one Quinn talked to remembered the boy Patrick had been, but they all remembered, very well, the cop who had hung himself.

The more questions he asked and the more people he talked to the angrier Quinn got. When people asked him what he was doing, he was as vague as possible, but it did not take long for several people to figure out who he was talking about.

"Isn't that the building where the cop went nuts and hung himself?" people would ask. Quinn would have to make excuses and turn away before he lost his temper and did something stupid.

He stopped at a small, faceless burger joint and got something to eat at dinner time. He checked his watch after every bite, waiting for nine o'clock to come around so he could go and follow up on the one useful thing he had stumbled on during this farce he was trying to refer to as an investigation.

After what seemed like an eternity and several glances from the staff at the burger joint indicating they might want him to leave, Quinn stood from the table and walked outside. The sun was a vague glow in the west, and night was falling rapidly. He stood in the parking lot, feeling the stares of the burger staff on his back, and looked at the darkening sky.

He remembered standing on the stained carpet of Patrick's apartment, trying to feel what the boy had felt in his last moments. Is this what he felt? A darkening of the light as a rope pressed against his neck.

Quinn shivered at the imagined memory. With a last look at the sky, he got into the Pontiac and pulled out of the parking lot.

The drive across the tracks and into Slaterville took a few minutes, and soon Quinn pulled over to a wide spot in the road, a few hundred meters from the ruins of the old hospital. A few faces pulled back filthy curtains and peered at him as he got out of the car, but he paid them no attention. He did not bother to lock the Pontiac before he walked away. There was nothing in it to steal. If someone wanted it that bad he did not think the detachment would care.

He checked the gun at his hip, his other gear and the an-cient dagger beneath his shirt at the small of his back. He found everything in place and easy to access, as he reached the hospital grounds and started across them.

As he got closer to the burned out buildings, he encoun-tered a blue construction fence. It did not take him long to find a gap big enough to squeeze through and he carried on deeper into the grounds. There were no operating street lights here. He pulled a small flashlight from his pocket and used it to guide his way. His stealth would be vastly reduced if he stepped in a hole and broke his ankle.

He came around a charred and crumbling brick wall and got his first close look at his destination. The building that had once been the insane asylum, marked building 'F'. The 'F', he thought as he looked at the building, must have stood for 'fucking creepy', even back in the days before the building was abandoned and left to ruin. The front entrance had grey stone pillars on either side that met in an archway above the door. In the centre of the arch was some kind of stone angel, look-ing down with a benevolent gesture. Above the angel was a stone gargoyle, leering at Quinn as he neared.

The windows were square, but small, the ones that were not boarded up showed thick white bars. He shuddered to think what it must have been like to stand in one of those rooms and grip the bars as you looked out on the hospital grounds, locked in with the tortured voices in your own head.

Quinn wiped at a bead of sweat on his upper lip, even though the night was relatively cool. Memories, dark and sudden, flashed across his mind of another building. Joe Robowski's house, where Quinn and his friends had faced down the demon, had much the same feel as the old asylum. Quinn felt his mouth go dry at the memory, and he licked his lips. The same weight, the primal fear, that had worked its way into his bowels and made him hesitate, that urged him to flee before he went into Robowski's house, visited him again. He felt like he had lead in his boots as he stared at the front of the building.

He had pulled himself together and entered the house two years ago, but this time he did not have Dave at his shoulder, lending him courage. This time he was alone, and if he did not come out no one would know where he had gone.

Quinn checked the grip of his pistol again and gritted his teeth. Now was no time to bitch, he told himself. Now was no time for cowardice. He had spent the last two days wandering around this shitty little town, scratching his nuts and getting yelled at. Here, finally, was something for him to do. He could not quit.

He visualized himself reaching down into the pit of his stomach and pulled at his deeper strength. He plucked at that string until it hummed. Once it was playing a tune he liked, he stepped forward.

The entrance had once been sealed with plywood, but now stood open, the original doors swinging inwards on rusted hinges. Quinn stepped through and immediately to the right. He was in a wide hallway that stank of wet dirt and rot. There were puddles of water on the black and white tiled floor, and he moved forward cautiously, using the flashlight to guide his way. He tried to avoid making too much noise.

Despite the stink, the hallway was relatively clear of major obstacles. The neglect was obvious. Everywhere Quinn looked was peeling paint, sagging drywall and small scatterings of debris on the floor.

The building looked and smelled deserted. Quinn saw no signs of life among the dust. As he moved deeper into the hallway, he found a set of stairs leading up.

A narrow trail of scuffs in the dust lead from the bottom of the stairs to a door at the back of the building, one that Quinn had not seen previously, but could make out now by distant street lights shining through the windows. He shone his light around the floor and saw more scuffs in the dust and grime, giving further evidence to the occupancy of the derelict building.

Cautiously, Quinn set a foot on the first stair and started to climb up. He stepped slowly, trying not to make too much noise, and looked upwards as he ascended. The top of the stairs was not visible from the bottom, and he came to a landing, requiring him to reverse direction to continue his climb. At the top of the stairs was another, broader landing, a set of open double doors with windows in them and a trash littered hallway leading into the dark.

He carried on, his hand resting on his pistol as he swept the flashlight beam side to side down the hallway. He peeked into the open rooms he passed and saw nothing but more junk and rot lying in heaps in all the corners. The scuffed footprints were everywhere, growing more plentiful the further he went on, but there was no other sign of life.

As he neared the halfway point between the staircase and the end of the hallway, he though he saw a light ahead of him. He depressed a button on the back of the flashlight, turning it off, and confirmed the glow, like candlelight, from the last room on the left side of the hallway. There was no sound, only the faint, orange light.

Quinn eased up to one side of the door and held his breath, listening for movement, but heard nothing.

He turned around the corner and stepped into the room. He saw a small square table on the far side, beneath a barred window, with a single, thick, black candle burning atop it. As he paused, looking at the candle, a hand reached out of the shadows and clapped on top of it, plunging the room into darkness.

The moment the light died, Quinn heard shuffling and foot falls on either side of him and felt hands grasp at his shoulder and chest from the right side. He dropped the flashlight on the dirty floor and slapped his hand down over the hand that held him, stepped forward, and twisted the wrist sharply. Quinn heard a cry and then the sound of a heavy body hitting the floor as the owner of the wrist lost his footing and tumbled away. As his first attacker fell, another set of arms wrapped around him from behind. He could hear grunted breath in his ear. Gritting his teeth, he threw his head backwards as hard as he could and felt the back of his skull connect with a nose. There was a loud crunch and another wail. Quinn grabbed one of the arms that had now loosed its grip and surged forward, bending at his hips to throw a heavy body over him.

Quinn spun, swinging his fists wildly to keep back any further attack.

"No! Stop!" A voice shouted from the back of the room.

A bright light flared from near where the candle had been. Quinn put one hand up in front of his eyes, while he drew his pistol with the other. In front of him, two men, dressed in black leather with heavy boots and dyed black hair, lay on the ground, moaning. At the back of the room, beside the recently lighted, battery powered lamp stood a young man in a black trench-coat, with hair so blonde it was white. He had pale blue eyes and a long, carefully styled beard the same colour as his hair. The rest of the room held a scattering of leather-clad youth, all of them staring at Quinn with wide-eyed shock.

"Show me your fucking hands," Quinn shouted as he raised his pistol. Some of the youth moved to obey his command, holding their hands out in a supplicating gesture. Others continued to stare.

"I said, show me your hands, or I'll blow your fucking heads off," Quinn shouted, louder this time. "You're all under arrest for assaulting a police officer." He reached into his pocket to pull out his cell phone so he could call for some back up and haul all these freaks down to the detachment.

"No, Officer Sullivan, wait," said the man with the nearly white hair. He stepped forward, his hands held out where

Quinn could see them. "That's not necessary."

Quinn turned the muzzle of his pistol towards the blonde man. "That's Corporal Sullivan, and how the fuck do you know my name?"

The blonde man gestured to one of the people in the room. Quinn looked and saw Mandy, the girl from the front counter of his hotel, standing to his left. She was dressed all in black, a corset leaving absolutely no secrets about her figure, with large amounts of black lipstick and eyeliner making her pale skin even whiter in comparison. She had one hand at her throat, her eyes darting between Quinn's face and the pistol in his hand.

"Mandy told me about you," said the blonde man. "The new cop who showed up in town, and we figured we might see you."

"Who are you?" Quinn asked. The man's manner had not been threatening, but Quinn kept his pistol pointed at the skinny chest in front of him, his eyes moving among the stunned, speechless people in the room.

"My name," the man said, laying a long fingered hand on his own chest with a little too much dramatic flair, "is Alastair Bane."

Quinn looked him up and down. "What? No, shithead, what's your real name?"

The man looked indignant. "That is my—"

"Cut the shit," Quinn said. "Or I'll come over there and rip that stupid beard off your face."

The blonde man touched his beard self-consciously and glanced around at the other people in the room. They were looking back at him, waiting expectantly for his answer. Quinn had it in mind that they believed him when he gave his ridiculous moniker.

The man still did not answer and Quinn took a step forward.

"Okay, okay," the blonde man said. He held up his hands, retreating until his leather-clad back hit the wall behind him. "My name is Edward Robertson."

There was a collective sigh of mass disappointment from the other people in the room. Quinn could not help but grin. "Okay, Eddie," he said, and tucked his gun back into its holster. "Tell me what the fuck you're doing here." He pulled the flyer he had found in Patrick's apartment from the pocket of his jeans, and flapped it until it unfolded. "And who you gave this to."

Edward squinted and leaned forward, peering at the paper in Quinn's hand, then took a couple of steps forward and peered again.

"Why don't you put your glasses on?" Quinn asked.

The skinny man glared at Quinn, then took another step and looked at the paper. "That is one of my flyers, yes. I give them out at many places in this backwards little town."

"Okay. Why did I find one in a dead kid's apartment?"

"Ah," Edward said. "You're here about Patrick. I understand now."

Quinn worked his mouth for a moment, letting his mind shift between shock and smug self-satisfaction. He knew this flyer was important, but he did not expect anyone on the other end of it to admit knowing Patrick. "You knew him?"

"Of course we did," Edward said. "He was one of our circle." He gestured to the other people in the room who nodded. "He was dear to us, and his loss has been a terrible blow to our little family."

"What the fuck are you talking about?" Quinn said, his anger rising now, thick and hot as it climbed up his chest and into his throat. "Patrick wasn't into this shit." He looked around, giving his most disgusted expression to the people in the room. "You weren't his fucking family. We were."

Edward crossed his arms across his narrow chest. "If you were his family, where have you been the last six months, when he needed you?"

The skinny man's words hit Quinn in the face like a blow, and his arm itched to move forward and strike back. Edward sighed and waved his hands in the air as though he were washing the last few minutes away.

169

"No," he said. "We can't do this. It's not right. Not for us and not for Patrick." He took a few steps forward and turned to face the other people in the room. "You all go home. I'll speak to Corporal Sullivan."

"I think my nose is broken," said the one who was still bleeding.

The two youth who had jumped Quinn were back on their feet. One had an obviously broken nose and the other rubbed what was likely a sprained wrist.

Edward turned to Mandy. "Can you take him to the hospital? I'll come by there, later."

Quinn stepped forward. "What was that all about, anyway? You're lucky all I did was break his nose. What were you thinking, jumping a cop?"

"We didn't know you were a cop when you came in here," Edward said with a shrug. "We're a group of people living an alternative lifestyle in a small-minded, redneck town, Corporal. You're not the first person who has come, uninvited, to one of our gatherings. Usually there is violence and ridicule involved. We've learned to take precautions." He turned and looked at the bloody face of the youth in front of him. "I don't know why you didn't just come and talk to me."

"How the fuck would I get a hold of you?"

Edward turned back and snatched the paper out of Quinn's left hand. "My cell number is on the flyer," he said, pointing to the bottom of the page.

Quinn's face burned with embarrassment and he looked away. In his search to make someone wrong in Patrick's death, he had overlooked something obvious. He could not help but wonder how many other times he had done that in the last two days.

Edward waved one of his hands, and passed the flyer back to Quinn. "This isn't a big deal. A broken nose will heal." He looked around him to the other people in the room. "Okay, everyone out. I'll email you all later and tell you what happened."

Reluctantly, the other leather clad youth slouched from

the room. Mandy lingered longest, making airs of helping the youth with the broken nose. She studied Quinn with intense interest, looking him up and down like a housewife picking out a new vacuum cleaner.

Once the room was clear, Edward checked down the hallway, and then came and stood in front of Quinn. "What can I do for you, Corporal?"

Quinn looked down at the flyer in his hand, folded it again and put it back in his pocket. "How did you know Patrick? Where did he get your flyer? And why did I find it in his apartment?" He looked around the room, then held up his hands and shrugged. "And what are you people doing here?"

"Some of your questions are going to require complex answers, but as to where Patrick got the flyer; it could have been any number of places. He's been coming to see us for several months, so that particular flyer isn't likely to be new. We always meet at the same place, at the same time. I send out the days we're going to meet via email."

Quinn took in Edward's black garb, his Goth appearance and the silly fake name he used, and thought that the use of email did not seem to fit with this image. "And what is it you do when you meet here? That Mandy girl said something about fighting the corporate overlords."

"Really, what I'm trying to do here, Corporal, is just provide a place for people to be who they want to be. To show them it's okay to not drive a pickup and listen to country music, or spend your life working in a mill. It's okay to experience a different kind of art, and different music, and you don't have to feel like a freak because of it."

He stuck his long fingered, delicate hands in the pockets of his black trench-coat, and flapped the fabric. "Growing up in a town like this, where people throw things at you and call you 'faggot' because you don't chew tobacco and watch a lot of football, is hard. I managed to pull myself through, without any support from anyone, and decided I didn't want that to happen to anyone else and tried to put this thing together. We come here, we hang out, we watch the movies and listen to the music we want. We try and think a little independently and push away the concepts promulgated by popular culture and mass media. When you live on the fringe of a small red-neck town, there is safety in numbers."

Quinn nodded and began to get an idea of where Edward was coming from. His own childhood had not been easy. He had been the short, fat kid growing up and had been constantly bullied until he had discovered karate and grown eight inches.

"I see what you're saying," Quinn told him. "But what's up with the fake name. Alastair what's-his-fuck?"

Edward flapped his coat again. "I'm still trying to make my way, too, I guess. No one wants to hang out with Edward Robertson, so I created a pseudonym when I started publishing my little magazine and founded this group. The name helps."

"Okay, Edward, I get it, but I need you to tell me where Patrick fits in to all this. How well did you know him?"

The skinny man turned, his coat flapping around his calves, and walked towards the table where the candle still stood. He took one hand from his pocket and rubbed his chin, then turned again and leaned against the table. "I guess I knew Patrick as well as I could after only three months. The first time I'd met him, I was handing out those flyers in the centre of town, outside a coffee shop and he was off duty. He took it and asked some questions about what we were doing.

"Initially, he said he needed to do some kind of project for his police training that examined a community group. I said our little group wasn't really a part of the greater community of this town, but told him to come hang out with us anyway. He was the same age as most of the kids that come here and he fit in. Pretty soon he went from interviewing us for his project to coming here every time he could just to be among friends. He even came in uniform a couple of times, when he was working."

Quinn was finally getting some of the information he was looking for, but instead of being relieved, he was heartbroken. He had always looked at the Mounties as a family. He had been taken in by his coworkers since he was transferred to Resolution. It should have been Patrick's watch-mates, his co-workers, that took him into their fold. He should not have had to look elsewhere for friendship. If he had had more support from within his own team, or from Quinn and the others in Resolution, perhaps he would still be among the living and Quinn would never have had to complete this file review.

The weight of Patrick's death, anchored with chains of guilt, pressed down on Quinn. He had to shake himself to make this thoughts form into anything but a black mass.

"Are you all right, Corporal?" Edward asked.

Quinn realised he had been staring at the floor.

"I'm fine, and you can call me Quinn." Edward smiled and Quinn struggled to get his thoughts moving in the right direction again. "How had Patrick been in the time you knew him?" he asked. "What was his mind-set like?"

"I don't think he was happy here," Edward said, pulling his hands from his pockets and crossing his arms. "He liked police work, but he said this detachment wasn't like the one at home, where you're from. I don't think it turned out to be what he anticipated when he came out here."

"Did he take a downturn that you noticed? Was there any event that really got to him?"

"No," Edward said. "I don't think so. I'm no cop, but I from what I could tell, Patrick was competent, and was probably really good at his job. It wasn't the work itself, but I think he was having trouble with someone at the police station."

"He was? Who?"

Edward shook his head. "He would never actually tell me. He just mentioned that someone was on his case a lot and it had something to do with his dad being a boss of some kind. The other people he worked with didn't like him much, or so he said, and he thought it might be because of what this person was saying about him."

The guilt that had been weighing him down was replaced by a slow, seething anger, and Quinn clenched his teeth together. If Patrick had been bullied to the point where he felt the only answer was to take his own life, then Quinn would see the person responsible answer for it. Either inside the law or out. He took a deep breath through his nose and tried to keep his anger in check. There were still questions he needed to ask and he wouldn't be benefitted by losing his shit just then.

"How was he before..." Quinn paused, hesitated with the words. "Before he killed himself?"

Edward rubbed under his nose with a skinny finger and took a deep breath of his own before answering. "He was troubled, Quinn," he said. "Whatever had been getting to him at work was getting to him even more, and he was not handling it well. He talked more than once of quitting his job and going home, but said he'd never be able to face his friends, or his father."

More understanding flooded Quinn. Patrick was embarrassed by his experiences at work, so instead of reaching out for help, he hid his misery and tried to push through. Quinn wished he had been a better friend to Patrick. He wished he had called, checked on him, seen how he was doing.

"You cannot blame yourself for this, Quinn," Edward said, as though reading Quinn's thoughts. "I tried to help him as much as I could, but I don't work your job and didn't really know what to say. So, I told him, more than once, to call home, to call you—even though I didn't know who you were—and get some advice. Every time he refused, saying he wanted to take care of things on his own. Even if you'd called him every day, I don't think he'd have told you anything."

The tone of Edward's words was reassuring enough, but it did nothing to make Quinn feel better. He looked at the ground, his questions exhausted.

"Patrick was a good friend," Edward said, after they'd been silent for several moments. "We're going to miss him."

"Yes, we are," Quinn said. "I'm sorry to bust in on your gathering, Edward. Apologize to that kid with the broken nose for me."

"I will," Edward said, and nodded. "If you want to come

back here, a friend of Patrick's is always welcome." He stuck out his hand and Quinn gripped it.

Quinn turned, striding through the grime and debris, and fled the building as though Patrick's ghost chased him.

CHAPTER 13

The good news is," Doctor Stovern said, as she threw a chart down on the bed where Kord lay, "this man's arm is not broken. The bad news, Corporal Raife-"

"Sergeant Raife," Raife said, from where he stood beside Kord's bed.

"Whatever. The bad news is you're still an ill-mannered baboon."

"I missed you too, Doc," Raife said, a smile lifting his mustache.

The plump, pretty woman pushed her dark hair away from her forehead. "Why is it every time I see you, I get the distinct impression you're up to something?"

Raife shrugged and did his best to act innocent.

Doctor Stovern put one small fist on her hip. "How did this man get injured? He's been hit hard enough that he'll be black with bruises tomorrow, and you look like you got in fist fight with a wrecking ball. What the hell is going on here?"

"Does he need anything, Doc?" Raife asked, as he pointedly ignored the Doctor's questions.

She rolled her eyes. "You people are impossible. He needs rest and anti-inflammatories. Other than that he'll be fine. For you, I'd like to prescribe a stiff kick in the ass."

"Get in line, Doctor dear," Raife said, and gestured to

Kord to get off the bed. "As always it was a pleasure to see you."

Doctor Stovern gave Raife a glare that would scratch glass, picked up her chart and bustled from the room in the same manner as her arrival.

"She is not a fan of yours, is she?" Kord asked.

Raife shrugged. "She's warming up to me. I'd say five more years and she won't want to punch me in the mustache anymore."

Together the two men walked down the hallway out of the emergency treatment area and into the waiting room. Sandy and Dave stood at the back of the room, talking with their heads together. Gerritt had a chair pulled up to a small, plastic picnic table, helping Abby fill in the lines of a colouring book. It was long past the end of their shifts, but Raife had phoned them once he had reached an area with cell reception and told them what happened on the mountainside. They had all agreed they best stay armed and in the policing loop, and hauled the recruit along to keep up appearances.

There had been questions as to why they had not signed off and gone home. Raife had explained to the night shift watch commander that he had gone to check the campsites, in a proactive manner, for whatever freak had attacked and eaten Dean Springer, and had found a man who had gotten into a confrontation with some campground partyers and needed transport to the hospital. Dave and Sandy, he had explained, were staying on to help him look into the matter and possibly make an arrest if a suspect could be identified. It had been an easy sell. The night shift people were glad there were some more uniforms around after the second set of gnawed bones had been located behind the Welcome Beaver.

"How you making out?" Raife asked as they joined the other members.

Dave looked up at him and shook his head. "Not good, boss. They found more."

"More what?" Raife asked.

"More bones," Sandy said. "Behind a homeless shelter. But

not a complete set, only what looks like an arm and part of a hand. The rest," she paused, pulling in a big breath. "Was carried off."

"It is the creature," Kord said. "It was injured after our battle and it is feeding to recover."

Raife turned to Kord and raised a fist with a pointed finger extended. "You were awfully quiet on the ride back here, my strange little friend. You know a fuck of a lot more than you let on. So you start yapping, right fucking now, about what you know about this thing and what it plans on doing with your kid. We've had several people eaten in this town and it's gonna stop."

Kord rubbed at his injured arm and looked down at Abby. She stared back at him, her blue eyes wide. Gerritt looked from her to Kord, took in the look on Raife's face, then gently reached out to turn Abby's chin towards the colouring book and tapped the page with one finger. Raife remembered where he was and looked around for other patients, then grabbed Kord's good arm and steered him across the room, Sandy and Dave following.

"You saw what my girl can do, Sergeant," Kord said, once Raife released him.

"I did," Raife said. He folded his arms across his chest, leaning forward so his face was close to Kord's.

"Wait," Dave said. "What does she do?" Raife had only told them of the confrontation, not the details of it.

"She...moves things," Raife said, answering him while still keeping his eyes locked on Kord's.

"Moves things?" Dave asked, screwing his face up like he'd tasted something bitter. "What the fuck does that mean?"

Sandy poked him under the arm and he stopped talking. They both leaned towards Kord, who appeared extremely uncomfortable under their scrutiny.

"Abby can open doors," Kord said, his eyes moving across the ring of faces around him. "She opens doors to other places, and can send things through them, or bring them out."

"Okay," Raife said. "How?"

Kord shrugged, his hand still on his wounded arm. "I don't know, to tell you true. It has something to do with that amulet she wears. It was her mother's, and her grandmother's before that. You take that thing away and she can't do it. Give it to someone else and they get nothing. We've tried every possible thing you can think of, but only Abby, and the line of women that came before her, can use it."

"So, what does this thing want with her?" Sandy asked.

"I don't know for certain," Kord said, a slight smirk on his face. "I've never actually sat down and asked it, but I can only assume it wants her talents." He stood on his tip-toes and looked over Raife's shoulder, turning his head to check for nearby ears. "Things like the creature we fought today, demons, they come from another plane of existence, or so I understand. It takes an extremely strong creature to push through the fabric that separates our worlds, and an even stronger one to disguise itself as human and walk among us."

Dave shifted his weight, checking over his shoulder as well. "We know some of this, Kord. We dealt with something like this before."

"Yes," Kord said. "You and the Guardian. That is why we came here."

"The Guardian?" Sandy asked, glancing at Raife. "Is he talking about Quinn?"

"Yes," Raife said, then turned back to put the full weight of his attention on Kord. "Carry on."

"These things, these creatures," Kord said, "are always alone, because it is so difficult for them to push through into our world themselves that they couldn't possibly bring another along. Unless they turn a human into their Thrall, they are companionless."

"Yes," Raife said. "And?"

"I believe," Kord said, "that this thing wants Abby so it can open a door to its own plane of existence."

"Oh, fuck," Dave said. "It wants to invite a few of its friends over for a party."

Kord looked from Dave's face and back to Raife's. "Yes.

Exactly."

Raife looked across the room at the small child who pointed to the page of her colouring book while chatting with the Mountie hunched next to her, and shuddered. He had seen what a demon looked like, felt its breath on his face. The one he had met had been too weak to leave the safety of Joe Robowski's basement, and it had nearly killed three of them. If Quinn had not had the glowing knife he used to stab the fucking thing and burn it to ash, they would all be dead. They were barely able to handle one. Raife could not imagine what would happen if the doors to Hell were thrown wide open and all its occupants were given a free ride out.

"God help us," Raife said, still looking at the girl. The thoughts of Quinn triggered another memory and the big man turned from looking at the child, and back to Kord. "When that thing showed up, you pulled out a set of brass knuckles and they glowed, just like a knife Quinn has. What are they?"

Checking again to ensure they weren't being watched, Kord reached into his pocket and pulled out the brass knuckles. "They've been with my family for generations," Kord said, as he held the brass knuckles out to Raife and dropped them on his palm. "My family, just like that of Abby's mother, have been a part of this struggle for as far back as we know. That weapon," he pointed to the object in Raife's broad hand, "has been carried by a dozen men of my family. Where it came from, I don't know, but whenever demon-kind gets near, it grows hot. It's the only thing I've seen that can really harm one of the creatures."

"This shit gets weirder and weirder by the minute," Dave said.

The brass knuckles were far too small to fit Raife's massive hands, even if he had been inclined to try and take them. He handed them back to Kord.

"What do we do now, Raife?" Sandy asked.

Raife took in a long breath through his nose. He knew two things for certain: the demon that attacked him—and was busily eating people—must not get its grubby hands on the girl, and he wished Quinn were back.

"We gotta call Quinn," Raife said. "And we gotta get Kord and Abby someplace safe until Quinn can get back here and we can hunt that fucking thing down and put an end to it."

"Right," Dave said. "Where is that gonna be?"

Raife could not help but grin. "I know someone who has a house guest. I'm hoping she won't mind a couple more."

"You've got to be kidding me, Raife," Carrie said, looking down at the big sergeant as he stood at the bottom of the steps to her front door. "Who the fuck are these people?" She looked past Raife to where Kord and Abby stood, side by side. "No offence," she said to them.

"It's only going to be for tonight, Carrie," Raife said. "Until I can get something else going for them."

"I don't even know what's happening. Quinn is gone to some God-forsaken shit-bowl town and you're bringing strangers to my house. What the fuck is going on?"

Raife looked at the two refugees behind him and then back at Carrie. "Have you been watching the news?"

"Yeah, why?"

"Did you see the story about the human bones that were found?"

"I don't like where this is going." Carrie crossed her arms.

"Well, the thing that did that might be coming for them next."

"The 'thing'?" Carrie asked, her voice climbing in both pitch and volume. "What thing? What thing ate someone? I saw the inspector on the news. He said the whole human teeth marks were only a rumor. What thing are you talking about, Raife?"

Each word she spoke brought panic closer to the surface of her speech. Raife held up his hands and made the same gentle sounds he would use if he were confronted by an angry rattle snake. "Don't worry," he said. "We're gonna leave a member with you."

"So you're saying we need someone to protect us? You still never told me what 'thing' you were talking about."

Raife smoothed his mustache and then rubbed a hand over his bald head. He had not anticipated this being so difficult. "Okay, Carrie," he said, deciding he was going to have to throw some truth out there and see where it landed. "I'm going to be straight with you. We got a freak in town eating people."

"People? That means plural, Raife. How many people have been eaten?"

"Well, three, that we know of."

"That you know of?" The panic lifted in a thin bubble from the surface of her calm.

"Have there been more, Sergeant?" Autumn said, walking up behind Carrie and looking over her shoulder.

"You knew about this?" Carrie asked, turning towards Autumn. "You never said anything before."

"Carrie," Raife said, slowly, his voice pitched low.

The black haired woman ignored him. "You've been here all freaking day, hiding from someone and you didn't tell me you knew about a freak eating people?"

"Carrie," Raife said again, a little louder.

"Wait..." Carrie said, still ignoring Raife. "You're here hiding, too. Is the freak coming after you as well? Are we on the menu?" She turned towards Kord and Abby. "And what about them? Are they going to be eaten, too?"

"CARRIE!" Raife bellowed, loud enough to make the thin windows in the old house rattle.

"Why are you yelling?" Carrie turned to Raife. She looked at him as though he had lost his mind.

"Jesus, Carrie, calm down a second," Raife said. "No one else is going to be eaten. Yes, these people I've brought you are in danger. That's why I brought them to you. No one knows they're here and they can hide. I've known you since you were in high school, and you know me well enough to be sure I would never do anything to bring harm to you or your boy. I just need a safe place for these people to lay up for a night so I can find this freak and sort this shit out."

Carrie crossed her arms again, which Raife thought an improvement, because at least she was not waving them around. "Okay," she said after staring at him for several seconds. "You're sure this freak isn't going to come here?"

"Yes," he said. His conscience winced as the lie flowed past his lips. He was not, in fact, certain the creature—this new demon—would not find Kord and Abby at Carrie's house. It had found them in a campsite fifty miles from anywhere, so it was completely likely it would find them again, eventually. He just had to get Quinn back here and hunt the bastard thing down before it did.

"Okay, so who are you leaving here?"

"Gerritt!" Raife called over his shoulder. The slump shouldered recruit got out of the front seat of Raife's truck.

"The half-wit? Don't I rate better than the half-wit?"

"I brought a colouring book from the hospital." Gerritt held the book up proudly. "One of the nurses said I could have it."

Carrie slapped her forehead and gritted her teeth, while Autumn gave Raife a sick look.

"Don't worry," Raife said. "You won't even notice him. He's really here for your piece of mind." Really, he was there to get him out of the way so the rest of the team could be about the messy business of demon hunting.

"I'm going to live to regret this, aren't I?" Carrie asked as Raife said his goodbyes to Kord and Abby and pointed Gerritt towards the house.

Turning to walk back to his truck, Raife waved over his shoulder and said, "I hope so."

Quinn drove back to the Cranbrook detachment, a sick feeling roiling in the pit of his stomach while a small army of unanswered questions marched through his mind.

Over the past two days he had talked to more people than he could remember, read through a file that had killed a large forest to produce and had pissed off most of an RCMP detachment. Despite all the steps he had taken, he was still no closer to any answers, or the smallest sliver of peace of mind. His busily marching questions began kicking things over and acting like hooligans, defying any answers to come near them.

In this town, he had received several different views of Patrick Green. None of those views fit Quinn's memory of the young man, and it tore at the inside of his mind like a mouth full of broken glass. Why had Patrick been distant and troubled while he was here, instead of the jovial, charismatic youth Quinn remembered in Resolution? What had happened to that boy in the last year that his personality would have made such a shift? How was it that his friends—both old and new—his detachment and the whole organization of the RCMP had failed to save him from the fate he had devised for himself.

Quinn had heard it said before, until he was sick of it bouncing off the inside of his head, that you could not save someone who was truly suicidal. He hated the sound of that tired saying and resolved to break the arm of the next asshole who threw that line at him, before pushing him down a set of stairs. There had not been enough done for Patrick, not by Quinn or the other members in Resolution, and not by his new detachment.

Two years ago, before his confrontation with the demon in Resolution, Quinn had been forced to kill three people: first a boy shooting his classmates, then a homeless man—a man Quinn had known and liked—who shot up a strip-mall, and finally a drug addict in the thrall of the demon, who had attacked Quinn at Carrie's house. He carried the memory, the burden of those deaths, with him every moment of his life in the time that had passed, but the death of Patrick settled on him with a weight he could scarcely bear. During the drive back, he could not bring himself to look at the passenger seat for fear Patrick's ghost would be riding shotgun, there to remind him of his blame.

Those same people who would tell him you could not save

a suicidal person would also say he should not blame himself. Those people were idiots.

He pulled into the parking lot at the back of the Cranbrook office and shoved the gear shift into park. He looked down at his watch and saw it was just after ten P.M., but it felt like he had been awake for days.

He got out of the car and walked in the back door of the office, using the electronic fob attached to the car keys to open the door. He walked past the small cell block and into the main body of the office.

He wished he could think of something else to do, some other step he could take that would bring some kind of closure to Patrick's death. No matter how hard he thought – and he thought until he feared his brain would dissolve and leak out his ears—he came up with nothing. All he had discovered during this awful experience was that Patrick had been miserable in his new life, and Quinn—along with everyone else—had failed him horribly.

As he walked into the general duty pit where he had left Patrick's file, he saw Gerry Barnes and the two other members he had spoken to the previous day, sitting at office computers, presumably working on their files. When Quinn walked into the office, Gerry turned his chair away from the computer, folded his arms and looked at Quinn with barely concealed contempt.

"You find what you were looking for there, Corporal?" Gerry asked. His face was close to a sneer. Quinn waited for it to fully materialize so he could wipe it off with the bottom of his boot.

Shaking away his anger, trying desperately to keep himself together, Quinn ran a hand over his face. "Yeah, I'm done."

"Any other questions I can answer for you?" the heavy man asked.

Forcing his hand to relax from the fist it had bunched into, Quinn shook his head. "No, thank you."

Gerry snorted and turned back to his computer.

Quinn had thought to leave the keys to the Pontiac in the

office and ask one of the members on duty for a ride back to his hotel, but decided a cab would be a better option. He feared that in his frustrated state, with all his anger at himself resting in a red ball at the base of his neck, he would say, or do something stupid; or perhaps violent. He dropped the keys to the Pontiac on the desk beside Gerry's elbow.

As Quinn turned to leave the general duty pit and head towards the front door, something against the wall caught his eye: a series of mail slots sat in a tall column, the name of a member below each one. It took Quinn only a moment to find the one that said 'Cst Green' on it. He looked inside and found an unopened pay stub and some random, miscellaneous paperwork. He looked at the paystub and thought of Patrick's father. If there was anything at the detachment belonging to Patrick, Quinn should take it now and save Donald Green the pain of seeing the place his son had worked. It had been the inspector's fondest dream to see his son follow in his footsteps, walking into this place would likely break the man's heart.

"There is something you can do," Quinn said, turning back to Gerry Barnes.

The heavy man turned his chair away from his desk again and raised an eyebrow.

"I need to get into Patrick's locker," Quinn said. "If he has any effects here I'll take them back to his family."

The vague smirk that had been waiting to form on Gerry's face departed entirely, and he nodded. "Yeah, okay," he said and got up from his desk. He left the pit and went into another office. Quinn heard a file drawer open, then close a few seconds later. Gerry reappeared holding a piece of paper and an empty banker's box. He handed the box to Quinn.

"I've got the master combination list," Gerry said, holding up the piece of paper. "I'll show you Patrick's locker and open it for you."

Quinn nodded, following Gerry wordlessly through the office.

The locker room for Cranbrook detachment was a small, cramped affair; a square room with a bench in the middle and dull brown lockers bolted to the surrounding walls. Gerry walked directly to a locker in the far corner from the door, consulted the list in his hand, and then spun the combination lock several times. He pulled the lock open, the metallic click echoing off the aluminum doors of the other lockers. He stepped back without taking the arm of the lock from ring.

"I'll leave you to it," he said simply. He turned and walked from the room.

Quinn set the banker's box on the floor beside the locker, lifted the lock free and pulled open the door. The contents were unremarkable: several sets of uniform shirts and pants, a pair of boots, Patrick's duty belt and a scattered selection of toiletries and personal items. Quinn looked through the contents on the top shelf, where the toiletries sat, just in case there had been a note of some kind.

Shaking his head, Quinn stopped his search and sat down on the bench in the middle of the room. The members who investigated the file certainly would have checked the locker for a note and had also taken Patrick's duty pistol.

He had not expected it to, but looking at Patrick's locker stung Quinn in a way he had not yet experienced during the exercise in futility he was loosely referring to as an inquiry. He imagined what the boy had felt each time stood in front of that locker and put his uniform on. For Quinn, each day had been a new and spectacular adventure. For Patrick, who had apparently had so much strife and trouble in his first six months, it must have been a struggle to generate the enthusiasm to lace up his boots.

Fighting back tears, Quinn stood and began taking the items out of the locker, placing them in the box. He cleaned out the top shelf first with its collection of toiletries and tins of boot polish. Then he carefully folded the pants and uniform shirts and laid them in the box as though he was putting them in a coffin. Finally, he took out the boots and the duty belt.

He rolled the duty belt into a coil and stooped to set it on top of the other items in the box when he paused and looked at it. The sight of it caught him funny. There was something off about it, something unfamiliar. He stood up and unrolled the belt, then held it flat on his hands and studied it. After a moment he realised why it looked funny, different than his own; Patrick had been left handed and the holster was on the opposite side.

A small thought, like a trickle of sand, rolled down the hill of Quinn's mind. Those few grains dislodged a couple of heavier pebbles, and soon there was an avalanche of horrid realization.

Quinn turned and ran from the locker room, down the hallway and into the general duty pit. When he burst into the room Gerry Barnes stood from his desk.

"You all finished?"

Quinn ignored him and shoved past, heading for the desk where Patrick's file lay. Gerry squawked in protest and fell back into his chair. Quinn ripped the lid off the box and began rifling through the file, until he found the folder marked 'images.'

"What the fuck are you doing?" Gerry Barnes asked from behind him, getting off his chair.

Still ignoring Gerry, Quinn sat and carefully opened the folder, his heart hammering in his chest, blood rushing to his face, making it feel tight and swollen. He turned the pictures over, slowly, one at a time, until he found the image that showed all of Patrick's body, his neck oddly elongated, as he hung from the ceiling fixture.

Once he had found the picture, Quinn pressed his thumb and forefinger to his eyes before he studied it, his hands shaking slightly as he feared what he might find. Once his hands were steady again and he had slowed his breathing, Quinn opened his eyes and looked at the picture.

The scalpel Patrick had used to carve meaningless symbols in himself was gripped in his right hand.

Patrick was left handed.

Trying without success to keep his breathing even, his hands shook so badly they made the paper rattle, Quinn turned through the rest of the pictures of the crime scene. He needed to be sure it was not a glitch in the photography making the picture appear backwards, but the rest of the pictures were the same, each one showed the scalpel in Patrick's right hand.

As Quinn turned the pages, his face burning so hot it made his eye sight blurry, he came to the pictures of Patrick laid out on a steel examination table and the close-ups of the symbols carved on his body. Through the haze of his vision, he noticed something that had not been apparent when he had viewed the pictures previously; he thought he recognized some of the symbols.

He turned the photograph upside down and looked again. Once he looked at the photos with this new perspective, he knew there was no mistake and he recognised three of the symbols: the characters that Autumn had thought were Japanese, were, in fact. The characters for the word 'Bushido,' or 'The Way of the Warrior', were carved, upside down and out of order, on Patrick's stomach. They were symbols that he knew, that he had seen several times before, and he cursed himself for not recognizing them sooner. They could be found between the covers of the book, 'The Hagakure,' that he had given to Patrick when he left for Depot.

He stood from his chair, pushed, once again, past Gerry Barnes who stood behind him, and snatched the keys of the old Pontiac off Gerry's desk.

"What the fuck is going on?" Gerry asked, his round face a vivid shade of red above his uniform shirt.

"Patrick was left handed," Quinn said, and turned to run from the office.

CHAPTER 14

A burning certainty thrummed through Quinn's chest as he hammered his foot down on the accelerator of the groaning Pontiac and pulled out of the parking lot of the detachment. In the passenger seat beside him, he could almost see Patrick's ghost smiling in approval.

Patrick had not killed himself. If he had, he would not have died gripping the scalpel he had used to mark himself in his off hand. Someone else had carved Patrick up, hung him from the light fixture and then put the scalpel in the wrong hand. He was certain of it.

Knowing, however, was a long way from proving. If he went to Inspector Ferguson, or anyone else, with only the fact that Patrick was left handed, it would not be enough to prove a murder or even reopen the investigation. There was too much evidence to the fact that Patrick was possibly depressed. What Quinn had was not enough. He needed to find something else.

He blasted along the mostly deserted streets of the town, doubling the speed limit in most places and racing through red lights when he was sure he would not kill anyone. Within a few minutes he brought the wheezing Pontiac to a lurching stop in front of the building where Patrick had lived. He got out of the car, slammed the door and ran to the front entrance of the building.

He thought about smashing the glass of the door, but calmed himself enough to search the occupant listing for the building manager and pressed the buzzer. After he had pressed it several times, he heard a burst of static from the speaker above the panel of buttons.

"Who is it?" a wavering voice asked. "Do you know what time it is?"

Quinn looked down at his watch and saw it was eleven p.m.. He leaned toward the speaker. "This is Corporal Sullivan from the R.C.M.P. I need to get into the building."

There was a pause. "How do I know you are who you say you are?"

"Come down to the door and I'll show you my badge."

Another pause, followed by a pronounced sigh. "All right. Let me put some pants on."

Several minutes later the elevator doors at the back of the lobby opened and a rumpled man with a wispy comb-over, dressed a wrinkled t-shirt and stained blue work pants, shuffled towards the front door. Quinn stood with his hand on the door handle, waiting.

The skinny man rubbed at the white stubble on his slack face as he took long, obvious looks at the badge on Quinn's belt and the pistol on his hip. He took his hand off his face and pointed at the badge. "How do I know that's real?"

The eighth of an ounce of patience that Quinn desperately clung to broke apart like an iceberg in warm water. "Open this fucking door," he shouted. "Before I break it down and arrest you for being an asshole!"

The old man jumped, then reached out a shaking hand and pushed down the latch on the door. Quinn felt mildly guilty for yelling at the wizened man, but did not have time to play silly bastard with him.

"Do you have a master key for all the suites?" he asked the manager, who had backed away, fearfully.

"I do," the man said, his voice cracking slightly. "What suite do you want to get into?"

"The one that belonged to Patrick Green."

The old man looked less intimidated and rubbed at his chin again. "You mean the one that belonged to the dead kid?"

The man's nonchalance about Patrick sent a hot, vibrating flare through the centre of Quinn and he had to take in a deep, shuddering breath to bring his temper in check. "Yes," he said through his stiff jaw. "That is the one."

The old man shrugged and walked towards the elevators. "All the other cops have come and gone from there already, so I don't know what you want with it, but I'll let you in if it suits you."

"Thank you," Quinn said, as he thought that pushing this man down a steep staircase might suit him. He shook his head as he looked at the old man's back and thought his awful thoughts. It was not this man he was angry at, or who deserved his fury, it was someone else. It was the someone who killed Patrick who was going to be on the receiving end of Quinn's wrath.

When it came it would be awful.

They entered the elevator and the old man pushed the button for the fourth floor. They rode in silence, the old man sneaking glances at Quinn, while Quinn did his best to focus on the job before him and not the anger associated with it. He needed a clear head when he stepped into Patrick's apartment.

Now that he truly believed someone had murdered Patrick, he had a whole new perspective on the inquiry; a perspective that no one had possessed at any point during the investigation. It would have been obvious to the initial investigators that Patrick had hung himself. The reports said the apartment was secure, there was no sign of forced entry and no reason to believe anyone else had been there. There had been no sign of restraint or trauma – other than the apparently self-inflicted wounds – to Patrick's body, and no indication he had fought or struggled with anyone.

Now, after his discovery, Quinn would be looking at this

from a different angle, and he hoped he would find something he could use to prove Patrick was murdered.

The elevator doors opened and Quinn followed the old manager into the hallway. The man shuffled at an infuriatingly slow pace, while he took a heavy ring of keys from a clip on his pants and began sorting through them. As they reached the door to Patrick's apartment, the old man selected a key and unlocked the door.

The old man twisted the knob and shoved the door inward. Quinn felt a small breeze stir across his face. It felt like a set of humid, rotten fingers caressing his skin. He bunched his shoulders as a small shiver darted up his spine, and took in a deep breath as he prepared himself to step inside with his eyes and his mind open.

In the moment Quinn spent gathering his focus about him, the manager stepped into the apartment, one hand making a gesture of dismissal while the other hand flicked on the entry-way light switch. "Like I told you before," he said. "There's been a dozen cops in and out of here already, so I don't know what—"

On the old man's second step Quinn leaned forward and grabbed the skinny arm making the dismissive gesture. He yanked the old man back through the door and into the hallway. The manager gave a startled little yelp as Quinn nearly pulled him off his feet, and then cringed as Quinn pushed him to arm's length and stood in front of the doorway.

"I'll be fine from here," Quinn said, letting a healthy dose of menace creep into his voice. "That will be all. Thank you."

The old man rubbed his arm and looked at Quinn with a wounded expression. He opened his mouth to say something, took in the look on Quinn's face and closed his mouth with a click. He nodded, then turned and walked down the hallway.

Once he was sure the manager was gone, Quinn turned and stepped through the open door of Patrick's apartment.

Though he had been there already that day, the small dwelling looked completely different to Quinn. The feeling of the place had taken a shift. It was no longer a morgue where

Quinn had come to mourn the dead. It was now an arena where he was taking swings at Patrick's unseen killer. Somewhere in these lonesome walls Quinn would find something to prove what he knew in his core; that Patrick Green had not taken his own life, but had it taken from him.

Quinn carefully checked the closet immediately inside the door and found a few coats and pairs of shoes, but nothing that would indicate that anyone else had ever been there. He moved from there and into Patrick's small bedroom. He looked beneath the bed, under the mattress and in the drawers of the nightstand. He found nothing except dust and a couple of DVD's Patrick would likely not want his mother to find. Quinn searched the dresser drawers, carefully examining each piece of clothing, checking to see if there was anything that was an odd size and would not have belonged to Patrick. Finally, he checked the small closet, rummaging through the footlocker in the back and flipping through the garments suspended from the wire hangers. Still nothing.

His phone buzzed in his pocket, but he ignored it, cursing at the interruption.

Panic and frustration began play on Quinn. His mouth dry, he could hear his own heartbeat in his ears. The space between his shoulder blades began to tingle, as though Patrick's ghost were in the room staring at him, bearing witness to his failure. *There had to be something here*, Quinn thought as he flipped through the garments in the closet a little quicker, his hands starting to shake.

Once he had gone through everything twice, he moved from the bedroom and into the small kitchen. The reek in the narrow space had gotten worse over the course of the day. Quinn felt a surge of annoyance; a bitter sensation that made the big muscles in his back quiver. Couldn't the lazy fucks who investigated this scene the first time have taken out the garbage? Shouldn't they have realised that Patrick was left handed and noticed he gripped the scalpel in the wrong hand? Didn't they give a fuck?

The annoyance burned away beneath a hot flare of anger.

Quinn roared and slammed his fists against the front of the refrigerator, giving voice and body to his rage. The appliance rocked and crashed against the wall, and the whole room rattled. Quinn lowered his hands and looked at the twin dents he had left in the top door of the thing. He stepped back and rubbed hand across his forehead, wiping away a bead of sweat. He was starting to lose it and had to bring his focus back so he would not skip over anything in haste.

He closed his eyes and shut his mind to the thump of his own pulse and the muffled, angry voices of the occupants in the suite below him. He pushed away the imagined figure of Patrick's ghost, and pushed off the horrid weight of the young man's coffin. A few moments of clarity, of reason, were all he needed, and he knew he would find what he sought.

When he opened his eyes again his breathing was even and the red mist that had obscured his vision was gone. He stood in the kitchen, carefully looked around him, and decided there would not be anything there he had not seen before. He turned to his right, into the living room, where Patrick Green had died.

He walked slowly into the room, feeling the transition from the hard linoleum of the kitchen to the soft carpeting of the living room under his boots. He tried to open himself, to spread his senses wide, to take in everything that was in the room. Now that Clara was not there, with her impatient stare and regardless manner, it was easier.

Sliding his feet forward, Quinn moved deeper into the room, skirting the blood stain on the floor and moving around the perimeter - as much as the furniture would allow – and studied the spot where Patrick had died, from all angles. He turned away from the stain and checked behind and under the couches. He lifted the seat cushions, dug his hands down the small crevices, and came up with nothing but lint and some crumbs.

The last place he had to look now, the only thing left, was where Patrick had died. Quinn took the few steps needed to reach the blood stain. He looked up at the broken light fixture, then down at the round, broad stain of blood. He circled it, like a dog circling an enemy, but saw nothing to indicate it was anything other than what it was. He got down on his hands and knees and peered at it closely. There were no drag marks and no foot-prints that looked like they'd been made when the blood was fresh and Patrick was still hanging there. He did not find anything.

Nothing.

Quinn sat back, kneeling before the blood stain, hands on his thighs. There was nothing here for him to find, not with his own eyes and street cop's experience, anyway. He suddenly felt as though he were in over his head, and that he was drowning in this task and should have been given to a better man; someone who knew this kind of work and would see the problem from angles Quinn could not even fathom.

As he sat, staring down at the blood stain that had revealed nothing, Quinn could feel Patrick's ghost creeping down the hallway, staring at him. There was blame in the spectre's stare.

Quinn raised his head and fought the tingling in his nose and eyes that were the prequels to the tears that wanted to run down his face. As he raised his head, he saw a familiar book spine on the small shelf behind where Patrick had hanged himself – or been hanged – and Quinn got to his feet.

Carefully avoiding the round stain, Quinn moved to the bookcase and took a book off the shelf. *The Hagakure.* The book Quinn had given Patrick, the same volume that contained three characters Quinn had seen in the pictures of Patrick.

Why did those characters appear in Patrick's skin? If the boy really had killed himself would he have remembered the characters, but put them out of order? Would he have looked down at himself and carved those characters, which would be correct from his viewpoint, but upside down to everyone else? What did the boy take from reading this book that made him remember those three symbols at such a time? Quinn flipped through the first few pages, reading the short, powerful passages, as confusion warred in his mind with a hot, burbling anger.

Had he been looking for a wrong so hard that he had jumped on the first thing he had seen that was out of place and called it murder. Was he making too much of a leap in thinking Patrick must have been murdered if he was holding the scalpel in his off hand? He shook his head as he flipped through the pages, hoping to find answers to his questions in the wisdom of long dead warriors, but he found nothing. As always, more nothing.

As he flipped through the book, Quinn found the page with the three symbols for 'Bushido', the three characters on Patrick's stomach. It was a photograph of a painting done by a long dead samurai. Quinn traced the letters with his fingers, the lines familiar. He wondered, hopelessly, if remembering these symbols brought Patrick strength in his final moments. He was about to let the book snap closed, when he noticed something on the bottom of the page, in close to the spine, where you would have to open the book wide to see it.

Quinn felt heat build in his chest as he stepped away from the bookshelf and into the light cast by the fluorescent bulbs in the kitchen. He opened the book as wide as it would go, the spine cracking audibly, and held it up to the light.

There, on the page, in the rusty colour of dried blood, was a single fingerprint.

Quinn strode quickly from the apartment, head down, scanning the rest of the pages in the book. He had tucked *The Hagakure* under his arm and flipped through several of the other books on the shelves, but had not found anything else. Really, he thought, he didn't need anything else as long as he had that one print.

He shuffled around the possibilities as he walked, playing them through his mind like pieces on a game board. Right now, Quinn was gambling that Patrick would not have needed to consult the book to remember the symbols. It was a long bet, but it was the only one he had. The first thing he needed to do was to compare the fingerprint in the book with Patrick's own prints, to ensure he was not wrong and the print belonged to someone else.

Then the real work—the monumental task of figuring who the print actually belonged to—would begin.

He got into the old Pontiac and drove it, shuddering, back the way he had come less than an hour previously. The urgency he'd had while traveling to Patrick's apartment was nothing compared to what he felt as he drove back to the office with a piece of actual evidence on the passenger's seat beside him. He blasted through stoplights, hardly slowing down, and took corners at speeds that threatened to rip the dilapidated car apart.

In a matter of minutes, he arrived at Cranbrook detachment and came to a stop in a four wheel drift in the centre of the parking lot. He got out, ran into the office and into the general duty pit.

Gerry Barnes and the two other members were still there, standing in a circle and talking animatedly.

"There you are," Gerry said when Quinn strode into the room. "What the fuck are you on about? What did you say when you left?"

"I said Patrick was left-handed," Quinn said, looking around. "Where are the member's personal files kept?"

"Over there," one of the other members said, pointing to a closed door in the hallway.

"What?" Gerry asked, turning slightly to cast a glare at the member who had spoken. "Never mind that. What are you talking about?"

Quinn ignored him and walked over to the closed door. Gerry hurried to intercept him and stepped in front of him, blocking Quinn's access to the door.

"Get out of my way," Quinn said, dropping his chin slightly.

"Fuck that," Gerry said. He poked one finger into Quinn's chest. "You're gonna answer me first, asshole."

Quinn sighed in resignation. He really did not have time

for this.

Gerry opened his mouth to speak, but his words turned into an inarticulate yell when Quinn reached up, grabbed the back of Gerry's hand, turned the palm towards him with a sudden twist, and pushed hard. Gerry tumbled backwards, his free arm pin-wheeling as Quinn shoved against his wrist. Gerry hit the ground, the air whooshing out of him from the force of the impact. Quinn stepped forward and tried to turn the doorknob, but it was locked.

"Where's the key for this room?" he asked the two other members, who stared at him, their mouths in round 'O's' of shock. "I said, where is the fucking key for this room?" he shouted when they did not respond. The two men both took hasty steps backwards.

"Call the inspector," Gerry croaked from the floor, while he struggled to stand up and find the breath that had deserted him.

"Ah, fuck it," Quinn said, as he turned and kicked in the door.

The knob and latch blew apart on the first kick and the door banged open. Quinn stepped into the small room, not much more than a closet, and groped about beside the door until he found a light switch. Over his head, a pair of fluorescent tube lights flickered to brightness and showed a tall bank of file cabinets down the left hand wall. The drawer of each cabinet had a name tucked into the card slot on the front, and it only took a moment for Quinn to find the one that said 'Green, Patrick.'

Quinn pulled open the drawer. There was only a single file folder in the drawer, which stood to reason as Patrick had only been in Cranbrook for six months and would not have built up much paper in his personnel file. Quinn pulled the folder from the drawer and laid it on top of the chest-high filing cabinets. He opened the cover and flipped through the contents— Patrick's performance records from Depot, his recruit field training assessments, his emergency contact information— until he found what he was looking for: the green fingerprint form that every member had to submit, with a set of Patrick's prints on it.

Opening the book and cracking the spine, Quinn laid the *Hagakure* on the filing cabinet so he could see the bloody fingerprint. He looked at the print closely and then looked at the set of prints provided by Patrick. He checked each digit on the form and compared it to the print in the book. He was no expert, but there was no fucking way any of them matched.

He experienced a sick sort of excitement, but tamped it down. The job was not done yet. He had to eliminate anyone else who had been in Patrick's apartment during the investigation; anyone who might have come in contact with Patrick's blood after he was dead and then picked up the book. If that had happened it would prove nothing more than sloppy police work, and Quinn would be back where he was when he arrived. Which was no place at all.

He went back out to the desk where he had left the investigational file. The other three members who had been there when he went into the file room were gone. Quinn was alone. He had to operate under the assumption that they had gone to get some back up and there would be a large body of angry men coming to the detachment to kick his ass. He had to work quickly.

He grabbed a blank note pad off a desk and rifled through the file box until he found a file folder with a label that said 'notes.' Every member who was part of the investigation, from the guys who did scene security to the primary investigators, would be required to submit a copy of their notes. Quinn flipped through the pages in the folder and wrote down the name of every cop he found there. When he was done, he had nine names on his list.

He searched around the general duty pit until he found a hand held magnifying glass, and then went back into the file room. One by one, he pulled the files of all the members on his list and compared their prints to the one in *The Hagakure*. He used the magnifying glass to make the job easier. His conviction that he was on to something increased with each set of prints that did not match. He came to the last name on the list and opened the folder as a formality, certain that none of the prints would match.

He let out a scream of frustration as he checked the first print, the left thumb. It was a perfect match to the one in the book. The name at the top of the page was Clara Morgan.

How could she be so fucking careless? Quinn thought as he dropped the magnifying glass in the middle of the book, making the bloody fingerprint pop upwards as though it were mocking him with its presence. A sudden rage laid hold of Quinn and he spun, kicking the wall at the back of the room. His foot went through the drywall and he tore open a jagged hole the size of a garbage can lid when he pulled it out. That further increased his temper and he punched his hand through the wall, showering his face and head with a puff of drywall dust.

"Fuck!" he yelled. He thought about the slap he was going to give Clara for fucking up a crime scene.

That thought triggered another and Quinn stopped his raging to lay hold of the memory that skittered across the surface of his mind.

When he had gone to Patrick's apartment the first time, with Clara, she had told him she had not been into the apartment before and that other members had examined the scene. She had never been inside.

If she had not been inside the apartment, how did her bloody fingerprint come to be in this book?

A feeling, a dark, terrible, ugly feeling grabbed hold of Quinn and squeezed him until there was no breath left.

"Oh, dear God," he said to the dusty cabinets around him.

"Sullivan!" A shout came from down the hallway. It was quickly followed by the shape of Inspector Ferguson filling the doorway to the file room, the three other detachment members behind him. The inspector looked at the scattered papers, pieces of drywall and general carnage that Quinn had wrought and his mouth dropped open.

"Sir, I need to speak with you," Quinn said.

"What the fuck are you doing?" Ferguson shouted. If he had heard Quinn he gave no indication. "You assault my members and then destroy my detachment? You're under arrest."

"Ah, fuck," Quinn said as the inspector stepped into the file room.

Ferguson lunged at Quinn, trying to grab him. The other members, following their boss's lead, tried to crowd into the room as well. Fortunately, for Quinn, the room was too narrow to allow more than one of them in at a time. He grabbed hold of one of the inspector's reaching hands and yanked the lighter man toward him. The inspector stumbled forward and Quinn slipped his right arm under Ferguson's armpit and then reached around so he could grip the inspector's neck. Quinn squeezed hard. The inspector gurgled as his arm was sucked up against the side of his face and the carotid artery on one side of his neck was cut off.

"Listen to me!" Quinn shouted, his roar nearly deafening as it echoed in the small room. "I don't think Patrick killed himself. Something about this is all fucked up, and I can prove it."

The inspector was still struggling to get away and one of the members in the hallway had his pistol out and was pointing it at Quinn. He needed to plead his case quickly or he was going to get shot.

Keeping the inspector between him and the Mountie with his gun out, Quinn shoved back against the press of bodies and pushed the inspector's face to where *The Hagakure* lay open on the file cabinets.

"Look at the bottom of the page," Quinn yelled, raising his voice to be heard over the cacophony in the small room. "I found that book in Patrick's apartment." He saw the inspector's eyes move across the page and land on the fingerprint that was conveniently enlarged by the magnifying glass. Once Quinn was sure he had seen it, he dragged the inspector to the right and pushed him down again. "That is the fingerprint form for Clara Morgan. The left thumb matches the print in book. The blood hasn't been tested but I'd wager my left nut that it belonged to Patrick Green."

The inspector stilled in Quinn's grip and ceased fighting. He waved his free arm at the other members who slowly got the idea and backed up a little. They still had their guns out, all pointing at Quinn's forehead, but he did not think they would shoot him now. Slowly, Quinn released his grip on the inspector and stepped away.

Inspector Ferguson gave Quinn a glare that nearly scorched the five o'clock shadow off the younger man's face, then picked up the magnifying glass to carefully examine both the open book and the fingerprint form.

"Fuck me," the inspector said after several quiet seconds. "It's a match." He put the magnifying glass down and looked at Quinn. "Okay, what do you think this proves? That Clara fucked up the scene and handled the book while she had Patrick's blood on her hands? So, one of my members doesn't understand crime scene management. Write us up and go away."

Quinn shook his head. "No, that's not what I'm getting at. When Clara showed me Patrick's apartment this morning she said she'd *never* been in there before. That she hadn't gone when the file was first investigated. If she wasn't part of the team managing the scene, then how did her fingerprint appear in a dead kid's blood?"

The frown that was already on Ferguson's face deepened. "You must be mistaken," he said. "Where's the file?"

"On a desk in the pit," Quinn said, and pointed out the door.

Inspector Ferguson snatched the copy of the *Hagakure* off the filing cabinet and slipped it into his coat pocket as he turned and walked towards the file. Quinn tried to follow, but was blocked by the other three members, all of whom still had their pistols in their hands. Quinn did not think it would be a good idea to start another fight now, so he stood in the doorway to the file room while the inspector sat at the desk and looked through the file.

After a few minutes, Inspector Ferguson stood up. "The

prick's right," he said as he walked over and held up several pieces of paper. "These are Clara's notes, and they don't ever mention her going to the scene."

Quinn tried to step closer to the inspector, but the other members blocked him, so he satisfied himself with standing on his tip-toes and looking over their heads. "There is no way she could have handled that book previously, either. She told me she'd never been in Patrick's apartment, which I thought was kind of odd."

Gerry Barnes frowned. "Why is that odd?"

Quinn looked down at him. "Since they were friends, I'd assumed that she might have been in his apartment previously."

"They weren't friends," one of the other members said.

Quinn turned his head towards him. "What?"

"Clara hated Patrick," Gerry said. "She was always on about how he was a lazy piece of shit and only got through training because his dad was an inspector. Said she knew someone who'd met Patrick at Depot and told her he'd been a useless prick and was always yapping at people about who his old man was."

"Did Patrick seem like that when he got here?" Quinn asked.

"Well," Gerry said, his eyes moving around the faces of the men about him. "No, he didn't. He was just a quiet kid as far as I could tell. He did his job, and he seemed like a hard worker. Just a little weird. He'd pissed Clara off something fierce though. Every time he fucked up, she'd come and let us know about it."

"Inspector," Quinn said. "When Clara Morgan picked me up from the airport, she told me how close she and Patrick were, and then she cried."

Gerry looked at Inspector Ferguson. "What the fuck?"

A thunderhead was brewing above the inspector's eyes and he glanced down at Clara's notes. "Let him out, Gerry." The other members stepped back, and the inspector met Quinn's eye. "Okay, Sullivan. What else did you find?"

Stepping past the inspector, Quinn rummaged through the photographs littering the desk he'd been using, and grabbed the picture of Patrick hanging in his apartment. "The scalpel is in his right hand," Quinn said, holding the picture out and tapping it with his finger. "But Patrick was left handed. Right?"

Gerry nodded as he put his pistol back in its holster.

"So, why would he hold a scalpel in his right hand to carve himself?" Quinn asked.

The inspector took the picture from Quinn and examined it. His brow grew darker with every heartbeat. "How the fuck did we miss this?" he asked no one in particular.

Another thought struck Quinn. "Who was in charge of the file?"

The inspector looked up at him, his mouth crunching over to one side. "Initially, it was our senior plainclothes guy, a corporal, but when he had a look and it was ruled a suicide, it was passed off to one of the junior members to complete the final report."

"And who was that member?" Quinn asked.

"Clara," Gerry said, looking down at the picture of Patrick in the inspector's hand.

"I think I'm going to be ill," one of the other members said, turning away, his hand over his mouth.

"This cannot be," Ferguson said. "I cannot believe that one of my members killed another."

Quinn believed just that. He did not know why, but everything he had seen was coming together and pointing at Clara Morgan as Patrick's killer. It was her who gave Patrick a hard time at work and made his life miserable. It was her who had turned all of Patrick's coworkers against him. It was her who was in his apartment and carved him with random symbols, some of which she took from Patrick's own books, and it was her who hung him up and left him to die.

A sick feeling punched at Quinn's stomach as he remembered his first visit to Patrick's apartment. When he had stood in the spot where Patrick had hung and tried to imagine what the boy's last sights had been like. He had been furious when Clara Morgan stood in front of him and spoiled his feeling.

Now, he realised, Clara was likely the last sight Patrick had seen.

"Even if she didn't kill him," Quinn said to the inspector, "then at the very least she knows more than she is telling. There is something very fucked up here and we need to sort it out."

Inspector Ferguson nodded. "You're fucking right we do." He turned back to the table where the file lay and set the picture of Patrick on the pile of others. "Gerry, you come with me. We're gonna go talk to Clara."

"I need to be in on this," Quinn said, stepping forward into the inspector's space. "This is my investigation. I found this stuff. I need to be there." He looked over at Gerry and back to the inspector. "Besides, Patrick was my friend, and I'm not gonna let him down twice."

Quinn held his breath while the inspector studied his face, grey eyes narrow as he searched Quinn's. "Okay," he said after a few moments. "You're in and you ride with me."

CHAPTER 15

The inspector walked down the hall to his office and came out a minute later wearing his pistol on his hip.

"You two hold the fort down 'till we get back," he said to the two other members. They had distinctly confused, somewhat worried expressions on their faces.

Quinn followed the inspector out the back door of the detachment to his work vehicle, a grey Ford Escape, and got in the passenger side. Gerry hurried out behind them and climbed into a fully marked Ford Crown Victoria patrol car, the springs of the car squeaking in protest as the heavy man threw his bulk in.

"Do you know where her place is?" Quinn asked as the inspector drove out of the parking lot and made a right hand turn.

"I do," Ferguson said. "Whenever a member gets a new place I make a point of taking them a gift, so I know where they live in case I need to find them for something."

Sneaky bastard, Quinn thought, even though it was a really good idea.

"What are we going to do when we get there?" Quinn asked. His first instinct would be to kick down the door and arrest Clara, but he would freely admit that his style was a little blunt.

"I'm going to show her this," the inspector said and pulled *The Hagakure* out of his pocket. "And I'm going to ask her how her bloody fingerprint came to be inside." He looked over at Quinn. "Then I'm going to hear her out and make a decision after that."

He was not sure how big a fan he was of the whole 'hear her out' part of the inspector's plan, but Quinn did not think it would be wise to argue with a man who only just recently decided he was not an asshole. No, that was not accurate. The inspector might still think he was an asshole, but he was now a believable asshole.

The inspector drove down several residential streets into a relatively affluent neighbourhood and came to stop in front of a single story house with a tightly manicured lawn.

"This is it," Inspector Ferguson said as he put the Ford into park, then pointed a finger at Quinn. "You let me do the talking. You keep your mouth shut unless I ask you something. This is one of my people and I'll get to the bottom of this. Do you understand me, Corporal?"

Quinn wanted, horribly, to point out that the file had lain dormant and fucked up until he had come and looked into it, but once again decided he had like to keep some credibility with the inspector until this matter was sorted out. He kept his mouth shut and nodded.

"Good," Ferguson said and opened his door.

Stepping out onto the street, Quinn saw Gerry bring his vehicle to a sharp stop behind Ferguson's Ford with a squeak of the police car's tires. Gerry climbed out and walked over to them, brisk for a man so portly, and joined the inspector as Ferguson crossed the lawn to the front door.

The house had a broad front porch, complete with a swing and a welcome mat. Following behind the inspector and the heavy constable, Quinn checked the front windows but saw no movement and no light. It did not look like anyone was home. The place was still as a grave.

The inspector rang the doorbell twice then pounded on the door with the bottom of his fist. "Clara," he yelled. "Clara, it's Dan Ferguson. I need to talk to you. Now."

There was no answer from inside.

Quinn looked at the driveway. The Nissan Clara had been driving sat there, the light from the nearest street lamp reflecting in orange circles off the hood.

"I don't think she's home," Gerry Barnes said, stepping off the porch to peer in the living room window. "Where would she be at this time of night?"

"Wait," the inspector said, holding up a hand. "Do you smell that?"

Quinn looked at the inspector, and then took a deep breath in through his nose. Nothing. He did it again, and got a whiff, a small one, of what the inspector was talking about. The smell of rot, of decaying flesh, was in the air, and it came from the house in front of them.

"We need to go in there," Quinn said.

"Yes, we do," Ferguson said and drew his pistol and pulled a small flashlight from his pocket. Quinn and Gerry both followed suit. The inspector stepped to one side of the door and nodded at it. "Kick it, Sullivan. I'll be first through."

Quinn nodded and kicked the door as hard as he could.

The wooden door crashed backwards into the wall of an open foyer so hard the window in the centre of it broke. The stink that had tickled Quinn's nose while he was on the porch, bashed him in the face like a brick in a tube sock once the door was open. He had to open his mouth to avoid breathing through his nose as he followed the inspector in the open door, Gerry Barnes at his back.

Inspector Ferguson swept right into an open living room. Quinn stopped, watching a broad hallway in front of him that looked like it led into a kitchen and a narrower hallway on his left where he could see rows of doors. He struggled to concentrate while he watched the hallway, but the smell in the house distracted him. He had been into some reeking houses, with some extremely putrid dead bodies, but they were nothing compared to this.

"Clear," the inspector said once he had searched behind

the furniture. He came back towards Quinn and slipped in behind him, then squeezed his shoulder to let Quinn know he was ready. He had done this before and was no slouch at it.

"Clearing forward," Quinn said. He stepped into the broad hallway in front of him. He did not have to look back to know the inspector would have moved up and would be watching the narrow hallway.

The broad hallway led into a dining room area, with a kitchen on the right and a wide family room area on the left. Quinn cleared the kitchen with a glance, and then moved into the family room and looked behind the couch and T.V. stand. "Clear," he shouted, when he did not find anyone.

"Go, Gerry," Inspector Ferguson said once Quinn had spoken. He heard the sound of doors opening down the narrower hallway. He walked out of the living room and took up position at the end of the hallway to see the inspector going into one room while Gerry came out of another. Gerry waited a moment until the inspector came out of the room, looked up and down the hallway. He shook his head.

Gerry nodded and moved into the last room at the end of the hallway. Inspector Ferguson lowered his pistol and relaxed his posture as he looked down the hallway at Quinn.

"There's nothing here," Ferguson said as he holstered his pistol.

Quinn heard the sound of a shower curtain behind drawn back and then a surprised yell from the last room at the end of the hall. "Holy fuck!" Gerry shouted.

Inspector Ferguson ripped his pistol from his hip and Quinn lunged the few steps down the hall. Both men slammed into the room, nearly knocking each other over in their haste to get inside. Quinn saw Gerry standing beside the bathtub, his hand clamped over his mouth as he stared downwards, his flashlight on the floor and his pistol hanging limp in his other hand. The stench was doubly thick in the tiny room and Quinn feared what he would see once he moved past Gerry's bulk.

Inspector Ferguson reached behind the open door and

flicked on a light. Quinn steeled himself and stepped forward.

In the bathtub, its wrists and ankles shackled to eye-bolts embedded in the wall, was a rotting corpse. The outer extremities were hard and mummified, but the centre of it was still wetly bloated. Maggots writhed in the sockets where the eyes used to be and Quinn noticed a buzz in the air as flies swirled above the body. The skin of the thing was black with decay, but the hair on the twisted head was a fine, pale blonde.

"Dear God," Inspector Ferguson said, his words muffled by the hand over his mouth. "Clara."

The body had been deceased for several weeks, Quinn estimated by the sight of it.

"If that is Clara," Gerry said, speaking Quinn's thoughts aloud. "Who have we been working with?"

"I thought you'd never come, Guardian," a voice said from behind them. It was a tone and timbre Quinn recognized. Two years ago he had heard the same imitation of a tortured cat in the basement of a run-down house in Resolution Cove.

A heat bloomed in the centre of Quinn's lower back, as though someone had laid a hot skillet against his skin. "Ah, fuck," Quinn said.

Slowly, Quinn turned. Behind him, filling the doorway, was something that bore a striking resemblance to the Clara Morgan who had picked him up from the airport. Only the thing in front of him was not the same. The creature was several inches taller and its broad shoulders nearly touched each side of the door jamb. Where slender limbs previously existed, hard, bulging muscles rolled beneath grey-tinged skin and covered arms that were disproportionately long. When the thing moved into the light, Quinn looked at the face and recoiled. It looked like something had peeled Clara Morgan's face off her skull pulled it on over the head of an animal.

As they watched, the face rippled and the nose and mouth elongated with a wet popping sound. The shoulders swelled even further and the arms lengthened with a crunch of expanding cartilage.

"So much work," the thing hissed, as it rolled its shoulders and flexed its hands. "So much planning to get you here. I feared you'd not come."

The thing wearing Clara's face looked at the two horrified men crammed into the bathroom with Quinn. Gerry struggled to move backwards, the heels of his boots clanging into the side of the bathtub, while Inspector Ferguson stood, staring in limp horror.

"You've brought friends," the thing said and smiled, producing a mouth full of jagged teeth, some human and others reptilian. As it smiled, its eyes glowed a horrible red.

'So much work to get you here,' the thing had said. This was all a plan, a scheme to get him to Cranbrook. Patrick had been targeted, used as bait to lure Quinn to the site of his death. The thing had concealed itself here, replacing Clara so that it could carefully work away at Patrick, ruining the young man's confidence and belief in himself until, ultimately, it killed him.

Quinn had been tricked. He had been played. There was only one reason he could think of: to get him away from Resolution.

Without a word he raised his pistol and started shooting.

The blast from the pistol was deafening in the small space, but Quinn had no care for the noise. A stinging, breathless anger gripped him and all his senses were blanketed with a red mist of fury. He could barely hear the report of the gun in his hand through the steady drone of his hate.

The creature threw up its elongated arms in front of its face and stepped backwards, out of the bathroom. Dark gouts of blood sprayed from the puckered wounds where the bullets punched into its massive body.

When Quinn's gun locked open, empty, Inspector Ferguson stepped forward, in front of Quinn, and started shooting. Behind them, Gerry Barnes dropped his pistol in the bathtub with a clang and tried to pry open the small square window above the rotting corpse.

Quinn reloaded from the single magazine on his belt and racked the action of his gun with a practiced motion. He stepped forward, just off the inspector's right elbow, and started firing again. The demon, still wearing a distorted mask made from Clara Morgan's face, reeled backwards, screaming in pain as its clawed hands scraped at the air in front of it.

With a click, Quinn's pistol went dry and locked open at the same time as the inspector's gun. Ferguson slapped his hand on his belt and around his waist, looking for another magazine but failing to find it.

"Gerry!" Ferguson shouted, his voice high with panic. "What are you doing? Shoot it!" Gerry carried on as though he had not heard him, clawing at the pebbled window while a high, keening whine leaked from his throat. The inspector yelled in frustration and lunged for Gerry's belt, trying to pull loose the pistol magazines there. Still, Gerry ignored him and trampled the corpse of the real Clara Morgan, his boots squelching in the putrid flesh.

Quinn looked down at the empty pistol in his hand and up at the demon. The creature, realizing the barrage of bullets had stopped, lowered its arms and glared at Quinn, who met its red stare evenly. This thing had cost him and the people he considered family much in the last week, and he did not even know why. He could not let this thing stand.

He dropped the pistol on the ground. This was not a fight for firearms. Slowly, his eyes never leaving those of the demon, he reached beneath his shirt and drew Donnell's dagger.

The dagger pulsed with a bright, vivid white light, the heat of it searing Quinn's hand. He ignored the pain and held the dagger in front of him, bathing the room, the hallway and the demon in the harsh light.

"Come, then," the thing said. It waved him forward with one hand, black blood dripping from the clawed fingers. "Come on and bring that sliver with you. Let us see what you can do with it, Guardian." The thing grinned, Clara Morgan's lips splitting over jagged teeth.

Roaring out his hate, Quinn launched himself forward and slammed into the demon. He felt clawed hands grasp and scrape at him, but the pain was muted by the blanket of anger that lay over him. He pushed and churned with his legs, and used his momentum to force the bigger body of the demon down the hallway and into the living room. As he pushed, he stabbed with the dagger, his arm pistoning back and forth, ramming the searing blade into the misshapen body. With each fall of the blade, a small squirt of flame jumped from the wound. Quinn could smell charred flesh below the stench of rot.

In the broader expanse living room, Quinn shoved the demon away from him and faced his opponent across the open space. The demon staggered away, its hand held to its side where Quinn had stabbed it. It lifted its hand from the wound and looked at the black blood on its palm. It smiled at Quinn with jagged teeth and ran its tongue over slick fingers.

If the demon was trying to intimidate him, it failed. Quinn gave a grin of his own, his face so tight it felt as though it might crack. "Come on, then," he said, using the demon's own words. "Come on," he screamed so loud his voice cracked. "Come on and die!"

The Demon lunged towards him, its right arm streaking out. Quinn slipped forward smoothly and ducked under the swinging arm. He struck once with the dagger, low, slashing across a meaty thigh, then again, higher, ripping a gaping wound in the thing's back. The demon turned, staggering to maintain its balance as black blood ran in streaming bands down its twisted body. Its red eyes were wide, and less vivid than before.

Quinn grinned all the harder. The demon was afraid.

He went on the attack now, feinting left then right, then lunging straight forward, ramming the dagger into the heavy body. The demon roared in agony and flailed uselessly with its arms as Quinn jabbed the dagger inwards and then ripped it down. Yanking the dagger clear of the gnarled body, he grabbed the back of the thing's head and pulled it forward while driving the dagger upwards into its neck. The thing gurgled and hot blood blasted against Quinn's arm. Sawing furiously, Quinn dragged the glowing blade through the neck, severing bone and tissue, until he grabbed a handful of stained, blonde hair and ripped the head free.

The torn body slumped forward against Quinn's legs as he lifted the head and looked into its dead face. He yelled, staring into the vacant eyes of the demon, screaming until he thought his throat would rip apart. When he ran out of breath he flung the head away into a far corner of the room.

He stood, his chest heaving while his throat burned, looking down at the ragged, torn body of the demon. As he stared, it began to shrivel. The arms shortened and the joints shrank with wet, popping sounds. The muscles deflated and the skin on the body started to hang, slack and loose. After a few moments, the body that lay before Quinn was well diminished, smaller even than it had been when the demon wore the guise of Clara Morgan.

As the demon shrank, so did Quinn's fury. The red mist that had clouded his vision began to fade and his heartbeat slowed. With the demon's death, the dagger's light faded and the handle grew cool in his grip.

"What the fuck was that?"

Quinn looked over to the hallway, to see Inspector Ferguson, pistol in hand, looking at the shriveled corpse. His gun hand was shaking slightly.

"Where's Gerry?" Quinn asked.

The inspector gestured back down the hallway without taking his eyes off the body at Quinn's feet. "He's still in the bathroom." Ferguson moved out of the hallway and came to stand beside Quinn, the pistol in his hand still pointed, shaking, at the demon's limp form. "I asked you, what is that thing, Sullivan? What just happened here?"

"It's going to be hard to explain," Quinn said. "But I'll make it simple. That," he pointed at the body, "is a demon. Just like from fairy tales and ghost stories you heard when you were a kid. Where it came from, I'm not sure, but it assumed the identity of your member and killed Patrick."

Ferguson stood, trembling, his legs shaking so hard Quinn could hear the keys in his pocket jangling. The pistol in his hand never lowered, but the muzzle danced in time to the quaking of his body. Fearing the inspector would accidentally shoot him, Quinn stepped forward and gripped the older man's gun with a hand that was black with the demon's blood.

The inspector stared at the demon, his eyes locked onto its shrunken form, until Quinn moved into his field of vision and pulled the pistol from his grip. Ferguson's eyes flickered down to his now-empty hand, then up at Quinn's face.

"It can't be," Ferguson croaked. "It can't be what you say."

"It is, sir," Quinn said.

The inspector's shaking legs finally gave way and Quinn had to sling an arm around him and guide him towards the couch on the other side of the room to prevent him from falling on his face. Once Quinn released him, Ferguson sat, with his elbows on his knees and his head hanging down for several moments, saying nothing. Only able to guess at what thoughts were spinning through the other man's head, Quinn stood silent and waited.

"Why is it here?" Ferguson asked, finally, raising his head to look at Quinn. "Why would it want to kill Patrick?"

Quinn looked down at the body. "It said it was planning to get me here. It killed Patrick and carved him up in strange symbols, knowing I would come. And I think it did it to get me away from Resolution."

The inspector rubbed his hand over his pale, sweating face. "I don't understand any of this," he said, his voice strained, on the point of cracking. "Why would it want to get you away from Resolution?"

He had a decision to make, Quinn thought. He had to decide how much he could trust the man in front of him. He looked down at the body again and figured the inspector had already seen him stab a creature that wore the faces of other people and shrank when it died, so they were not going to get much closer than they were at that moment.

"I've seen something like this before," Quinn said.

"There are more of these things?"

Quinn nodded. "Not exactly like this one, but yes. I don't

216

know the intricacies of it all, but these things live on another plane of existence, and they can push through into our reality. We had one show up in the basement of an ugly house in Resolution. Do you remember all the shootings we had there two years ago?"

The inspector met his eyes and nodded.

"It was because the thing that appeared in Resolution made people nuts. It nearly killed one of our members. I found it, with two other guys, in the basement of a house and killed it. With this." He held up the dagger.

"So why did it need to get you away from Resolution?" Ferguson asked.

"I don't know, and that scares me. These things think I'm special, that I'm some kind of Guardian that defends Resolution. If they wanted me gone, there has got to be a reason."

The inspector looked away from Quinn's face, and back at the shriveled body. "There's got to be an ugly fucking reason."

"And I need to get back there. Now." He looked at the inspector. "Can you help me?"

It was asking a lot, Quinn knew, to have the inspector process what had just happened. To have him believe and accept that a demon, a creature of fairytales and bad horror movies, had killed two of his members and in turn lay dead in his city.

Inspector Ferguson stood up, slowly, then turned away and ran both hands over his slicked back hair, sucking in a deep, audible breath. He paced for several moments. Quinn felt his chest grow cold with a chill anticipation, wondering if the inspector was going to lend a hand or slap him down.

"Do you think there is another one of these in Resolution?" Inspector Ferguson asked, pointing at the demon.

Quinn shrugged. "I don't know enough about this to say one way or another. The one I faced before was alone, but that doesn't mean this one is."

"Okay." Ferguson turned away, running a hand over his face, as he gradually reclaimed some of his colour. "I think I can help you out, there, but we have to sort this," he gestured to the demon, "out first."

"What do you have in mind?"

Ferguson stopped in the middle of the living room, looked around, then nodded. "You go get Gerry. I think I have a plan."

Quinn found Gerry still in the bathroom, sitting on the floor with his hands covering his face. The heavy man's boots were covered in reeking grime, and the desiccated body in the tub beside him had been churned into a mass of bone splinters and torn, rotting flesh.

Stopping to pick up his discarded pistol from the floor, Quinn knelt down and put a hand on Gerry's arm. The heavy man gave a muffled cry and jerked away from Quinn's touch, but looked from behind his palms. His eyes were red and puffy. Quinn saw that Gerry's fingernails were ragged and bloody from clawing at the window.

"Are you all right, Gerry?" Quinn asked, his voice low.

Gerry shook his head, his pallid cheeks shaking. "No. I'm not. That thing…it killed Clara. It *was* Clara…"

"It's gone, now." Quinn ran his hand over Gerry's quaking arm, noticed it was still black with the demon's blood, and tucked it behind him.

"What was it?" Gerry leaned forward, and looked down the hallway towards the living room.

Quinn didn't think it would be wise to attempt and explain to the traumatized man what the demon had actually been. Instead he put on his best reassuring smile. "It's gone."

Gerry looked down the hallway, up at Quinn's face, at the broken body in the tub, and then covered his face with his hands again.

They sat like that for several moments until Quinn heard a dull clunking in the hallway, Ferguson's hasty footsteps. The inspector shuffled into the bathroom, carrying a large, blue plastic container, about as big as the trunk of a mid-sized car, complete with a lid.

"What's that for?" Quinn asked as he stood.

Ferguson pointed at the corpse in the bathtub. "It's for her. I think I know how we can sort this out, but we have to take her with us."

"Clara is dead…" Gerry said from the floor.

"He's fucking cracked," Quinn said, looking down at the heavy man.

"Make no mistake, Sullivan," Ferguson said as he pushed the plastic container past Gerry's feet and against the side of the tub. "I'm only holding myself together on the thinnest of lines. If I see one more fucked up thing today, I'm gonna get down on the floor with him."

Quinn shook his head. "Okay. What are we doing?"

"We're moving quick. With all the gunshots we let off, I'm guessing we have another five minutes until every cop in Cranbrook is out of bed and on their way here. Five minutes after that, the fire department will be here." He pointed towards the bathroom sink. "Get yourself cleaned up."

"Wait," Quinn said, while he turned on the tap and started scrubbing his hands. "Why the fire department?"

"'Cause I am going to burn this house to the ground." He pulled a set of kitchen gloves out of his back pocket and pulled them on.

Before Quinn could ask any questions, the inspector pulled in a very deep breath, then leaned down into the tub and fit his hands under twisted mass of the corpse. With one motion he pulled the broken body over the side of the tub and into the plastic container. He stood up, turned away, sucked in another breath and went back for the bits that weren't attached.

Quinn thought the air in the small house couldn't get any fouler, but once the body was moved, he discovered he was wrong. He shook water from his hands, and then lifted his arm to cover his face.

Once the entirety of the body was in the container, Ferguson peeled off the kitchen gloves, dropped them inside the container and then fitted the lid snugly into place. He placed one hand in the middle of the lid, and sniffed loudly. "I know this sucks, Clara, but it's the best I can do."

"What do you mean; you're going to burn this house to the ground?" Quinn asked.

"It's the only way I can think to hold this place together, Sullivan." Ferguson began dragging the plastic container through the bathroom and into the hallway. "Anything else leaves too many questions that people are going to want answers to." He stood up from the container. "That's what you did in Resolution, wasn't it?"

Quinn remembered, vividly, the fire that had ripped through the broken-down house in Resolution. "It wasn't exactly intentional," he said. "But, yeah, the house burned down."

"Okay," the inspector said. "Here's what we do. We cannot let that thing," he jerked his thumb over his shoulder, "ruin the memory of either Clara Morgan or Patrick Green. If we try and report that a shape-changing devil was responsible for both deaths we'll lose all credibility and no one will believe us.

"We're going to bury Clara's real body and leave the other body here as the official remains. It won't be her, but no one needs to know that. We'll say that whoever killed Patrick also killed Clara, planting evidence of her involvement at the scene of Patrick's death. We'll have to live with people thinking there's a cop killer on the loose, but I'd rather have that than anyone thinking she did something wrong."

"I can live with that," Quinn said.

"Good." Ferguson took hold of the plastic container and continued dragging it down the hallway. "Get Gerry out of here. I'll take care of the rest."

Nodding, Quinn squatted down beside Gerry again. "We have to leave now," he said, as gently as he might if he were calming Shawn after a particularly bad nightmare.

Gerry looked at him, then past him down the hallway, and swallowed thickly. "The thing. Clara. Is it gone?"

"Yeah, Gerry," Quinn said. "It's gone. And now, so are we."

Quinn took hold of one of Gerry's meaty forearms, pulled it away from his body, and slung it around his own neck. With an effort that made his back creak, Quinn stood, hauling Gerry to his feet. Half dragging and half guiding the heavy man, Quinn made his way stumbling down the hallway.

As they reached the living room, Quinn realized that the house was filling with smoke. He looked into the kitchen and saw the inspector with a large, clear bottle, filled with white powder. A significant portion of the kitchen's back wall was already on fire. Wherever the inspector flung the white powder, a fresh gout of flame shot up. He dashed it on the walls, across the wooden floors and finally onto the body of the headless demon.

"What's that?" Quinn asked, as he began coughing through the smoke.

"Regular coffee whitener," the inspector said, also beginning to cough. "It burns like hell, and it'll be enough to get this place really going without smelling like gasoline." He pointed towards the door. "Okay, let's get out of here."

Still supporting Gerry, Quinn staggered to the front door and yanked it open. As he stepped out of the fetid air of the small house and into the blissfully clean air of the night, he could hear the distant screech of sirens. As Quinn looked around, he saw that almost all the nearby houses had lights on, a few with huddled shapes peeking through windows.

Behind him, Inspector Ferguson stooped through the doorway, hauling the plastic container. "Help me, Sullivan," he called over his shoulder.

The clean air seemed to pull Gerry out of his near catatonic state. He blinked and looked around, wiping a thick palm across his pale face.

"Gerry, can you stand?" Quinn asked. The heavy man gave no reply, but stood on his own and continued to wipe at his face and press the heels of his hands against his eyes.

Quinn turned back to where the inspector dragged the blue container across the lawn. Quinn picked up the opposite end and together they hustled their burden to the other side of Ferguson's grey Ford, opened the rear hatch and tucked the container inside.

"What are you going to do with her?" Quinn asked, as the inspector slammed the hatch.

"I'll find a place she can rest." Ferguson turned away from the truck and breathed deep through his nose, smoothing back his disheveled hair. "I'm the only one who will know she's there, but that's a load I'll just have to carry, isn't it?"

Unable to think of a suitable reply, Quinn nodded.

"Gerry," Ferguson said, stepping briskly across the lawn, apparently in control of himself. "Gerry, are you all right?"

The heavy man stopped rubbing his face and stared at Ferguson. "Yeah…all right." He glanced over his shoulder at the house. The structure was fully involved now, the fire arching through the roof vents and into the night sky. "Clara's dead."

"That's right, Gerry," Ferguson said. "But we're going to do right by her. When everyone else gets here, I'll do the talking. Does that sound okay?"

Gerry nodded and Ferguson turned towards Quinn. "You're right. He is fucking cracked." He reached into the pockets of the light coat he wore. "Oh, and you're probably gonna need these." He pulled his hand from his pocket and held out two loaded pistol magazines. Quinn glanced over at Gerry, whose magazine pouches were empty. Quinn accepted the offerings gratefully, drew his gun, reloaded it and shoved it back in the holster.

Moments later two marked RCMP patrol cars skidded to a stop in front Clara Mogan's house. A uniformed constable scrambled out of each vehicle, their pistols in hand.

"Inspector, there was a report of shots fired," one of the young constables, the same man who had been pointing his gun at Quinn earlier, said.

"Get on the radio," Ferguson said, his voice booming through the dark. "Call everyone. This shit has gone sideways."

If there was one thing Quinn could say for Dan Ferguson, it was that the man could talk. Within twenty minutes he had another handful of Mounties at the scene, the entirety of the Cranbrook Fire Department, as well as members of the local media, all eating out of the palm of his hand.

He sold them a story about how Quinn's investigation had revealed new evidence in Patrick Green's death, which had led them to a confrontation at Clara Morgan's house. It was discovered, the inspector said with a showman's flair, that an unknown third party had been responsible for Patrick's death, and had also killed Clara Morgan. Ferguson praised both Quinn and Gerry as heroes in the gun-fight that had ensued during the confrontation with Clara's and Patrick's murderer, but that the man—and here the inspector gave an innocuous description of a dark haired Caucasian male—had ultimately escaped and was still at large.

Quinn stood by with his hands clasped behind his back, nodding in all the appropriate places. Gerry Barnes stood on the Inspector's other side, watching the fire fighters battle the inferno that had once been Clara's house.

As the inspector finished the explanation required for them to get out of this mess, Quinn stepped away from the crowd and pulled his phone from his pocket.

"My office is going to be getting anonymous tips about dark haired men for months," Ferguson said after he was finished. "Have you made contact with any of your people in Resolution?"

Quinn shook his head. "I tried, but there was no answer on anyone's phone." He had tried Carrie, Raife and Dave, but received no answer anywhere, and it was starting to freak him out.

The inspector looked down at his watch. "It's after midnight. They're probably all sleeping."

Quinn nodded, wanting to believe what the inspector said, but not really buying it. "I need to get back there to check."

Ferguson nodded, and then beckoned the other two night-shift constables to him. He gave whispered directions, to one of the young men, pointing to Gerry—who was still watching the house burn—while he did it. The young constable nodded, then took Gerry's arm and steered him towards one of the patrols cars.

"Come on, Sullivan," Ferguson said as he walked briskly towards the driver's side of his grey Ford. "I've done all I can here. I gotta get you home."

As he followed, Quinn looked at the back of Gerry Barnes and wondered, even though Gerry had survived, had the evil that followed him to this small town claimed another victim.

After a brief stop at Quinn's hotel to change his clothes and pick up his bag, Inspector Ferguson drove him out of town and towards the airport. The Ford flew down the highway at a worrying speed and Quinn put his hand on the dash to steady himself as the inspector shoved the accelerator to the floor.

"I gotta get back to the scene so I can manage it," Ferguson said when he caught Quinn casting worried glances at him from the corner of his eye. "I gotta make this trip quick."

Quinn said nothing in response. He continued to grip the dashboard and hoped he did not die in a Ford hybrid, which would be terribly embarrassing.

They arrived at the airport very quickly. The gate was open but the parking lot was nearly deserted. No flights were scheduled at this hour of the night. The inspector drove past the terminal and onto a service road that lead away from the main body of the building. The service road passed several closed hangers and planes on the tarmac, and Quinn looked through the rear window as the terminal grew distant behind them.

"Where are we going?" he asked, facing forward again.

"I know a guy," the inspector said.

"Whenever I've heard someone say that, it has never turned out well," Quinn said.

"I know a guy who owes me a favour." Ferguson glanced over at him as the SUV screeched down the narrow road. "Don't worry."

"That phrase never leads to anything good either."

The inspector smirked and continued driving.

Near the end of the runways, out of view of the main terminal, the inspector stopped the Ford in front of a small hanger with a trailer beside it. "We're here," he said, as he put the Ford in park and got out. Quinn grabbed his bag from the back seat and followed the inspector towards the trailer that resembled a construction office.

"Jody!" the inspector yelled as he approached the trailer. "Jody, it's Dan Ferguson. Get out of bed."

There was no response from inside.

The inspector climbed the wooden steps and pounded on the door. "Jody, get up."

Quinn looked around, getting a little nervous and heard movement from inside the trailer.

"Who is it?" a voice grumbled from inside.

"It's Dan Ferguson, Jody," the inspector said. "Get up, we need to talk."

"About what?" the voice asked.

"You owe me, Jody," the inspector yelled at the trailer. "You owe me a solid and I'm calling it in."

There was silence inside the trailer for several seconds and then Quinn heard heavy footsteps. The door opened a crack and a frugal beam of light leaked out. "What do you want?" the voice asked.

"This is Quinn," the inspector said. "He needs a ride."

"A ride?" Jody asked, opening the door a little more to look at Quinn. He was a big man, with a shaggy blonde beard and unkempt hair. "A ride where?"

"To Resolution Cove," Ferguson said.

"Where the fuck is that?"

"Out on the coast."

"No, Ferguson. No fucking way." Jody closed his eyes and shook his shaggy head.

"Jody," Ferguson said, crossing his arms. "We had a deal. You owe me. I know what you've got sitting in this hanger and it's just what we need. You gotta do it."

Jody pulled open the door all the way, revealing wide,

heavy shoulders, and a hairy protruding gut above a pair of rumpled boxer shorts—the only article of clothing he was wearing. "C'mon, man. You know I can't do that. I'll get fucking fired."

"Jody," Ferguson said slowly, putting on a reasonable face. "If I tell your bosses what you were doing last month, you'll get fired, too. Help me out. You have a chance to get away with it. You don't help me, you're getting tossed for sure. What do you wanna do?"

The big man ran a grease stained hand through his shaggy hair. "You're an asshole, you know that? You people are like the fucking Mafia. You owe a favour once and you owe for life." He shifted from one foot to the other for a couple seconds, apparently thinking over his options. "Okay, fuck it," he said. "I'll do it if it'll get you off my back." He disappeared inside the trailer and Quinn heard a great deal of rummaging.

"What was that all about?" Quinn asked Ferguson when they were alone with the noise of Jody's grumbling.

"Jody owes me a favour. A big one."

"What kind of favour?"

Ferguson scratched his chin. "Jody works for a family that owns a number of high producing mines throughout the province. They have a summer home here and keep their private plane at this hanger. Jody is their airplane mechanic; one of the best in this part of the country, and a reasonably good pilot, too. About a month ago, Jody met a young lady in one of the bars in town and, in order to impress her, took her up in his boss's plane and flew her around long enough to saw a piece off.

"Jody's only problem, is one of the security guards for the airport called the detachment saying someone has taken off from the airport in an expensive-looking plane. I happen to be in the office that night. I came out here to see Jody pulling the plane back into the hangar and sending his new friend on her way. What he did wasn't technically illegal from a criminal standpoint, but if I talked to the right people he'd probably lose his pilot's licence, and he'd certainly lose his cushy job.

"In trade for my silence, he agreed to owe me a favour, and this is it."

Quinn decided that his previous assessment of the inspector as a sneaky bastard did not even scrape the surface. "What kind of plane is it?" he asked.

"A really fast one," Ferguson said.

Jody came out of the trailer a few minutes later, dressed in blue jeans and a grey t-shirt covered in grease stains, his wild hair stuffed under a Pittsburgh Penguins hat. He had a chart of some kind in his hand, as he walked briskly towards the doors to the hangar. "Come on," he said. "Show me where this fucking place is so we can get there."

Jody stood under a broad lamp that illuminated the outside of the hanger and unrolled the chart against the metal door. It was a map of the province, Quinn saw, and he pointed out where Resolution was. Then the shaggy man rolled up the chart again and, still grumbling, opened the hangar doors.

What Quinn saw inside left him open-mouthed. "What kind of plane is that?"

"It's a Cessna Citation Mustang," Jody said. "Where ever you need to go, it'll get you there quick."

"How long will it take us to get to Resolution?"

"Once we get into the air, about three hours, give or take." He looked at his watch. "It's about twelve-thirty now. We'll be there shortly after three." Jody connected an airplane tug to the front of plane and began pulling it from the hangar.

Quinn turned to Inspector Ferguson and held out his hand. "Thanks, I appreciate this."

Ferguson gripped his hand. "No, Sullivan. It's me who appreciates your help. If you hadn't come here and shown me something was wrong in my detachment, there is no telling what that thing would have done or how bad it would have gotten. I think we'd have to say I owe you one."

"This isn't about owing," Quinn said. "We were both there, we both saw what it was, and we both know what it did to Patrick and to Clara. The only people who are owed anything are them."

Ferguson nodded in agreement. "You're correct. We'll do right by them. I'm gonna make sure that everyone knows that Patrick didn't kill himself. We'll put the story out there, don't you worry."

"I won't."

Dan Ferguson looked at Quinn for a moment, then nodded and turned back to his truck. He got in, started the engine and very quickly sped back the way he had come.

As the tail lights faded in the dark, Quinn turned back to where Jody stowed the tug back in the hangar.

"You ready?" the hairy man asked as he stepped to the front of the plane, which was now clear of the hangar. He pulled open the door and a set of stairs lowered with a hydraulic hiss.

"Sure," Quinn said, as he walked towards him.

"So, why is it you need to get back to this place so fast?"

"I'm not sure," Quinn said, truthfully. "I'll find out when I get there."

CHAPTER 16

S till no answer," Raife said, as he looked at Dave and Sandy. He hit the 'end' button on his phone. "Why isn't he fucking answering?"

They stood in the parking lot of Resolution Detachment, gathered around the hood of Raife's truck, all of them still in uniform, all of them worried.

"Could he be busy with this review thing?" Dave asked. "Didn't he say he was going to try and finish it tonight so he could fly back tomorrow?"

Raife looked down at his watch. It was after ten PM and he had been trying to get a hold of Quinn for the last hour since he had dropped off Kord and Abby at Carrie's house. He needed to update the boy on what they had seen and what was happening, but Quinn would not answer his phone. "Okay," he said, glaring at his phone as though it could personally be blamed for Quinn's absence. "We can't stand here and do nothing. We gotta try and find this thing."

"How do you plan on going about that?" Sandy asked.

"We could get a really big box," Dave said. "Then get a stick and a length of rope. We'd just have to find something to bait the box—"

Raife cuffed him in the side of the head.

"Be serious, boy," Raife growled.

Dave rubbed his ear and put on a wounded expression. "I was being serious."

Raife wanted to hit him again, but did not think it would do any good. "I don't know, Sandy," he said, doing his best to ignore Dave. The man could be on fire and still crack jokes about it. "But we have to get out in front of this thing, before it eats anyone else or finds out where we've stashed that kid."

"What are we going to do if we do manage to find it?" Sandy asked.

"Yeah, Boss," Dave said, all levity gone from his voice. "You remember what it was like the last time. We put enough lead in that thing to use it as a pencil and it didn't go down until Quinn stabbed it with that glowing knife. I haven't checked recently, but I'm pretty sure those aren't standard RCMP issue."

That was a problem Raife had been considering carefully for the last several hours. He remembered the first demon they had faced that had nearly put an end to them all. The cuts and bruises from his most recent confrontation were still fresh and throbbing, along with the bite marks from the horribly changed dog he had encountered at Dean Springer's house the day before. Nothing he had done had put down either one of the creatures. It had come down to Quinn. Even Kord, with the glowing brass knuckles he produced, did not do much to slow the thing that was coming for them. "I wish I knew what it was about him that makes him so special in this..." he twirled his massive hand in the air. "This...fucking...thing."

"My mother always told me I was special," Dave said.

"We don't need short bus and hockey helmet special, Dave," Sandy told him and flicked his ear.

Dave laughed out loud and clapped a hand over his ear as his phone rang in the holder on his gun belt. "Hello, Dave here," he said when he pulled it out. He listened carefully, nodding as the jovial expression flew from his face as though it had been slapped off.

Raife felt a ball form and tighten in his gut. "What is it?" he asked when Dave hung up the phone.

"More bones," Dave said.

"Sweet Jesus," Sandy said, placing a hand on her forehead.

"Well, I shouldn't say that," Dave said.

"What should you say, then?" Raife asked.

"Well," Dave said. "Apparently someone heard screaming and came across one man eating another man. There is a great deal of freaking out about it, as we speak, and they've asked that we come down and help out."

"At least we know where to start looking," Raife said, walking around the hood of his truck and towards the driver's door.

Fire. If there was one thing he hated it was fire, and these people, these...*humans*...always brought fire. Fire in their hands. Fire from their guns. Fire in their old magic. It was always fire.

He crouched in the doorway of a dark building, beside a filthy alley. He rubbed at the puckered scars on his chest where the big man, the *Mountie*, had shot him with his guns, and the rippled marks where Kord McRae had bashed him with that fiery fist. It irked him that these common men could still cause him pain when they were so pitiful and useless in their short, trifling existence. They were only rough spots in the long road of his life. Soon he would wipe them smooth and leave them forgotten.

His mood was not helped by the interruption of his last meal. Being hungry made him feel old and he needed to feed to regain his strength. There were too many of these men, these Mounties, among the streets of this town tonight. He could not afford too much attention. The old wench who had stumbled across his last feeding had started caterwauling as though she was the one who had been shot and beaten with searing fire.

No wonder these humans were so weak: they were stupid.

He was sore and tired. He needed to feed again before finishing the task he had come to this place to complete. He had glimpsed the girl, the first time he had done so in more than two years of trailing her and her father. She was almost in his grasp. She would have been, if the big Mountie had not arrived at her hiding place moments previous to his own arrival.

Once he had the girl—and all those who tried to protect her were dead—there would be no end to the possibilities. He would, very quickly, turn this whole valley to a haven for his kind. From here they could go anywhere. He would walk from this place with an army at his back. He would bring this world to its knees. He would be transformed from a wanderer to a conqueror. He would be king.

He was getting too far ahead, he chided himself. The proper steps were laid out and must be followed. Deviation from his carefully crafted plans would spell disaster.

First of all, he must feed to regain his strength, but that was a job easily completed. He would be more careful this time and would not be interrupted. Then he must gather others to him. He could not leave anything to chance. He must have reinforcements for the next job that needed doing.

He could only assume the Guardian of this place would be dead by now. The ruse had worked and Quinn Sullivan was far away and would soon meet his end. His counterpart in the town near the mountains would find the Guardian distracted by his grief, to pull him apart and consume him.

Yes, everything was working out as planned. This time there would be no failure.

He stood from the stairs he had occupied for the last hour and stepped out of the doorway into the dark alley. He looked up and down, seeing an open street at one end and a wall at the other. He was about to start for the open street when he sensed movement in the corner by the brick wall.

He would not have to go far for a meal, he thought, as he stepped eagerly forward. He was disappointed when all he saw was a skinny mongrel dog, the slats of its ribs protruding through its mangy skin. He could not eat this. There was no power there. He started to turn away, when a wonderful idea came to him. Why should he wait to start gathering a force about him? It would not take so much power that he would not be able to hunt. He might as well start now.

He crouched down in the reeking wetness of the alley and wiggled his fingers at the dog. The beast lifted his scruffy ears and came forward willingly, sniffing the outstretched hand.

He stroked the grizzled head and looked into the animal's eyes, casting his will down into it. Beneath his hands the dog began to ripple and change. He grinned in satisfaction.

Soon, this conflict would be settled and he would have what he wanted. Very soon, indeed.

The long silences across the small kitchen table in Carrie's house were almost too much for Autumn to take, tapping her fingers nervously on the arborite surface. She and Carrie had come to a comfortable truce. The tension between them was minimal, but the strain increased dramatically when Raife dropped off Kord and Abby on Carrie's doorstep before fleeing into the night.

Raife had told Carrie that the thing that had been eating people, the thing that came to Autumn's shop looking for Kord and his daughter, was still hunting them. When Autumn thought about it too hard, about how close she had come to death at the hands of the creature, she felt bile creep up the back of her throat that threaten to choke her.

In the hours since Kord and Abby had arrived, there had been almost no discussion of why they were here. Carrie prepared food for them, turning out handmade dough and cooking pizza in her oven, sending Abby into the living room with Shawn to watch television. The Mountie, Gerritt, who Raife had left to guard them—although Autumn suspected that he was there to be watched as much as he was there to watch over them—sat on the couch with the children and laughed at the television as he shared their pizza.

Abby—who was absolutely fascinated by the movies Shawn was so accustomed to—showed very little evidence that anything was wrong in her life. She seemed to be, more or less, made of rubber. Kord, however, looked very worried.

It was obvious he had been in a fight that night, evidenced by his puffy face and slow movements, but he seemed reluctant to speak of it. He stared at the tabletop as he sipped the tea Carrie brought him and picked at a slice of pizza. Autumn was deeply curious by her very nature and had many questions for the slender man. Why was he running, and why did this demon want them so bad? Kord's reluctance to speak, however, kept the questions from her lips, but there came a point where she could stand no more.

"Kord," she said, leaning forward, her hands wrapped around a steaming mug. "Are you all right?"

The slender man lifted his bruised face and looked at her. He gave a wan grin and nodded. "I'm okay. Nothing is broken, or so the doctor told me."

"No, that's not what I meant," she said. She glanced over at Carrie, who seemed relieved that someone spoke and leaned forward with interest. Autumn was unsure if she should be cautious around the dark haired woman; even though she held Quinn's heart, Autumn did not know how much she knew about the events of two years ago.

"What I mean," Autumn said, looking back at Kord, "is that you look troubled. Worried. Is there anything I can help you with? Anything I can say to ease your mind?"

The slender man looked back at the tabletop and shook his head. "No, there isn't. I'm tired, Autumn. I'm tired of running. Especially when I know I can't run far or fast enough to get Abby clear of this." He looked into the living room where his daughter sat, staring transfixed at a talking cartoon animal on the television.

"Get clear of what?" Carrie asked.

"Of what is hunting us," he said, still looking at his daughter.

Carrie glanced over at Autumn. "What is hunting you? Is it this guy who's eating people?"

Kord looked back at her, before turning his eyes to Autumn. "She does not know?" he asked.

"Know what?" Carrie asked, sitting up straight, her slender

234

eyebrows drawing together.

This was no time for deception or half-truths, Autumn decided. They were taking refuge in Carrie's home, and if she did not know what they were hiding from, she probably should.

"Carrie, how much do you know about what happened here in Resolution two years ago?"

"You mean when Quinn was nearly killed - twice?"

Autumn nodded. "That's what I mean."

Carrie crossed her arms, and narrowed her blue eyes slightly. "Quinn doesn't talk about it much, or at all. I know it was fucked up; way beyond the realm of normal. I know that some little junkie freak, that was way bigger and meaner than he should have been, broke into my house and stabbed Quinn. Then Sandy shot herself and Quinn had to go to that house in the south end to try and sort it all out. I don't know what he needed to do, but I know it's not something that I would have understood at the time."

"At the time?" Autumn asked.

The dark haired woman shrugged and leaned her elbows on the table. "Quinn came home with claw marks in his neck and burns all over his body. He had a knife with him that he's carried everywhere with him since. He still has nightmares every now and then, bad enough that I wake him up. I know something happened in that house, something he doesn't want to talk to me about. It kills me that he's keeping a secret, but I trust him enough to believe that he'll tell me about it when he's ready to. I know it changed him. That he saw something in that house he couldn't un-see. But when he came out, Sandy broke out of the coma she was in and this town started to go back to normal."

Kord looked at her. "And do you know what it all meant?"

"I think," Carrie said. "There was something in that house making this town sour and Quinn went and killed it."

"You're right, Carrie," Autumn said. "He did. He made things right again." She did not know how to explain what she believed was in the basement of that house, just as she did not know how to explain to Quinn what she believed, either. In the end, she decided to cast the truth before her and see where it landed. "Do you believe in demons, Carrie?"

Carrie's eyebrows drew together. "You mean, like Satan?"

"Not exactly," Autumn said. "I mean, do you believe that beings who are purely evil could walk and live among us? Could you imagine something whose core is so black it taints everything it comes in contact with?"

"I don't know," Carrie said. "Should I?"

"You really should," Kord said, looking at his daughter.

"When Quinn went to that house two years ago, he was, indeed, going to sort something out. A demon, like a boogeyman from a children's story, had come to Resolution. That was why we had so much violence, then. That was why Quinn had to shoot two people, and was then attacked here, in your home."

"A demon?" Carrie said. There was no incredulity in her voice, only a seeking of confirmation.

"That's right."

Carrie looked down at her mug and sighed. "I have an urge for something stronger than tea." She looked up at the two other people at the table. "Are either of you interested?"

"I would not refuse," Kord said, pushing his mug away slightly. Autumn nodded her assent as well.

Carrie got up from the table and rummaged through the cupboard above her stove. After several moments, she produced a round, dusty bottle of scotch and three wide-bottomed glasses. She poured a measure of each of them and then sat back down.

"Are you going to offer a snort to the Mountie?" Kord asked.

Shaking her head slightly, Carrie took a small sip from her glass then swallowed slowly. "No," she said. "If Raife caught him drinking on duty he'd strangle him. Besides, I'm not sure he's old enough to drink."

Kord smiled at that, the bruises on his face shifting.

"I need to be perfectly clear on this," Carrie said, taking

another small sip. "You're saying that there was a demon living in someone's basement? And Quinn, with Raife and Dave, were there to kill it the night the house burned down and they were nearly caught inside?" She glanced back and forth between Kord and Autumn. "And the story the Inspector put out about them trying to rescue the guy who lived there was all bullshit?"

"A deception designed to protect them," Autumn said. "The man who lived in that house knew the demon was there and was in thrall to it. He was aiding it, keeping it safe, bringing it people to feed on."

"To feed on?" Carrie asked. "You mean like this thing that's in Resolution now?"

Kord shook his head. "No. Each demon is different. From what I know so far, the demon two years ago only fed on part of the person they came in contact with. It took away, consuming, what made them sane. It removed anything that made them human, sending them back out into your town as soulless creatures with nothing inside them to stop the anger and hate the demon had left in place of their reason.

"This one consumes flesh. He is powerful and greedy and wants *everything*. He eats until there is nothing left, and then seeks more."

"You sound like you know this thing pretty well," Carrie said.

"I do," Kord said, nodding. "It killed my wife trying to get to my daughter."

Raife pulled up to Resolution's newest crime scene, another alley in the poorer end of the business district, and put the Tahoe in park. Where normally there would be a handful of cars and several members on scene security, there was only one uniformed member in a marked car and one plain clothes investigator taking pictures of the scene. The detachment resources were running very thin and there were not enough bodies available for all the work that needed doing.

"This is getting sad, Boss," Dave said as he looked through the truck window. "We're going to be arming the janitor and sending him out to hold scenes soon."

"Steve Faulk has called for more bodies from other detachments, but they're not likely to arrive until morning, so we'll have to hold down the fort until then." Raife got out of the truck, followed by Dave and Sandy, and approached the plain clothes member. Bill Davis lowered the Nikkon D-200 camera he held and gave Raife a nod.

"How's it going, Bill?"

"For us, a little better. For him," he nodded at a mangled corpse at his feet, "not so good."

"What is better for us?" Sandy asked.

"This is the first person, other than Dean Springer, we've been able to identify," Bill said and snapped another picture. "There was nothing left of anyone else. The only way we identified Springer was through his dental records. There isn't even a sniff of who the other bodies belong to, so having their teeth doesn't help us."

He stepped forward and crouched down beside the body that lay in a heap against the wall of a drycleaner's business. Raife gritted his teeth and smoothed down his mustache. He'd seen some ugly things in his time on the job, but this was particular sight was in the running for first place. The body was torn and bloody, the clothes in tatters and the limbs all snapped and bent at unnatural angles. It was a man, Raife could see through the gore and bone splinters, with an untrimmed beard and a layer of dirt beneath the splattered blood.

"I think I recognize him," Dave said, talking with a clenched fist held in front of his mouth. "It's one of our homeless guys."

Bill nodded. "That's what we figured the other victims were, since Resolution has more than its fair share of people jumping off boats in the harbour and living in the local alleys, but we couldn't be sure. While the only person identified is Springer, we can assume the rest were homeless and unaccounted for, because there haven't been any missing person reports to go with the continually appearing bodies."

"So who is this guy?" Raife asked, leaning forward to take a closer look. He coughed, trying to work his way past the smell of shit and terror that accompanied a torn open torso. There were identifiable teeth marks in the neck and upper chest, but the torso below was nothing more than a mass of torn flesh,and a great quantity of it appeared to be missing.

"Ronald Jack," Bill said. "Or so the expired drivers licence in his wallet says. The face is torn up so bad I can't say if the picture is the same guy, but we'll be going with that until I run the fingerprint I got from one of his remaining digits through the database in Ottawa."

"This one was interrupted, wasn't it?" Sandy asked.

Bill stood up and nodded, checking the last picture he took on the screen of the camera. "It certainly was. We have a witness, some old lady who lived above the dry cleaner and found this when she was taking out her garbage. She's down at the office now, giving a statement to one of my guys."

"Any description of the suspect?" Raife asked.

"Yeah, but it's pretty vague: a man of medium height and build, long dark hair, wearing a torn red work shirt and dirty jeans." Bill gazed down at the display screen of the digital camera. Raife gave Dave and Sandy a surreptitious glance and a barely perceptible nod.

"There was one other weird thing," Bill said.

"You mean this has the ability to get weirder?" Dave asked.

"The witness said there was a smell. A really strong animal smell, like she was outside the bear cage at a zoo. Said she never smelled it here before and it was gone when the guy ran. She insisted it wasn't just human body odour. She was adamant it smelled like an animal."

"You think she's full of shit?" Raife asked, knowing the woman was not.

Bill shrugged. "Fucked if I know. The woman saw a deranged serial killer eating another person. I'd probably be seeing unicorns and smelling rainbows if that happened to me."

"What's the time delay now, Bill?" Raife asked.

"I'm gonna say about an hour," Bill said, looking at his watch. "Can you guys give me a hand for a few minutes with some neighbourhood inquiries? I'd have my guys do them, but they're all tied up with other miserable tasks. I've called for help from the guys at 'E' Division headquarters, but they have to come from Vancouver and they won't be flying in until to-morrow morning."

"No problem," Raife said, pointing Dave and Sandy to one side of the street while he took the other.

The area they were in was primarily a business district, but almost all the buildings had apartments on the upper floors. Raife climbed several sets of stairs and knocked on a handful of doors. Almost all his queries received answers, but no one saw much of anything. Everyone he talked to had the same story: they had been home and had not heard or seen any-thing until the old lady started screaming. By the time they had come out the bad guy was gone.

"Is there really someone eating people?" a skinny girl in her early twenties asked him. Her equally skinny boyfriend stood on his tip-toes to look over Raife's shoulder.

"I can't comment right now," Raife said. "But don't leave your house at night, and don't leave it alone during the day." When he said that she slammed the door and he heard several locks click into place.

An hour later he had talked to everyone within ear shot of the alley. No one had anything useful to add. He was not sure what he was doing out here, except for the simple fact that he needed to do something. He had to find this thing before it killed and ate anyone else, but he did not know where to look. The thing was like a shadow, a hungry ghost, and it kept ap-pearing out of nowhere and disappearing just as quickly. Raife knew he needed a starting point so he could find where this thing was hiding during the day. He had to run it to ground, keep it penned until Quinn got back and they could all go and deal with it properly.

He met Dave and Sandy back in front of the crime scene tape and gave Bill Davis the results of their canvass, which was this side of fuck all.

Bill nodded as he listened to what they had to say, making a few marks in his black, ledger-sized notebook. "I'm going to have to leave the scene and get back to the office, and hope like fuck this doesn't happen again." He was still scribbling in his notebook when the phone on his belt rang.

"I hope he didn't speak too soon," Dave said.

"Sergeant Davis," Bill said as he answered the phone. He listened for several seconds and his face tightened until his mouth was a thin, barely perceptible line.

"Yup," Dave said. "Too soon."

"You gotta be fucking kidding me," Bill said into the phone. "No, I'll head over there now. No, I'll be fine. Raife and a couple of his guys are standing in front of me. I'll ask if they can roll with me."

Raife nodded and Bill nodded back.

"Okay," Bill said, still into the phone. "I'll call you when I get there and see what's what." He hit the red button on his phone and stuck it back into the leather holster on his belt. "Shit, fuck, piss, bugger, damn!" He shouted and palmed his own forehead.

"Another body?" Raife asked, already knowing the answer.

"Yeah," Bill said, hoisting his camera case on his shoulder. "And I think things are getting stranger, as though they weren't strange enough as it is."

"My enthusiasm for more good news is starting to wane," Dave said, to no one in particular.

"What have you got?" Raife asked.

"I don't know if I can even explain it," Bill said. "You better just come and see for yourself."

Raife nodded and turned for his truck, Dave and Sady following in his wake. He did not like the tone of Bill Davis' voice. He did not like it at all.

Five minutes later Raife stood beside Bill, about two blocks away from the Welcome Beaver, his eyes moving between a mass of piled and broken bones and the wall of the alley.

Dave stood next to him, his mouth open. Sandy's mouth, also, was open, but she had the good manners to cover hers.

"Do you have any idea what this means?" Bill Davis asked as he snapped several pictures of the wall.

"No clue," Raife lied. He knew very well what the drawing on the wall meant—painted in a dead man's blood, but he did not want to say it out loud. Not to Bill, anyway.

Above the littered mass of bones, in broad, bloody strokes against the grey stone, was a silhouette of a child; a girl with pigtails.

Kord's daughter, Abby, did not have pigtails standing up off the sides of her head, but the meaning was clear enough. Raife chewed back the sick feeling in the pit of his stomach. He turned to Dave and Sandy. "We have to go. Now." The two members nodded and started towards the truck.

"Go?" Bill asked. "Where are you going?"

"I have to check on something," Raife said over his shoulder as he took long strides towards the driver's side of his police truck.

"Raife, you can't leave," Bill said as he hurried after the bigger man and grabbed his arm. "The most prolific and psychotic serial killer in years is operating in your town and you have to check on something? I need you here."

"I have something I need to do, Bill." Raife looked down at the hand gripping his hairy forearm. "Now you let go of me or this is going to go south, in an awful big way."

"You're fucking insane," Bill said, as he released Raife and stepped back.

"If this is nothing," Raife said, as he climbed into the truck. "I'll be back in a few minutes, and we'll do whatever you need us to." He pointed to Dave and Sandy and they scrambled into the passenger side of the vehicle, Dave in the front, Sandy in the back.

Bill stood, his jaw clenched tight, staring at Raife as the big sergeant put the truck in gear and sped away from the curb and down the street.

"What are you thinking, Boss?" Dave asked from the passenger seat as Raife surged down the deserted streets of Resolution's core.

"I'm thinking the same thing you're thinking, Dave," Raife said. "I'm thinking we never should have left those people alone, or tried to hide them in Quinn's home with his family. I think we made a horrible mistake."

"Maybe they're fine," Sandy said from the back seat. "Maybe that drawing didn't mean what we think it meant."

Raife said nothing in response, but concentrated on keeping the big vehicle between the sidewalks as he drove much faster than was safe, but far slower than he needed to. He knew what the picture in the alley meant as well as his constables did. They were wrong to think they could hide those people from this demon. He was wrong to think they were safe. He could only hope they were not too late.

Autumn sat, transfixed and terrified, as Kord told them the story of his life. He cast constant, nervous glances at the living room, checking to see if Abby listened or watched him while he spoke, but she paid them no mind, giggling on the couch beside Shawn.

"We always knew that Abby was going to be different from the women in our family," he told them, rolling his glass of scotch between calloused fingers. "We always walked with one foot in a world that most people don't understand, both of our families, my wife and me, but when Abby came along we knew that everything was going to change.

"We brought her up in our traditions. My family—my father and his father before him—were fighters, and I learned their ways. As I grew up, I fought with my cousins, and then in a ring for money, always knowing that I was preparing myself to fight for my own family one day. When I came of marrying age and was properly deemed a man, my father gave me this."

He reached into his back pocket with his good arm and produced a set of old, tarnished brass knuckles, and laid them on the table. "I'm no Guardian, but one of my ancestors was, and he carried these.

"My wife learned her family's lore and secrets, and carried the amulet that Abby now wears around her neck, once she came of age." He took a sip from his glass and looked over at the living room again.

"When we were kids, young and in love, we thought it was all a game. I trained to be a knight and Diana, my wife, was my queen. We were married, and shortly after that Abby was born. It didn't take long to figure out that she was different, that she was special.

"She walked before she was a year old. She was talking in sentences by two. She was reading out loud at three, and could remember the name of every person she ever met, every story she'd ever read. Usually, the amulet is passed to the next woman in line when she gets old enough to marry, or even on her wedding day. With Abby, she could use it when she was five, and was more proficient with it than any person in memory by the time she was seven. We weren't the only ones who noticed.

"Our family are Travelers. We made our money how we could: fighting, healing, telling fortunes, odd jobs, whatever we could find. One day, two years ago, we set up camp on the other side of the country. At sunset a stranger walked up to us. Said he'd heard about a fortune teller and wanted his palm read.

"We knew there was something wrong with him. The sight of him was fine, but there was something about him that made him look...greasy. And a smell. He smelled like—"

"An animal," Autumn said, cutting Kord off. "He smelled like a wild animal."

Kord nodded. "Diana took his hand in hers and flipped it over, then pulled her own hand back. He had no life line, you see. He was already dead, or had never lived. She knew, then, it was a demon."

Carrie shifted uncomfortably in her chair and took a long pull from her glass.

"It told us it'd heard about our daughter and wanted to see her. Diana said no, he could not see her and I felt a burning in my pocket where those were." He pointed to the brass knuckles. "When I pulled them out they glowed bright white and I knew he was a demon, too.

"Abby was special, it said, calling my child by name. It said she had a destiny we could never understand and it would take her to her calling."

"Her calling?" Carrie asked.

"With that amulet, Abby can do a lot of things: she can heal the sick, find things that are lost, but the most important thing she can do is open doors," Kord said. "She can open them anywhere and move nearly anything."

"And the demon wants her to open a door, doesn't it?" Autumn asked.

"A door to where?" Carrie asked.

"I don't know," Kord said. "I've never asked it, but I can only assume it wants to open a door to where it came from."

"And bring others through," Autumn said.

"Other what?" Carrie asked. "Other demons?"

Kord and Autumn both nodded and Carrie blew her breath out through puffed cheeks, pouring herself another drink.

"What happened the night it came to your camp?" Autumn asked. She did not want to pry into Kord's story, but he needed to finish it, as much for himself as for anything she might be able to learn from its telling.

"That night, Abby was playing with her cousins in a playground within sight of our camp. The demon knew her by sight and ignored us as it walked towards her. Diana, always brave, tried to stop it, to get in its way. It struck her, only once, like it was slapping away a gnat, but she was so crumpled when she fell that I knew she was dead without checking." He paused , laying his hand on top of the brass knuckles on the table and closing his eyes. He took a deep breath and lifted his head a little.

"I fought it in the centre of our camp. All I remember of the fight was fire and screaming, either mine or the thing's. I was good, but I was no match for it and I was beaten into the dust as well. I didn't stop it, but I slowed it enough that the rest of our clan poured in to help. The men attacked it with what weapons we had and the women brought what power they had to bear. In the end, it was not enough to kill it, only to hurt it a little, to slow it down.

"My father picked me up and told me to run, to take Abby and run. I grabbed my girl from the playground she stood on, threw her in my van and fled. I left my wife's body in the dirt and my family fighting an enemy we'd always prepared for, but did not at all understand."

He raised his eyes, red rimmed and full of tears, looking first at Carrie, then Autumn. "I don't even know if any of them still live," he said. "I don't know if they laid my wife to rest, or where she is. I ran and I didn't stop running. Never staying anywhere for more than a day, always moving, scrounging money where I could, but only ever enough to feed us and put gas in the van."

"How did you find this place?" Autumn asked.

"It was Abby," he said, looking over at the child who was still transfixed by the television. "She can hear things on the wind, read them in the trees. She says the rain speaks to her and I do not think she lies. She's told me about things that haven't happened yet, and later come to be. She knows where we can go to make a little money, who will hire me, when to buy the right piece of junk at a garage sale so I can sell it to a pawn shop for enough money to keep us alive for another month.

"A month ago, she told me the name of this town and that we had to come here - that this place had a Guardian. I knew what that meant, but I don't think she really understood or how she knew."

"This Guardian you keep talking about," Carrie said. "Is that Quinn?"

"Yes, it is," Autumn said.

"Don't take this wrong, because he's mine and I love him, but what makes him so special?"

"Quinn has asked me that himself," Autumn said. "I cannot explain it any more than I can explain why Abby is so talented. All I know is Quinn was drawn to this place by the fates, like metal to a magnet, because this is where he is needed. He was needed two years ago when a demon appeared here and he is needed now when another comes to take a child."

"Can he stop this thing?" Carrie asked. The hand holding her glass quaked slightly.

"I hope so," Kord said. "Nothing else has been able to."

"And what if he can't?" Carrie asked.

"Then that thing will have my child," Kord said, his voice dead and flat.

It had grown late as they sat and talked, Autumn thought, looking at the clock on the kitchen wall. It was after midnight now, closing in on one o'clock. The sounds from the living room had grown more infrequent until all she could hear was the drone of the television and the deep breaths of sleeping children. She stood up and stretched, her lower back making several satisfying popping noises.

"I have seen the strength of Quinn Sullivan," she said to Kord once she had lowered her arms from her stretch. "He will not fail in this. He did not fail before. You don't have to worry."

"I hope you are right," Kord said. He drained off the last of his scotch in one swallow.

"We should all get some rest," Carrie said and stood from the table, gathering up the empty glasses and Kord's uneaten pizza. "It's been a long day."

"Some of us are way ahead of you," Kord said, as he stood stiffly, rubbing his left arm.

Autumn followed his gaze and saw that the three occupants of the living room were all sound asleep; Gerritt in the middle of the couch, one of the children under each arm, and

Gus, Quinn's tomcat, curled on his lap.

"Raife's gonna tune that kid up for falling asleep on the job," Carrie said, standing with one had on her hip, leaning against the kitchen counter. "C'mon. Let's wake up Captain Awesome and find everyone a spot to spend the night."

She walked past Autumn and bent to touch Gerritt's arm, but she stood upright and backed away. "Autumn?" she said.

Not liking the tone of her voice, Autumn hurried to her side and immediately saw what she was looking at. Gus had stood and was puffed up to twice his normal size, his ears laid back and a growl blooming in his throat. His wide yellow eyes were focused on the front door. The growl turned into a screech.

"Wassappening?" Gerritt said, as he woke and looked at the howling cat in his lap.

"Oh, be damned," Kord said from behind them.

Autumn turned and saw him reach for the brass knuckles on the table. They were glowing bright white.

She had a moment to register fear, then panic, before she heard a chorus of howls coming from every direction, surrounding the house.

"Oh good God," Carrie said. "What the fuck is that?"

Gus leapt off Gerritt's lap in a burst of fur and claws. The Mountie yelled in pain and surprise. Both the children were awake now. Shawn went to the window while Abby grabbed hold of Kord's injured hand, the one that was not wearing the glowing set of brass knuckles.

"Mum," Shawn said, turning from the window. "There are a bunch of dogs on the lawn. What's going on?"

"I'm not sure, baby," she said. Carrie held out her hands for him and he ran to her.

The howling grew in pitch and frenzy, and Autumn heard a frantic scratching at the front door. "Is there any way out?" she asked no one in particular.

Gerritt was on his feet now and had his gun in his hand. "I think we're in trouble." He looked over at Carrie. "Aren't we?"

"Even the new guy knows," said Carrie. She released Shawn and ran down the narrow central hallway of the house, leading to the bedrooms.

Gerritt reached down to the radio mic hanging from the 'D' ring on his vest and hit the transmit button. He pressed it several times before shaking his head. "My radio don't work."

Kord stepped to the back window in the kitchen and looked out. "They're back here, too. Dozens of them. There is no way out. We have to fight." Kord began shaking his arms out and threw a few experimental jabs in the air with his bad arm. He winced, but he kept shaking it. "Are you any good with that?" he asked, tipping his head at Gerritt's gun.

The younger man looked down at the pistol in his hand and swallowed thickly, his Adam's apple bobbing.

Carrie came back down the hallway, a big, black pistol in her hands, with a barrel as wide as Autumn's index finger. She had several spare magazines in the front pockets of her jeans.

"You know how to use that?" Autumn asked, feeling suddenly very useless and very helpless.

Carrie nodded. "Quinn taught me to shoot and bought me this pistol after he was nearly killed, just in case something like that ever happened again." She held the gun up and rammed a magazine into the handle, then yanked on the top with metallic clank. When she held it up, Autumn saw '.45 Sigsaur' stamped on the side. She did not know anything about guns, but thought that sounded good.

The howling outside grew louder, as did the scratching and snarling outside the back door by the kitchen. There was no way out, Autumn thought. The guns held by Carrie and Gerritt might stop the dogs circling the house, but not the demon if it was with them. It would only laugh as they shot it and kill them all anyway. She was going to die here if they did not have a way out.

She looked around, frantically, trying to think of something to help them, and her eyes stopped on Abby. The girl gripped her father's leg with one hand, the bronze amulet around her neck with the other.

"A door," Autumn said. "We need a door."

"There are two doors," Gerritt said, looking at her as though she were an idiot. "But neither one is any good."

"No," Autumn said, and turned to Kord. "Can Abby make us a door?"

Kord shifted from foot to foot for a moment, looking from the surrounding windows down to his daughter. "I don't know," he said, finally. "I've never heard of anyone ever sending a living thing through one of the doors. I don't know what would happen. I don't think it's a good idea."

"Why not?" Autumn asked, fear lending a piping edge to her voice she did not care for.

"A couple of times, the things we tried to send through didn't come out," Kord said.

"What happened to them?" Carrie asked, still gripping the pistol in both hands before her.

Kord turned to her and shrugged. "That's the problem. We don't know."

The howling outside ceased, casting the interior of the house into an odd, tangible silence.

"McRae!" a voice outside shouted.

"There it is," Kord said, raising his fists and tightening his grip on the brass knuckles.

"McRae," the voice said again, lengthening the name in a sing-song manner. "All I want is the girl, McRae."

Autumn went to the front window and looked outside. On the front lawn, surrounded by frantic, gnashing dogs with oddly elongated snouts, stood the creature that had invaded her home.

"If you let me have her," the creature continued. "I'll let everyone else in the house go. You'll never hear from me again."

There was a pause and the dogs started howling, as if on cue.

"If you don't let me have her, McRae, everyone inside that ramshackle little dwelling will die. Horribly. What is one small child compared to the lives of everyone in that house? Think about it, McRae."

"We don't have a choice," Autumn said. The tension in her neck and shoulders made her feel as though she were about to crack. "We need a way out."

Kord said nothing, his face flat, as he continued to look towards the two doors that were now rattling and shaking from the clawing outside.

Autumn crouched down so her face was close to Abby's. "What do you think, kiddo? Are you willing to try? It doesn't have to be far, just a little ways away from here."

Abby shrugged and looked up at her father.

Autumn looked up at him as well. "If it doesn't work, Kord, it won't matter. We'll all be dead anyway."

As though emphasizing he point, the voice from the front yard yelled. "Come out now, you pathetic sacs of nothing. Or I'll come in and I'll be bringing friends with me."

Kord looked down at Abby. "Do you want to try?"

The girl looked up, gripping her braid in one hand and the bronze amulet in the other. She tilted her head to one side, considering, and then nodded.

"Okay, Abby. Go ahead. Concentrate."

The child moved to the middle of the room and crouched down on the floor. She put her hand down on the kitchen tile, closed her eyes and lowered her head. After a moment, a brilliant source of bright light appeared beneath her palm.

The spot of light grew bigger, spreading out from her hand like water rippling on hot cement. As the light got larger, the centre of it started to darken, until just the edges glowed and the middle looked like a pool of cold ink.

"Where does it go?" Autumn asked the girl. There was no response. Abby kept her eyes closed and her head lowered. Small beads of sweat popped out on her smooth forehead. Autumn stood and tried to wipe the worry from her mind. The time and opportunity for questions was over. Now, there could only be movement.

"We have to hurry," Autumn said. She reached down and picked up Shawn. He slung his arms around her neck. He was a solid kid, but rank fear and adrenaline made him feel like a bag of crumpled newspapers.

"That's it," the voice outside called. "Your time is up."

"We have to go through," Autumn said, her voice climbing. "Now."

Everyone shifted towards the edge of the glowing doorway, reluctance making their movements stiff. Carrie still held her pistol up, pointed at the front door. Gerritt stood beside her, his pistol up as well, his eyes darting between the front door and the hole in the floor.

"Wait," Kord said, his voice cracking. "If Abby holds the door open for us, how does she get through?" He looked down at the child, who hadn't moved, had not even appeared to breathe, since she opened the doorway to nothing. "No," he said, waving his arms, the glowing brass knuckles leaving streaks of after-image across Autumn's vision. "This isn't going to work. Abby, stand up."

As he reached down for the child, there was a crash and the front door flew open, splitting apart from a great impact. The demon stood in the doorway and wild dogs, their eyes tinted red and their shoulders massive and misshapen, struggled and snapped at each other to wriggle by him.

Carrie lifted the pistol smoothly pulled the trigger. The roar of the big gun slapped Autumn in the ears like a hammer and the flash from the muzzle left after-images as striking as Kord's weapon. The demon threw a hand across his face and several of the dogs were torn apart by the gun's heavy bullets.

One of the dogs shot between the legs of the demon and lunged at Gerritt. The young Mountie yanked the trigger of his pistol several times, the bullets punching into the body of the dog, but it collided with him anyway. Wet jaws snapped closed on one of his arms. The momentum of the animal unbalanced him and he stumbled, staggering into Kord, who bent over to grasp Abby and bring her to her feet. Kord lost his footing as well, his grasping hand missing Abby's elbow and he crashed into Autumn. She gripped Shawn to her, squeezing tight by instinct and put her hand out to hit the floor.

There was no floor beneath her, only a black space rimmed in sharp light. As she passed through where the floor should have been, she had a sensation of being run under cold water, and then felt nothing, the distant crash of gunfire still ringing in her ears.

CHAPTER 17

Raife cleared the last corner leading up to Carrie's house in a four wheel drift and thought, for a moment, the truck might flip. He twisted the wheel with a practiced hand, evened out the vehicle and then hammered back down on the accelerator. The big engine howled.

They came in sight of the house. Raife's worst fears realized. The lawn was covered in twisted, rapidly moving shapes. It was only when they got closer that Raife recognized they were dogs.

"What the fuck are those?" Dave said. He hit the release for the new shotgun Raife had acquired from the office and pulled it from the rack attached to the roll bar above their heads.

"They look like dogs," Sandy said. She unbuckled her seatbelt and put her hand on the door release.

"They used to be dogs," Raife said, flexing his wounded arm and remembering the beast that had once been the good natured friend of Dean Springer. "Not anymore."

The animals had the house surrounded and the front door was ripped apart, chunks of wood sagged on its hinges. The rapid pop of gunfire came from inside the house and a hot surge burned the inside Raife's chest. Instead of stopping, he gunned the engine and drove through the squealing pack of dogs, feeling several satisfying thumps as he drove over them. He cranked the wheel hard and pinned the accelerator, causing the rear wheels to spin on the lawn and the back end of the truck to swing around. Raife hit the brakes again and brought the truck to a lurching stop with the bumper almost touching the steps to the front door.

Dave pumped the shotgun and threw open the passenger door. A dark shape lunged at him. He stuck the barrel of the shotgun into a dog's mouth and pulled the trigger. Then he was out and moving, the shotgun roaring in his hands as he turned and fired at anything that came near him.

"The radio is fucked," Sandy yelled, depressing the key on her mic as she pulled her gun from her holster and threw herself out the rear passenger-side door of the truck.

Raife cursed as he opened the driver's door, his own pistol in his hand. He ran around the front end of the truck and up the stairs. "Carrie?" he called as he shot a dog that came near him, pulling the trigger several times. "Carrie!"

He gained the top stair and had one foot on the floor of the hallway, when a dark shape streaked from inside the house and slammed into him. The impact knocked the wind from his lungs and the gun from his hand. Raife spun through the air to land in a painful heap on the lawn. He raised himself on one elbow and looked at the house through the white spots in his vision. In the doorway, silhouetted by the light behind it, stood the demon. He had an extremely smug look on his face, a bundle over one shoulder and another tucked under his arm as he walked calmly down the stairs. Raife groped in the churned up dirt of the yard for his gun. If he could manage to see straight, he was going to shoot the smug look off the fucking thing's face.

His big hand closed on the grip of his pistol and he tried to rise, but a wave of vertigo seized him and sent him face first into the dirt. He tried to rise again, lost his balance and tumbled back to the earth. The demon laughed at him as it passed.

A shape moved out of the dark and stood in front of the

demon. Sandy, her gun raised, pointed at the Demon's face. "Stop right there, asshole," Sandy said, her voice even and her hands steady.

The demon laughed an awful sound that made Raife's ears want to bleed. It shifted slightly so the bundle on its shoulder covered its face. Raife looked at the limp form and realised it had a head of long black hair, a portion of which was plastered to a bloody skull. The demon had Carrie and beneath its arm was the squirming form of Abby.

"I wouldn't be so hasty," the demon said, a mocking note in its voice. "You wouldn't want to hit your little friend, would you?" He tossed Abby into the air as easily as he would a pillow and caught her by one leg. It dangled her back and forth in front of him like a pendulum. "How good is your timing, bitch? Do you think you can make the shot?"

Sandy hissed in frustration, her hand wavering as she grew more panicked. Raife pawed at his radio mic, thinking now would be a good time to call for help, but when he keyed it all he got was a blast of static.

"Resolution, we're ten-thirty-three," he yelled. Or at least he thought it was a yell, but he could not tell through the ringing in his ears. He keyed the radio again. "Resolution, this is Charlie Five-One, Sergeant Raife, do you copy?" There was no response. Gritting his teeth against the waves of dizzy pain that wracked his body, he tried to find his feet again.

As he struggled to rise, another shape came around the front of the truck. Dave moved into his line of sight. The lean man was torn and bloody, his body armor gone and his uniform shirt hung from him in tatters. His face grim, Dave moved quietly behind the demon while the thing mocked Sandy and gloated.

"Come on, then," it said, swinging a squealing Abby by the leg. "I've not got all night."

Dave crouched behind the creature and pressed the barrel of his shotgun to the back of its left leg.

"Eh?" it said and looked down.

In answer, Dave pulled the trigger.

The demon screeched, a sound like a piece of sheet-metal being torn in half, as the blast of the shotgun shattered its lower leg. It dropped both Abby and Carrie as its arms flailed and it tumbled sideways. It landed in the dirt, directly beside Raife. The big man reached out calmly and placed the barrel of his pistol near the side of the thing's head and pulled the trigger.

The thing saw Raife and jerked away at the last second. Raife's gun popped and dirt showered his face. It leapt to its feet with unnatural strength, lunging forward, weight off its shattered leg. It slammed into Dave, who knelt, sending him crashing into the dirt. It snatched up Abby from the ground and lunged at Sandy, who still had her pistol up. Sandy back-pedaled, lost her balance and landed in the mud as the thing swiped at her. The demon glanced back at them, fleeing as quickly on its injured leg as a fast man could run to disappear into the night.

"Dave, Sandy, are you alive?" Raife called as he struggled to one knee.

Sandy stood up and came to grab one of his arms and help him to his feet. He managed to get up, but had to reach out and put a muddy hand on the truck to steady himself. Dave slowly got up as well, with a great deal of cursing.

"Check Carrie," Raife said, pointing at the crumpled form on the ground a few feet away.

Sandy knelt down beside Carrie and felt her neck. "She's alive, but she's unconscious. She's a goose egg on her head the size of an apple."

"Can we call for help yet?" Raife asked.

Dave keyed his radio mic, got a clear beep indicating he had the channel, and started speaking while he nodded. "Resolution, this is Charlie Two. I need EHS forthwith. I have an unresponsive female, suffered a blow to the head. I also need any available member to our location."

Raife did not wait to hear the dispatcher's responses, but turned and staggered towards the front of the house.

"Where are you going?" Sandy asked, putting out a hand

to steady him.

"We need to clear the house," he said through gritted teeth. It was hard to breathe and he was beginning to think he had broken a couple of ribs in the fall. He tried to suck in a deep breath, but if felt like someone was squeezing his body in a vice. "Come on," he said, the pain making his voice sound garbled in his own ears.

He managed to make it up the stairs and found a charnal house of gore inside the front door. There was a Sigsaur .45 calibre on the floor of the kitchen with two empty magazines and more than a dozen spent shell casings littered about. In a circle around where the gun lay, were the bodies of several mutated dogs, their elongated jaws hanging limp and bloody. Dark pools of blood spread beneath bodies that were torn by the bullets from the big gun. Raife nudged the carcasses of the dogs as he went, making sure none moved and they were all dead. There was no movement in the house and that worried him even more than if one of the dogs had still been alive.

With Sandy at his heels, he staggered through the house, trying to catch his breath as he searched the rooms. He did not find any other bodies, which was good, but he could not find Autumn, Kord, Shawn or Gerritt, which was not.

"Do you think they got out?" Sandy asked, as they finished searching the house and found nothing.

"I hope so," Raife said, clutching at his chest which was starting to hurt. "They wouldn't have been eaten that quickly, so they must have."

"Boss, are you okay?" Sandy asked, laying a hand on his arm. "You're really pale."

"I'm fine," he said, trying to stand up straight. "We have to find Autumn and the others. We have to figure out where that thing took Abby. She won't have much time."

"Raife, I think you need to wait for the medics," Sandy said.

"God damn it I said I'm—" His tirade was interrupted by a fit of coughing. He put his hand up to his mouth and felt hot wetness splatter against his palm. He pulled his hand away and it was covered with blood. He looked at Sandy and tried to walk to the door, but his legs faltered beneath him and he sagged down the wall.

"Raife," Sandy said as she tried to lower him down. "Dave! I need you!"

Coughing again, Raife saw more blood splatter against the front of his vest. He could still see Sandy in front of him, although she became a tad fuzzy. She kept talking, but all he heard was a steady buzz. "Maybe I don't feel so well after all," he said, but did not hear a thing.

Hard ground rushed up out of the dark to meet her and drove the breath from Autum's lungs. She cradled Shawn to her and felt a heavy body land on her, forcing out even more air and prohibiting her from sucking any in.

She felt cold and her skin tingled. She had vague memories of a glowing circle in the floor and flashes of colour in an extremely dark place. Shawn's hair was slightly damp beneath her face, the moisture frigid.

"Abby," Kord said as he struggled to get off Autumn and look back the way they had come. There was nothing behind them except for black sky and the side of a house, dim and tall in the dark. The glowing circle, the doorway the child had opened was gone and there was nothing to see. "Abby!" Kord yelled.

Autumn disentangled herself from Shawn and helped the boy to his feet. A few feet away, Gerritt pawed the grass and stood up once he had put his hands on his pistol. "What the hell just happened?" he asked. She did not know herself and could offer no answer.

"Where are we?" Kord asked, frantically looking around. The brass knuckles were still on his right hand, but they were dark.

Shawn wiped a hand across his damp, dirty face. "Um, we're about a block away from my house," he said. "My school is that way and my house is just over there."

Kord looked at the direction the small finger pointed and started running.

Autumn took Shawn's hand and started after the slender man. "Come on, Gerritt," she called over her shoulder. The lanky Mountie followed.

They passed through several yards, causing motion sensing lights to blink on and dogs inside dark houses to bark. The barking reminded Autumn of the howling in Carrie's yard and she slowed. "Kord," she called to the man running in front of her. "Wait! Kord!" she called again when he did not slow.

She turned to Gerritt. "Is your gun ready?"

He gripped his pistol in both hands and nodded.

"Good," she said. "You need to be ready, too." She carried on as fast as she could, Shawn running easily at her side, his hand gripping hers. They passed around the corner of a house, following the disappearing shape of Kord.

Autumn stopped, her breath catching in her throat and her legs going soft beneath her.

The front lawn of Carrie's house was churned to ruin with a police truck in the middle of the yard. Everywhere Autumn looked, she saw dead dogs, their bodies unnaturally misshapen through the demon's influence and torn with bullets from the Mountie's guns.

There was a figure in the broken yard; Dave McLeod knelt over another, crumpled form.

"Where's Abby?" Kord shouted as he passed him. Dave looked up as the other man ran by, but did not get up and continued attending to the person in front of him. When Kord did not receive an answer from Dave, he carried on past the police truck and into the house. "Abby!" his shout echoed out the front door.

Autumn approached Dave who looked up when she knelt down in front of him.

"I don't know what to do for her," Dave said. Autumn looked down at the body on the lawn and saw Carrie's pale face, clots of blood pasting her raven hair to her skin.

"Is she...?" Autumn did not have it in her to finish the

question.

"No, she's alive," Dave said. "But she's hurt bad and I'm not sure what to do."

Autumn placed her slender fingers under Carrie's jaw and found a strong, even pulse. She looked in the mats of hair and found a long gash in Carrie's scalp, but no other injuries. " I think she's just been knocked out," Autumn said. "I think she's going to be okay."

"Dave?" Sandy's shout came from inside the house. "Where the fuck are you? I need some help."

Dave moved to stand, but Autumn put a hand on his arm. "You stay here, I'll go," she said and stood.

Autumn searched around for Shawn. The boy knelt by Carrie's head, tears rimming his dark eyes. "Shawn, your mother will be fine. Just stay here and watch out for her." The boy nodded, one of his welling eyes breaking, tears leaking down his face.

Stepping over dead dogs and around the nose of the big police truck, Autumn hurried into the house. She could hear the frantic crash of Kord rummaging through the dwelling, searching for his daughter, and found Sandy kneeling over Sergeant Raife near the entryway.

"What happened?" Autumn asked as she knelt down beside them.

"I don't know," Sandy said. Autumn could see she was doing her best to remain calm, but her voice was on the brink of a sob and her hands were shaking. "He got hit really hard by the...by the thing, and he started coughing up blood a few minutes ago."

"How long have you been here?"

Sandy looked down at her watch. "I don't know," she said, her voice cracking. "About ten minutes, I guess. Maybe more? I don't know."

Ten minutes they had been gone, Autumn thought. Ten minutes surrounded by darkness and flashes of colour to make a journey of one block that felt like it took only a moment.

Autumn shook herself free of the dark feeling of wonder at

where she had been and focused on the broken body in front of her. She felt Raife's neck and for a moment feared he was dead when she could not find a pulse. Then she felt it, a faint fluttering beneath her fingers. Then, as she waited for the pulse, the big man pulled in a shallow hitching breath. His skin was dreadfully pale, his lips and chin covered in dark blood. She ran her hands over his limp body and found that his ribs felt oddly squished, collapsed, on his left side. With her hands on his face, she could almost feel his life trickling through her fingers.

For the past two years, since Quinn had nearly been killed, Autumn had focused all her time and energy on building her ability to heal. She had studied old texts and practiced old lessons in anticipation such a day would come when she would need to heal Quinn and keep him alive. Raife was not the Guardian, but he watched over Resolution just the same and she must do what she could for him.

She placed her hands on the centre of his chest and lowered her head. She reached out into the air around her and gathered every mote of power she could find, drawing it in. She took that energy and focused it under her hands, and then let it flow from her into Raife's shattered body.

She reached out with tendrils of power, searching out for the hurt in Raife. There was so much of it. She clamped her teeth together as a jolt of Raife's pain flashed through her. The incredible will that kept the big man alive through so much damage awed her.

She reached deeper, past the pain to the injury itself. Everywhere she looked was cracked bones and torn tissue, but in his side was the hurt that was killing him. The ribs on the left side of his body had all been shattered, one of them puncturing his lung. She wrapped the tendrils of power, like seeking fingers, around the shattered bones and willed them straight. She focused on them, straightening, healing, smoothing away the damage, until her own heart thumped in her chest and sweat spilled down her face.

When the strain became too great and she could do no

more, she lifted her hands and sat backwards, her legs splaying in front of her. Raife was still unconscious, but some of the colour had returned to his face and his breathing was even.

"He will live," Autumn said. "I think."

"What did you do?" Sandy asked, as she rechecked the pulse at Raife's neck.

Autumn wiped a hand across her sweaty face. "Everything I could," she said.

Blaring sirens announced the arrival of an ambulance and Autumn struggled to her feet, exhaustion making her want to fall forward onto her face. She saw Kord, standing behind Sandy, the slender man appeared more shattered than Raife.

"My daughter is gone," Kord said, his voice pitched up with strain.

Autumn could find no words and only nodded.

"What are we going to do?" he asked.

She sighed. There was nothing they could do. With Raife near death there was only one person who could bring the child home. "We need Quinn," she said. "He is the only one who can help us now."

CHAPTER 18

Quinn sat beside Jody in the cockpit of the plane and stared at the array of instruments in awe. He kept looking for the button that said 'start', but it was lost amid the hundreds of dials and switches.

"Where did you learn to fly a plane like this?" Quinn asked. It was nearly two hours into the flight and they had said very little. Jody was taciturn and grumpy, and had only spoken a couple times; once to confirm their destination and once more to tell Quinn where the bar on the plane was.

"If I'm gonna steal a plane," Jody had said on the second occasion of speech, "then it probably won't matter if you drink some of the booze. It's good shit, too."

Quinn had refused the offer, thinking he should keep his head as clear as possible since he did not know what he was walking into once he stepped off this plane. He had, however, pillaged the tray of snacks he had located near the bar, since it had been many hours since he had eaten. Jody had possessed no compunction about sharing the bounty.

The big, shaggy man tossed a handful of peanuts in his mouth. "Been around planes all my life," he said. Bits of half chewed peanut flew from between his lips. "My old man was a pilot in Korea and flew commercial after that. I could fly a single prop by the time I was ten and take the fucker apart by the time I was eleven. Ain't much I can't fly and nothing I can't fix." He shrugged and downed another handful of nuts.

"You borrow the plane often?" Quinn asked.

Jody snorted. "More than Ferguson knows about. Only got caught because I was drunk."

Giving the older man a worried look, Quinn wondered to himself how much Jody had been drinking that night, prior to getting behind the wheel of this plane. The plane flew smoothly enough and there was no quake in Jody's hands as he manipulated the controls. Quinn did not think he was in a position to be demanding too many answers.

"So, why you need to get back to this place so fast, any-way? I ain't never even heard of a place called Reputation."

"Resolution," Quinn corrected.

"Whatever," Jody said, sniffing loudly. "It don't sound like much. Why you gotta get back in such a hurry."

"I'm not sure, myself," Quinn admitted. He was not cer-tain there was going to be trouble in Resolution when he ar-rived, but based on what he had seen in Cranbrook, he thought the odds were better than even. "I had some problems in Cranbrook. I'm worried they might have spread to my hometown."

"Yeah?" Jody asked. "Some pretty heavy problems to travel all that way."

"They are, indeed."

"What you gonna do if you get there and find the trouble waiting for you?"

Quinn touched the butt of the pistol at his hip, a move-ment he did not know he was making until it was done. He glanced over at Jody and back through the dark windshield. "I'm gonna sort it out."

Jody glanced down at the pistol, then at Quinn's face. "I imagine you are," he said.

They passed another hour in silence. Quinn stared out the window at the deep black beneath them. At sporadic intervals there would be small specks of light below them, but they were few and far between as they got closer to the coast, where the towns grew to resemble wide spots in the road.

Rubbing his eyes, Quinn fought against the fatigue that lay across him like a lead blanket. The last two days had been whirlwinds of grief and pain, punctuated with moments of gut turning horror. He could not wipe the memories of standing in Patrick's bloody footprints, of experiencing the young man's last few, miserable weeks from his mind. Nor could he forget the reeking demon who took such pleasure in that remembered pain. There was so much about the last few months that Quinn wished he could go back and change. He wished he had been a better friend to Patrick. He wished he had been there for the young man so none of this would have happened. He wished he had never had to drive away from Resolution, leaving both it, and the people who resided there, vulnerable to the dark that seemed to be crowding in on them.

But, as Raife often told him, wish into one hand and shit in the other, then see which one fills up first.

Quinn did not realise he was falling asleep until he was jolted awake by the sound of Jody's voice and the sharp banking of the plane.

"I copy you, Resolution tower," Jody said into the microphone of the headset he wore. "Coming in now, and I won't be staying long."

The small plane dropped quickly. Quinn felt a sharp reduction in speed as Jody did things with the controls that Quinn did not even attempt to follow. They landed smoothly and Jody taxied the plane over to the single building near the narrow runway: a mobile trailer that served as a terminal. Jody stopped the plane within twenty meters of the building, killed the engines, then slid from his seat and opened the passenger door.

"Get out," he said, jerking a thumb towards the opening.

Thinking it pointless to say anything else, Quinn grabbed his bag and moved towards the exit. He offered his hand, but Jody ignored it and waved him down the stairs.

"Come on, man," the shaggy man said, looking at his watch. "I gotta get this thing back and refuel it before the sun gets too high and anyone notices it's missing."

"Thanks for the lift, anyway," Quinn said as he stepped down the stairs.

"Good luck with your trouble, man," Jody said as he pulled the door up. "If you're ever in Cranbrook again—"

Quinn stopped and turned towards him.

"—don't come to my house, and don't tell anyone you know me."

Shaking his head, Quinn turned and walked towards the small building. Behind him, the engine of the plane started and Jody was on his way.

Quinn pulled his phone from his pocket and looked at the screen. It was just after three A.M. The flight had taken less time than predicted, but it was still a long time since he'd had any word from anyone in Resolution. He felt his heart rate spike as he dialed Carrie's number. His call went directly to voicemail. He did not leave a message, but dialed again. Still he received no answer. He tried Raife's phone. It rang several times before Raife's recorded baritone voice asked Quinn to leave a message. Quinn snarled in frustration and hit the 'end' button on his phone. He tried Dave's number, his heart thumping, and prayed to anything that would listen that his friend would pick up.

"Quinn?" Dave's asked on the other end of the line.

"Yeah," Quinn said, excitement nearly turning the affirmation into a shout. "I've been trying to get a hold of everyone but no one is answering. What the fuck is going on?"

"Where are you?" Dave asked.

"I'm at the Resolution airport. Where are you?"

"How the hell did you get to the airport?"

"It's a long story," Quinn said. "Where are you? Why can't I get a hold of anyone?"

"I'm at the hospital," Dave said.

Quinn felt his heart tumble downwards through his chest and land behind his navel. "What happened?"

"I'm coming to get you," Dave said. "There is too much to tell over the phone. Carrie is hurt, but she's going to be fine.

We don't know about Raife. I'll be there in ten minutes."

The line went quiet as Dave hung up and Quinn looked down at his phone. He stared at it for several long moments, his eyes focused on a picture he and Carrie had taken together that spring, her cheek pressed into his face as she looked at the camera while he nuzzled into her hair.

He closed his eyes and clenched his fist until he heard the screen on his phone crack.

"So, tell me why you broke your phone again?" Dave asked as he guided Raife's truck, surging and floating with speed, down the road from the airfield and into Resolution.

Quinn glanced down at the screen that had taken on the appearance of a drunken kaleidoscope and tossed it in the back seat. "Fuck. I don't know. Never mind." He rubbed a hand over his tired face and sighed heavily. "Tell me what happened, again. Slowly...and in English this time."

He listened carefully as Dave recounted the events of the last two days, starting with the man, Kord, and his daughter coming to Autumn's shop looking for the Guardian, and ending with the fight at Carrie's house where the child had been taken. Quinn sat in silence once Dave had finished, his elbow on the arm rest of the truck. "Tell me why this kid is so important?"

"She opens doors or something. Raife said she put her hands on a big-assed rock and it disappeared and reappeared over top of the demon and smashed the fuck out of it. After the thing came to Carrie's house, Autumn said the kid opened a door to allow them to escape. She said it felt like they were gone for a moment, but it must have been more like ten minutes."

"And this thing," Quinn said, "this new demon, wants her to open a door for him."

"That's what we figured," Dave said.

"A door to no place good."

"No place good at all."

Dave had the truck's lights and sirens on and in minutes of reaching the outskirts of town they were drifting into the parking lot of the hospital. Quinn had his seatbelt off and the door open before Dave had brought the truck to a full stop. Quinn was out, sprinting across the parking lot, his urgency suddenly increased with the nearness of his goal. Dave flung open his own door and raced after him.

He burst in through the doors of the hospital to many startled looks from the people sitting in the emergency room and an annoyed glare from the triage nurse.

"Can I help you?" she asked.

Quinn looked side to side, realizing he had no idea where Carrie or Raife were and turned when Dave came in behind him. "Where?" he asked, knowing he did not need to elaborate.

Dave, still in uniform, passed wordlessly past the ancient security guard who sat behind a particle board desk beside the door to the minor treatment area. The guard's eyes flickered up once as Quinn went past, but he said nothing. Quinn followed Dave, matching his long legged strides, —wishing the lean man would run—down the hallway, past the trauma room and into the surgical area. In the waiting room sat Autumn, one bangled arm around Shawn's shoulders, as the boy leaned into her, his dirty face blank as he stared down at his hands. When Quinn walked into the room, Shawn turned his eyes up.

"Quinn!" the boy shouted. He threw himself from the chair and into Quinn's embrace.

Sandy and Gerritt were in the room also, bandages and tape criss-crossing their bodies from a horde of minor scrapes and scratches. Quinn looked at them over Shawn's shoulder as he gripped the boy.

"What's going on?" he asked. "Where is Carrie? What's happening with Raife?"

Sandy stood up, her arms folded. "The doctor just came out and talked to us. Carrie is going to be fine; just a concussion and a few stitches."

Quinn waited for more, but didn't get it. "What about Raife?"

"He's in surgery," Autumn said, standing slowly. Her hands reached out to touch the arm that Quinn had wrapped around Shawn. "He's got several broken ribs and one of his lungs had been punctured. He had a lot of internal bleeding. They're not sure he is going to survive the surgery."

Quinn felt as though someone pulled out his kneecaps and his legs buckled. Only his fear of dropping Shawn kept him on his feet. "Oh no," he said into Shawn's hair as he gripped the boy tighter. "Oh, dear God, no."

"He'd already be dead if not for Autumn," Sandy said. "I thought he was done at Carrie's house, but she put her hands on him and he kept breathing." Sandy looked at the blonde woman. "I don't know what you did, but I'm glad for it."

Autumn nodded her head and looked at her feet.

"The demon did this?" Quinn asked. Fury and pain made his voice waver. He knew it was a stupid question as soon as it came out of his mouth. Whether it had been the thing's own hand that had injured Raife, all of this was its doing. The murder of Patrick and Clara Morgan by its counterpart in Cranbrook; all the people who had been killed and consumed here in Resolution; Raife lying on an operating table fighting for his life; all were the sole responsibility of this demon. It would be held to account.

"Where is this Kord guy?" Quinn asked.

"No idea," Dave said. "He took off into the night after his kid. Whether he has any idea where the thing is going or not is anyone's guess."

Quinn turned his attention to Autumn. "Do you have any idea where it might be taking the kid?"

She shook her head. "I don't know, Quinn. This demon is so different, so much more powerful than the one you faced before. It doesn't need a den, and it can make itself look like a man. It could be anywhere."

"Is there anything you can do?" he asked. "Is there any way you can track it?"

Autumn ran a hand through her long hair and shook it out. "I don't know. Maybe. I'm not sure."

Dave's eyebrows drew together. "Uh, what does that mean?"

Sighing heavily, Autumn rubbed her eyes with the first two fingers of each hand. "There is a way," she said. "I just don't know if I can do it. It might be beyond me. Even if I can, I need some of its blood."

Quinn looked around at the gathered faces. Dave shook his head, Sandy turned her face down in a frown and Gerritt just looked worried. "There has to be something we can do here," Quinn said. "We can't leave that kid to die."

"Sullivan?"

Quinn turned at the voice behind him to see Inspector Green, his uniform rumpled and dark circles under his eyes.

"Quinn, when did you get back?" Green asked. He took off his hat and tucked it beneath his arm. "And what kid? Steve Faulk called me at home, said Raife had been hurt and the town is in shambles. What the fuck is going on?"

"Sir," Quinn said, putting Shawn on the floor. "It is difficult to explain, but I need to speak with you."

"You're damned right you do," Green said. "I need some fucking answers."

"No, sir. I need to talk to you about your son."

The inspector had his right hand up, pointing finger extended and his mouth open to speak, but whatever he was going to say died before it cleared his throat. His face seemed to droop, as though he had forgotten his son's death for a moment and the returning memory was a weight hooked into his skin.

The inspector seemed to shake himself slightly before standing a little straighter with obvious effort. "You have news about my son, Quinn?" His voice was even, but Quinn could hear a tension across the surface of it, a sheet of ice on the verge of cracking.

"I do," he said. "Best shared alone, I think. Then you can tell people the truth of it when you're ready."

Quinn saw Dave and Sandy look at each other. Dave shrugged, and they both focused their attention back on Quinn. Gerritt simply looked confused as his eyes roamed around the room.

"Very well, Quinn," Green said, ignoring the questioning looks from the constables around him. "Let's talk a minute."

Green turned from the waiting area and walked down the hall. Quinn glanced at Dave and Sandy, shook his head slightly, and followed.

The inspector walked a few paces until he passed a room with the door ajar. He stopped, looked in the room, then flicked on a light switch and jerked his head at Quinn. The younger man stepped into the room and found himself in a broad supply closet with a fluorescent light in the ceiling. The inspector closed the door behind them, squared his shoulders, adjusted the hat tucked beneath his arm and looked up at Quinn.

"All right, Quinn. What did you find out?"

"There is no easy way to go about this, sir, so I'll speak plainly." Quinn pulled in a deep breath through his nose. "Patrick did not commit suicide. He was murdered."

Inspector Green nodded slowly and sniffed. "How do you know this?"

Now, Quinn thought, came the really hard part; the news he could scarcely stand to give. "Do you remember two years ago when Dave, Raife and I went into Joe Robowski's house, and you've carefully avoided asking exactly what happened there?"

"I would not forget that, Quinn."

He nodded, and then sucked in a deep breath through his nose. He knew the time for avoidance and falsehoods was over, but the truth might make him look like a mental patient. "In the basement of that house we found a demon. I cannot explain how it got there, but we found it and we killed it. I didn't know it at the time, but it wasn't the only one."

The inspector turned away to face the shelves behind him and passed a shaking hand over his balding head. When he turned back, his face had lost much of its colour. "I knew you met with something strange in that basement, Quinn. I didn't ask you because I did not want to know. But a demon? Come on, son."

Quinn shook his head slowly. "I'm not addled, sir. We found something evil, something that had no place on this planet in that basement, and I found a creature that was much the same in Cranbrook."

The inspector waved his hand vaguely in front of his face. "Whether I can believe you or not, what does this have to do with Patrick?"

"I don't know exactly how to tell you this, but one of these things killed Patrick. It did it to get at me, to get me out of Resolution."

"Quinn, are you telling me someone killed my son because of you?"

"Not some*one*, sir. Some*thing*."

"I don't understand, Quinn. What are you talking about?" The inspector flipped his hat onto a shelf beside a stack of white linens and pressed the palms of his hands against his eyes. When he pulled his hands away his eyes were red and brimming with tears. "Why would some*thing*," the inspector said, his voice choked with something between a growl and a sob. "Need to get you out of Resolution?" The older man took in a deep breath and clenched his fists until they shook. "How are you involved with the death of my son?"

Quinn rubbed his own hand against his face, and then flapped his arms, feeling helpless. The display of emotion, the righteous fury of a grieving father, robbed him of his words and he felt his own eyes tingle with the beginnings of tears.

"I don't know how to explain this to you, sir, but believe me when I say if I'd know what would happen to Patrick, that I would gladly have traded places with him."

The inspector reached forward and grasped Quinn's shirt, balling it in his fist. The other hand gripped the back of Quinn's neck, and pulled the younger man down until they were almost nose to nose.

"If you tell me the truth I will believe you, Quinn," the inspector hissed. "But tell me true." The hand on the back of Quinn's neck tightened and shook. "Tell me what killed my son."

Quinn met the inspector's eyes and blinked back his tears. He took in a deep breath and searched the recesses of his exhausted mind for something to say – something that would convince Donald Green he wasn't mad. "It was a black thing, sir. Evil. Something that should not walk the earth. I cannot tell you exactly what it was, but I can tell you it killed Patrick."

"But, why?" The inspector released Quinn and turned away, wiping at his eyes. "What is so special about you that this thing would kill my son?"

"I'm not sure myself, sir. These things, they think I'm a threat to them. That there is something about me that makes me able to kill them when no one else can." His own voice sounded hollow in his own ears; a weak explanation for something he could not pretend to understand. "I didn't ask for this, sir, and I don't want it now."

"I cannot say I believe you, Quinn. This is too much, but I don't think you're lying either." The inspector sniffed and turned back towards Quinn, wiping a hand under his nose. "So, what now? What is going on in Resolution that my son was killed for?"

Quinn rubbed a finger across his lips and cleared a throat that felt dry and very tired. "I believe the thing in Cranbrook drew me away so that I couldn't oppose another of its kind here, in Resolution. I think that is what has been killing people."

"There's another one of these things in my town?" The inspector's eyebrows climbed while his voice dropped to a growl. He clenched a shaking hand and pointed to the floor in front of his feet.

"There is," Quinn confirmed, fighting the urge to step back in the face of the inspector's anger.

"And what about the thing that killed my son?"

"It's dead," Quinn said. The words brought back a twinge of the fury he'd felt only hours ago, in Clara Morgan's house, and helped push back his fatigue.

"What about Patrick?" the inspector asked. "What about his memory? Will people still believe that he killed himself, or will they know he was murdered."

Nodding, Quinn cleared his throat again. "The detachment commander in Cranbrook, Inspector Ferguson, knows the truth of what happened. He won't be able to tell the whole of it, but he will make sure that Patrick is honoured."

At the word 'honoured', Donald Green lifted his chin, forcing some of the slouch out of his spine. He retrieved his hat from the shelf and tucked it back underneath his arm. "We will speak more of this later, Quinn, and we'll see if we can't find some meaning in all this. For now, let us, you and I, move forward with the understanding that you have my faith, if not my belief. Can we do that?"

Quinn drew in a deep breath. "We can," he said after several moments.

The inspector nodded. "What needs to be done now? What do we have to face? Is there still something in my town? Is that what hurt Raife so bad?"

"It is," Quinn said. "It also has a child, the daughter of a man Autumn Donnelly knows."

"And we need to get the girl back from this thing, do we?"

The inspector, faced with a task he was able to understand, seemed to be recovering both his colour and his composure.

"We do," Quinn said.

Green reached past Quinn and pulled open the door. "All right, son, don't forget that I expect us to sit down over this later. For now, we've got a job to see to." He stepped from the storage room, but paused on the other side of the door and looked back at Quinn.

"The thing that killed Patrick," the inspector said. "You said it was dead. Were you the one who killed it?"

"I was," Quinn said, meeting the inspector's eye, another

sliver of his remembered anger returning. "I cut its head off."

With a deep, whistling breath through his nose, Inspector Green clapped his hat back on his head. "Good man," he said, and turned to walk briskly down the hallway.

Quinn caught up to him and the two men entered the waiting area, side by side.

Everyone waited, standing, in a tight circle in the middle of the room. Autumn held Shawn, the boy's arms around her neck, while she rocked slowly side to side. When Quinn and Inspector Green walked into the room, Autumn set Shawn on the floor and all attention was focused on them.

"All right," Green said. "What needs doing?"

"We have to find this child," Quinn said. "But I don't know how."

"I have an idea," Dave said. "But we have to go out to the truck."

"How many people are you going to need to drop this thing, Quinn?" the inspector asked. "How do we stop it?"

"This isn't going to be a 'we', sir. I need to stop it myself."

There was a loud chorus of dismay at Quinn's words, as he had expected, but he shook his head at the people surrounding him.

"I'm the only one who can stop this thing," he said. "I'm the only one who can kill it."

"If you'll recall," Dave said, putting on indignant airs. "You weren't exactly alone last time."

Quinn shook his head. "No. This time is different. This thing, this demon, is different than the last one. I'm supposed to be the Guardian, this is my job."

"How are you even going to find this thing, Quinn?" Sandy asked. "It's been hiding in town and eating people for a week, but no one has actually seen it except for us."

"Dave said he had an idea about that," Quinn said.

"I'm not telling you fuck all if you insist on leaving everyone behind," Dave said, folding his arms.

"Don't be an asshole, Dave, just fucking tell me," Quinn said, anger making his voice climb.

Glaring, his jaw clenched, Dave said nothing for several moments, obstinance painted on his face.

"Dave," Quinn said, trying to keep his voice even. "This isn't the time to argue."

Dave worked his mouth as though he tasted something sour. "Fine. Fuck," he said. "I shot that thing, right up close, with the shotgun." He pointed down at the spots on his filthy uniform shirt. "Some of this blood is from the demon, and there's got to be more on the barrel of the shotgun."

Quinn turned to Autumn. "Does that mean you can find it?"

The blonde woman sighed and ran her hand through her hair again. "I don't know, Quinn. I can try."

"That might be the best we can hope for," he said.

He was about to demand the keys to the truck from Dave, when a familiar form bustled into the waiting area. Doctor Stovern pulled a surgical cap off her head and ran her fingers through her sweaty hair.

"Do you have any news, Doc?" Dave asked when he saw her.

The doctor opened her mouth to speak and then stopped when she saw Quinn. "Constable Sullivan, I should have known you'd appear wherever Mr. Raife showed up."

"It's actually Corporal Sullivan now," Quinn said.

"Oh really?" Doctor Stovern said. "Will those little stripes on your uniform make you a bigger idiot than you were before?"

"No," Dave said. "Your idiocy doesn't increase until you get commissioned."

"Careful, McLeod," Inspector Green said.

Dave grinned, and winked at the inspector.

It was an incredibly odd time for a joke, Quinn thought, but the smile that crept onto his face felt good. It was a piece of normalcy in a world that had gone incredibly wrong. As the laugh came out and was joined by the others, Quinn felt okay for the first time since he had learned of Patrick's death. If laughter could still come, even at a time like this, then per-

277

haps the world was not too far gone to be set right.

"Never mind these baboons," Inspector Green said, glaring at the other people in the room. He tried to put on a hard face, but it was ruined by the smile that kept trying to form at the corner of his mouth. "What can you tell us about Carrie and Raife?"

"Ms Dawson will be fine," Doctor Stovern said. "She took a nasty bump on the head, but the CT scan showed no bleeding or damage. I've got her sedated just to keep her calm as she wakes up."

"What about Raife," Quinn asked, his face feeling flushed and full from the relief spinning in his head.

"Mr Raife is..." the doctor paused and ran her hand through her hair again. "He's a tough call. We got his lung reinflated and relieved the pressure on his organs, but his liver is badly lacerated and he has lost a lot of blood. He's about the toughest man I've ever seen, but he's in rough shape. He's going to be in intensive care for the foreseeable future. That he even survived long enough to get to the hospital is a miracle in itself." She moved her gaze over each of the drooping faces around her. "Hope for the best, but prepare for the worst."

"Can I see him, Doc?" Quinn asked, stepping forward slightly.

"He's not awake," she said.

"That doesn't matter, I just need to see him a minute."

"If I say no, are you going to wait until my back is turned and run in there anyway?"

The accuracy with which the doctor read his mind gave Quinn a bit of a shiver, but he kept a straight face. "I make no guarantees either way."

The doctor rolled her eyes. "Okay. Come on."

"And Carrie, too?" Quinn winced a little as he asked, knowing every word he said was likely a saw on the doctor's already frayed and extremely limited patience.

She turned. "Why is it every time I see you, you quickly become a massive pain in my ass?"

"He has that effect on everyone," Dave said.

Quinn glared at him, to no effect, and turned back to the doctor. "I'm sorry, Doc. I know I'm asking a lot, but I need to leave and go do something. It would mean a lot of if I could see them first."

"Why do I have the feeling I'm going to be seeing you back in here later, but with something for me to put stitches in?"

"Please, Doc," Quinn said. "I'm gonna marry one, and the other is family."

The doctor snorted and turned down the hallway.

Assuming the snort was code for assent, Quinn followed.

She showed him first into a room with a single bed and lone occupant. As Quinn walked into the room, Carrie's eyes fluttered open.

"Quinn?"

"I'm here, Carrie." He hurried to the side of her bed, clenching his teeth together to suppress a sob that wanted to burst from his throat at the sight of her bruised, puffy face and tangled hair.

"Where's Shawn? Is he okay?"

"He's fine," Quinn said. He sat on the edge of the bed and reaching out to cup Carrie's bruised face in his hands. "He's with Sandy and Dave in the waiting room right now."

"Something came to the house, Quinn." Her words were slow, her mind laboring under the meds Doctor Stovern had given her. "It took the girl that Raife asked me to watch out for. I tried to stop it, but I couldn't."

"It's okay, Carrie." He brushed several strands of black hair away from her face. "I'm going to get her back, right now."

"Is everyone else okay?"

Quinn looked over at Doctor Stovern, who stood in the doorway of the room with her arms crossed. The Doctor gave a minute shake of her head, and Quinn took her meaning.

"Everyone is fine, babe," he lied. "There is nothing to worry about."

The sedatives were having a heavy effect on Carrie; her eyes kept drifting closed. "What happened in Cranbrook?" she asked, her voice thick. "Did you find what you were looking for?"

"Yeah," he said. "I guess you could say that."

"Don't leave me again, Quinn,"she said, her voice soft, pleading. "Promise you won't leave."

He leaned towards her and kissed her forehead as her eyes fluttered closed. "I have to do something, but I'll be back soon. When this is over, I'm going to make you my wife and I'll never leave you again."

He did not know if she had heard his last words. Her eyes were closed and her breathing even, the lines of worry melting from her face. He kissed her again and then stood to face the doctor.

"Where is Raife?" he asked.

Doctor Stovern tilted her head down the hallway and walked out of the room. Quinn followed.

The intensive care unit was dark, most of the lights turned off at this time of night. Raife lay on a bed in a glass walled room, blinking machines surrounding him like metal sentinels. The big man's face was pale and he seemed to be diminished, as though a piece of him were missing.

"Wow," Quinn said, finding himself unprepared for the sight of his friend lying broken in a hospital bed. "Tell me true, Doc, is he going to make it?"

Doctor Stovern crossed her arms and sighed before running her fingers through her hair again. "I can't say for sure. By all accounts, with the severity of his injuries he should already be dead. I don't know how he made it this far, but he's hanging on, somehow. We've done everything we can. Now the rest is up to him."

"Did anyone call his wife?" Quinn asked.

Doctor Stovern nodded. "I believe the in-house social worker is on her way over there to pick her up and bring her here. Usually, we'd ask your crew to do it, but it seems you've had your hands full."

Quinn stepped into the room and moved between the machines until he was next to the bed, looking down at Raife's sallow face.

"I'm sorry I wasn't here, Boss," Quinn said, his voice pitched low, his eyes tingling. "I'm sorry I wasn't here when you guys needed me, but I'm not going to let this stand." He reached out and gripped Raife's limp hand. "This will be answered for."

Releasing Raife's hand, Quinn turned for the door. "Thanks for letting me see him, Doc."

As he tried to walk past, Doctor Stovern snagged his arm. "Are you going to tell me what this is all about?"

"No," Quinn said, looking down at her.

The doctor shook her head. "Will you at least tell me you'll be careful?"

"I can't do that either."

"It's too bad you're such a stubborn boor, Sullivan." She squeezed his arm, and then let him go. "I'd almost be convinced you're a good man."

"I do what I can, Doc."

He turned and left her standing in the doorway of Raife's room and walked quickly down the hallway. When he entered the waiting room, everyone looked up at him. He stopped in the center of the room, and beckoned Dave, Sandy and the Inspector them towards him. They stood in a tight huddle, their heads close together.

"How are they?" Dave asked, folding his arms and standing by Quinn's right hand.

"Carrie is asleep and fine. Raife looks rough."

"What now, Quinn?" Inspector Green asked. "What do we need to do?"

"I told you, sir, there is no 'we.' I'm going to go and find this thing and get that kid back."

"Bullshit!" Dave said, his voice almost a shout. "You are not going after this thing alone." Quinn opened his mouth to interrupt, but Dave slashed his hand through the air in front of his face. "No, don't fucking argue with me. I might not be the Guardian, or whatever the fuck you're supposed to be, but I can still come with you, watch your back, slow this fucking thing down, something! I'm not letting you walk out of here alone."

"None of us are letting you walk out of here alone," Sandy said, standing beside Dave.

"Someone has to stay with Shawn," Quinn said. "We can't leave him here by himself."

"I'll watch him," Inspector Green said. "I'll wait for news about Raife, fend off the media, and keep the boy with me until you're done."

"That's it," Dave said. "We'll leave Gerritt here with the Inspector in case something happens and everyone else is with you."

Gritting his teeth, Quinn surveyed the faces around him. He wanted to say something compelling, but he knew arguing with Dave once he had fastened his mind around something was useless. It was like trying to pry open the jaws of a pit-bull with a toothpick.

"I don't like it," Quinn said. "But if that's the way it has to be, let's go."

Autumn stood well behind Dave, holding Shawn's hand. She did not look up or take part in the conversation when Dave argued with Quinn. She looked anywhere but at Quinn's face as the Mountie walked towards her.

"Autumn, are you all right?" he asked.

She nodded and pushed her hair back from her face. "Yes, Quinn, I'm fine." She said nothing else, but stood gazing at the top of Shawn's head.

"Are you sure?" Quinn prodded.

"No, Quinn, I'm not sure." She lifted her eyes to his face. "I'm terrified. I don't want to do this. I want this all to be over." She looked at the faces of those around her. "I'm afraid we won't come back from this. This creature is too strong. It was in my home and I felt the darkness flowing off of it. I don't want to go after it. I am not a warrior. I'm no Guardian. I don't think I can do this."

Quinn looked down to where Autumn's hand gripped Shawn's and saw it was shaking. He reached out to clasp both her hand and Shawn's in his own. "I know you're scared. I am, too, but that demon has a child and almost killed Raife. We cannot leave this be. We have to go."

"I know," she said.

"I cannot do this without you," he said. "I need you to help me find this thing. Are you with me?"

"Yes, Quinn," she said, slowly. "I am with you."

He bent down and kissed the top of Shawn's head. The boy wrapped his arms around his neck, squeezing tight for a moment. When Shawn released him, Quinn stood up and faced his friends.

"All right," he said. "Let's roll."

He turned quickly and walked down the hallway, unwilling to give himself another moment to look at Shawn and hesitate. Dave caught up to him, walking at his shoulder, while Sandy and Autumn walked side by side, one pace behind. Anyone who stood in their path in the hallways of the hospital moved immediately upon seeing them. If his face at all reflected the hot anger thrumming in his chest, Quinn could only imagine what he looked like.

Once outside the hospital doors they all strode for the police truck in the parking lot. Dave unlocked the doors with a remote control, then opened the door and slid into the driver's seat. He put the key in the ignition and turned it enough to make the radio power on, then hit the release button for the shotgun rack and pulled the long gun free.

"Here it is," Dave said, holding the gun out to Quinn.

Quinn took the gun and examined the barrel. There were dark flecks on the first few inches of the cool metal, and it looked to him like it was blood. He looked at Autumn. "Can you do something with this?"

Her lips were pressed into a thin line as she examined the gun without touching it. After several moments of silence, she nodded. "I think so. I hope, anyway." Her eyes flickered to Dave. "You're sure this is from the creature?"

Dave shrugged. "I think so. I did a lot of shooting at a whole pile of shit, but I remember blood hitting me when I shot that thing in the leg. I can only assume some of it landed on that gun."

"Okay," Autumn said, bitting her lower lip a moment. "Let's see what we can do." She licked the first two fingers of her left hand, and then rubbed the digits on the dried blood spotting the shotgun barrel. Once she had a red smear on her fingers, she drew one single line down the back of the index finger on her right hand.

She glanced at Quinn. "Okay, now the hard part." She extended her right hand, index finger stretched and pointed into the night. She closed her eyes and began to speak, her voice so low it was nothing more than a droning mutter, her lips moving subtly. As she spoke, sweat popped out on her forehead and her voice gradually grew louder until she spoke in a loud, commanding voice, in a language Quinn did not understand. As her voice reached a shout, she began to turn, pointing her finger in all directions. When she pointed west, towards the water, the line of blood on her finger began to glow with a dull red light.

Autumn's eyes snapped open. "There," she said. "I can feel it."

Quinn took her elbow in his hand and started to guide her towards the passenger seat of the truck, his mouth opening to congratulate her, when a growl, in the darkness beyond the lights of the parking lot, made his mouth shut with a click. The sound was deep and awful, making the hair on the back of his neck feel like it was trying to crawl up to the top of his head.

He released Autumn's arm and shouldered the shotgun he still held, hoping Dave had reloaded it. He turned to face the sound of the growling. In the dark, just on the edge of the light, was a pair of bright eyes glowing with the vaguest hint of red.

"What the fuck is that?" Quinn asked as he racked the shotgun. Relief flooded into him to see a shell leap from the magazine tube and into the chamber.

"It's another one of those dogs," Dave said, his gun ap-

284

pearing in his hand. "That fucker must have mutated every stray dog in Resolution."

"I thought you said you killed them all," Quinn said, remembering Dave's account of the fight outside Carrie's house.

"I think it fairly obvious I was wrong," Dave said.

"You didn't miss any," Autumn said. "It is sending them."

"What?" Sandy asked. "Why? How?"

Sweat ran down Autumn's face, her hand trembling as she kept it pointed west. "These dogs are broken, savage, wild, just like the demon. It's gathering these animals and making them its brethren."

As Autumn spoke, Quinn saw several more pairs of eyes appear in the darkness. The growling grew to a chorus of savage aggression. "Why?" he asked. "Why are they coming here?"

"They came for us," Dave said, his pistol steady but his eyes darting as more bright specks appeared. "They came to finish us off."

Instinctively, they formed a circle, back to back, guns pointed outwards. Then, as Quinn's mind churned, trying to decide on the best course of action, the sliding glass doors that led to the interior of the hospital opened and two women dressed in blue nurse's smocks stepped out. Before Quinn could shout a warning, the women had taken several steps into the parking lot. A feral dog, misshapen and insane, lunged out of the shadows between two parked cars and slammed into one of the women from behind, knocking her to the ground.

Seeing the woman go down, Sandy took a handful of running steps, raised her pistol and fired. Her bullet caught the dog in the hind quarters and it jumped backwards, snapping at the air near its rear legs. Sandy fired several more times, each shot hammering into the dog, hurling it to the ground.

"Get back inside," she yelled at the two women.

Both stared at her, their mouths open in wide 'O's' of surprise. The standing woman helped her prone friend, hands scraped and bleeding, to her feet and they scuttled back inside, sobbing dramatically and clutching at each other.

The sets of eyes that surrounded the hospital parking lot faded slightly when Sandy started shooting, but Quinn could still see dark shapes moving back and forth in front of them. He suddenly thought he understood how a wounded water buffalo on a nature documentary felt while a group of hyenas circled it.

"What the fuck do we do now?" Dave asked as Sandy rejoined them.

"We need to call for help," Quinn said. "We can't leave Raife and Carrie, or the people in the hospital alone with these things out here."

"There's no more help, Quinn," Sandy said. "Everyone's already working."

Dave nodded. "And they're busy as fuck with all the shit that's happened in the last two days. There isn't anyone else to call. I think Steve Faulk even called a couple of the retired guys in town and asked if they were willing to work."

"Fuck," Quinn said, his eyes moving between Dave and Sandy. "You'll have to stay here. Someone has to guard the hospital." He held the shotgun out to Dave.

"What?" Dave asked, looking down at the shotgun but not reaching for it. "Fuck, no! You can't do this by yourself, you stubborn bastard. I'm not going to let you run off and get yourself killed."

"He's right," Sandy said. "We have to separate. There just aren't enough of us."

"No," Dave said, shaking his head. "We'll get Gerritt to guard the doors. I'm coming with you."

"You can't leave that kid here alone, Dave," Quinn said. "He couldn't lead a one man raid on an out-house, let alone be held responsible for the lives of a couple hundred people, and I don't trust him to keep Raife and Carrie safe. You have to stay here." He held the shotgun up a little higher and shook it for emphasis.

His mouth set in a grim line, Dave stared him down until Quinn was certain the other man was going to hit him. "Mother fucker!" Dave shouted in frustration. He slammed his pistol back in his holster and snatched the shotgun from Quinn.

"Autumn," Quinn said, turning to the blonde woman who had been watching the exchange between the Mounties with her hand held carefully in front of her, so as not to disturb the smear of blood on the back of it. "Get in the truck." She slid into the passenger seat, and he slammed the door after her.

He ran around the front of the truck, keeping his gaze on the glowing eyes skirting the limits of the parking lot, and climbed into the driver's seat. Before he closed the door, he opened the glove box, took out two five-round boxes of shotgun ammunition and passed them to Dave.

"Be careful, Quinn," Sandy said, as she retreated towards the hospital doors, her pistol gripped in both hands before her.

"You and I are going to talk about your fucking hero act once you get back here," Dave said, tucking the shotgun into his shoulder. "I plan on slapping you around a little, Corporal, so make sure you come back intact."

Quinn felt a sudden pang of regret that Dave was not in the truck with him. There was no one else, with the possible exception of Raife, who he would rather have at his back when fuckery of this particular intensity started happening.

"I will," he said with a nod to his friend. "I promise."

"I'll hold you to it," Dave said. He turned to trot towards Sandy.

Slamming his door, Quinn yanked the gear shift of the truck into 'drive' and looked over at Autumn. "Which way?"

Her face was pale and drawn, lines of exhaustion and worry pulling at the corners of her eyes, but her hand was steady as she lifted it and pointed west. "That way," she said. "Towards the water."

"Okay," Quinn said. "Hang on."

He jammed his foot down on the accelerator and the big engine of the truck roared as Quinn sent it lurching over the sidewalk that ringed the parking lot. The words of a nearly forgotten Depot driving instructor came back to him as he yanked the wheel and veered towards a group of the mad, feral dogs: 'Drive it like you stole it, not like you own it.'

The dogs scattered, but Quinn managed to catch one and felt a satisfying thump beneath the tires of the truck as he pushed the gas pedal down further and steered towards the waterfront.

CHAPTER 19

Quit your sniveling," the demon said as it looked down at the child at its feet. The girl had her knees drawn up to her chest and was rocking back and forth on the dirty concrete floor beneath her, her face pressed into her thighs. "If there is one thing I cannot stand it is the way you humans whine. It is enough to turn the stomach."

A deep feeling of satisfaction filled the demon's belly and it could not help but smile. Many years of pursuit, of effort, of planning had finally come to fruition with the prize that sat before it, crying silent tears.

For several human lifetimes it had walked this world, the majority of those years spent without purpose. Like many before it, it had found a place to pass through its own plane and into this one, and its wanderings had taken it all across this watery rock the humans so revered. It had started wars, spread plagues, sown misery, aggression and hate, and it had basked in the scent of it all like it was the finest cologne. Making men scream was fun—like going to a carnival—but it had needed something more. It had needed something bigger. It had needed a goal.

That goal had come when it had found this child. It had been able to feel her ability from the moment it saw her. Plans, a purpose, had sprung fully formed into its mind and it had tried to claim her. Her parents had been more resourceful than it had expected, and she had escaped, but not now.

The girl's father, the demon knew, would attempt to seek a safe place for the child. It was the way of humans to want to form alliances with other stupid humans. When the demon had heard of a Guardian coming into being in this sad little town, it knew exactly where the man, Kord, would flee, and he had run right into its hands.

It had not been hard to find another, although assuredly lesser, of its kind and bend it towards the necessary tasks. The plan had come together and fallen smoothly into place. It was not difficult, really. Humans are, after all, nothing if not stupid.

This town had come with some surprises, however, but only enough to make things interesting. The big man who had thwarted it had come as a surprise. He was not a Guardian, but he was formidable nonetheless, and had managed to interrupt the demon's efforts and cause a significant wrinkle in its plan. The wrinkle had been smoothed, though, and now things were going as they should have in the first place.

Delicious anticipation curled up through the demon and it licked its lips. The Guardian was surely dead by now, the big man had been laid low, and the savage allies the Demon had created—the half starved dogs that were only one step away from their wolf ancestors—would surely finish the big man and his companions. There was nothing to stop it, no loose ends needing to be snipped and no one left to stand in its way.

The smile on its face grew wider and it crouched down in front of the weeping child.

"Listen to me, girl," it said, pouring honey into its voice. "I am not going to harm you. Not one golden hair will be split, but I need you to look up at me, now."

The girl only continued rocking back and forth, her face hidden.

"I SAID, LOOK AT ME, YOU LITTLE BITCH!"

The demon's scream struck the child like a blow and she jerked as though she had been shocked. The sound, so horrid it hurt the demon's own ears, bounced about the inside of the large, metal-walled warehouse they were in and continued to buffet the girl.

Slowly, her eyes red rimmed, wide and terrified, the child lifted her head and looked into the demon's face.

"That is better," it said, the cloying sweetness in its words once more. "Now, I need you to focus. There is something we are going to do."

"Are we getting close?" Quinn asked. He guided the truck through the deserted streets as quickly as he could manage.

Autumn held her hand up in front of her face, her fingers spread wide, with her index finger pointed forward as she looked down it like the sights on a pistol. "Yes," she said. Her eyes focused on the dully glowing line of dried blood on the back of her finger. The light pulsed, growing stronger as they grew nearer to the water. "Very close, indeed."

The residential area ended and the run-down houses grew fewer and further apart. Soon they were in the wide streets of the industrial complex near the harbour. On both sides of the street were manufacturing shops and shipping warehouses, almost all of which were deserted at this time of night.

"Slow down, Quinn," Autumn said, glancing over at him. "The thing is close." She refocused on her finger and pointed it to the left. "Go that way."

Quinn guided the truck down a narrow road that ran parallel to the water. Creeping along at a slow speed, he glanced at Autumn for queues. The further they got away from the harbour, the more run down and ramshackle the warehouses and shops became. Eventually, the buildings had the windows smashed out and stubby trees growing up through cracks in the parking lot.

"Where are we?" Autumn asked. Her gaze flickered up from her finger to take in her surroundings.

"This is the abandoned sector of the docks," Quinn said. "There was a big boom here in the mid-eighties when the

Alaskan cruises started to get popular and there were hundreds of tourists pouring into town every day. Retail businesses bought up all the real estate right off the harbour and the industrial companies had to move further out. Once the boom calmed down and the retail stores moved back up into town, all these buildings further out were abandoned and left to rot."

"Old ghosts and broken hopes," Autumn said. "A fitting place for a demon to hide."

Quinn nodded as he remembered Joe Robowski's rundown house with the demon living in the stone-walled basement beneath it. "It certainly is."

The line of blood on Autumn's finger pulsed again, bright enough that it made Quinn squint. "This is it," she said, pointing to a warehouse building in front of them. "The creature is in there."

Flicking off the knob for the headlights, Quinn put the truck in park and turned off the engine. "Are you sure?"

Autumn nodded. "I can feel it, Quinn. Even without this," she lifted her glowing finger. "I would know it is here. This old trick just got us close." She wiped her finger vigorously with her skirt, smothering the glow. "If you open yourself, you'll be able to feel it, too."

He wanted to tell her now was not the time for one of her kooky lessons, but then he felt something. It was a strange, foreign feeling that he could barely identify, let alone describe. It was as though his chest grew loose and tight at the same time. It was like he had pins and needles on the inside of his veins. He could not quantify it, but he knew what it meant: the demon was close.

"I feel it," he said, looking through the windshield of police truck at the building. "I can feel it, too."

Out of the corner of his eye he saw Autumn smile and nod her head once. "You're beginning to understand. I knew you would."

Over the past three days, Quinn had seen things—most of which he did not want to see, and hoped fervently to forget— that he never believed would have been possible. For the past two years, since he, Raife and Dave had faced down the demon in Joe Robowski's basement, Autumn had been trying to prepare him, school him, guide him into the role he had not asked for. He had been trying to convince himself that the battle with the demon two years previous had been an isolated incident, something he had only have to experience once. Now he knew that was not, and could not, be true. He also had a feeling, very deep in the pit of his gut, that things were going to get worse before they got better.

As he reached for the door handle of the truck, he thought things were going to get very bad indeed.

When he opened his door, Autumn did the same and he reached out to grab her arm. "No, Autumn, you stay here. If I'm not back with the kid in ten minutes, start the truck and drive back to the hospital. If anything besides me comes out of this building, don't wait for ten minutes, just go."

She shook her blonde head. "You cannot ask me to do that, Quinn."

"I can and I will. I'll handcuff you to the steering wheel if I have to."

In the two years he had known her, Quinn had never seen Autumn angry. Mildly frustrated, yes - and only when Quinn made her so by being an obstinate pain in the ass - but never full-on angry. The emotion that bubbled to her kind, finely lined face now was a close cousin to complete fury.

"I'm not fucking waiting here while you go in there and die!" Her voice was barely above a whisper, but there was so much heat in it, Quinn felt as though his eyebrows had been singed. "What if you face this thing and win, but lie in there bleeding? You want me to drive away and leave you and the child alone where no one can find you? It will not happen, Quinn. I'll stay out of your way, but you cannot ask me to sit here while you go alone." She leaned back, the conflagration of her anger burning down to a hot smolder. "Besides, that child was my responsibility. I was supposed to protect her, but she was taken from me. I cannot leave a job like this half done."

He thought about arguing with her, about making good on his threat to handcuff her to the steering wheel of the truck, but in the end he only nodded. He realised he was scared, terrified, in fact, of what he would find inside that building. Besides the enemy that waited for him, he feared he would find his failure. Worse than his own death would be the death of the child.

He wished vehemently that Raife and Dave were with him, shoring him up like they had before, pooling their courage, their collective will, to allow them to do what needed to be done, but they were not here, and as Raife had told him before: "If wishes were horses, then beggars would be shitting all over us."

Autumn, however, was here and wanted to stand with him. She was not like Raife and Dave with their hard edges and capacity for violence, but the fire of her will burned no less hotter than theirs. He felt her courage creeping beneath his own skin and adding iron to his spine.

"Okay," Quinn said, after studying her for several long moments. "But you have to stay behind me. No heroics. If you get an opportunity to grab the kid and get out, then you run. Don't think twice about leaving me behind. Agreed?"

He thought she would protest, but she nodded. "Agreed."

He pushed his door open and slid out of the driver's seat. "Stay close and stay quiet." She nodded and opened her own door, stepping out onto the cracked surface of the parking lot.

He drew his gun from its holster and gripped it in both hands as he walked around the front of the truck to stand beside Autumn to study the building.

"Where's Donnell's dagger?" the blonde woman asked. "You know your gun won't kill the creature."

"No," Quinn agreed. "It won't, but it will certainly surprise the fuck out of the prick and give me time to stab it. Besides," he said as he pulled his small flashlight from his back pocket, "shooting demons has almost become a habit."

His pistol held up at eye level, Autumn one step behind him, Quinn stalked quickly towards the abandoned warehouse. The clouds overhead were low and thick. The bright lights of the harbour reflected off them, giving the sky an unnaturally bright, orange colour. There were no operating street lights in this part of the warehouse district, but the clouds reflected enough light to walk by. Quinn did not need to turn on his flashlight.

He moved between the short trees sprouting through the cracks in the asphalt parking lot and made his way towards the corner of the building. As he got close, he ran into a pool of cold air so stark in its contrast that he felt as though he had walked beneath a waterfall. He remembered the bitter cold that had gripped Resolution Cove two years ago when the other demon was marshaling its strength and clamped his teeth together to hold back the wave of fear that rose in his throat.

"Is this what it was like before?" Autumn asked, her words choppy as she took small panicky breaths.

He realised he had stopped when he hit the pocket of cold air. He glanced back over his shoulder at Autumn and nodded. He tried to speak, but the cold seemed to have frozen his tongue and sucked all the moisture out of his mouth.

"I'm sorry, Quinn. I didn't know what I was asking of you." She reached out and touched the back of her shaking hand to his face. Her fingers were warm, and the warmth in them spread from his face and down his neck to set his heart beating again.

He turned his eyes back to the warehouse. With a force of will he started his feet moving again. Autumn followed.

When he reached the corner of the building, he pressed himself against it. The doors in the front were all boarded up and he had to look for another entrance. He peered down the long side of the building and saw several darker shapes in the shadows that might be the outlines of unblocked doors.

He knew he needed to keep moving, to push forward, but his heartbeat crashed in his ears like a series of consecutive thunderclaps. He took a deep breath, willing his body to settle and his heart to slow. Once it did, he gripped his pistol tight and took several steps towards the first of the doorways.

The first door he came to was boarded over. The second was not, but when he tried the door knob, gripping it and gradually adding pressure, he found it would not budge. He walked further down the long warehouse, coming to the last doorway before he reached the opposite corner. This door, he could see, was unblocked and stood slightly ajar. He reached out slowly to give it a tentative push as a figure, a darker shape against the shadows, came around the end of the warehouse.

The figure had a faintly glowing object on one hand and stopped when it saw Quinn. The Mountie's heart lurched, a hot blast of panic shooting through his chest. He brought his gun up, the glowing sights of the pistol unnaturally bright in the dark. He began pulling the trigger as he leveled the sights at the centre of the dark shape.

"Kord?"

Autumn's hiss of recognition stopped the travel of Quinn's trigger finger, and he depressed the button on the back of his flashlight, shining the bright, LED beam at the dark shape. Before him was a slender man in stained blue-jeans and a torn plaid shirt, the shadow of a dark beard forming on his jaw, beneath unruly dark hair. There was a set of brass knuckles on his right hand. Even in the bright beam of the flashlight they glowed like Donnell's dagger, which was producing a steadily growing heat from its sheath in the small of his back.

"Who is this?" he asked Autumn, his voice pitched low, while he kept his eyes on the man in front of him.

"This is Kord MacRae," Autumn said. She leaned over his shoulder and spoke into his ear. "The father of the girl we've come for."

Quinn took his eyes off the man in front of him and looked back over his shoulder at Autumn, allowing his pistol to drop, but not very far. "Are you sure?"

She nodded, her blonde hair swaying. "You see the object on his fist? It carries the same type of power as Donnell's dagger. A demon could not bear to hold it."

After his experience with the demon in Cranbrook assuming the identity of another Mountie, Quinn was deeply skeptical, but he had no choice except to trust Autumn and her judgment. There was no time to interrogate the man.

"Kord, how did you find us?" Autumn asked.

"I was about to ask you the same thing. I tracked the demon to the waterfront from the house we were hiding in, but lost the trail when it began running between these warehouses. I've been checking each of these buildings, looking for my child."

"Tracked it?" Quinn asked. "How?"

"The thing was bleeding badly when it fled with Abby. The trail was easy to follow for a while, but the blood stopped and I've had to guess." The slender man looked past Quinn to Autumn. "Is this the Guardian?"

"He is. Kord, this is Quinn Sullivan."

The slender man nodded. "You are as I imagined you to be."

Quinn wanted to make a response, but had nothing to say that did not sound idiotic as it bounced around the inside of his skull.

Kord saved him further embarrassment. "Have you come for my daughter?"

"I have," Quinn said. "Among other things." It was a matter of course, for Quinn, that he try and get this child back from the demon. He could not leave her to whatever the thing would do to her, but there was another matter he had to discuss with the creature. The tab left by the death of Patrick Green was very long and Quinn would see the account settled.

"What do we do now?" Kord asked.

Quinn had no illusions that they would be sneaking up on the demon. Their approach had been too loud, had taken too long, to dream of any kind of stealth or surprise. He would have to work under the assumption that he had be walking into a stand up fight, but the churning anger living beneath his breastbone and his rank desire for vengeance called out and welcomed the confrontation.

"Where did you get that?" Quinn tilted his chin toward Kord's right hand.

The slender man held his fist up, the glowing brass knuckles gripped tight. "They've been passed through my family for years. Came across the sea from Scotland with one of my ancestors. You have something similar, don't you?"

A hot pulse in the small of his back was a constant reminder of Donnell's dagger, and Quinn nodded. "Do you know how to use them?"

"I'm not a Guardian, though I wish I was, but I'm no slouch either. I won't be useless to you, and I won't get in your way."

"All right," Quinn said and glanced back at Autumn. "Our plan doesn't change. If you get an opportunity to grab the girl—"

"Abby," Kord interrupted.

Quinn nodded. "Autumn, if you get a chance to grab Abby you do it and get out. The keys are still in the ignition of the truck. Take her to Inspector Green. He'll be able to see her safe, even if he doesn't know why." He nodded at Kord. "We worry about the demon."

The slender man said nothing, but flexed the fingers through the holes of the brass knuckles and sniffed loudly.

"Okay," Quinn said. He pushed his shoulder into the already open door.

The inside of the warehouse was dark, the strange half-light reflecting off the clouds came through the broken windows. Quinn moved sideways, out of the open doorway, as his nostrils filled with the damp stink of rotting drywall and the acrid tang of rust. In the sparse light, he could see heaps of debris, jagged spears of twisted metal reaching up out of the gloom like clawing fingers. There was no clear way forward. Quinn waited, hoping his eyes would adjust a little, while Kord and Autumn slipped in behind him.

"Do you see anything?" Autumn whispered, the sound like a shout in the eerie stillness of the warehouse.

Both Quinn and Kord glared at her and she clapped a

hand over her mouth. Quinn noticed that Kord had the hand with the glowing brass knuckles stuffed into the pocket of his jeans in an effort to conceal the light. A faint glow was still visible through the material, but not enough to give them away unless something were to look right at it.

Quinn was trying to decide which way to go when he felt a tap on his shoulder. He turned his head. Kord pointed a finger towards the right side of the warehouse – the side closest to the water. It took Quinn a few heartbeats to see what the other man pointed at, but eventually he could make out a faint glow that was a different shade of orange than the light filtering from the windows. He nodded, acknowledging he had seen it, and started towards it, trying to pick his way through the debris in the near dark.

Every step Quinn took caused some small piece of garbage to shift on the damp cement floor, and every small scraping sound sent a jolt of hot adrenaline streaking through his chest. He was reluctant, even, to breathe deeply, fearing the sound of it would give away their position in the warehouse. Every shadow, every piece of junk, could conceal the demon they had come to find. It was likely waiting to kill them all.

They slipped in single file, between two heaps of trash. The source of the light came into view. Attached to a catwalk, high on the wall closest to the water, was a platform of metal grating with an old kerosene lamp sitting on it. Beside the lamp was a blonde haired girl, about ten years old, her hair in a long single braid. Her hands were bound in front of her and her mouth was tied with a rag.

"Abby!" Kord McRae shouted, as he darted past Quinn and ran up a set of stairs leading to a branch of the catwalk.

"Kord!" Quinn hissed as he tried to grab him. "No!"

The slender man reached the top of the stairs and turned left, towards the platform. Quinn saw a shadow, barely illuminated by a sparse tendril of light from a broken window, shift on the right side of the catwalk, behind Kord, where the slender man could not see.

There was no time for Quinn to shout a warning. The

shape burst from the shadows, moving with unnatural speed and slammed into Kord's back, sending him pin-wheeling off the catwalk and into the debris below. Abby tried to scream through her gag, but the sound was drowned out by the strangled cry that erupted from Kord as he struck the ground.

Quinn lifted his pistol and began firing at the dark shape on the catwalk. The muzzle flash left blinding streaks in his vision and the bark of the gun was ear-splitting in the enclosed, echoing space of the warehouse. He saw the shape jerk and then turn to flee towards the girl. Quinn stopped firing, fearing he might hit the child and charged up the stairs to the catwalk, doing his best to keep the dark shape in his sight. From the corner of his eye, he saw Autumn run through the warehouse to where Kord had landed.

The demon darted down to where Abby was bound and snatched her up like she weighed nothing and turned to face Quinn. The creature held the girl, one of its arms around her chest, while the other hand gripped her throat. Quinn, his pistol held up at eye level, stalked forward, the glowing sights of his gun trained on the centre of the creature's forehead.

"You're supposed to be dead, Guardian," the thing said, its voice pleasant, almost conversational. "Why are you here? How did you get past my other in the east?"

Quinn continued forward while the demon talked, his pistol steady despite the thrumming of his heartbeat in his ears. When the thing mentioned 'the east', Quinn thought of Patrick and the demon in Cranbrook who had murdered him to draw Quinn away. As he thought of Patrick, of the images of the young man hanging dead, the last few cold fingers of fear were pried off his heart and replaced with the searing heat of the anger that had been smoldering there.

"Stand where you are," the thing said, its voice rising. "Another step and I'll rip her pretty head off."

He was within eight steps of the thing and he took two more. While he did not doubt the thing was able to kill the child with its bare hands, Quinn did not think it would. "You're full of shit," he said. "You're not going to kill that kid, but I'm certainly going to kill you."

"You cannot kill me," the thing said. Laughter burbled out of its throat like raw sewage from a broken pipe. "Your friends have been making a pathetic effort at it for days and haven't come close. I've settled with Kord McRae. I've laid low the big man you call Raife. I've done for that pallid little cur you called Patrick and very soon I'll do for you."

"Why did you have to kill Patrick?" Quinn sensed it was a bad idea to talk to the thing, to give it the satisfaction of knowing he hurt, but the question was out of his mouth before he knew it.

"You bloody humans and your constant, consuming questions. Why did I kill him? So I could kill you, of course. Or at least so my *other* could. I cared less about that miserable little bastard than I do for the dog shit on my boot heel.

"The only thing more insufferable about you humans than your question is your ever-present compassion, your infuriating pity. I knew that man you answer to would send you out with questions when his son was dead, and because you are weak I knew you would go. Without their tame dog to guard them, the mewling sheep in this town were ripe, begging to be taken. The boy was nothing, only a means to an end."

While the demon was on its diatribe, Quinn had been taking small, shifting little steps forward. He now stood three paces from the yapping creature.

"Patrick was something else that you forgot," Quinn said, as he closed his left eye, sighting down the pistol with his right.

"Oh, yes? And what is that?"

"He is the death of you." He squeezed the trigger of his pistol and the bark of it silenced the demon's half-made retort. The bullet punched into its right eye, throwing its head back and causing it to release Abby.

Quinn lunged forward, dropping his pistol on the catwalk as he reached to the small of his back to rip free Donnell's dagger. With his empty hand, he grabbed Abby's bound wrists, hauled her to her feet, and pushed her, stumbling, towards the stairs.

"Autumn!" he shouted as he drew the dagger. He held it up, the harsh, white glow of it blinding in the dim interior of warehouse, the grip burning in his fist.

The demon took only a moment to recover its balance and turned to face Quinn. There was a bloody mass of pulp where its right eye used to be. Quinn watched, his limbs frozen by dread fascination as the pulp began to swirl and then reform until, after a handful of heartbeats had passed, there was a milky white ball filling the socket. The demon's other eye, whole and undamaged, glared at Quinn. A slow grin spread across its mouth.

"You are not unskilled, Guardian," the demon said, its voice clear and silky. "I'll acknowledge that, but I've come too far, seen too much, planned too long, to be stopped by the likes of you." The creature stood up straight and rolled its shoulders, producing loud, pronounced popping noises. As Quinn watched, it expanded, the muscles of its neck and shoulders growing like rising bread, its limbs and fingers elongating and taking on an animalistic, crooked appearance. It shook its head and stretched its jaw, producing another loud crack as it jutted further from its head. It settled in a crouch, meeting Quinn's gaze with one red tinged eye and flexed its long, clawed hands.

"If we'd met some days ago we'd have a contest, you and I, but I've been in this place too long. I've fed off its denizens and drunk of the raw power of this valley, and now..." It shrugged, its massive shoulders lifting. "Now, I'll break you and drink of your power as well."

The dark part of Quinn's brain, the part where his cave-dwelling ancestors still lived and remembered what it was like to crouch around a fire in the dark with superstitious dread, believed the demon. It believed, completely, that there was no standing against this creature, and he was simply going to die.

"You'll meet your Patrick soon enough, Guardian," the demon said, the silk gone from its voice, replaced with a rasp of sandpaper dragged over a bleached skull. "When you meet him in Hell, you can tell him of your failure."

Quinn had been taking a shaking step backwards when he heard Patrick's name and stopped. The word, the name of the boy, hit the frightened part of him like a slap in the face and sent it tumbling away. Left behind was anger, free now of the dampening effect of the rank fear. Quinn fed every ounce of strength he had left into that flickering flame and willed the heat to grow. Instead of stepping back, he ground his foot into the metal of the catwalk and crouched, holding Donnell's dagger in front of him. The light of it cast a shield to ward off his fear.

"I may have failed Patrick," Quinn growled. "But I will honour him with your death." He yelled, giving vent and voice to all the fear and shame and hatred that had been welling in his chest for days.

The demon flinched.

Quinn charged.

The demon thrust forward to meet him, but the Guardian changed direction, lunging low and to one side, as far as the rails of the catwalk would allow, and ducked under the demon's swinging arm. He slashed the dagger across its gnarled body. The dagger bit through muscle and bone. A pulsing red flash erupted as the ancient steel met flesh.

The demon whirled, seemingly unaffected by Quinn's strike, and surged forward with supernatural speed. Quinn tried to dodge out of the way, but the demon was too quick. It caught him with a glancing blow to the side of the head. Stars burst into his vision and he was thrown sideways, towards the rail of the catwalk. The momentum of his body carried him over the rail and he dropped the dagger in a frantic scramble to keep from falling, but tumbled over anyway.

His stomach lurched in his gut as he plummeted through the dim light to crash with teeth-rattling impact into a pile of debris. His vision swimming, Quinn struggled to make his battered limbs obey him and stand upright, but could not find purchase in the pile of sliding rubble and did nothing more than flail towards the edge of it. He heard the impact of a heavy body falling into the pile near where he landed, and scrabbled away on his hands and knees.

As he reached the floor, still crawling, Quinn looked over his shoulder to see a broad shape, silhouetted in the light of the lantern on the landing. He saw it jump high in the air and threw himself forward on his belly, barely avoiding crushing impact as the demon landed where he had been a moment before.

He flipped over on his back and scrambled backwards, his hands grated bloody on the rough floor, until he collided with a stack of pallets and could move no further.

"No more talk, Guardian," the demon said as it stomped across the floor towards him. "It is time to die."

Quinn pressed himself into the pallets, trying to escape, as the demon stopped beside him and raised one booted foot up above the Mountie's head. With his boot-heels scraping in the dust, Quinn Sullivan gritted his teeth and waited for the impact.

A scream from the demon's right side drew its attention. Autumn Donnelly appeared out of the gloom, her blonde hair flying behind her as she charged. She had Donnell's dagger held up in one hand, the glow of the weapon muted but still present. She collided with the creature, which still had its leg up while it stared at her in quizzical disbelief. She slashed downwards as they tumbled to the floor.

With the demon distracted, Quinn felt a small, warm hand grip his wrist and he snapped his head to the side. Peeking around the edge of the pallet was Abby. She slipped her father's brass knuckles into his hand.

Quinn jammed the weapon onto his fingers and clamped his hand closed. The glow of the weapon flared to brilliance in his grip, and he thrust himself upwards, pulling his feet beneath him.

As soon as the demon hit the floor, it thrust Autumn away, almost casually, sending her spinning into the gloom. It surged to its feet and started in pursuit of the woman, but Quinn lunged forward, hammering its face and head with the weapon in his fist. Hot light flared with every blow and the demon's clawed hands scraped wildly as it backpedaled, trying to escape Quinn's attack.

Triumph and hope burst in Quinn's chest as he struck the demon again and again. That hope died as suddenly as it was born, as the demon regained its composure and reached out to catch Quinn's fist and hold it tight in its own.

Quinn could hear the flesh of the creature sizzling as it held both his hand and the weapon fast in the massive bulk of its fist. The demon gave no indication it was in any pain and showed Quinn a mouth full of jagged teeth in a gross parody of a smile. The demon stepped forward, forcing Quinn back, the crushing power of its grip so great that the Guardian felt as though his hand were pinned beneath the tire of a truck. The demon's other hand streaked out to latch about Quinn's neck, hauling him bodily from the ground. Quinn kicked and thrashed and beat at the demon's arms with his free hand, but he might as well have been attacking a tree for all the reaction his struggles produced.

The demon hammered him downward into a pile of debris and pain rocketed through Quinn's body. He could taste blood in his mouth and smell the fetid breath of the demon as the creature brought its red-eyed face close to his. His vision narrowed, growing dark. The demon before him faded from view. He began to think of sleep, of how tired he was, and how long he had been awake and fighting. He longed to let his eyes close and think about Patrick Green and his wasted death no more.

A light, dazzling in the gloom of the warehouse, caught the corner of his eye and Quinn forced himself to look at it. Behind the demon, where it could not see, stood Autumn Donnelly. She shuffled forward, her face a bloody mask of pain as one arm hung limp and useless, but her blue eyes were clear and she met Quinn's, holding up Donnell's Dagger in her good hand. Quinn stretched out his own hand, his fingers splayed wide. Autumn tossed the dagger with an awkward, underhand motion. The dagger tumbled through the air and

Quinn reached out, his fingers grasping.

The knife landed in his hand and he closed his fingers about the blade. The glowing steel flared with new, intense heat and Quinn felt the edge bite into his palm and fingers. The searing pain of the cut snapped him out of his semiconscious state. He locked his eyes on the two glowing orbs in the demon's face—the ruined eye now whole again—and held the creature's gaze without flinching. The demon flicked a look down at the knife now in Quinn's hand, then snarled and squeezed the Guardian's neck all the harder. Unable to reach past the creature's long arms, Quinn shuffled his hand along the knife until he held it by the grip and then rammed the glowing blade into the soft underside of the arm holding his neck.

The demon howled in agony as it released its hold. Quinn ripped the dagger free and slashed at the hand holding his fist, once, twice, until that came free, as well. His limbs felt leaden and weak as he sucked in great, shuddering breaths, but he pushed forward, swinging his glowing fist and dagger as hard as his weary arms could manage.

With each blow Quinn struck there was a burst of flame.

The demon staggered. It would not go down.

"Autumn!" Quinn shouted between painful, wheezing breaths. "Take the kid and run." He needed them to get out while he could still hold the demon off. It was too strong, he could see now. He would not be able to kill it. It was the best he could do to buy them some time.

He received no response to his shout, and found himself defending instead of attacking. The time he had taken to call out to Autumn gave the demon an opportunity to come at him. He parried and dodged the whistling blows that hurtled towards him, the demon seemingly undiminished despite all the damage Quinn had inflicted upon it. As he back pedaled, he collided with a metal support pole and had to duck quickly around it as the demon lashed out with a swinging blow that set the pole ringing.

Quinn stumbled, but managed to keep his feet, and turned

to face the creature. He held the dagger in one hand and the brass knuckles in the other. He tried to bring them up in front of his face and at least give a vague impression he was ready to fight, but each of the small objects might as well have been a cinder block. His arms quaked as he clenched his teeth against the strain.

"Hold still, you sniveling little shit," the demon snarled as he stalked around the support pole and flexed its long fingers. "You're hard to kill, Guardian, I'll give you that, but you're only drawing out the inevitable."

Quinn wanted to make a witty retort, but his brain was solely occupied with the task of staying on his feet. "Go fuck yourself," was the best he could manage.

The demon simply grinned and took a leisurely step forward.

Movement behind the demon caught Quinn's eye. Autumn, Abby's small hand clasped in hers, appeared again between two piles of debris. She released the child's hand and pointed downward with her one working arm. The child, terror and dirt smeared across her features in equal measure, nodded and crouched down with her hands on the floor. A spot of searing light appeared beneath her palms, as bright as the light from Donnell's dagger. It spread quickly outwards. The light grew, turning from a spot into a circle, and in the centre of the circle was the blackest dark Quinn had ever seen.

As the circle expanded and silently consumed the floor, any debris lying on it fell in and disappeared, winking out of existence in the endless black of the opening. Autumn looked at Quinn, and when his eyes met hers, she waved her good arm once, towards the hole. Instantly, Quinn understood.

He stood up as straight as he could and sucked in a deep breath. "You think you can kill me, you piece of shit? Bigger and badder things than you have tried. I cut the head off the cunt that killed Patrick, and I'm going to do the same to you."

The demon, its red eyes focused on Quinn, still had not seen the hole behind it. It continued to stalk forward and tilted its head back and laughed. "You think my other in the east was my equal. It was a cub compared to me. You know nothing of real power, Guardian. You know nothing of pain, but I promise I'll teach you before you die."

With a howl, the demon lunged forward. Simultaneously, Quinn summoned the last of his strength and charged as well. As they were about to collide, Quinn dropped and slid forward on his knees, letting his momentum carry him into the demon's legs. He latched on and slashed wildly with Donnell's dagger. The Demon screamed as the blade bit deep into the back of one leg. Quinn dropped the dagger and wrapped both arms around the creature's other leg and heaved until he felt as though his spine would burst through his skin. The leg came free of the floor and the demon staggered backwards, its hamstrung leg faltering and its hands grasping at nothing as it tumbled towards the hole.

As it fell, the demon shrieked and twisted in the air like a cat, flailing at the ground with its clawed hands. Its legs disappeared into the hole, but its claws found purchase and it started to pull itself onto the floor. Quinn struggled to rise, to throw himself forward and push the demon into the gap, but his whole body shrieked in protest and his limbs would not respond.

From the other side of the hole, Autumn leapt, her hair flying wildly around her face, and landed on the demon's back. There was a jagged piece of metal in her hand and she stabbed at the demon's face with it, screaming as she drew new howls of fury from the creature.

"Close it, Abby!" Autumn shouted as she stabbed and flailed at the demon. The child had her eyes closed tight, the strain of keeping the portal open plain on her face. She reacted to Autumn's voice without seeing, lifting her hands from the floor.

"Autumn, no!" Quinn screamed as he flung himself towards the gap, his hands out in front of him. Before he could reach her, the gap began to close and the demon's claws came loose of the floor. Howling in rage, the creature tumbled backwards, Autumn still clinging to it. With a pop like a gunshot, the portal snapped shut and they were both gone.

Quinn sat, stunned and staring, the silence around him broken only by the ragged sound of his own breath. He reached out a shaking hand and touched the concrete floor where the portal had been, and found it solid and unyielding. "Oh, no," he whispered into the silence. "Autumn...no..."

The sound of sobbing cracked the hard surface of his shock and he saw Abby kneeling with her forehead pressed against the floor, her hands covering the back of her head.

Quinn struggled to his feet, squinting to see in the dim light cast by the lamp still perched on the catwalk. Every fibre in his body protested vehemently against the movement, ordering him to lay back down. He took a few staggering steps to where Donnell's dagger lay in the dust and bent down to pick it up. The weapon was cool to the touch, as was the set of brass knuckles still covering his right hand. He slipped the knuckles into the pocket of his ragged jeans and put the dagger back into its sheath before turning to shuffle towards where Abby lay.

"Abby," he said, kneeling down stiffly beside the child. "You have to open the door again. I can't leave Autumn in there with that thing."

The child did not move. He knew she was still alive by the shaking of her narrow shoulders as she cried, but she gave no response to his voice.

"Abby," he said and shook her slender body. "Please. You have to open the door again. Abby, please!"

The child lifted her head. Her face was streaked with tears, her eyes red and puffy. "I didn't mean to," she said, her voice a cracking whisper. "I didn't know she was in there."

"It's okay," Quinn said, cupping her face. "Can you open the door again so I can go after her?"

"I don't know," she said, looking around as though seeking someone to rescue her. "I don't know if it will be the same place or not."

"We have to try," Quinn said.

The child looked at him, her face a mask of pain and bone breaking weariness. She did not know Quinn—this was the first time he had ever spoken to her—and she looked as though she were already about to break. It hurt him to ask more of her, but he could not leave Autumn in that black place.

"What if you don't come back?" the girl asked. "I'll be here alone."

"Your dad is still here."

She turned her blonde head slowly and looked in the direction Kord had fallen. Abby looked back at Quinn and shook her head side to side once. Without asking, he understood her meaning.

"I'm the Guardian," he said, trying to be reassuring. "Your father told you about me?"

The child nodded.

"Then you know I'll come back. Now, please, Abby, we have to try."

The child let out a weary sigh and then leaned forward and put her hands on the floor. She closed her eyes and her face screwed up in concentration as a glow appeared beneath her hands, but it was weak and muted. It flickered for several seconds and then went out completely. A thick drop of sweat fell from Abby's face to splattered on the floor. Her small body shuddered with the effort, but the glow did not return and Quinn let out a helpless growl between his clenched teeth.

"Stop, Abby," he said, reaching out to the child. "Stop. You've done enough. You need to rest." The girl stopped quaking and fell against him in an exhausted heap. He gathered her up, cradling her against his chest and heaved himself to his feet, the effort so great he nearly passed out and dropped her.

Taking small, staggering steps, he walked to where Kord lay. Quinn needed to look for only a moment to know the man was dead. His spine was bent the wrong way and his head lolled too far to one side, the eyes wide and staring.

"We're not going to leave him there," Quinn assured Abby

as he started shuffling towards the exit. "We'll come back for him."

The truck was undisturbed and he deposited Abby on the passenger seat. He walked slowly to the driver's side, opened the door and hauled himself in by the steering wheel. As he started the vehicle and turned it towards the centre of town, he saw Abby turn her head and stare at the building they had left. It occurred to him that the child had left more than just her father inside. A piece of her was left on the dusty floor as well.

They cleared the maze of run-down buildings and the first rays of the rising sun struck Quinn in the face, making him squint in the glare. Normally, first light was welcome; the symbol of a new day, perhaps the end of a long night shift. Now, it seemed to illuminate his failure.

He had failed Patrick in not keeping him safe from the demons that had come to kill Quinn by using the boy as a tool. He failed Abby when he let Kord run up the catwalk and be killed by the demon. He failed Autumn when he let her fall into the black and left her for dead. It would be better if the sun went out, he thought as he drove. Then the rest of the world would feel as cold and hard as he did.

CHAPTER 20

R eturning to the hospital to meet Dave and Sandy, Doctor Stovern had taken one look at Quinn and immediately admitted him. He tried to protest, insisting that the doctor have a look at Abby instead. The doctor ignored his pleading, plucked Abby out of his grip and passed her to Sandy, then called over two medics who unceremoniously bundled him onto a gurney and wheeled him into the bowels of the hospital. X-rays and tests revealed he had several cracked ribs, a concussion and a badly sprained shoulder.

Everyone else was fine. The dogs that surrounded the hospital had drifted away, Dave explained, shortly before sunrise. They had been prowling at the edge of the light, where Dave could not get a good shot at them, and had disappeared as suddenly as they came.

Once Quinn had been treated and Doctor Stovern had been talked into letting Inspector Green and his teammates into the room, he carefully explained, with every detail he could remember, what had transpired after he and Autumn had left the hospital. Everyone sat around his bed and listened without interrupting. The only movement anyone made was when Sandy reached out to grip Quinn's hand as he described Autumn's death and began to weep.

"You cannot blame yourself for this, Quinn," Donald

Green said softly from the side of his bed when Quinn's story was finished. The older man's eyes were red rimmed, the lids sagging, but his voice was steady. He laid a gentle hand on Quinn's arm and patted it slowly, "I can see in your face that you think this all to be your fault, but believe you me, it isn't."

Quinn said nothing. He simply stared at the lumps of his feet beneath the hospital bed sheet.

"The inspector is right," Dave said, his voice a hoarse, wavering crackle. "It's not your fault Autumn is dead. It's that fucking thing's fault." He looked out the window of Quinn's room, then sniffed loudly and rubbed his wrist beneath his nose. "If it hadn't come here to steal that kid then you wouldn't have had to fight it and Autumn would still be alive. We know where the blame lies, and it isn't with you."

"You saved this town, Quinn," Inspector Green said. "If you hadn't gone and faced that thing down, if it had gotten that kid and opened up whatever door it wanted, then we'd all be dead, every one of us, and who knows where it would have gone next. You did the best you could, son, and so did Autumn."

Sandy nodded, and slipped an arm around his neck, pulling him into a clumsy embrace. "Autumn did what she felt she needed to, what she believed was right. You can't take that away from her. You can't blame yourself."

Despite his friend's arguments, Quinn felt as though he might as well have killed Autumn himself, but he did not voice his objections. He did not have the will.

Donald Green stood up and ran a hand over his thin hair. "Once I manage to put this town back together we'll sit down and talk about this some more. All of us. For now, you," he pointed at Quinn, "get some rest. Dave, Sandy, I'd like to send you home, but I think we need to go and collect the body of Abby's father. He deserves better than to lie alone in that warehouse."

Dave nodded. "Any idea how we're going to explain all this?"

The inspector shrugged. "I'll sort it out. Don't you worry.

For now, suffice it to say a member of the general public informed you of an insecure premise at that warehouse and you needed to investigate. We'll sort the rest out later."

"We'll see you later, partner," Dave said as he turned to go. Sandy kissed Quinn on his hair line and followed.

"Inspector?" Quinn said, as Donald Green moved to leave the room. "What about Abby? What are we going to do with her?"

The inspector stopped and rubbed his chin a moment. "I've got room at my place," he said. "She can stay with my wife and me for now. Since Patrick left for Depot my wife has been saying how empty the house feels. Anyway, I think she'll be glad of the company. It might do them both good."

"What about Raife, and Carrie?"

"They're both fine, Quinn. Carrie will likely be able to go home today. Raife is going to have a long road ahead of him, but he's going to live." The Inspector walked back to Quinn's bedside and laid a hand on his shoulder. "I know you've got so much pain in you right now that it feels like you'll never breathe right again, but you will, trust me. And when you're back to yourself you need to be ready for what comes, because I have a feeling this whole thing ain't over. There is more work for you, for all of us to do." He reached out, tenderly, and touched the top of Quinn's head. "Get some rest now, son. We'll talk more later." Taking his hat from where he still had it tucked under his arm and slapping his hat on his head, the inspector turned and strode from the room, leaving Quinn alone.

He lay still, staring at the bright world outside his window, thinking about all the miserable dark that hid where the light could not see. He had faced more of it than he ever thought could exist, far more than he ever wanted to. The thought that the inspector was right – that there was more black waiting for him, that his job was not done - made him so weary he thought it would break him.

But, he thought, as he lay still, he was not broken, and he was not dead. He could not dishonour Autumn's memory by crawling under his bed to give up. No, he was not built that way and it could not be done.

If there was more dark for him to face, more darkness coming to Resolution, let it come, he thought. It would find him ready, and it would be the dark that trembled when he stepped into it.

Countless miles from where Quinn lay seething in his hospital bed, several people sat in a small room. The room was warm with the press of bodies. Each face dripped sweat down eyelids that were closed in concentration.

The centre of the room was occupied by a woman. Her face lined from a lifetime of many smiles, and long curly hair, once blonde but now more grey, burst off her head in a puff of ordered chaos. As she sat, her meditation was broken. Her eyes, pale blue and clear, snapped open.

She felt a loss. It was far away, but she felt it just the same, and it was dear.

Wiping a hand across her face, she stood up fluidly and every other set of eyes turned to look at her.

"A sacrifice has been made," she said as she met every set of eyes around her. "We must go west."

ABOUT THE AUTHOR

Award Winning Author, Tyner Gillies,
works and lives in Surrey, BC, with his
beautiful wife, Ewa, and two moderately
chubby cats.

http://www.tynergillies.com